USA TODAY best[...]
nominated author[...]
romance. She tea[...]
in creative writing[...]
Extension's prestigious Writers' Program, where she
finally gets to utilise the MA and PhD in English
Literature that she received from the University of
York in England. She currently lives in the Pacific
Northwest, with her very own hero and too many
pets. Visit her at caitlincrews.com.

Nicola Marsh is a *USA TODAY* bestselling and
multi-award-winning author who loves nothing better
than losing herself in a story. A physiotherapist in
a previous life, she now divides her time between
raising two dashing heroes, whipping up delish meals,
cheering on her footy team and writing—her dream
job. And she chats on social media. A lot. Come say
hi! Instagram, Twitter, Facebook—she's there! Also
find her at nicolamarsh.com.

If you liked *Unleashed* and *Play Thing*
why not try
King's Price by Jackie Ashenden
Look at Me by Cara Lockwood

Discover more at millsandboon.co.uk.

UNLEASHED

CAITLIN CREWS

PLAY THING

NICOLA MARSH

MILLS & BOON

First Published in Great Britain 2018
by Mills & Boon, an imprint of HarperCollins*Publishers*
1 London Bridge Street, London, SE1 9GF

Unleashed © 2018 Caitlin Crews

Play Thing © 2018 Nicola Marsh

ISBN: 978-0-263-26653-5

MIX
Paper from
responsible sources
FSC™ C007454

This book is produced from independently certified FSC™ paper
to ensure responsible forest management.
For more information visit www.harpercollins.co.uk/green.

Printed and bound in Spain
by CPI, Barcelona

UNLEASHED

CAITLIN CREWS

MILLS & BOON

To Iceland, the most magical place I've ever been.

CHAPTER ONE

"I'M SORRY," THE overly polite receptionist said from behind the polished surface of the gleaming marble desk in Hotel Viking's iconic lobby. "The weather has turned foul. There will be no possibility of returning to Reykjavík tonight."

Professor Margot Cavendish squared her shoulders as if the woman had taken a swing at her, and forced a smile. It wouldn't do to let her irritation get the better of her, especially when she was mostly—okay, entirely—annoyed with herself.

She'd seen the weather with her very own eyes. She'd known that coming all the way out to this remote village was a risk, especially when there'd been no indication that the man she'd come to see would take a few minutes out of his busy schedule of sin and temptation to meet with her. He hadn't condescended to answer her emails or bothered to return her calls. And yet she'd gone ahead and come all this way anyway.

This was what she got for being spontaneous, she told herself darkly.

"It was snowing on the way here," she said, as if she could argue her way back to the little flat she was renting in central Reykjavík during her semester sabbatical. "It was a little slippery, but fine."

That wasn't entirely true. The road over the mountains had been treacherous. The snow had been coming down much harder up high than it had been in the city. But her taxi driver had been undeterred. And Margot was used to blustery Midwest winters at the University of Iowa, where she'd taught in the humanities department since completing her doctorate a few years back.

She wasn't afraid of a little snow. But she'd never spent a winter this close to the arctic, either.

"It's a developing storm, I'm afraid." The woman typed ferociously on her keyboard as if she was transmitting that same information to the public as she spoke. The tag on her chest read *Freyja*. "These winter storms are so unpredictable. It might very well clear up by morning."

"By morning?"

Margot's voice was too loud in the hushed, expensive lobby, which made her want to cringe. There was something about this place that got under her skin: its epic pageant of ice and fire on display wherever she went; elves and trolls and sagas wherever she looked, in one form or another. Like this hotel, a monument to sin that its reclusive owner somehow made seem attractive when Margot thought it should all be seedy. She could imagine the sort of things that must go on here, even if she hadn't seen much of it besides this damned lobby.

She forced her shoulders down an inch from where they'd crept up toward her ears. "You can't be suggesting I stay here overnight?"

She might or might not have emphasized the word *here* a bit too much.

The previous owner of the famous Hotel Viking, larger-than-life Daniel St. George, had died in a dramatic car accident in Germany some months before. His will had divided up his boutique hotel properties to the sons it had always been rumored he'd littered about the globe, though he'd never acknowledged them while alive. One of those assets had been Hotel Viking, the remote Icelandic hotel and resort that billed itself as the first and last stop in international fantasy. And it was only a couple of hours outside Reykjavík in good weather, so Margot had decided she had to go see it for herself.

Her current research project was all about Iceland and its reputation as the most feminist country in the world. Specifically, she was interested in sex and how Iceland's famous and highly alcoholic hookup culture intersected with those feminist principles—because to Margot's mind, those things didn't go together. She'd been in Reykjavík for almost a month already, consulting with colleagues at the University of Iceland and conducting interviews with as many locals as she could convince to talk with her on any given late night out there on Laugavegur—the famous street where so much of Reykjavík's nightlife happened—as they stumbled from bar to nightclub in the cold.

The name that kept cropping up was Thor Ragnarsson, the brand-new owner of the iconic Hotel Viking and the eldest of Daniel St. George's sons and heirs. Thor, who they whispered personally practiced all the many wicked things his guests got up to at the hotel. Thor, who seemed to embody all the things Margot liked least about men—in bed and out.

Overtly sexual. Too physical.

Not that it mattered what kind of sex the man had in his private life, of course. Margot wanted to know what he thought about sex in general, that was all.

Of course that was all. Even if she was trapped here.

His secretary had politely refused all requests for an interview when Margot had started calling instead of emailing. So she'd decided to just show up today and see what happened.

But she hadn't gotten past the lobby. Freyja had been polite but firm. The hotel proper was accessible only to its guests because complete privacy was its central promise, and Mr. Ragnarsson was unavailable for even a five-minute chat. It had been foolish for Margot to come here.

And now she had to pay for it.

"There are worse places to be snowed in," Freyja was saying. "After all, we're a hotel. There are those who get stuck in the snow out on the roads in these conditions and must hope for rescue."

"Yes, but…"

"Why don't you go and sit in our bar," Freyja suggested. "Have a drink. Relax. And I'll see how we can accommodate you tonight."

It wasn't as if Margot had a choice. She could see the way the snow was beating down outside. It swirled around on the other side of the glass entry doors with visibility of about an inch, leaving her well and truly trapped. She'd let herself grow complacent this past month in Reykjavík, clearly. She'd imagined that she could handle the snow the way the locals seemed to so easily.

And it had certainly never occurred to her that she could find herself stranded in a sex hotel. The whole building felt swollen with dark passions, with an undercurrent of sensuality weaving in and around everything, even the cheerful flower arrangements that adorned all the tables.

It was…disconcerting.

Margot had always viewed her body as an afterthought. She was a woman of intellect, not rampant, unchecked desires. She liked sex the way anyone did. Meaning, she enjoyed it. At its best it was fun. But she didn't *hunger* for it. She certainly wouldn't check into a special hotel to have particular kinds of operatic sex—mostly because she didn't like opera that much when it was sung, much less acted out in the flesh.

But Margot kept her thoughts on sex hotels and operas to herself. She nodded stiffly at Freyja, then made her way from the reception desk across the lobby toward the great, high doors on the far side that looked like they belonged on a Viking longhouse and led into the bar.

Hotel Viking was beautiful, as befit the exorbitant cost of even a single night's stay. It married the typical Scandinavian starkness of this part of the world with opulent details better suited to something more traditionally European and decadent, and somehow made it all work. And Margot found the hotel itself seemed to soothe her as she walked, not unlike a cool caress from a—

Get a grip, she ordered herself. She was not going to succumb to the sensual promise of this place. She wasn't a guest here. She didn't need a pageant with her orgasm when she could come happily and quickly and move on. She was an academic observer, that was all.

And she didn't like the fact she had to remind herself of that.

Almost as if she was afraid of what would happen if she surrendered to this place. As if the lure of it was that powerful, even while she was doing nothing more salacious than walking across a lobby.

Margot dismissed that notion almost in the same instant. She wasn't *afraid*. She was a tenured professor back home, a position that had required single-minded determination to achieve. She was a strong and capable woman, wholly self-reliant, to the point that her two last attempts at relationships had complained bitterly about her independence on their way out the door.

Good riddance, Margot had thought, once the

sting of each departure had faded. Because she didn't believe that independence was anything to be ashamed of.

And she certainly didn't think that finding herself snowed in for the night in a sex hotel was any reason to fear she might lose that independence.

Annoyed with herself, she pushed through the double doors that looked like something out of *Beowulf* and walked into the bar. She couldn't remember a time she'd ever needed a glass of wine more.

Inside, it was far more ornate than the lobby. Deep reds and golds somehow merged with a kind of industrial feel that, once again, shouldn't have worked as well as it did. The light was dim and suggestive. There were seats grouped together in intimate little clusters, taking advantage of the deep shadows. Unearthly Icelandic music played while various configurations of hotel guests talked. Flirted. And maybe did more than that under the stout wooden tables where no one could see.

Stop seeing sex everywhere, she ordered herself.

Margot ordered a drink from the friendly bartender and carried a gratifyingly large glass of wine to a little booth facing the windows on the far side of the bar, where she couldn't begin to figure out the relationships on display at all the other tables even if she wanted to. Instead, she had a front-row seat to the storm wreaking havoc outside.

Every now and again she saw glimpses of the surging sea far below, pounding against the obsidian volcanic rock the way it had done forever on this remote, northern island. But everything else was the snow. The wind rattled the windows, but it wasn't threatening now that she was sunk deep into a comfortable seat, safe and warm.

And yet a kind of threat seemed to roll over her anyway, making her skin prickle.

"Excuse me, I—"

Margot stiffened. She lifted a hand without looking up, stopping whatever was happening before it started.

"Thank you," she said coolly. "But I'd prefer to be alone."

"You are trapped in an isolated hotel in the middle of a blizzard," came the amused, decidedly male voice again, English spoken with an Icelandic accent that kicked its way down her spine like another caress. "It would be difficult to find more solitude than that."

"I understand that this is a sex hotel," she said crisply. She turned as she spoke, twisting around in her seat. And then looked up. And up further. And then still further, until she found the face of the man towering over her like a Viking god of old. "But I'm afraid I'm not a sex tourist. I'm just an accidental visitor."

The man standing beside her seat laughed. Loudly and deeply, as if he might break the windows in another moment if he let himself go. And Margaret was surprised to discover that his laughter seemed to move in her, too. It washed down her back, then spiraled even lower, settling like a fierce heat between her legs.

"This isn't a brothel," he said, all that laughter a kind of honey in his voice, and pooling in her, too. It made her feel almost…sticky. It made her very nearly wish that she really was a guest like everyone else. Like him. "What dark tales have you been reading?"

"The reputation of the Hotel Viking speaks for itself."

Margot was used to traveling alone. It rarely took more than a few cool words and an unapproachable expression on her face to deter unwanted male advances. Especially in Iceland, which prided itself on its civility. But the man standing over her was…different, somehow.

He was so big, for a start. Iceland was filled with tall men, broad of shoulder and long of leg as befit the descendants of Viking raiders. This man was all that, but something else besides. Something *more*. Every inch of him was packed with lean muscle, as if he carried a leashed danger in every sinew and held it in through sheer force of will.

And yet the way he stood there was easy. Lazy, almost.

Margot was meant to be a clear-eyed observer of humanity in all its complexities, damn it, so she was forced to acknowledge the simple fact that this man was easily the most striking she'd ever seen. He was beautiful, in fact. His hair was a tawny gold, worn in a careless length that looked as if he spent his days raking his fingers through it—or more likely letting others do that for him, if he spent time here.

And he had the face of a saint.

Nordic cheekbones. A carnal mouth.

And eyes so blue they burned.

Good lord, she burned.

"Exactly what have you heard about the hotel?" he asked in that same boneless, effortlessly suggestive way.

Margot tried to school her expression to her usual academic disinterest, but she couldn't quite get there. Her pulse seemed to be everywhere, too hard and too fast. She fingered the stem of her wineglass and sat back in her chair, hoping she looked as irritated as she wished she felt.

"The hotel is the premier international destination for extremely high-class pursuits of pleasure," she said, well aware that she was practically quoting from the website. "In whatever form they might take."

"Perhaps you misunderstand the word *pleasure*," he replied, but Margot doubted it. Not when she was looking at his mouth, hard and sensual. "A 'sex hotel' suggests a certain lack of consent. Prostitutes, for example. There's none of that here. The Hotel Viking caters to consenting adults."

"And of course there are no blurred lines," Margot said, as if she was auditioning to be a Puritan, all pursed lips and clutched pearls, when all she really wanted to know was how he made the word *consent* sound so hot. "Not in such a fine establishment as this."

"Some lines are better blurred." There was a gleam in the wild blue of his eyes that made her think of the northern lights that danced in the skies here, unworldly and impossible all at once. "But lines are not laws. Laws, you will find, are taken very seriously here."

She felt breathless, which was ridiculous. As if something about the simple fact of this man standing next to her table had reached inside her and scraped her hollow. Margot felt something like...jittery.

It was the storm, she told herself. The unpleasant novelty of finding herself stranded when she couldn't fix it. She couldn't walk away. She couldn't simply call a cab. There was no amount of intellect or cash that could beat back the snow.

Of course she didn't like it.

Margot told herself that was why she was reacting to this man the way she was. As if he was electric, when she didn't believe in that kind of thing. She didn't want it—it was messy and she hated opera and she had no interest in sex hotels on remote Icelandic peninsulas. She had too much work to do.

It was more than time to send him on his way. "It wouldn't matter if this was a convent. I'm not interested."

He laughed again, louder and longer than before. And once again, Margot could feel it everywhere, licking all over her like flames against her skin.

"I admire a woman who speaks her mind so distinctly. So there can be no mistake. You would be surprised how many people do not possess that particular talent."

"And yet here you still are."

"Forgive me," the man said, and that mouth of his curved into a smile that Margot absolutely did not feel directly in her breasts. Or in between her legs. Because she liked sex that was fun while it was happening but didn't interrupt her life afterward. Or even her schedule. She did not like…this. "I didn't come over here to ask you for a quick little fuck while the snow rages down, as diverting as that sounds. I am Thor Ragnarsson. I believe you're here to see me."

He pulled out the seat beside her and settled himself into it, while Margot couldn't seem to do a single thing but stare in shock.

Her heart was pounding in her chest, and her mind was spinning, desperately trying to figure out how she hadn't recognized him, while her body was getting a little too…operatic for her peace of mind. It was the angle, maybe. She'd seen pictures of him straight on, not from below, looking up. She might as well have been kneeling before him, head tipped back to receive his cock—

She sat up straighter, ignoring the fact her ears felt red and singed with the force of her embarrassment.

It had to be embarrassment that made her flush like that. It couldn't be anything else.

"Yes," she said, stiffly, casting around for her lost

professionalism. "Mr. Ragnarsson, of course. I've been trying—"

"This is Iceland. We are not so formal. Call me Thor."

He was watching her intently and she told herself that was why his name seemed to sit there on her tongue like sugar. It wasn't an unusual name, not here. But there was something about him that made her think less of Icelandic naming traditions and a whole lot more about his namesake. The god of thunder.

The god of sex, they'd called him back in Reykjavík, with those suggestive little laughs.

She fought back a little shudder.

"Thor, then," she corrected herself. "I've emailed and left a number of messages. I am—"

"I know who you are. The American professor who wants to talk about sex."

There was no reason that should have sounded the way it did—intimate, suggestive—when it was the simple truth.

"Sex in a cultural sense, not a personal one," she clarified. "In case that's unclear."

His mouth curved again and its effect was even more pronounced when she was this close to him, tucked away in these high-backed chairs that concealed them from the rest of the bar. It was impossible not to notice how beautiful he was, there next to the howling storm outside. As if they were made of the same fury.

"Noted," he said, those eyes lit with suppressed laughter.

And something else she chose to ignore, because it felt a little too much like a kind of aria, lighting her up from the inside out.

Margot fumbled with her bag, reaching for her notebook. "I have some questions to ask you. I'm mostly interested in how you think this hotel complicates the feminist reputation of Iceland's women, particularly in a sexual sense."

But when she wrestled her notebook to the table and looked up again, Thor was only sitting there in the same lazy way, studying her as if she fascinated him. As if she was the subject under consideration, not him.

Which she should not have found at all sexy.

"That is a very boring question."

She'd been staring at his mouth, so it took too long to process his actual words. "I beg your pardon?"

"Is that really what you want to know? You could have put that in an email. Instead, you took it upon yourself to drive out from Reykjavík. You tried to argue your way past my reception desk. All this because you wanted to know such a tedious thing?"

There was something fluttering deep inside her, making her entirely too aware of the growing heat and softness between her legs.

"So your answer is that you find feminism silly?"

"Not at all. I celebrate it."

He lounged there in his seat as if it was a throne and she was entirely too aware of him. The way his shoulders fit in the jacket he wore over a T-shirt that clung to the sculpted planes of his chest. How very long his legs were, thrust out before him. The way his hands moved on the arms of his chair, his fingers long and clever. He looked like what he was: a very confident, even arrogant man, who clearly imagined himself the winner in any game he chose to play.

But Margot had never been very good at losing.

"How exactly do you celebrate feminism?" she asked, her gaze steady on his, because she was the professor and he was the pervert, no matter the odd little scenarios that kept playing on repeat in her head. If she really did kneel. If he moved a little closer, here where no one could see. If he pressed into her from behind, her skin flushed and hot against the cold glass of the windows... But she had to stop this madness. "Is it by throwing one of your sex parties?"

"There's nothing I love more than a woman who knows her own mind and every inch of her own body," Thor told her, his teeth flashing in a grin that was much too dangerous for a man who looked so at his ease. Or maybe it was just too dangerous for her, because she couldn't seem to breathe past it. "I find nothing sexier than equality, particularly in bed."

It took everything Margot had not to squirm in her seat. She didn't want to think about him in bed.

And she couldn't seem to think about anything else.

"By your response, am I to assume that you think feminism is a sexual act?"

"It is when I do it," he said, amusement flickering

over his face. "But perhaps not for you, of course. You have my condolences."

"I would prefer if you keep things professional," she said, but for the first time in her academic life, she wasn't sure that was true.

"I know all about your research, Dr. Cavendish," he said, and Margot was certain she detected a mocking inflection to the way he said her name. Because, of course, Icelanders did not use titles or even surnames for that matter. "I've been receiving reports of you almost from the very moment you set foot on our little volcanic island."

Margot frowned. "Reports?"

"If it had appeared that your questions bothered my customers, I would have had to encourage you to conduct your experiments elsewhere. You understand."

Margot's frown deepened. "You can't think—"

"But all you have collected are stories."

There was something in the way he said that that made her stop protesting. She found herself leaning forward, as if compelled against her will, except that couldn't be right. Margot made it a point never to do a single thing she didn't want to do.

Did that mean she wanted this? Him?

Because when Thor smiled at her, all thunder and heat, she just wanted to melt.

"Have you ever asked yourself what would happen if you stopped recording secondhand stories and found out for yourself?" he asked idly.

Though there was nothing idle about the way he looked at her.

She sat straighter, because it was that or succumb to the madness coursing through her veins, making her imagine…all kinds of things. Operas and perversities, decadent and lush, and his hands all over her while they did them. "Let me guess. This is where you offer to get into my pants, for the good of my research."

"Icelanders fuck, Dr. Cavendish." He lounged there, as intent and watchful as he was boneless. "They do not waste all this time talking. Fuck first, then, if it is any good, perhaps talk a little. Haven't you already discovered this in all your research?"

She nodded, trying to pull herself together. "It's that exact permissiveness that interests me."

"There are some things that intellect cannot help you with. I think you'll find that sex is one of them."

Margot sat back in her chair. "I see no one has told you the most powerful sexual organ in a woman's body is her brain."

"You say that," Thor said, a rich vein of laughter in that deep voice of his. "But I've had a remarkable amount of success with the clit."

Which meant she could do nothing but feel that laughter in hers.

"Exactly what are you offering?" she asked, perhaps more harshly than necessary, crossing her legs against the intense throbbing sensation where she least wanted it. "If you wanted to hit on me, you should have said so from the start."

"This 'hitting' on you," he said, as if he was unfamiliar with the term. "As if attraction is an assault. Is that how you see sex? Is that an American thing—or is it you?"

Margot didn't like that his comment landed, hard. It made her feel a little dizzy. "It's a figure of speech."

"Surely an academic such as yourself loves nothing more than to dig her claws into figures of speech."

"Because you have a vast interest in academic pursuits, of course."

"In pursuits, yes. Not necessarily of the academic variety."

"They told me at the reception desk that I was trapped here for at least the night," Margot said crisply. "Possibly more than one night, if the storm rages on. Is this the price of a room? Sex with you?"

The amusement in his gaze shifted, growing darker and more focused at once. For a long moment, he didn't speak. He only watched her, and she thought she could see a muscle tense in his lean jaw.

Holding her gaze, Thor reached into the pocket of his jacket and drew out a key. It was an old-fashioned key with an exuberant flourish on its end. He placed it on the table between them with a decisive click.

"This is your room key," he told her quietly. She was riveted by the thunder that stormed around beneath those seemingly soft words. "There is no price. You may stay until the storm blows itself out, with my compliments."

"Did I… Did I offend you?" she asked, not certain

why that possibility seemed to tilt madly inside her, as if she was on some kind of roller coaster.

"It is my mistake," Thor said with a faint smile. "This is a cultural thing, I think. Icelanders talk very openly about sex. Having it, not having it. Who they wish to have it or not have it with. Offers are made, accepted, rejected. This happens all the time. I would have thought you'd know this, given your field of study."

Once again, Margot felt off balance, and she hated it. "Is this the part where you try to make me feel bad, as if I'm somehow unsophisticated and re-pressed for calling you out?"

"You can call me whatever you wish," Thor said, his voice deeper, somehow. Or maybe that was just how it felt inside her, where her body was acting as if it belonged to someone else. Someone who wanted sex to be a whole lot more than *enjoyable*. "I do not require payment for kindness. It insults me that you might think otherwise, but I understand. You come from a place where sexual politics are significantly more adversarial. You cannot help but fight, no mat-ter what it is that you want."

Margot didn't know which was drier, her lips or her throat. Especially when he shrugged as if she was that easily summarized. That easily understood.

"And I suppose you're here to tell me what it is that I want?"

"I don't think it's accidental that you chose to come to my sex hotel." And the way he said those words, *sex hotel*, was like sharp blades. "On the day of a storm."

"You think I planned to strand myself in a snow-storm?" Margot laughed and told herself it wasn't the least bit forced. "For this? For you?"

He didn't laugh. "I like sex. I'm not afraid of it."

"I'm not afraid of sex."

But there was something in the denial that made her wish she could snatch the words back. Especially when his blue gaze seemed hotter. Wilder.

"Maybe you are and maybe you're not." He shrugged. "What I know about you is that you have done nothing but watch. What I can offer you is the opportunity to do a little fieldwork."

"Fieldwork?" She blinked. "Is that a joke?"

"I never joke," he said, deadpan. "I'm far too per-verse. Do you need to get to know someone before you sleep with them?"

"You say that as if it's a bad thing."

"Not at all," Thor said. "But in Iceland, that's back to front. I could sit here and tell you my life story or you could come to my rooms with me and I will show you. It will be there in the chemistry between us, or not. Every answer to every question you have, laid out before you clearly and inarguably."

"Because you're that good in bed."

Thor laughed, though it was quieter than before. And somehow, she thought, more volatile. "I don't believe in 'good in bed.' Either people connect or they don't. One woman's sex god is another's dud. It is all chemistry."

"What if we have no chemistry?"

He smiled at that and it felt like fire. Then he leaned forward, putting his hand on the table, his palm up.

"Maybe we don't." He nodded at his hand. "Why don't you touch me and see."

Margot ordered herself to remain calm. She couldn't remember the last time a man had tied her into knots the way this one was doing so effortlessly.

Was that chemistry? Or was she in over her head with this latter-day Viking?

This was her opportunity to put them back on proper footing. Before things spiraled even further out of control.

But Margot wasn't one to back down from a challenge. Instead of turning it over and over in her head the way she probably should have, she leaned forward and slid her hand over his.

She expected him to be strong. For his hand to be warm and to envelop hers the way it did. But the contact jolted through her like a flash of lightning, and she had to bite back the involuntary little noise she made.

Not that it mattered. She could see from the burning thing in his gaze that he felt it, too. And more, that he had heard her.

As if he could feel that same lightning. As if it crackled in them both.

"Here is your opportunity to be less American and more Icelandic," Thor said, his voice rougher than before. Lower. "You've been trying to talk to me for weeks now. This is your opportunity."

"You're not offering to talk."

"Oh, don't worry," Thor murmured. His palm slid against hers as he flipped her hand over. "I'm fluent in all kinds of languages."

Margot fought the urge to yank her hand away from his. Because there was too much sensation, suddenly. Because she'd completely lost control of this interaction. Because there was a part of her that didn't quite know what to do with all the wild things she could feel storming around inside her, competing with the swirling snow outside the windows.

Be practical, she ordered herself. *Think this through.*

It was unorthodox, certainly. But she would be lying if she tried to pretend that she hadn't wondered what it would be like to be one of those Icelandic girls, casual in ways she had never quite managed to be.

Margot had never had sex with a stranger. She wasn't the kind of woman men tended to pick up in bars. Because she was generally unimpressed with drunken attempts at conversation. And because she preferred to spend her time in libraries and classrooms. The men in her life had always been like her, academic and intellectual and more interested in an intense conversation than sex.

Not so intensely physical and overwhelming that she'd forgotten they weren't alone in the room.

Maybe it was time to see what all the fuss was about. And who better than Iceland's god of sex?

"It would be for research purposes only," she heard herself say.

Thor's impossibly carnal mouth curved. But his eyes were like flame. "Of course."

"Just sex," Margot said. "And only during the storm."

"If you insist."

"I do insist." There was something about the way he was regarding her then, leashed and ready, as if he knew something she didn't. As if he knew her better than she knew herself, which Margot didn't like at all, no matter how wet the notion made her. "And no kissing."

She wasn't sure he would agree to that, and the more she stared at his mouth, the more she wondered why she'd said it in the first place. Because the urge to lean forward then, to crawl across the table between them and set her mouth to his, was nearly overwhelming.

But that half smile of his only deepened.

"No kissing," he agreed.

"Great," she said brightly, as if they were discussing the kind of sex she studied, not the kind she was going to have. "I'm sure one round with the self-styled king of fantasy will be a perfect experiment."

Thor took his time standing up from his chair. He didn't let go of her hand, so Margot found herself standing with him. For a moment it was awkward, and then he pulled her toward him until she was *this close* to falling against his big, broad chest.

And worse, wanted to.

"I do love an experiment," he said, in a kind of drawl, all command and blue fire. "But prepare yourself, Professor, because it won't be just once."

CHAPTER TWO

THE PROFESSOR HAD purple hair.

Well, it was more properly a deep lavender. It cascaded over her shoulders and caught the light, and was almost impossible not to reach out and touch.

But he managed it.

It wasn't as if Thor had never seen brightly colored hair on a woman before. Still, he had never met a woman so determined to present herself as profoundly serious while supporting such…unserious hair.

The contrast intrigued him.

But then, everything about Margot Cavendish was intriguing.

Why had she come all the way to his hotel in the middle of a storm, for example, only to pretend that it was some kind of accident? It wasn't as if Thor was a hermit. He made it into Reykjavík often. It would have been easy enough for this American professor to camp out in one of his city clubs if she really wanted to run into him.

Thor did not believe in accidents. He'd been running Hotel Viking for almost six months now, ever since the man he did not consider his father in any real sense had left it to him in that odd will. The same will that had also presented Thor with two half brothers he'd never met—and wasn't sure he wanted to know. And one thing he'd learned in his months as the proprietor of the world's finest and most remote purveyor of fantasies was that no one rolled up to this place by accident.

Oh, they might tell themselves otherwise. They might make up all kinds of stories to convince themselves they hadn't meant to come here. As if it was possible to accidentally end up in Iceland. Or to take a wrong turn in the middle of Reykjavík and end up hours away on a lonely little peninsula that was near absolutely nothing but the pitiless sea.

It never took long to reveal that, in point of fact, they'd been heading for Hotel Viking all along.

Thor led the prickly, lavender-haired professor out of his sumptuous bar, built to be an endless celebration of luxurious sin. He nodded at the bartender as he went, smiling when he saw that one of the guests—a Mr. Oliveras from Portugal—was chatting Kristjan up.

"Do you let your employees date your guests?" his professor asked as they passed.

Thor was fairly certain that was a touch of judgment he heard in her tone. But that wouldn't surprise him. Thor had yet to meet an American—no matter how supposedly liberal—who didn't carry that country's moralistic roots inside themselves somewhere.

He allowed that he found that just as fascinating, having not a shred of the puritanical anywhere in him. At all.

"Some establishments that cater to the kinds of sexual fantasies we do have all kinds of draconian regulations about the behavior of staff toward guests, but Hotel Viking isn't one of them." Thor smiled down at her and wondered why he so badly wanted to taste that intriguing little furrow between her eyes as she frowned at him, very obviously *thinking* at him. "Our staff are encouraged to follow their passions as they like."

"That sounds problematic."

"Only if you find happy, satisfied and loyal employees problematic. I do not."

He kept one hand in the small of Margot's back as he moved her through the big bar doors and back into the gleaming lobby, as much to maintain contact with her as to guide her anywhere.

And also because he suspected any hint of chivalry would irritate her. The more irritated she was, the more likely she was to stay off balance.

And Thor had a powerful urge to rattle this woman, just a little. Just enough. To peel away her composure and see beneath it.

He had thought she was attractive from the first moment he'd laid eyes on her, stalking across his hotel and then sitting as far away as it was possible to get from the place while still being in it. But it was something else again to talk with her.

Especially when she'd been so committed to shutting down what she'd seen as his unwelcome advances. Thor couldn't remember the last time he'd been rejected. He'd enjoyed the experience, if he was honest.

And he'd enjoyed her.

Thor liked her brain—especially when he could *see* her using it.

At him.

He'd always had a thing for smart women, but he found himself particularly intrigued by Margot, who seemed to be so delightfully unaware of her own body's needs and the way she was broadcasting them. He could feel her anticipation even now. It was like a hum just beneath her skin and he could feel it in the fingertips that grazed her back.

Thor led her across the lobby, smiling at Freyja behind the main desk, and headed for his private elevator far in the corner.

"Let me guess. You're taking me to your dungeon."

Thor studied Margot as they stepped into the lift and she put as much distance between them as it was possible to get in such a small, enclosed space.

"I can tell that you are joking," he said after a moment. "But perhaps not entirely joking, yes?"

"Of course I'm joking." She sounded fierce. But Thor noticed that it wasn't until the elevator doors were closed behind them and the lift moved upward that she released the breath she was holding. Her shoulders inched down from around her ears.

"Professor, you must trust me on this, if nothing else," he murmured, enjoying himself far more than he should. "You are in no way ready for the dungeon."

He was fascinated anew by the flush that stained her cheeks and swept down her neck. And the suggestion of heat—and a thousand questions—in her gaze.

And more than all that, the fact she didn't reply.

Thor felt certain that her silence said a great deal more than she likely wished to reveal.

"Why no kissing?" he asked mildly as the lift rose, slow and steady. He lounged across from her, crossing his arms and his legs at the ankle as if they were off to discuss something prosaic. Numbers, perhaps. Or taxes.

Margot frowned. "You agreed."

He couldn't quite hide his smile. "I agreed, yes. I'm wondering why."

"Because it made more sense that way." She blinked, as if she hadn't wanted to say that. Or not quite that way. "Kissing is too..."

"Intimate?"

He watched another flush of color move over her face, deeper this time, making an interesting counterpoint to the lavender of her hair. It made her look prettier, though that shouldn't have been possible. It made her look delicate, and oddly young in contrast to the scowling severity she had exuded down at the bar.

And he felt that like a long, hot lick down the length of his cock.

"Kissing is something you do in a relationship," Margot declared as if she had a doctorate in the subject. It was possible she did. "It has no place in this sort of arrangement."

"You say that with great authority. Have you had many such arrangements?"

"We already agreed that this is for research, Mr.—" She stopped herself. "*Thor.* There's no need to confuse the issue."

He shrugged. "I cannot say that I have ever found kissing confusing."

"You also consider sex to be about as intimate as a handshake. It's possible that you're not really the ideal control group for this experiment."

That amused him. "I can tell the difference between sex and a handshake."

He wondered if she realized that she had crossed her arms over her chest, too. Mirroring him, perhaps. Or Thor supposed it was possible she was simply naturally defensive. Either way, that awkward bristling, endearing as it was, melted away the more professorial she got.

He filed that away.

"You said downstairs that you get to know people through sex."

"There is little that's more revealing. I mean that literally, of course." His mouth curved. "As the participants are usually naked."

"And modesty is not a huge concern here, is that right?"

"It is my belief that false modesty has no place

anywhere," Thor replied. "But Icelanders spend a lot of time in the baths, as I'm sure you know. We are used to seeing all sorts of different body shapes. It is not like America, where you are bombarded with images of unhealthy bodies constantly. It's a wonder that Americans ever take their clothes off at all."

Margot nodded as if he'd confirmed something for her. "So your position is that sex ought to be as casual as a trip to the hot tub. And you would prefer to start with sex rather than beginning with a coffee or a dinner date, which I'm sure you know is more common in other countries."

He laughed. "It must surely be far more awkward to share a meal with someone who, for all you know, will completely fail to satisfy you in any way sexually. Why waste all that time?"

Thor was being somewhat facetious. But there was something about the way she frowned at him. There was something about the way her theories seemed broadcast across her face. He could *see* her turn over the things she thought, one after the next. He wasn't entirely sure why he thought it was so hot.

And why not play into her ideas about their cultural differences? She wasn't entirely wrong. Thor had spent a very informative year in America when he'd been of university age. He had been amazed at the gulf between the permissiveness of the American media, in all its forms—like bikini-clad models on hand to sell a hamburger—and the actual behavior of its citizens in private.

"Do you consider yourself a sexual libertine?"

she asked him, in a matter-of-fact tone of voice, as if the word *libertine* was one people usually threw about so casually in conversation.

"Are you asking for personal reasons, given what we're about to do? Or is this more of your general research?"

"Research. Of course."

"I have been called many things in my time," Thor replied. And then laughed. "Why do you ask?"

"Yours was the name that came up repeatedly while I was doing interviews on Laugavegur. I'm trying to decide if you're different from the average Icelander or if you're a decent representative of Icelandic mores."

"I consider myself a unique little snowflake, of course."

"Well, there are a lot of those in Iceland," she said. She smiled. "Snowflakes, I mean."

Thor liked that. He liked the glint of challenge in her hazel eyes that looked gold in the elevator light. And he was looking forward to getting his hands in all that hair.

"There is a great deal of snow in Iceland, it is true. Just as I believe there are a legion or two of purple-haired women in your precise demographic. Is that not so?"

Margot reached up and tugged on a strand of her hair. "I like it."

"But why do you like it?" Thor asked, mildly enough. "Isn't this the sort of thing you study? Why it is that certain habits or choices—casual sex, let us say, or the sudden rise of purple-haired women—suddenly sweep the planet?" He studied her as she stared back at him. "Perhaps we all like what we like, Professor."

He wasn't sure she liked that too much, but then they arrived. The elevator doors opened smoothly and delivered them directly into the owner's penthouse that rambled over the entire top floor of the hotel.

Thor walked in, turning on a light here and there as he went. He didn't look back to see if Margot was following him. He didn't have to. He could hear her feet in her heavy winter boots on his blond wood floors.

"This is…" He could hear the nerves in her voice, making her sound huskier than before. It made him that much harder. "Stark."

"Nordic, I think you mean."

"This seems excessively Nordic."

Thor stopped in the center of the vast living room and looked around. It was all open space, exposed steel beams and floor-to-ceiling windows that let the best and worst of the weather in. The furniture was low and spare with a modern edge. Geometric shapes, designed to make the most of the space and to enjoy what little light there was for half the year. The living area was designed to feel three times its size, and it did. But then, Thor was a very large man, a credit to his Viking forebears. He wasn't fond of tight, cramped little spaces with low ceilings and no air.

"The rest of the hotel veers toward the lush," he said, looking back at her. "I prefer something a little more austere."

"Clearly." But she kept walking toward him, even though her arms were still crossed over her chest. "I imagine that tells me all kinds of things about you."

"That I am a product of my environment?"

"I was thinking more...lush in the streets and stark in the sheets."

Thor let out a laugh at that and watched Margot blink, as if she hadn't expected it.

"I don't think *stark* is the word, but you will have to let me know what you think after you've experienced my sheets, I think."

Thor led her all the way across the living room and then into the bedroom on the far side. It featured a wall of windows with mechanized shutters to keep out the white nights in summer, thick rugs on the floor, and his bed wasn't the least bit clean and spare. It was a towering four-poster monstrosity that looked as if it could entertain the entire hotel.

"Better?" he asked. "Less offensively Nordic?"

She stopped just inside the door and swallowed convulsively. He watched the way her throat moved and felt it ripple through him like some kind of honey.

He moved over to the wall that faced the bed and set about building a fire in the large fireplace that was set halfway up one wall, sleek and smooth.

By the time he had the flames crackling, Margot had inched a little bit farther into the room.

He took that as a good sign. "You look remarkably nervous for a little research trip."

"I'm not nervous at all."

"Professor." Thor was still squatting there before the fireplace. He turned without rising so he could keep his gaze trained on her. "This is not going to be very much fun if you lie to me."

Her brows drew together. "I'm not lying."

"Perhaps you do not mean to lie." He shook his head. "But look how you are standing. Stiff. Tense. Profoundly unwelcoming. What am I to make of this body language?"

"Why do you have to make something of it?"

"Margot." Thor liked the way she reacted to her name in his mouth. He more than liked it. He felt the air between them ignite. "I am not in the habit of fucking women who look about as excited at the prospect as they might a trip to the dentist."

She actually jolted at that, then scowled, which he already understood was her natural progression in all things.

"You're reading me completely wrong." But her voice was flat, contradicting her own words.

Thor stayed where he was. "Am I?"

"I told you. This is supposed to be about research. And the research is not about me."

"You are the one doing the research," Thor pointed out. Patiently. "With me. And I prefer a little more enthusiasm. It is a requirement, in fact."

"I'm enthusiastic."

"You are quite obviously nothing of the kind."

"I don't think you have the slightest idea what you're talking about."

"Probably not." He lifted a brow. "Prove me wrong, then."

He wasn't sure what Margot would do. But then again, that was precisely why these situations fascinated him. How better to know a person than to see what they would do in unforeseen, fraught circumstances?

Thor shifted back on his heels and stayed where he was. He could stay there all night, watching Margot *think*.

And he wondered what it would be like to know her better, to be able to tell what sort of thoughts they were that made her frown like that; that made those clever eyes of hers glitter.

She pressed her lips together as if she was girding her loins for a potentially unpleasant task, and then she marched toward the huge bed.

When she reached it, she threw a look at him as if she expected him to comment on what she was doing, but Thor only smiled. And waited.

Margot tossed her coat onto the leather chair next to the bed. She threw her bag down beside it. She did both with a level of aggression that Thor would have laughed at, had he not felt the moment was perhaps a little fragile.

So he said nothing. He waited.

Holding his gaze, Margot sat down on the edge of the chair and began to work at the laces of her boots. They were the high kind, with fur around the tops, and it took her a moment to loosen each side, then pull her leg out.

Again, she looked at Thor as she took each boot off and set it beside the chair with a certain ferocious precision.

And again, he only watched. And kept his own counsel.

"Are you just going to sit there?" she demanded.

"I am," he replied. "I don't think it's *my* enthusiasm that requires proof, is it? After all, I'm the reason we're here and not exchanging barbs and very little wine down in the bar."

"You're the one who said consent was sexy."

"I beg your pardon." He kept his gaze on hers, steady. Demanding. And had the great pleasure of watching that telling flush move over her face. "Do you not find me sexy?"

She didn't answer him with words. But there was no noise in the room, save the crack and pop of the fire, and so he heard the breath she let out. In a rush.

Thor felt that was answer enough.

Her chin tipped up in another show of whatever this was. Aggression. Nerves.

Or, something in him murmured, *how little she knows her own desires.*

His were far more straightforward and he wasn't in any doubt about them. He wanted to get inside her. He wanted her astride him, that lavender hair cascading all over the both of them as she rode him. He wanted his hands on her breasts and he wanted to hear what she sounded like when she came.

The sooner, the better.

She held his gaze then, steady and sure, which he doubted she knew was perhaps the sexiest thing she could do.

Her hands were busy with her clothes. She pulled off the jumper she wore, a thin merino wool. Then the base layer she wore beneath it. She stood there a moment, as if reveling in the fact that she was standing in front of a stranger wearing nothing but a pale blue lace bra that cupped a good-sized pair of breasts, round and plump. Her waist nipped in, then out again, to the flare of her hips.

Thor's mouth watered.

He let his gaze track over her. He estimated she was around five feet seven, and she wasn't skinny. She had the sort of athletic build that Thor liked best—muscled, capable and solid. She looked like a woman who could walk anywhere, hike a mountain if she felt like it and then spend a long, hot night with a lover.

Perfect, in other words, for a man like Thor, who liked to sweat in a variety of settings.

When he didn't say anything, Margot went to work on her trousers. She pulled off what looked like snow pants, revealing another base layer. When she pulled that off, too, she worked her socks off at the same time, and then he watched as she carefully, ferociously, folded every item she'd peeled off and set it on the chair in a ruthlessly neat little pile.

And then his professor with the magical hair turned back around and stood before him in only her bra and a surprisingly suggestive pair of thong panties in a bright pink leopard print.

Thor's mouth went dry.

Her legs were as lean and muscular as the rest of her, and long enough to give him particularly bright fantasies of how they would feel looped over his shoulders.

"Well?" she asked. In her voice that was both huskier than before and more than a little belligerent. "Are you satisfied?"

"That you know how to remove your clothes?" He did nothing to keep the amusement from his voice. Or the heat. "Yes, I am satisfied. But if this is enthusiasm, Professor, I am tempted to imagine you do not know the meaning of the word."

The look she gave him then was something like murderous, so Thor wasn't sure why it made him want to laugh. He thought better of it.

Margot made a frustrated sort of noise in the back of her throat. Then she moved again, unbuckling her bra and throwing it on the chair beside her. Then she hooked her fingers in her panties and tugged them down her legs, before kicking them off.

Then she was naked.

And it was like the blizzard that raged just there outside his windows disappeared. As if the world narrowed to this single woman in this shadowy room lit by the fire.

He took a long moment to appreciate the way she gleamed while the firelight licked and danced over her lean curves and gently sculpted limbs—and to make sure he was completely in control of himself despite the storm of need that pounded through him.

She was pale. She had a tattoo that wrapped around her left side, a series of typewritten words declaring her persistence. She wore a little silver ring in her navel.

And in between her legs was a triangle of strawberry blond curls.

Thor felt his pulse batter at him. In his temples. His chest. His heavy cock. He took his time lifting his gaze to hers again.

"Is that your natural hair color?"

"That's a personal question," she retorted.

"It was a rhetorical question. I feel certain nature did not gift you with purple hair, no matter how, exactly, you persist."

Her hazel eyes looked like dark gold coins in the firelight. And they narrowed as she stared at him.

"Yes," she said stiffly. "Sometimes I'm a red-head."

Thor stood then. He was aware of the way she tracked his every movement. The way her gaze dropped to play over his chest. Then bounced back up to his face again, as if she felt guilty for taking pleasure in him.

"Explain to me what is intimate and what is not, please," he said as he moved toward her. Slowly. Almost lazily. "You do not wish to kiss on the mouth. But you're already naked. Your nudity is not intimate, but a question about hair color is?"

She scowled at him. He didn't know why he found that...delightful.

"We're supposed to be having sex," she said, her voice ripe with impatience. "Not playing these ridiculous 'get to know you' games."

"Oh, Professor," he murmured. "I haven't even begun to play games."

Margot breathed harder the closer he came. He liked it. It told him more things about her than he imagined she knew she was giving away, and he liked that, too. He moved over until he stood next to the bed, facing her.

Still holding her gaze, Thor reached out and patted the mattress beside him.

She swallowed again, visibly, and he watched in fascination as she fought with herself. He could actually see the fight. It was as obvious to him as if she was taking swings at herself.

Her fists clenched and released. Once, then again.

Then she moved, jerkily, and climbed up to sit on the very spot that he'd patted with his hand.

He moved so he was standing at the side of the bed, then. He moved himself between her legs so she was forced to open them even wider. Thor leaned forward, planting his hands on either side of her as she fell back, catching herself on her elbows.

He wasn't even touching her. But he could smell her arousal. He could see it in that telltale flush that moved down from her pretty face to cover the whole of her chest. Her breasts sloped slightly to the sides and the nipples were already pink and hard. Flushed, they seemed to gleam like heat.

She was breathing as if he was already inside her.

"Why is this a struggle for you?" he asked with deliberate politeness, as if he'd offered to call her a taxi.

"It's not a struggle at all."

"Liar."

That flush of hers got brighter. Redder.

"I don't know," she whispered.

"That's not good enough, Professor. Try again. Use that brain of yours."

"I've never done this before." She said it in a rush, as if it was a confession. "I've never— You're a stranger."

"You have researched me already. You know far more about me than if I was merely a stranger you met in a bar."

"I don't pick up strangers in bars."

"You didn't pick me up, either. It was quite the opposite, if you'll recall."

She stared at him a moment. Then that chin of hers tilted up again.

"Is this why you got me naked?" she demanded. "So we could talk?"

Thor laughed at that, and even that made his impatient cock ache. He shifted so he was leaning over her more, bearing her back against his bed.

"Remember," he told her sternly. "You're not allowed to kiss me no matter what happens. This is your rule."

She frowned at that, as he had known she would. She was sucking in a breath, no doubt to share her indignation, when he dropped another inch and took one of those pink nipples in his mouth.

Finally.

And whatever she might have said was choked off. Then turned into a cute little sound of need that Thor liked.

A lot.

Margot moaned something, but he didn't pay attention to it.

He paid attention to her gorgeous body instead. He lavished that first nipple with attention, testing the lush, perfect shape of the other with his hand.

Then he switched places, and as he did, he learned her responses, her taste. The way she writhed beneath him, shifting her legs and lifting her hips. She slid down off her elbows and arched her back, offering him more of her.

More access. More of those hot little noises.

More.

But it got even better when she lifted her hands and sank them into his hair, not to stop him or guide him, but as if she couldn't help herself.

And after a while, Thor could feel the ache of his own need edging toward pain in his cock. But he didn't hurry anything along. He explored her, reveling in his own delayed gratification.

Because his ornery American was giving herself to him, and he wanted to marinate in every single moment of it.

He moved from those velvety nipples down to her soft belly, where he amused himself with that belly ring of hers and her shuddery responses. He tested the span of her hips with his hands, and when he was tempted to bury his face between her legs and drink her down, he thought better of it.

For the moment.

He flipped her over onto her belly instead.

She made a low sound as he crawled up onto the bed and dropped down closer to her. He set his mouth behind her ear, then made his way to the nape of her neck.

He found that he could make her squirm.

And he did.

Thor followed a meandering path down the length of her spine, then made her shiver and buck a little when he found the sweet curve of her ass.

He let his thumbs graze that dark furrow and the sweeter heat beneath, but he didn't go deep.

He didn't know why he was restraining himself until she made a low, hot sound of protest. He grinned, then nipped at her nape, using his teeth lightly until she was shuddering all over again.

Only then did he turn her over yet again.

He ran his hands along her legs, enjoying the play of her quads and her calves. He found her ankles and then lifted her, draping her legs over his shoulders.

Margot was breathing fast then.

Heavy, hard.

And there was a wildness, a glorious heat, in her gaze that hadn't been there before.

He held her ass in his hands again, levering her up off the bed so she was at an angle.

And it was impossible not to notice that she was exactly the right size, scaled to fit him perfectly. He could lift her. He could play with her. And soon enough, he would be so deep inside her it would feel like coming home.

Thor was actually shaking a little, he wanted to fuck her so badly.

"I want to lick you until you scream," he told her, and his voice was gruff. He felt so greedy and insane with need. "It's my preferred version of a handshake."

"Oh my god."

"I am named for a god, it is true. Are you calling out my name, Professor? Or is that a prayer for deliverance?"

She sucked in a breath that sounded like a moan and writhed in his grip. Her hair was spread out around her, a bright tangle on the bed.

"Why are you talking about it?" she demanded, her eyes too dark and too gold, and furious. Thor could relate. "Why don't you just *do* it?"

"If you want me to do something, Margot," he told her, clipped and dark, "you need to ask for it. By name."

CHAPTER THREE

MARGOT'S ENTIRE BODY was rioting.

Everything seemed connected. Her breath. Her pulse. The wild heat that stormed through her and made her want to do things she couldn't even name—things she'd never thought she'd have the slightest interest in before tonight.

Before Thor.

She didn't understand what had happened. One moment she'd been in complete control. She'd been aware that he was baiting her, but that had been fine. She'd had more than a little anxiety about what she was planning to do, and the fact that Thor kept challenging her helped. She'd undressed as she wished, making certain that the entire exercise felt like what it was: work.

Then everything had shifted, rendering her something like drunk when she'd barely tasted her wine. But that was how it felt. The imposing walls of this penthouse of his had seemed to slip and slide, and the heated floor beneath her feet had seemed to buckle.

It was something about that arctic blue gaze of his

and the way he fixed it on her, as if he didn't care what that kind of intense focus might tell her about him. It was the way he'd stayed there, low before the fire as if he didn't hum with all that lethal energy and had done nothing but…watch.

Even thinking about it made her shudder where he held her, lifted up and off the bed though her shoulders were still pressed into the mattress.

And Thor was still dressed.

Somehow that made it all hotter. Dirtier. He was fully clothed while she writhed about, flushed red and naked and wide-open to him.

Imagining what she must look like to him made her shudder again, perilously close to another wild shattering.

"I don't beg," she panted out at him, trying to force a little more air into her chest.

The look on his face was too wicked to name.

"If you say so. But I did not ask you to beg. Just ask me for what you want, Margot. Ask me, or I will simply hold you here. Like this. Forever."

She believed him. She wasn't sure why, because it didn't make any sense that he would actually do something as ridiculous as what he'd threatened when the entire point of them being here was to have sex. Not stand around in odd positions.

But the truth was that her body didn't find anything about Thor ridiculous.

Not one thing. Not even his sensual threats.

She pushed herself up onto her elbows again. She told herself she was uncomfortable, that she was cold and in a strangely angled position—but even if that was true, she couldn't say she cared much.

Thor's hands were big like the rest of him, and he held her ass securely as if he really could do it forever. She felt almost as if he was burning her, his palms were so hot.

And her pussy was so wet it occurred to her that she ought to be embarrassed.

She told herself she wasn't, but a kind of electric shame flashed through her, telling her what a liar she was.

"I don't understand," she managed to say, though she could hardly hear her own voice over the roaring in her ears.

"You do."

"I don't see why I have to perform for you."

"You can either own your sexual desires or you can deny them," Thor said, that voice of his like gravel though it rolled through her like some kind of honey, pooling in all the dark places inside her she'd never acknowledged. "But only one of those things is going to get you off."

Something was building inside Margot then. It felt much too intense. It felt much too close, too scary—

But this is sex, she told herself. *It's just sex.*

And sex wasn't scary. It was sometimes awkward, or messy, or better in theory than in practice because penises never behaved as advertised and her own orgasm was often hard to chase down, but it wasn't *scary*.

Besides, she was here for research purposes. And

there was nothing scary about research. Why was she psyching herself out?

"Put your mouth on me," she blurted out, and it was as if she'd stuck her hands into an electrical socket. Everything went white-hot inside her, all over her, until even her breath felt edgy. Raw.

"Where?" Thor's voice was stern. Implacable.

"I can't…"

"If you can't name it, Margot, how can you truly enjoy it?"

"This is no time for philosophy."

He didn't relent. "Where, Professor? Where do you want my mouth?"

She was wide-open before him. He was lifting her off the bed as if he was prepared to serve himself a taste of her—and she was bright and hot and shuddery at the very idea. Her pussy was melting and wild, with a dangerous pulse all its own.

And it wasn't as if the rest of her was any better.

Margot pressed her elbows down against the mattress beneath her. Her hands were in fists against the comforter. She was tense and needy, sensations she'd never felt in her life shivering through her again and again.

"Between my legs," she whispered, because she had to know.

She had to know what it would feel like.

On some level she was appalled with herself for failing, yet again, to be as explicit as he'd been. Since when had she become so prudish? She was an academic. Not some sheltered adolescent tucked away in a convent somewhere, unable to form dirty words without imagining she'd be struck down from on high.

But she couldn't seem to make herself say any of the words she might have used. She couldn't seem to force herself to be more specific.

Thor shifted. He bent toward her, and her hips lifted of their own accord, but all he did was press his lips against the inner slope of one thigh.

"Is that what you mean?" he asked, and she could *feel* the words against her tender skin, as if he was tattooing them there with his own lips. As if there was no part of her he wouldn't mark. "I am between your legs, am I not?"

Another wave of heat swept over her. It even pricked at the backs of her eyes, and Margot was suddenly horrified at the notion she might actually cry.

Even more so that she would do it in front of Thor.

Here, while she was supposedly researching Icelandic sex traditions.

She didn't understand how he could be doing these remarkably physical things to her, but her body seemed to want to process them as emotions.

Too many emotions to bear.

Margot didn't *want* to understand.

But she was too hot. She felt raw and exposed, and greedier than she'd ever imagined she could feel. About anything.

It was as if she had never *wanted* before in all her life.

As if everything before this moment was pale. Insubstantial. As pointless as a single candle against the howling blizzard outside.

But she told herself that was the point.

She was here to try to understand this land of fire and ice in the most intimate way possible. The way the locals did.

"My…pussy," she forced herself to say, and managed to get the word out without stuttering like a child. "I want your mouth on my pussy, Thor. Please."

If he noticed that she'd come perilously close to begging after all, he didn't mention it. She felt his mouth curve, there against the soft inside of her thigh. Then he lifted his head and that was worse. Or better.

He looked like some kind of god. Old-world and elemental. Fierce and uncompromising, and entirely bent on destruction.

Margot had never wanted so badly to be destroyed in all her life.

"Your wish is my command," he told her, his voice dark and lazy, with an edge to it that made her wonder a little bit wildly what it would be like to choose to follow his commands.

In the sorts of very specific ways she imagined he practiced nightly in his own, personal dungeon.

He adjusted the way he held her, and she thought he would take the opportunity to make more challenging remarks. To draw this out even further—

But instead he bent and set his mouth there where she needed him the most.

He didn't simply lick into her.

He ate at her.

Thor growled as he feasted on her sodden, tender flesh, then sucked on her clit until she bucked.

He was greedy. Thorough. Impossibly hot. He went back and forth, keeping her on edge and unable to predict what he'd do next—

When the first wave hit her, it seemed to come from nowhere. Margot felt herself stiffen and then the ripples spread, getting more and more intense by the second, until she was jerking against his hold.

And Thor didn't stop.

He rode out her orgasm, as if he wanted to eat it whole, too. And something about that image made it worse—or made it more intense—and so it went on and on and on.

But so did he.

Margot thought she had stopped coming, or maybe it was one long orgasm with no beginning and no end, a rise and a fall and then a lush sweep right back into it all over again.

She went from peak to peak, rolling over and over, until she lost all awareness of herself. She didn't care if she was too bright, too red. She didn't care that she'd locked her legs around his neck, that she was arched up off the bed in total abandon or that she was grinding her pussy into his mouth.

All she cared about was this. Sensation after sensation, chasing each other toward something bigger. Brighter.

Too wild to name.

Eventually, the storm blew itself out.

Or he decided it had. Margot couldn't tell.

Thor pulled her legs from around him and settled her back on his bed, smiling a little as if he knew exactly how limp and wrung out she was.

Margot couldn't breathe. And the crazy part was, she didn't much care about that the way she knew she had before.

He straightened and stood there over her, and her heart pounded all over again as she stared up at that hard, wicked mouth of his. It was as if he was still pressed against her, his tongue and his teeth and that jaw of his driving her into madness.

How could it be that he didn't even have to do it again? That the memory of what he'd just done pushed her toward that edge all over again...

Margot felt dizzy, but she didn't want to analyze it.

It was easier to look at him instead. So big. So tall. Every inch of him a conquering Viking, packed with hard muscle, that tousled dark blond hair, and those gleaming blue eyes of his that burned wherever they touched her.

And he'd told her to ask for what she wanted, so she did.

"I want your clothes off," she told him, and her heart was still beating too hard, so she couldn't pay attention to how strange she sounded. How unlike herself. "Now."

Thor's mouth didn't move. But she could see the hard sort of smile in the blue of his eyes. He inclined his head and then stretched out his arms to the sides as if he was surrendering.

But she didn't think either one of them believed he was doing anything of the kind.

His eyes were the bluest she'd ever seen. "Do as you like."

It was couched as an invitation. So there was no reason it should have felt like an order.

But there was that fever in her, making it impossible for Margot to care about *feelings*. Not when she was still so wet and greedy.

Not when she still wanted him more than she wanted her next breath.

And the fact that she had never felt that way before—about anyone she'd ever been with or any sex she'd ever thought about having—

Margot couldn't let herself go there.

There were too many precipices littered about and she wanted no part of any of them. Not if considering their danger might make her rethink what she was doing.

She didn't want to rethink it. She didn't want to *think*.

Margot pushed herself up to kneel before him, and a little throbbing thing shook itself awake in a distinct sort of feminine pleasure at the fact he still towered over her.

Something in her shouted that it wasn't right to like this feeling. This strangely compelling sensation that she was small where he was so large, fragile where he was tough, everywhere—

Margot ignored it.

She pushed up the fine, soft T-shirt he wore and worked it over those massive shoulders of his. And her reward was that when she did, his chest was right there before her. His skin was hot to the touch. And he smelled so good it made her eyes water and her belly tighten.

She didn't care if it was right or wrong or what she ought to feel when she followed an urge she didn't recognize and bent forward, pressing her open mouth to the hollow between his pectoral muscles.

But he still wasn't naked and Margot was running out of patience. And nerve. Her fingers felt too big, too clumsy when she wanted to take her time. She wanted to explore every fascinating ridge of his abdomen and all those smooth, heavy muscles that gleamed in the firelight, but there was that dark need deep inside her, winding itself tighter and tighter.

She felt heavy with it. As if she might scream, or cry, or simply burst apart at the seams if she couldn't find her way to that...*more.*

"Why are you frowning?"

Margot hadn't realized she was until he said so. And the amusement in his voice didn't help. She didn't want to tell him that she was desperately trying to keep herself together. That she'd already come too many times and she couldn't seem to stop trembling, down low in her belly. That some part of her was terrified that there was more and that she wanted it so badly.

Or worse, that there wasn't. That she'd already

had her fun and Thor would be a disappointment the way she finally admitted to herself many other men had been.

It's unfair to call a mostly satisfying sexual encounter a disappointment, she lectured herself then, the way she always did. *There's no such thing as a sex god. You were there, too.*

But if he'd asked, she would have said that there was no way she could come and come and come again from a little bit of oral sex, either. It wasn't something she'd ever liked all that much, despite how many times her friends—and ex-boyfriends—had told her there must be something wrong with her.

Maybe there wasn't anything wrong with her. Maybe she just hadn't met Thor.

"I want you inside me," she threw at him, and only realized when the words hung between them that she sounded as if she was in the middle of a fight.

Because, of course, he had no idea that she'd just scared herself with her *thoughts*. His blue eyes gleamed too bright, as if he might laugh at her, and that was suddenly the worst thing that she could imagine.

So Margot tilted her chin up and doubled down. "Not your fingers. Not your mouth. Your cock, Thor. Now."

His smile was slow. Languid.

And so hot that Margot felt scalded.

"Yes, Professor," he murmured, as if there was a single part of him that was at all submissive when she could see perfectly well that there was not.

He stepped away and Margot bit her tongue so hard to keep from complaining that it actually hurt. She tasted copper but was happy she'd kept her complaints inside when all he did was move to the side of the bed, rifle through the drawer in his nightstand, then pull out a condom.

Then Thor crawled up onto the great big bed. She hadn't seen him kick off his shoes, but he was barefoot when he threw himself down in the center on his back.

He was also still wearing his trousers.

"Why do you still have clothes on?" she asked, and she could hear the greed and impatience in her voice.

And those other things she refused to acknowledge.

"You didn't take them off," he replied, entirely too much laughter in that voice of his.

Margot scowled at him.

"You should know that the more you do that, the more inviting I find it," he told her, and Margot couldn't tell if he was teasing her.

Or why it made that tight thing inside her seem to flex.

Then hum.

She was no blushing virgin. And yet that was what she felt like with him. Silly, somehow. As if she didn't know herself at all. As if the person who had walked through the doors into this hotel earlier this evening was a complete stranger to this naked creature who was literally panting for a man she'd just met. She wasn't sure she had the slightest idea what to do about that—

But right now she didn't care. She couldn't let herself care.

Margot kept her eyes on Thor's as she crawled toward him. She stopped when she was kneeling beside him, and she wanted—desperately—to conceal the fact that she was breathing so heavily. She could feel her rib cage expand and contract, and worse, she could feel the way her breasts swayed.

But there was no hiding such a thing. She didn't try, and she told herself that accepting it felt a little bit like power.

When really, the most powerful thing about her at the moment was that molten greediness between her legs. She felt like she was her own furnace.

"Is it your turn to beg?" she asked.

"If you want me to beg, all you need to do is ask me for it." His mouth curved, but it was more a challenge than a smile. "Like anything else on the menu."

Margot didn't have words for the thing she wanted.

Because she wanted everything.

She settled for putting her hands on the waistband of his trousers, still looking at him as she did.

"Are you waiting for me to stop you?" Thor looked almost offensively relaxed for a man who was as hard as he was. Margot could feel the heavy length of his arousal under her hands, leaving her in no doubt that the man was built…proportionally. But he only grinned at her and then folded his arms beneath his head as if he was on a beach somewhere. "Or to give you permission?"

Everything about this—about him—made her bristle.

But it also made her wet.

Wetter.

Margot decided to run with the latter and started to undo his fly. It was slow going because he was so damned hard his cock was pushing up against the fabric, distending the front of his trousers. She expected him to wince, or hiss out a breath or two, but not Thor. He stayed where he was, stretched out beneath her like some kind of boneless cat, watching her with those electric blue eyes of his at half-mast.

And then she didn't care what he was doing because she pulled the great, thick length of him free. Her mouth actually watered, when she would have called herself no more interested in performing oral sex than she was in receiving it. Both could be pleasant, but she believed they got in the way of the good stuff that she knew how to ride straight to her orgasm.

And yet Margot wanted to lean forward and suck the thick head of him into her mouth. She wanted to lick him like a Popsicle until he melted, too. She hardly knew who the hell she was, practically drooling over the man's cock like this.

But she was a reasonable, rational adult woman who owned her own sexuality and knew better than to expect Cirque du Soleil in bed, no matter how gloriously sexual and uninhibited Thor had claimed he was. And she wanted him inside her more than she wanted to taste him.

Margot told herself that it was giving in to damaging fantasies to imagine that she shouldn't have to choose between the two when she knew that biology was biology and masculinity wasn't made of Viagra.

Thor had tossed the condom down beside him when he'd stretched out on the bed, and she reached over to swipe it up then. She was aware of him watching her, but he didn't move. He didn't lift a finger. He didn't even shift his hips when she tugged his trousers down another inch or so to the middle of his thighs.

And somehow that made everything hotter. He let out a breath when she rolled the condom down over his cock, likely because it took a minute to make the edges roll down smoothly over something that big.

"What do you want?" he asked again when the condom was finally in place. And when, to her shame, Margot discovered she was breathing heavily all over again.

"You," she whispered.

"I think you can do better than that."

Later, she promised herself, she would unpack why it was she *wanted* to do better simply because he told her she should. Why she *wanted* to please him. Because all the strange, new things that were tight inside her, winding around and around and making her so shivery, were tied in to that wanting. To her hot, melting pussy, her aching clit and that empty space she wanted him to fill so badly it made her nipples hurt.

"I want…" Her tongue still stung, reminding her that she'd bitten it. And that reminded her that this was research. Fieldwork. An experiment. This wasn't *her*, really. This wasn't who she was or had ever been, and that was probably for the best. "I want to fuck you, Thor."

That wasn't the sort of thing Margot had ever said in bed before, because she'd never been much for talking, much less using dirty, potentially offensive words. She wondered why that was when Thor's blue eyes blazed. His hard mouth curled in one corner and his face seemed to tighten as she watched.

She didn't need him to tell her it was the same greed that throbbed in her, too. She knew.

"Do your worst," he told her, his voice low, dark and with a kick of wildness that seemed connected directly to her—deep inside her.

It felt like the storm outside, battering the windows. Battering her from the inside out.

Margot felt clumsy again, but that didn't stop her. She crawled over him, basking in the heat of him, the clean male scent. She threw her leg over his hips, propped herself up with one hand in the center of his chest, then reached between them to wrap her fingers around the thick head of his cock.

She didn't know what she expected when he shifted beneath her. Directions, maybe. Commentary, almost certainly.

But all Thor did was wrap his hands around her hips, his grip loose and his thumbs resting in the creases of her thighs.

And then did absolutely nothing as slowly, so slowly, Margot began to lower herself onto him.

It was as if everything slowed down with her. As if they were the storm hurling itself against his windows—and somehow every single speck of snow and ice as well.

Margot could feel everything. *Everything.* The way she filled herself with him, inch by thick inch, though she had to pause every other breath to let her body accommodate his size. She could feel the rough fabric of his trousers against her widespread thighs, and the hair that roughened his legs. She was too conscious of her own breath, loud and harsh, but she didn't let it stop her.

She was trembling when she finally took all of him and was flush against him, and she knew he could feel it.

For a moment she could do nothing but sit there, with Thor so deep inside her all she could do was melt and quiver around him. She braced her hands against his abdomen to keep herself upright, but still. It was as if she was caught in that gaze of his. As if she was burning alive.

"This is my favorite handshake," Thor murmured, a kind of inky, addictive darkness in his voice. "This is how you take the measure of a man, is it not?"

"I already know you talk too much."

He smiled at that, but there was something entirely too knowing in his gaze. "Whereas you only talk to hide. But there is no hiding here, Professor."

Margot wanted to object to that. She wanted to defend herself, somehow. Or make him take that back before it lodged inside her the way she could already feel it doing. She wanted to explain herself to him, somehow.

But that could wait.

Because he was stretching her. He filled her, hot and heavy, and that tight thing inside her pulled taut at last.

And she couldn't ignore it. She couldn't pretend it wasn't taking her over like its own kind of desperate fever.

She lifted herself up, then settled down again.

And she could feel that in her toes, her fingertips, her hair—and everything in between.

It wasn't the least bit disappointing, she was forced to notice.

Thor didn't say a word. His thumbs moved idly in that hinge between her thighs and her hips, but he didn't try to take control. He didn't wrap his hands tight around her and slam her down hard against him.

But the fact he could have done those things— that his ability to do it was written all over him and Margot thought she could almost taste it—only made it hotter when he didn't.

And the way he watched her with all that glittering blue male arrogance told her he knew it. Not only did he know it, he was using it against her.

Deliberately.

Because she was the one doing the fucking, but that wasn't what it felt like. She felt as if Thor was hammering into her, holding her down, making her scream and cry and writhe out this mad, red pleasure.

And every time she lifted herself up and slid back down, it was as if she could feel each and every one of those screams in the back of her throat.

Her breath was harsh and grew harsher. His matched.

Margot went faster and faster.

But it didn't matter how hard she went, how she rocked her hips, how she lost herself in the sweet hitch and the hot slide. There was no getting away from the fact that nothing about this felt appropriately academic.

She felt *alive*. She felt wide-open and exposed. She knew that he could see her—really *see* her—from that flush that rolled over her skin to the way her breasts jiggled as she worked herself against him. She wanted that to distance her from what was happening, what she was doing. She wanted it to throw up a wall.

She wanted something about this to feel the way sex normally felt.

Good, always good, but always *her*.

It wasn't that she didn't feel like herself with Thor, it was that she couldn't tell the difference between them. There was just that brilliant, blistering ache between them, and they were both a part of it.

It was heavy and it was dark. It was bright and it was hot. It was the place where they joined and it was all around them, like the eye of a storm and the driving snow at once, and there was no escaping it.

There was only going toward it.

She felt shattered already, she felt ripped into pieces and possibly broken, and that was before that crazy fire began to climb to its flashpoint inside her.

Again.

She thought he should have used his fingers. That it should take work, the way it sometimes did, instead of that too-good slide of her clit against him on her lush upstroke.

Margot kept waiting to crash into one of those walls—

But there was nothing there. Just too much sensation, the bluest eyes she'd ever seen and Thor surging inside her over and over again, pounding her out of her own skin and into the ether.

Once. Then again, those hands moving up to grip her waist as she came apart around him.

He held her there, still keeping that same hard pace, making her moans flip over into something that sounded perilously close to screams as he kept going.

And kept going, fucking her straight through that first shattering and into another, far higher and far more dangerous one, because she wasn't entirely sure she'd survive it—

This time he went with her, groaning out something in Icelandic as he pumped himself into her.

And Margot collapsed against that wide, hard chest of his, finally as boneless as he was, tried to catch her breath and waited for the shame of losing herself so completely to claim her.

CHAPTER FOUR

THOR HAD NO idea how long they lay there like that, heaped together on his bed as if neither one of them was likely to walk again under their own power. Or even breathe normally.

He wasn't sure he'd mind.

And it was a sign of how far gone he was that it took a moment for that thought to penetrate the haze he was in like the warning it was.

Margot was sprawled across his chest, her head tucked into the crook of his neck so that all he could see was the bright fall of all that purple. She was breathing deep and low, suggesting that she'd drifted off into sleep.

Or was still lost out there in the storm they'd built together that put the one outside to shame.

And Thor didn't know why he felt...different.

It was more than the simple release of a good orgasm. It felt...layered. Something a little too close to complicated.

As if this woman wasn't like any of the others he'd taken to his bed.

He didn't like anything about it.

He shifted Margot off his body, placing her gently to one side. He meant to jackknife up, head to the bathroom suite and wash the strange, lingering hangover from that truly excellent bit of sex straight off him before the strange layers stuck to him.

But he didn't move.

It took him a minute to realize that he was pressing the palm of one hand against his chest.

He stopped the moment he realized what he was doing. But he found himself frowning, there in his bedroom with the latest winter storm at the window and nothing inside but this confounding, surprising woman and the dance of the fire in its grate.

He felt almost…thrown. And he couldn't have said why, when he was a man very rarely lost for words.

It was something to do with the sheer honesty of Margot's responses. It was the way they'd fit together, the tight grip of her pussy around his cock so good and right it had felt nearly supernatural. It was the way she'd stared down at him as she'd ridden him, those eyes of hers gleaming gold with a kind of wonder in them.

He realized he was quickly becoming maudlin as he lay there. Something he certainly wouldn't have tolerated in anyone else and had no intention of allowing in himself.

Thor rolled to the side of the bed and sat there a moment, amazed that he really did feel as if he'd had too much to drink, even though he had trimmed back

on his excesses years before, the better to enjoy all
the many things self-control could give him.

He hadn't come close to losing control since.
Why did this particular woman test that? When he
couldn't recall the last thing that had?

"Are we done?"

Her voice was sleepy. A little bit husky and thick,
which lodged itself in Thor's chest as if he was still
rubbing his hand there.

He hated that he had to check.

"Do you feel that you collected enough data here?
Is your experiment at an end?" Thor wasn't sure he
recognized his own voice. He sounded…darker.

Different. Again.

When it was just sex. There was no reason he
should feel anything, and certainly not some intan-
gible *difference*. He rubbed his palms over his face
to wake himself up from whatever spell this was and
ordered himself to get a grip.

"I understand the limitations of male biology,
that's all," Margot said.

Thor couldn't quite place that note in her voice,
but he knew he didn't like what she was suggesting.
He turned his head so he could lift an eyebrow at
her over his shoulder.

She'd pulled herself up in the bed. Now she sat
there with the sheet wrapped around her, hugging
her own knees.

He would have thought she looked like a child
had he not had an instantaneous response to those

lush lips of hers that he had felt against his skin, but wasn't allowed to taste.

"I beg your pardon, Professor. What limitations do you imagine I possess?"

Margot's face changed as she gazed back at him, as if she had no idea what her mouth did to him. Her expression was equal parts wistfulness and something a lot more like resignation. "Everybody talks big, Thor. It's part of the game. And I understand it—the urge, anyway."

He found himself perilously close to a scowl and smoothed out his expression, faintly appalled at himself. "You are talking in circles. And I still don't know what you're on about."

"In the heat of the moment I guess it makes everyone feel better to imagine they can go all night long," Margot replied, and even let out a sad little laugh. If Thor was the sort of man who allowed his emotions to get involved with sex, the sound might have pierced him clean through. It was a happy thing indeed that he was not. "This is great as is, really."

"Great?" he echoed.

"Really."

For a moment he assumed she was needling him. Throwing down one of her challenges, because that was who she was—or who she thought she had to be, anyway. But the more he stared at her, there in the center of his bed, the more he was forced to face the disquieting notion that she was being completely sincere.

And it had been a long time since Thor had found

himself anything even approaching tongue-tied. After all, he'd made his way in the world on the back of his much-vaunted charm. His ability to talk anyone into anything. It was how he'd managed to build his own little empire at a time when Iceland's economics were shaky at best in the wake of the country's financial collapse.

He didn't really want to think about why it was that this purple-haired American was making him feel like a stranger to himself.

There was that hollow thing in his chest again that he didn't recognize—and more, wanted nothing to do with.

And he had the distinct impression that talking about it would make it a whole lot worse.

Instead, he reached over and took hold of Margot's arm. Then he pulled her toward him across the mattress, until she butted up against him. And the oddness inside him eased a little, because he liked the feel of her skin against his. Maybe too much.

"You could have asked me to come over to the side of the bed," she pointed out, though he could hear the breathlessness in her voice as well as he imagined she could, there in the stillness of the room. "You certainly didn't have to resort to caveman tactics."

"If I was a caveman, I wouldn't have been so gentle."

Margot laughed. Then looked startled, as if she hadn't meant to do that. And it was a different sounding laugh than the one before, as if she'd actually found him funny rather than finding the entire situation disappointing.

But what it meant to Thor was that he had one more item to add to a growing list of things he absolutely shouldn't have been feeling. He made people laugh all the time. It was part of his job, in fact. There was absolutely no reason why this particular laughter should wind its way through him as if he was terribly thirsty and the sound was water.

Why was she getting to him this way?

Thor was doing his own head in.

"Up," he clipped out at her, and when she didn't move fast enough to suit him, he scooped her up in his arms instead.

He stalked across the length of his bedroom while Margot clung to him, her arms going around his neck with an ease that suggested she wasn't as upset by his presumption as her expression suggested.

"Before you complain, a caveman would drag you by your hair, I believe. He would not carry you like this."

She sniffed, but she didn't let go of him. "I think you can agree that there is an inherent gender disparity in—"

"If you would like to pick me up, high against your chest, and then cart me across a room, Margot," he said silkily, "you are welcome to do so at any time."

Her face was so close to his like this, and he found his gaze drawn back to her lips. That mouth of hers that fascinated him far more than was likely healthy.

Thor had never thought too much about kissing. It was a part of things, yes. It was always on the menu. But he'd never been alive with the need to put his mouth on someone else's. He'd never found himself daydreaming about how another person might taste. He'd never thought the fact that he was forbidden to kiss a woman might very well kill him.

Until now.

"The world would be a very different place if I could do that," Margot said quietly, and he had the impression she'd spent longer than the last few seconds thinking about what it would be like to have a man's strength. "History would have taken a very different path."

"Perhaps." Thor walked them both into his bathroom, which featured a walk-in shower with a variety of showerheads, perfect for a very large man and any situation he might find himself in. He had endeavored not to think too closely about why his birth father, a known *libertine* of the first order, might have required such a space. "But would you truly wish to live in that world?"

"Yes."

"You seem so sure."

"I've been pretty sure about equality and how I want it since I could spell it. And I taught myself how to read, and spell, really young."

"Equality is a worthy goal, certainly. But that comes from inside. That is how we think. How we raise our children and what we demand of our leaders and fellow citizens, yes? It is in many ways an intellectual exercise. What we do with these bodies, that will never be the same no matter what we think—that is something else."

He set her down just inside the glass doors of the shower and smiled when the frown he expected to see on her face was right there, as anticipated. But the floors in the bathroom were heated the same way everything was in Iceland, with all that geothermal goodness, and Margot sighed a little as her feet hit the tiles as if she'd expected to find them cold and unpleasant. And as if she was almost shocked when they weren't.

That felt a bit too much like the sort of metaphor he had absolutely no desire to think about too closely, because sex wasn't about metaphors. It was about sex—or he was doing it wrong.

Thor reached in and fiddled with the water until it was pouring down from all directions and steam billowed up. And he shoved *metaphors* out of his head, then told himself he wasn't the least bit uneasy, or layered, or any of those other things he didn't want to feel.

Just because this woman felt different, it didn't mean *he* had to act any differently than he normally would.

He stepped inside the shower as well, nudging her to go farther when she hung back from the actual fall of the hot water.

"You look as if you might jump out of your skin at any moment," he observed.

Next to him, Margot smiled, though it looked

awkward. She slicked her hair back with both hands, making it look much darker with the wet and steam in it. And it was impossible, really, to notice anything on her face at all save her huge dark gold eyes. And that damned mouth.

Maybe, Thor thought then, he was the one who was damned.

"I'm not used to all this…naked time," she said after a moment.

Thor ordered himself to stop staring at her mouth like a crazed person. To try to summon up some of that charm of his he'd been so sure of down in the bar. "You don't get naked?"

"I get naked alone, yes. And I shower alone. I also dress myself alone, before you ask. I'm not sure how I feel about making it a communal activity."

"But we are all of us just bodies," Thor said. "Flesh and blood. Bones and sinew. Beautiful in our own ways."

And there was something about the heat, the wet. It sank into him, smoothing out the edges of that hollow place in his chest. Or maybe it was her. His suspicious professor. Maybe it was something about the way Margot tipped her head back to look up at him, and didn't seem to care that her mouth looked so vulnerable.

He had the disarming notion that it was entirely too possible that she didn't know.

"Of course," she said, but her voice had gone soft. Ragged. "Just bodies. Just a selection of interlocking parts. Nothing but a complicated handshake or two, the way people like to perform them."

Thor wasn't thinking. That was what he told himself, anyway. The water pounded down around them, locking them away in all the steam and heat. He reached over and found her hand, one and then the next. He laced their fingers together into a new kind of complicated handshake and then backed her up until she was pressed against the slickness of the far wall.

Her lips parted a little, just enough to drive him crazy. Vulnerable and challenging at once, and he… forgot himself. He bent his head and moved to fit his mouth to hers—

"No," she said, though the word sounded like more of a question. "No kissing, remember?"

Thor didn't want to remember. He wanted to taste her. He wanted to glut himself on her.

He *wanted* in ways as new to him as she was.

But he acquiesced, dropping his head to the line of her neck instead. And his hands rose almost of their own accord, lifting hers until he could pin them, one on either side of her head—and that mouth she continued to deny him.

"Thor…" she moaned as he made her shiver.

It was only sex. They were only bodies.

Or so he kept telling himself.

He didn't want to feel hollow. He didn't want to feel anything at all except sated. He dropped to his knees before her, finding her nipples again. He let go of one of her hands and traced his way down the length of her body as he sucked on one breast, exulting in the broken little moans she let out.

He found her pussy wet. Hot. And he didn't wait. He plunged his fingers deep inside her, using his thumb to drag against her clit on the outstroke.

Thor didn't know what he was proving. He didn't know what he was trying to do.

But then he didn't care, because Margot was so ripe and so lush and she came apart beneath his hands and his mouth as if she had been put on this earth for that purpose alone.

Just bodies, he told himself as Margot's cries echoed off the tiles of his shower.

Thor told himself that was what he had wanted. Exactly that sound she made. The way she clenched around his fingers. The sweet velvet of her nipples, the way she threw her head back, the line of her throat as she gave herself over to abandon.

That was what he wanted. Nothing else.

Because there was nothing else, he told himself sharply, no matter how beautifully she came for him.

He stood and didn't know what he meant to do next. There were too many competing things fighting for supremacy inside him. Too many of those layers he didn't want to admit were there.

It took a moment for Margot's eyes to open, but when they did, they were bright gold.

And she smiled—and this time there was nothing the least bit awkward about it. It felt a little too much like spring to a man who'd been raised in relentless winter.

She didn't say a word. She simply knelt down before him and tipped her head back so he could see the exquisite hunger all over her face. She wrapped her hands around his cock, smiled again and took him deep into her mouth.

"Look at you," Margot murmured after she'd sucked him in deep and then taken her time dragging her mouth off him again, scraping her teeth against the back of his head as she went. "You really do defy your own biology, don't you?"

But she didn't give him a chance to answer. And Thor couldn't think straight when she took him deep in that mouth of hers again and again.

Her mouth was so hot. Her tongue moved against the plump head of his cock, swirling and dancing and sending that crackling electric current all throughout his body. He leaned back against the wall of the shower, slightly concerned his legs might give out, and anchored himself with one hand sunk deep in her streaming wet hair.

But he didn't try to guide her. He wanted to see what she'd do, so he let her do her worst.

And Margot explored him. She licked him up and down as if he was dessert, and then she took him in deep, as if she was teaching herself how to deep throat right here in his own shower.

He meant to pull out. To give her warning or lift her up against him so he could ride her into completion again—but she didn't stop. It was as if she felt his balls tighten, his whole body stiffen, and she took him in even deeper—

Then listened to him groan as he poured himself down her throat.

And when he pulled himself out of her mouth at last, she was still kneeling there, her face tipped up to his while the water fell all around her, her smile wide and pleased.

Something gleaming brighter than gold in her gaze.

And Thor knew this was more than a run-of-the-mill hangover.

His professor was trouble.

CHAPTER FIVE

"YOU MUST BE HUNGRY," Thor said with a kind of easy courtesy that reminded her who he was. What he did.

And why she was here.

Margot was grateful. She was humming inside, as if she'd been tuned to a station she couldn't hear with her ears but could feel in every part of her flesh and deep into her bones. She didn't know what was happening to her, but that humming thing made it impossible to find that as terrifying as she might have otherwise. As perhaps she should have.

There was some kind of magic in this place, she couldn't keep herself from thinking, and it didn't seem to matter that she was a rational woman of scientific inquiry who didn't believe in magic.

There was some kind of magic in this man, too.

It wasn't that Margot had ever disliked performing oral sex, per se, because she didn't. She hadn't. It wasn't her favorite thing in the world to do, of course, but it was always the other aspects of the act that had gotten to her more than the main event.

Like the positions it required her to get into.

Kneeling, for example. So submissive and problematic, especially when a man wrapped his hands
in her hair as if he wanted to control her head—and
then often did.

Yet doing it to Thor had been a completely new
and different thing. She hadn't suffered through it
without getting much out of it herself because that
was what grown adults sometimes did in service
to their partners' needs, the way she always had in
the past.

She'd loved every second of it.

Margot was going to need to interrogate herself
at length about the things this man made her feel,
all those twisted things she'd thought she'd evolved
past years ago, but she still felt slippery. Her pussy
felt swollen into a kind of shivery ripeness. Her skin
was overly sensitive, all over, so that every brush of
the soft, cashmere wrap Thor had settled around her
sent spirals of pleasure all through her.

He had washed her. He'd used those big hands,
if not in the dark ways she'd wanted, and the soap
he'd made into a thick lather between his palms.
Something about the attention he'd paid to every
square inch of her body had tugged at her, but Margot
hadn't wanted to say anything to break the spell. She
couldn't say she'd enjoyed that fierce look of concentration on his face so much as she'd thrilled to it.

It had made her feel whole and even cherished in
ways she didn't know how to process.

And there was something wrong with her. Something terribly wrong, down into her wiring. She

understood it, but she couldn't seem to bring herself to analyze it the way she knew she should. But her *wrongness* glowed there, deep in her gut and splashed all over her skin.

What bothered her was that she didn't care about that, here with Thor, as much as she should have.

For one thing, she'd liked it far too much when she'd been on her knees in that shower, Thor's cock in her mouth. She'd wished that Thor had used that hand of his in all the dark, dirty ways she would have hated if anyone else had tried. She'd wanted to feel what it was like to be under his control, no matter how problematic.

He hadn't done anything with the hand in her hair except hold it there, and Margot had found herself entertaining wild fantasies, what-ifs… What if he held her head where he wanted it? What if he controlled the pace, the depth of each thrust?

What if he…took her over completely?

Her pussy ached even imagining it.

And she knew she ought to be ashamed of the way she melted more and more at each dark and dirty little *what-if* that she could come up with.

Letting him wash her had been much the same. *This is the ultimate objectification*, her brain had argued, but the rest of her hadn't cared. He'd tended to her as if she was his possession. Something precious to him, something he needed and cared for.

Something he owns, a voice in her had supplied.

And she knew that she should have been sickened by the very idea.

But instead, she had felt soothed. Adored, even. Thor had washed her everywhere. He'd even washed her hair. His hands were so big and she knew all the things they could do to her body, but there in the shower he had gently, carefully washed her clean as if doing so was his responsibility. His privilege.

And when they'd gotten out, he'd bundled her in a huge towel and dried her off as if that, too, was a part of this ritual he needed to perform. And despite all the words that crowded into her head—*infantilizing, condescending, daddy issues, problematic*—Margot had stood there and basked in his attention.

And that humming in her had continued.

Now she sat with her legs crossed on the low-slung couch to one side of the fireplace in his bedroom that should have been too big to feel cozy but somehow managed it despite its unwieldy size. He had exchanged the big, fluffy bath towel for this almost unbearably warm and soft wrap she wore now, and Margot told herself that she was merely drying her hair by the fire. That there was nothing to it but that.

That she wasn't watching Thor as he moved around the room. That she wasn't marveling in the things firelight did for a man as sculpted as he was. He was all muscle and sinew, cast in liquid gold thanks to the crackling flames.

"Are you in a trance?" he asked, and she realized with a jolt that he had been standing there, waiting for her response, for some time.

Margot cleared her throat. "Yes," she said, striving for that same overtly polite tone, the sort she'd have used if a waiter had caught her daydreaming in a fancy restaurant. "I think I'm starving, actually."

"I will send down to the kitchen for some food." She didn't know when he'd pulled on those athletic trousers he wore now, but they rode low on his hips, making it impossible for her to do anything but marvel at that ridge shaped like a V that pointed down beneath his waistband.

"Why are you taking care of me?" Margot asked.

And then wished she hadn't.

Thor's gaze found hers, something like affront in all that blue. He held up a finger, then spoke into the phone at his ear. Margot caught only the odd word here and there as he spoke in rapid Icelandic, never dropping her gaze.

When the call was finished, he dropped the hand holding the phone to his side as he regarded her for another long moment that seemed to scrape through her.

Maybe that was why she kept talking, when every word that spilled over her tongue made her feel more exposed. "I just mean that none of this is necessary. You're treating me like some kind of treasured guest when I'm not. It's supposed to be an experiment—"

"Yes, yes. Only an experiment. So you keep telling me. I was unaware that meant I should fuck you and then throw you out in the hall like rubbish."

There was an edge to his voice that Margot didn't understand. But she didn't particularly want to acknowledge it, either.

"I want to make sure that we're not blurring any boundaries here, that's all," she said coolly, and hoped that he couldn't see that she was blurry all the way through. So blurry she could hardly see straight.

That edge in his voice seemed locked on his mouth then. "Because I wish to eat? Because sex can work up an appetite? These are hard boundaries of yours that cannot be crossed?"

"You said yourself that Icelanders prefer sex to dinner dates."

"Think of it as fuel." His blue eyes glittered. She had the strangest notion that she had offended him, somehow. "After all, the blizzard rages on. And inside, it is warm and safe and the night is young."

"You can't possibly…" She drifted off, her gaze following that tempting V all the way down.

Where, if she wasn't mistaken, his cock was stirring yet again.

"How old are you?" she asked in disbelief.

And whatever tension had been building there between them, it shattered when he laughed. That same mighty laugh that reminded her where she was, tucked up here on the top of the world in this land of trolls and dark and men who were named for very old gods, she wondered if she could see in his face.

"Are you worried that I'm an adolescent boy?" he asked. "I regret to inform you that I haven't been anything like an adolescent in a very long while."

"If you say so."

"Adolescent boys have erections as easily as breathing, it is true." Thor was still laughing, and it was unfair, the things that did to his already too-beautiful face. "But it is like a summer storm. All that noise and carrying on, yet they do not have any control."

"But you do."

Another laugh, and it was just as dangerous as before. "Do you doubt it? I'm sorry. I must have lost track of how many times I made you come."

She felt her ears get hot. Some part of her wanted to curl into a ball and hide under the couch, but he'd told her about this. Icelanders talked about sex. With a frankness that made every last bit of Margot's Midwestern soul curl up and want to die.

But she told herself this, too, was part of the experiment she was conducting.

She inclined her head. "I counted."

His smile was delighted. And infinitely wicked. "I am pleased to hear that. I did, too."

"I suppose it could be the novelty," she continued, frowning a little. "As you said yourself, there's no such thing as a sex god. There's chemistry. But that always wears off, usually pretty quickly."

"Here is what I do not understand." Thor moved to sit down, and he didn't choose the chair across from the couch like a civilized person might have while discussing this research project they were undertaking together. Instead, he settled himself on the other end of the same couch where she sat, making it that much smaller in an instant. And he did it in that same languid, boneless way he did everything, lounging there and taking up more than his fair share of the couch, which only made Margot frown. "Your field of study is sex, is it not?"

Her frown deepened. "Well, sex is a fairly broad category, obviously, and my specialty is significantly narrower because I'm primarily concerned with—"

"I will take that as a yes."

"—human sexuality in cultural contexts. I'm specifically intrigued by the particular intersection—"

"Professor. Control yourself." And there was that curve in his mouth again, which meant that when she obeyed him it felt like some kind of caress. She didn't understand that, either, but it made that humming thing inside her grow deeper. Louder. "I don't want to debate your thesis. I'm sure it's fascinating. What specifically intrigues me is that you live and breathe sex in your work, yet seem singularly disposed to take the joy out of it. Why is that?"

"I don't think I do that at all."

"I have known you for a few hours and already I understand that you think sex is in many ways a chore, that you think chemistry comes and goes and cannot be depended upon. You think men cannot control their penises and you have a great many strange ideas about what any man is capable of in the course of an evening. You seemed astounded that I made you come at all, much less over and over again."

Margot felt as if she'd fallen, hard, knocking all the air out of her body. "I think you've read me wrong."

He lifted his shoulder, then dropped it, and even

as she struggled for breath, it was impossible not to notice how beautiful he was and, worse than that, how she could *feel* him in parts of her body that she'd never paid all that much attention to before.

"Who have you been sleeping with?" he asked in that same mild tone.

And ordinarily, of course, Margot would have been outraged at a question like that. A person's sexual history was no one else's business, unless she chose to share it of her own volition. But something about the way Thor had asked the question kept her from reacting like that.

His tone was so…cool. His gaze was clinical.

It was exactly what she should have wanted. She couldn't understand why she didn't like it much.

"I never pick men up in bars while drunk, if that's what you mean," she heard herself say. "Not that I'm suggesting that there's anything wrong with that. I support sex positivity in all its forms. Everyone should be able to enjoy sex wherever they find it, in whatever way they like it, as long as it doesn't harm anyone and assuming they're able to voice their explicit consent."

"Everyone should be able to do these things, yes. Of course. But you do not."

She didn't. She'd never really enjoyed sex that way, with the kind of cheerful merriment that she thought she should have, but Margot didn't know why it made her uncomfortable to say so. Out loud, anyway.

To Thor, who had made her come over and over

and over with what even she had to admit had seemed a lot like reckless abandon.

"I've had partners, Thor. I just met them under different circumstances."

"How mysterious. Did you grow them in a lab somewhere?"

"In a manner of speaking, yes. I spend most of my time on university campuses, after all. I've met most of the partners I've had through academics in one way or another."

"I see. You are usually seized with a sudden passion while flipping through piles of research books, or some such thing."

She frowned. "Not quite. I'm not sure I've ever been seized by passion, thank you. That sounds like something that ought to be checked out by a medical health professional." Thor laughed, and Margot kept going. "I meet a man. We talk. We usually talk quite a lot, in fact. How else can you possibly know if you suit?"

Thor's mouth curved. "You fuck them, Margot. You can talk until you're blue in the face. You can tell each other all manner of stories. You can compliment each other on your smart ideas and funny jokes. But if you have no sexual chemistry, then all you can ever truly be is friends."

"Not everything is about sex."

"Perhaps not. But I think you'll find that fucking usually is."

"You're obviously looking for a more physical sort of relationship than I am. I couldn't possibly consider someone as a partner if I didn't feel that we connected on an intellectual level, and I'd always choose a very good friend with an astonishing brain over a fuck or two."

"Why must you make that choice?"

She smiled at him. "You and I are different people. We look for different things."

"I can't decide if that was sad or patronizing."

"I'm not trying to insult you. You don't have to understand the things I need. I'm a tenured professor. You—"

She stopped herself, but it was too late. His dark blond brows lifted.

"I own a sex hotel and can therefore be assumed to have no intellectual interests whatsoever. A great and glorious *tenured professor* such as you, of course, is such a towering mind that you could never find yourself enslaved by the demands of the flesh." But he laughed. "Am I your intellectual equal, Professor? Because I suspect your body likes me just fine."

"It doesn't matter who likes what here. You're not my partner."

"Indeed I am not." That sat there between them. Margot told herself it was absurd that her pulse should racket about like that while he regarded her, all narrowed blue gaze and that humming thing inside her. "But you still haven't answered the question. Why do you study sex if you think it is little more than a physical expression of what sounds to an impartial observer like a series of very long, very boring conversations?"

"Some people are more captivated by the mind than the body."

"You are not one of those people." He shook his head when Margot scowled at him. "What fascinates me is why you think otherwise. Because you have a job that involves your mind? So do many others. Why do you seem to think that your body and your mind aren't connected? You can't have one without the other."

Margot drew the wrap tighter around her. "I think you're misunderstanding me."

"Proving, yet again, that I am not your intellectual equal, yes? Or is it that no one can be your intellectual equal? That must be convenient."

Margot's eyes narrowed. "I don't think I asked you to psychoanalyze me."

"I'm merely offering up my humble observations. It is my contribution to science, nothing more. After all, this is an experiment, is it not?"

And now there was a kind of prickly thing deep inside Margot that she didn't understand. She should have no interest at all in explaining herself to this man. She never had to see him again after the blizzard ended. In fact, she could demand that he give her that hotel key right now and let her go off to a room somewhere. She didn't have to tolerate any of this.

And yet there was something in her that wanted— needed—to explain.

The worst part was the little voice whispering that the need came from the same place as the part of her that had loved kneeling down before him. The part of her that had drifted off into the kinds of fantasies she normally strictly forbade herself to have, because they were remnants of patriarchal harm that every woman carried around inside her. They weren't real. She'd never allowed herself to believe they could possibly be real.

She should have forbidden herself this, too. And yet here she was, opening up her mouth.

"Sex is fascinating," she told him as if her life depended on it. As if she was on trial. "Why wouldn't I want to study it? You've built your life around sex, too, as far as I can tell."

"I built my life around pleasure. I'm not sure it's the same thing."

"What interests me are the ways that sexuality fuels change. If it does." She thought about the things she'd wanted him to do in that shower. The way she'd wanted to exult in his strength, his control. "What it means if it does. Can a philosophical need translate into a sexual one?"

"That sounds as if you think we are all able to pick and choose our sexualities."

"I don't think that." She shifted against the couch. "But I do think that we have a responsibility to make certain our expression of our sexualities doesn't betray our principles."

Thor sighed and ran one of his big hands through his hair. "You either think something is hot or you don't, Professor. It either gets you off or it doesn't. The end."

"I don't think it's that simple."

"Which is why you have created this life of yours that celebrates all the many ways you have complicated basic needs."

"Because you know best, of course. I can't possibly know myself or what I actually find hot. It can't be that people are different and want different things."

"I don't know about people in general," Thor said with that mildness that the heat in his gaze completely contradicted, and it made her stomach twist, then drop. "But I do know about you. Or maybe you've forgotten already."

"I had a few orgasms, yes," Margot threw back at him, and forced herself to unclench her teeth. "Forgive me if I don't think that makes you a god."

"I am not the one who considers myself a sex god. Nor am I the one who found each successive orgasm quite so overwhelming. This leads me to imagine that you are not so used to coming and coming and then coming again. And that, Professor, suggests that the kind of sex you are used to having is perhaps a little too intellectual."

"There's no such thing as *too* intellectual," she gritted out.

"If you say so."

"There's nothing wrong with intellect. Thinking is not a bad thing."

He didn't laugh, but she could see the gleam of it in his blue gaze. "I don't believe I said it was."

"I'm not embarrassed by the fact I'm more intellectual than physical. I like it that way."

Thor smiled. "And yet you are the one who appears upset. You are the one who feels there must be a separation between your head and your body."

Margot realized she was clenching her fists in frustration and forced herself to straighten out her fingers before she tore the airy cashmere draped around her.

"My father was an academic, too," she said after a moment, and she had no idea where that had come from. She never talked about her family. But tonight had been filled with things she never did. "He's a remarkably intelligent man who could spend days playing chess and conducting rousing debates. I was raised to prize that kind of intellectual engagement above all things. And I discovered as I grew that I agreed with the way I was raised. That I want the same things."

"Chess and a rousing debate."

"Yes." She lifted her chin. "I like people who arrange their lives around ideas."

"Let me guess. The only way your father gave you any kind of attention was if you proved your intellect to him."

Too late Margot realized her mistake. She didn't want to talk about her father like this. Or at all. She didn't want to tear apart her family's dynamics and expose them here in this powerfully strange place. She didn't want to talk about what it had been like to be raised the only child of towering intellect and swaggering academic genius Ronald Cavendish. She didn't want to recount the number of times she had fallen short of her father's expectations, confronted over and over again with her own limitations. Or the many ways she still did.

And she definitely didn't want to talk about her mother. Or all the ways Margot had learned since her earliest days that a marriage that wasn't between intellectual equals was like a stifling prison at best and something far grimmer than that at worst. She'd seen it with her own eyes. She'd lived it.

So instead she frowned at the door as if she could make their food come quicker that way. And so she didn't have to watch the way Thor was studying her and likely seeing far too much.

"Fathers are tricky," she said. "Take yours, while we're on the subject." He went very still at that, there beside her, but he didn't protest. So she forged on ahead. "Your last name, for example. Shouldn't it be Danielsson rather than Ragnarsson? Your actual father's name was Daniel St. George."

"Thank you. I am aware of Iceland's patronymic conventions." He sighed, but she'd been looking at the door. By the time she turned to him, he was only gazing back at her in that mild way that made her wonder how he got anyone to believe he wasn't wildly dangerous when it was that very studied languidness that announced it. "My mother married my stepfather before she had me, and when she did, they both decided to give me his name because my mother never expected to see my father again. And indeed, she did not."

It was as if being around this man had opened up dark pockets inside her that she had never known were there. Because she felt something like envy at his flippant, careless tone. The things he said should have been upsetting, surely. But Thor didn't look upset in the least. He merely lounged there, as if there was no story at all to how he came to be raised as another man's son.

Meanwhile, Margot couldn't say anything bad had ever happened to her outside of her father's disappointment in her. She hadn't been treated badly. Her needs had always been met. Her parents had supported her academic aspirations all the way. So why wasn't she relaxed and flippant in turn?

"I'm no tremendous intellect, but even a dullard like me recognizes an attempt to change the subject when it appears before him," Thor said quietly.

"I do not have daddy issues," Margot snapped.

"Then you would be remarkable indeed." His blue gaze was kind, and Margot found that unacceptable because it made her want to cry. "Are we not all stitched together by our pasts? And is the thread not often the color of the people who raised us?"

Margot could feel her heartbeat, each thud like a nail into a coffin. *Her* coffin, she had no doubt.

"I don't want to talk about needlework," she threw at him. "I don't want to talk at all. You told me Icelanders communicate with sex, not idle chitchat."

"I would not call something that makes you this upset *idle*, Professor."

"I'm not upset." When the elevator sounded from the main room, announcing the arrival of their food, she was almost pathetically grateful. She forced herself to smile. "But maybe I'm a little bit hungry."

Thor took his time getting to his feet. He kept his gaze on her, and Margot would have given anything to look away. To hide. To pull on her clothes and run.

But she couldn't seem to move.

"Very well," he said after a moment, when he was standing there before her again. "I look forward to all the epic, athletic, silent sex we'll be having once you replenish your energy stores and restore your delightful mood."

"That's why we're here, isn't it? I'm tired of all this talking."

Because she couldn't seem to help herself. And because anything was better than the unwieldy things sloshing around inside her, threatening to tip over and poison her there and then.

His smile was like a weapon. "I'll endeavor not to hold myself back any longer, then, shall I?"

Thor left her there as he walked toward the elevator, her heart like a lump in her throat and her body alive with a new sort of fire, wondering what fresh hell she'd dropped herself in this time.

And why she couldn't seem to do anything but stay right where she was.

Shivering with anticipation.

CHAPTER SIX

IT TOOK ABOUT three seconds for the silence to get to Margot. They both sat back from the meal having eaten their fill in a way that felt a bit too much like fueling for an ultramarathon.

Or perhaps it was less the silence and more the way Thor was looking at her from the other side of the table as he lounged there. It made her skin feel too tight. It made her entirely too aware of the way she was—or wasn't—breathing.

"I think this is a perfect opportunity to take a moment to reflect and reassess," Margot began in her best professor's voice, as if pretending she was delivering a lecture could help her feel a little safer in her own skin.

"This is a time for silence, Margot," Thor replied, cutting her off, his voice low and dark. Or not dark, exactly. It was astounding how much he seemed a part of the blustery night outside that made the windows shudder. "No more talking. Isn't that what you requested?"

She might have. She wasn't sure she could remember her own name when he looked at her like that, much less what she might have said earlier.

Thor stood without another word and came around the table. He took her hand and lifted her to her feet there before him. And Margot let him. She more than let him. She went as easily as if these were steps to a dance they'd choreographed and practiced a thousand times before.

"I can't promise I won't say something." Margot didn't mind that she sounded defiant. But it was the shakiness in her voice that she was afraid might haunt her forever.

"You won't."

Thor reached down and plucked something from the table. It took her a moment to understand what it was. An untouched snow-white cloth napkin.

And it took her still another moment to understand why Thor was offering it to her.

Something slammed through her, dark and mad.

"You can't be serious. You're not going to put…" Margot's words deserted her, especially when she saw all the *intent* in his gaze and the patience he wielded the way other men used their fists. "Why am I not surprised that you want to gag a woman?"

If she'd expected him to be offended at that, she was disappointed. His eyes gleamed as if she'd told a good joke.

"Women routinely beg me to gag them," Thor murmured. "Among a great many other things I suspect you would pretend to find appalling."

"I'm not sure I'd be pretending."

That blue gleam intensified. "Do women whose desires differ from yours deserve to have them met?"

Margot scowled at him. "Of course."

"I ask because I get the distinct impression that you use your academic reflections to judge these things."

"Academic reflection is a conversation, not a condemnation."

"What I think is that you hide in these words of yours. These ideas you have decided are true without having experienced them yourself. Meanwhile, you have no idea what your body wants because you talk yourself out of it." Thor ran a finger down her cheek as if he found her scowl delightful, and smiled when goose bumps prickled to life across her shoulders at the light touch. "What I am offering you is a chance to explore that directly. What if you can't speak? What would happen then?"

"I would be handing over my voice to a man, the way women have done for millennia. Why would that be appealing?"

"But this is not 'millennia.' This is here, now. Tonight. I am one man, not the whole of the patriarchy arrayed against you. And I don't want to take your voice from you, Margot. I want to hear what other things you have to say when you can't rely on your mouth."

She stared at him for what felt like nine or ten millennia, if not more, but Thor only gazed back at her as if he could wait forever.

And somehow that let her ignore all the shrieking things in her head and focus on the places where she melted and ached for him. She thought about the dark fantasies she didn't dare speak out loud and would have denied she had, if asked. The things she'd never told another living soul and hardly admitted to herself.

What he was offering was a chance to explore them. And if she couldn't talk, she couldn't talk herself out of it, could she?

"There has to be a signal," she said, still scowling at him. "I have to be able to tell you to stop if I want you to stop."

"There is a very simple signal. All you have to do is remove the gag. Then say whatever it is you wish to say. Tell me to stop. Tell me to never stop. Tell me whatever you like—but understand that the goal is to see if you can tell me all the things that go on in that beautiful head of yours without uttering a single word."

There was a different sort of tremor making its way through her then. Margot shook, but on the inside. Her eyes felt too glassy, and she worried that all the uncertain, off-center things tilting and slopping around inside her were close to spilling over and revealing her.

You've already revealed yourself, a stern voice in her head chimed in then. *Repeatedly.*

But Margot knew, somehow, that there was so much more.

And she was worried about the things he might do to her. She was worried she might hate them—

but if she was honest, she was far more concerned that she might not hate them at all.

And, most of all, she was worried that if she didn't do it, if she didn't take this opportunity no matter how it made her shake inside, no matter what it said about her or what it made her to even entertain the notion, she would regret it for the rest of her life.

It sat there between them, as stark and unrelenting as the coldly masculine room they stood in. As Thor himself, waiting there before her. As irrevocable as that pounding, swirling storm that beat at the windows and sounded too much like her terrified, deliriously wanton heart.

She didn't want to do this. She only knew she had to, or die.

And it didn't matter how many times Margot told herself she was being needlessly melodramatic. The feeling she had to do this—*she had to*—only grew the longer she stood there.

"What do you get out of it?" She hadn't meant to ask that question, but once she had, she found she desperately wanted to know the answer. It was her turn to study Thor for a moment, and she found herself lingering on the sharp blades of his cheekbones as if they were clues. "What do you like about playing games like this?"

"Other than the sex?"

But she didn't believe the lazy way he said that, as if all he cared about was getting his end away.

"This isn't about sex. Or not only sex. If it was,

you wouldn't be quite so concerned with how I use my voice or what words I choose."

"I don't know that I would consider sex a game at all. Intimacy is not a few sets of tennis on a summer afternoon, is it?"

Margot was tempted to comment on the game of tennis itself, and more specifically its scoring system that used *love* to mean *zero*, but refrained. She had a feeling that what sounded clever in her head would sound very different here in this cavernous room with her very own Viking.

"If you play at it, is it really intimacy at all?" she asked instead.

"I am not certain that I am the one playing," Thor said. He didn't back away as he spoke. He stayed right where he was, big and tall and taking up entirely too much space without seeming to try very hard. Or notice it. "You are the one who needs a university-sanctioned research project to allow yourself to push your own boundaries. I do not require these masks and charades. If I want to fuck, I fuck. The end."

It was something she knew firsthand now, though Margot found she still couldn't quite believe it. Not quite. No matter that she was close enough to naked and could still feel him all over her, like a new tattoo.

"But sometimes you do it with gags. And whips and chains or other such implements in a dungeon built for precisely that sort of transgressive sex, presumably."

"You seem unduly concerned with a dungeon you

have never seen." Thor laughed, a low, rolling scrape of sound that made her feel entirely too warm. "If you would like to experience it, Professor, you need only ask. Here in this hotel we exist to satisfy your every desire."

She ignored that last part and concentrated on the issue at hand. The issue that was literally still *in* his hand. "I don't think it's unreasonable to assume that playing sex games with gags operates as a training ground for the kinds of things people decide they need to do in dungeons."

"Not everything I do has an agenda." Thor laughed again, though this time it felt more like fire. "I am not a vaunted professor of human sexuality, after all. I am merely a lowly practitioner of the art."

Margot found herself smiling the way she did at unruly first-year students. "You and I both know what kind of power dynamic a gag indicates. Don't insult my intelligence by pretending that could be an accident on your part. What I'm wondering now is if that's part of who you are. Were you a sexual dominant before you came into possession of a sex hotel? Or is that something working here brought out in you? And how does sexual dominance work in a country filled with women so passionately feminist? Does that complicate it?"

Thor's laugh was louder than before, and this time when he reached out to move his fingers over her cheek, Margot could have sworn there was something affectionate in the way he did it. And in the way he gazed at her.

But she couldn't allow herself to dwell on that. This was about work, not her lonely little heart.

She was instantly horrified that she was thinking about her heart at all. Much less in those terms.

"I try not to complicate my sexual desires unnecessarily," he said drily. "And I'm not sure that I think the practice of sexual dominance and feminism are at odds anywhere but in the heads of skeptics who are more concerned with metaphors than with screaming, delirious orgasms."

"There is not a single submissive bone in my body," Margot gritted out.

And only realized once she did that he hadn't argued otherwise.

The curve in his mouth felt like an indictment. "If you say so."

"You know what strikes me as notably un-feminist? You believing you know what I want better than I do."

He was still so close, and that meant she could see the way his blue eyes gleamed. It made every hair on the back of her neck prickle, the way the dance of the northern lights across these far northern skies did. As if he was that elemental and otherworldly.

She told herself he was just a man. Nothing more and nothing less.

No matter that there was a part of her that wanted to make him a myth instead.

"What I believe is that all of us are made of a storm of competing desires and needs," Thor said, almost gently. As if he knew the real storm was the one happening inside Margot. "Some of us privilege one over the other. Some of us take pride in our labels, but these are always attempts to control the uncontrollable, are they not? You are the expert, after all. Surely you must know this already. People can talk. People can define themselves and others in any number of ways. But desire, passion, need—these things are not quantifiable no matter how we might wish they were. And for all our advances across the centuries, no one has yet figured out how to control them."

"I don't believe in that kind of passion," Margot whispered.

She didn't. She knew she didn't and she never had. She had written papers on the subject of passion and the many ways people tried to personify the feeling. Because if it was a kind of person, a being, they could blame it for all manner of things, like a demon of yore. A devil intent on their destruction.

If passion was responsible, the actual person in question need never be.

But there was something about saying it out loud, here, to Thor, that made her gut tighten as if she'd told him a lie.

"Passion is like truth, I am afraid," Thor told her, almost sorrowfully. "It does not require your belief to exist."

"You haven't answered the question."

He lifted the hand that held that bright white napkin, but the way he waved it between them had nothing to do with surrender. Or, at least, not his surrender. "And you have gone to great lengths to avoid this little bit of cloth, have you not?"

Margot's heart gave a terrific thump in her chest, or maybe it was in her belly. Or her pussy, where she felt a sharp jolt. It was everywhere. It was all of her.

She felt ripped wide-open. As if he'd wheeled in a giant spotlight and aimed it directly at her, so bright she could feel the heat of the light itself.

"If you are afraid, there is no shame in admitting it," Thor said in that same surprisingly gentle way she would have said he didn't have, which somehow made her feelings of exposure worse.

"Do I need to be afraid?"

"I would never dream of telling you what you need—lest I be accused of single-handedly imposing the will of the patriarchy upon you."

She glared at him, and at that dry way he talked about the things she'd spent years studying and considering and immersing herself in as if they were so much teenaged caterwauling.

"I would suggest that you view this as a test, nothing more."

Margot didn't tell him that she had always been excellent at tests. "What am I meant to be testing? How much I trust you?"

"I think the fact that you are here, naked and alone in my rooms, speaks to how much you trust me already." And there was nothing threatening in the way he said that. It was a simple statement of fact. And still, Margot felt as if he'd dropped a noose around her neck and pulled it tight. "In any case, this is not about me. It is about you."

"How convenient for you."

"Professor, you don't have to do anything you don't want to do. You never have to do anything you don't want to do. I thought we covered this already when we experimented with consent in the other room. Repeatedly."

"I can assure you that I never, ever do a single thing I don't want to do."

He didn't point out, again, that she was naked and alone with him and had already done things she really ought to be ashamed of. But he didn't need to when Margot was capable of doing it herself, did he?

"What I think is that you do want to do this," he said instead, with all that maddening, seductive patience. "And more, I think the fact you want to put this gag in your own mouth and see what it teaches you, that the very idea makes you wet and greedy, is what scares you most."

Her body was on his side, not hers. Her pussy swelled at his words, and she felt her own wet heat on her thighs.

Damn him.

"It amazes me that you think you can know anything about another person on so short an acquaintance," Margot said loftily, because she didn't know how to do anything but fight. "We are strangers. A state of undress doesn't change the fact that you don't know anything about me."

Thor smiled. "Here is what I know. You cannot

bear to let a challenge go unmet, no matter what it costs you. You will force yourself to do things that make you uncomfortable rather than risk losing face. You concentrate on the task set before you, simply because it has been set before you, rather than look inward to see whether or not you want to do it at all."

Margot stiffened. He didn't know her life. He didn't know all the committees she sat on at the university when she wasn't on sabbatical, all because she didn't know how to say no. He didn't know how many papers she'd agreed to coauthor for the same reasons. He couldn't possibly know that when she was so stressed out she thought that ache in her shoulders might never go away, she knew full well she had no one to blame but herself and her own stubbornness.

All he knew about her was how to find her clit. Not a bad skill to have. But not exactly psychic powers, either.

"I complete tasks because that's what adults do, generally speaking," she said. From between her teeth. "It's part of not being a coddled child. The alternative is leaving tasks undone, and *that* leads to chaos, in my experience. Maybe you like having the power turned off because you forgot to take the time to complete the simple task of paying the bill. I don't."

"You didn't have to remove your clothes simply because I asked you to." Thor was studying her again, that fierce blue gaze of his seeing far too much. "I asked you to prove something to me and you did. But why did you do it? Why should you have to prove anything? You could simply have said what you wanted, enthusiastically and repeatedly. But it made you feel safer to have an adversary, did it not?"

She felt dizzy. He might as well have kicked her, hard, in the solar plexus. It took her a long, desperate moment to catch her breath. "I don't think that's true at all."

"But you do think that wanting to experiment with things that have overtones that humorless people take great pleasure in excavating for evidence of wrongdoing makes you weak, somehow. I saw the expression on your face when I suggested that you turn your mouth off for a while. It intrigues you as much as it terrifies you." Thor's smile hurt her. It actually hurt. "You pride yourself on your mind and your mouth, do you not? Who are you if you cannot express yourself exactly as you wish, whenever you wish it? Are you afraid you will cease to exist? I can assure you, my suspicious professor—you will not."

She felt as if she couldn't breathe, but she knew that she could. That she was. She could feel her own chest rise and fall too rapidly. She could hear the ragged sound of her own breath, telling him everything he needed to know without her having to form a single word.

Proving him right.

"I don't think..." she began.

"But that is what we are arguing about. You are not a brain in a jar, Margot. What you think is not independent of your flesh. Your passion. One cannot destroy the other, no matter how hard you try."

"I don't understand what you get out of this. Is it simply that you enjoy the act of humbling—" She almost said *women*, then. But something in the way he watched her kept her from it. "Do you want to humble me? Is that what this is about?"

"I don't want to humble you."

"Then what? Why?"

"I like the things that sex can do above and beyond the act itself. I don't think it's a game. I don't think you can research it the way you might a cell or a virus. Humans are deeply complex and emotional creatures, are we not? Sometimes, if we push our own boundaries, we discover things we never knew were there."

"I have to tell you, Thor. That doesn't sound anything like a handshake."

He smiled anew at that, then took her hand as if he meant to shake it, though he didn't.

"Are you finished talking?" he asked quietly. "Or do you have more nerves to work through?"

Margot knew she had to do it. She had to try, anyway.

She knew other things, too. Such as the fact that somehow, though it shouldn't have been possible, this man really had discovered things about her without benefit of the usual narratives she told about what she liked and didn't like. About who she was or wasn't.

How had he seen all of that? How had sex given him that sort of key to her?

It made her feel restless deep inside.

But when all she wanted to do was open her mouth and comment on that, extensively and possibly with footnotes, she knew she was stalling.

She made herself reach over and take the napkin from him. And if he saw the way her hand shook, he didn't mention it, proving yet again how unexpectedly kind he was.

It burned through her with its own kind of heat.

It sank down into her bones. It shivered through her, like the blood in her veins. It made her want to cry.

She almost lost her courage, then.

Why are you doing this? that part of her she'd always considered her most rational demanded. *Why are you submitting yourself to something like this?*

But she wanted to see.

She wanted to know.

And Thor stood there before her, that patient intensity illuminating his bright blue gaze and tearing her up inside in too many ways to count.

As if this wasn't about the storm and never had been, but was about Margot herself—and he could wait forever if that was what it took.

It astounded her how much safer she felt when her gaze connected with his and held.

Or better yet, when approval flashed over his lean, fierce face.

Margot rolled the napkin into a long, thin tube, concentrating perhaps a little too hard on making it even. Then she lifted it to her mouth, took a deep breath and fit the napkin between her teeth like some kind of bit for a horse.

She wouldn't call it *surrender*. She wasn't certain she wanted that word in her vocabulary.

But either way, she caught the blue in his eyes. She felt all of that dark intent like his hands around her neck, a perfect storm in the form of a necklace she doubted she'd ever take off, and Margot stopped fighting.

She took a deep breath…and let go.

CHAPTER SEVEN

SHE WAS SO beautiful it hurt.

So brave it didn't merely make his cock hard, it made him worry that he didn't have the control he knew he needed to do this thing.

Because Thor knew that he needed to do it properly if he wanted to do it at all.

He fought to find his center. To calm himself down by focusing on her instead of that greedy fist of need that had him entirely too close to the edge already.

Because she might look at him with those bright gold eyes of hers lit with suspicion, but she trusted him. Although they had never met before tonight, he wasn't the only one who no longer felt as if they were strangers. As if they had never really been strangers.

As if she was more to him in ways he wasn't sure he liked.

It was such an odd sort of intimacy, but Thor didn't fight it. Because she had put that gag in her mouth for no other reason than that he'd suggested it.

She trusted him.

Not because she knew him or really anything about him. Not because she'd heard enough rumors about him from random people in Reykjavík to form a sketchy opinion that might allow her to engage in a quick, meaningless fuck. Not because he was Daniel St. George's eldest illegitimate son and somehow the most accessible of the lot—or so it seemed to Thor when the three of them had their stilted, careful conversations, as ordered by the father none of them had known or liked all that much.

Margot might have known a few broad details about Thor, the way everyone did since the will had come out and made him an international person of interest instead of merely one of Iceland's relatively few celebrities. But none of that was why she was willing to trust him tonight.

None of that was why she was standing before him, her eyes wide and that napkin distorting the shape of her lovely mouth.

She trusted him because of what had happened here, over the course of this deliciously endless night. She trusted him because he hadn't told her who he was, he'd shown her.

And now he had the opportunity to show her who *she* was, too.

It was a privilege.

Margot was breathing hard and a little too fast through her nose, and he could see the sheen of glassiness that made her eyes gleam ever more gold. Her hands kept forming into fists at her sides, then releasing. Over and over, as if she was *this close* to bolting.

But she didn't balk. She didn't break.

And when he reached over to liberate that wrap from around her shoulders, the only reaction he got was the faintest, finest little tremor snaking down her torso before she squared her shoulders and repressed it.

Out in the main, rambling room of his penthouse that he liked because it told visitors nothing about him, she looked like the finest of the art he collected and hung in the house he kept in the city. Except better. More precious.

Thor stood back from her and took a moment to admire her. All that fine, flushed skin. The upturned pink of her nipples, the strawberry blond curls between her legs. And the lavender hair that fell all around her, cascading over her shoulders in a kind of artless invitation.

And she trusted him.

It was enough to make him lose it right there, but he didn't.

Somehow, he didn't.

He took her hand and led her out from the seating area where they'd eaten, closer to the enormous fireplace that was built into one sleek wall and looked as if the fire rose directly from the decorative volcanic rock. But he didn't stop there. He kept moving until they stood before the giant window that in good weather looked out over the brooding sea. Tonight it would be much too dark and stormy to see anything even if he'd had all the lights on.

Which he didn't. So what he saw when he looked

at his window was Margot's reflection in the glass
and, here and there, hints of the driving snow outside.

He stood behind her for a moment, soaking in
the view.

He could also see that Margot didn't like it. He
saw the way her brows drew together, and that snap
in her gaze when it met his in the glass.

"See?" he murmured, snaking an arm around her
middle to haul her closer to him and enjoying the feel
of her, silky and warm. He held her with her back
flush against his front so she could feel his heat. His
strength. His greedy cock in the small of her back.
"Your nonverbal communication comes across loud
and clear. You do not want to look at yourself like
this. You do not want to be on display. No doubt you
have some concerns about objectification."

Her nostrils flared slightly. Then, slowly, she nodded.

Thor brushed her hair away from her neck on one
side and bent to taste her there, sweet and hot.

"Perhaps it is time we talk about the differences
between objectification and admiration," he said,
right there against her skin where he could taste the
way she trembled. "You assume that being on display makes you less, somehow, when we raise our
gods and our icons high, the better to adore them. We
elevate the things we cherish. We create pedestals,
cathedrals, museums. Why should it be any different between lovers?"

He put his hands on her skin, running one palm
over that tattoo on her side that declared her persis-

tence. And he moved the other higher on her rib cage until it rested just below her breast, and tried not to let the sight right there in the window before them roar through him unchecked, because he wasn't sure he'd be able to keep himself under control if it did.

"You were so concerned about power dynamics earlier," he continued. "But ask yourself this. Did I give you orders or make suggestions? And if I did issue an order, why are you focusing on the order rather than your need to follow it? Is it problematic if you want to do it or only if you think I want you to do it?"

He studied her face and that frown she still wore, though her teeth were clenched down hard on the napkin. He wasn't sure he'd ever seen anything prettier or more compelling than Margot fighting her need to tear that napkin from her mouth and light into him with all those mighty words she knew.

But it was his turn to do the talking.

"If we are two consenting adults and we both get something out of a power dynamic, why must it be considered problematic at all?" he asked. "Why do you imagine you get to decide how it is that other people get off in the first place?"

She made a little noise of protest and he smiled. "It seems to me that if a woman tells you that she enjoys submission, as you claim you do not, you are the one who is infantilizing her if you decide that the only way she can enjoy such things is if she has somehow betrayed herself. Or does not know her own mind sufficiently to make that determination.

If a woman tells you that she is no victim but you decide that you know better, who is truly victimizing her?"

Thor didn't glance toward her face to see if he could divine her answer from her expression. He didn't need to. He could feel the way she trembled in his hands. He indulged himself instead, shifting his palm so he could cover one of those velvety nipples that stood there, pink and proud.

He moved his palm in slow, lazy circles and kept his mouth at her neck.

"I think that no matter how you try to politicize sex or what good intentions you might have for doing it, all you truly end up doing is judging personal preference. And my suggestion to you, Professor, is that personal preference is none of your business."

And he punctuated that thought by finding her hot, wet pussy with his free hand.

He could hear the moans she made in her throat, sweet and needy. He could feel that same neediness in a rush of damp heat against his fingers.

Thor stroked her folds, gently playing with her clit. Almost as if it was an afterthought, and her hips moved as if of their own accord in time to his every light, teasing stroke. Her hands fisted and released at her sides.

Again and again.

"All this research you do. All these papers you write. All the many ways you try to convince yourself that this isn't real." He put his mouth to her ear and it was as if he could taste her arousal, all that delirious heat. He made his strokes longer, lazier, and felt the way her hips hitched. "Does it feel real now?"

She made another noise. Frustration. Helpless need. Thor reached over to take one of those convulsive little hands in his, then drew it between her legs.

And had the particular delight of feeling her freeze. Then bloom with heat.

Everywhere.

"Feel yourself. Your pussy doesn't lie, Margot." He was teaching her a lesson, and yet it was the first time he hadn't called her *Professor.* And that seemed to strike an odd little note in him, a ringing like a bell that seemed to move in all his limbs at once, but he shoved it aside. "You're either wet or you are not. Your pussy knows exactly what it wants. And it has no compunction about telling you. Feel your wetness. Feel how you quiver. Your body knows what it needs, what it desires. It is only you who are confused."

She made another one of those angry, frustrated sounds and he smiled, there in the crook of her shoulder where she could feel it.

"If you could talk, would you tell me that you are not confused at all? I think you would. But that's the trouble with words. They are indirect. They stretch across feelings and analyze them, contain them, change them in the telling. Your body is more direct. Uncompromising, you might say. There's a certain purity in a hard cock and a wet pussy. Everything else is a complication. Everything else is what we put on it, not what it is."

He slid his fingers over hers, there in all her slickness, and showed her exactly what he wanted her to do.

"Make yourself come," he ordered her, his voice like a growl. "And the beauty of the gag in your mouth is that you cannot tell me if that's possible or impossible. You can only do it."

She made another noise, but it wasn't a word. He wasn't sure it was even an attempt at words. He lifted his head so he could see the look of flushed frustration on her face in the window, and that ever-present frown of hers that he found he'd begun to crave. She looked as if she wanted to object. To argue.

But the truth was in that hand beneath his, buried between her thighs. She rocked her palm against her clit and she didn't stop. She didn't even pause, no matter how she scowled at him.

"The more you think, the less you feel," Thor told her, his gaze fused to hers in the reflection before them. "And if you are talking, you cannot be listening. So this is my challenge to you, Professor. Stop thinking. Stop talking—especially to yourself. Lose yourself in this."

And for a while there was nothing but the sound of her breath and the soft sound of her hand working between her legs.

Thor played with her nipple. He watched her face. "It either feels good or doesn't. You will either come or you won't. Does your body know what it wants? And if it does, do you give it what it wants or do you deny it out of some misplaced notion of what you *ought* to like?"

Her breathing was heavy. He couldn't tell if it was frustration or something else now, but either way, she didn't stop. He stood there behind her, the scent of her heavy in the air between them. It was a musky female arousal and a sharp, full vanilla that was all Margot. He wanted to taste her. He wanted to lift her up, tip her forward and settle her on his own aching cock at last.

But he waited, though he thought the waiting might kill him. He shifted to move his hands over her curves instead. As if he was settling and soothing her as much as he was attempting to excite her. He traced the span of her hips. He smoothed his palms up her sides, then along her arms.

He explored her as if he was committing her to memory, stroke by stroke.

And all the while she fucked herself with her hand, rolling her hips to meet her own palm.

Thor got to watch that delicious flush spread out over her skin, from the sweet triangle of her coppery curls to her lavender hair that fell down all around her, teasing the tips of her breasts. Her eyes drifted closed. Her head lolled back against his shoulder.

"Come," he ordered her, low and gritty. "Come, Professor. Now."

And when she obeyed him, it was like a tempest shook through her. He found himself gripping her hips to hold her steady. To keep her on her feet. Or better yet, to keep her from toppling over where she stood.

She shook and she shook. And when the shaking subsided, her hand dropped from between her thighs and she slid, boneless and still breathing hard, against him.

Thor turned her around in his arms, then picked her up and carried her over to the thick rug before the fire. He dropped to his knees and set her on hers.

And then he took his time and a good deal of care pushing her hair back from her face. He tucked the damp lavender strands behind her ears. And he didn't know what to call that weighty, complicated, knotted thing that squatted there in his chest and refused to be dislodged.

He didn't know what to call the urges that rolled through him then, none of them about the heavy need in his cock. None of them about pounding his way to oblivion.

The trouble with teaching lessons was that he couldn't avoid learning a few of his own while he did it.

And one of them was the simple fact that this woman was nothing like the many other women Thor had enjoyed in his past. He was too…involved. He was obsessed with that mouth he wasn't allowed to kiss. He was entirely too invested in the things he wanted to show her. About herself. About the pair of them. About sex itself. But he wasn't as removed as he usually was. He couldn't seem to find his footing or his usual distance.

Something about Margot was lodging its way deep inside him whether he liked it or not. As if she was leaving scars he wasn't entirely sure would ever heal.

Worse, he must have liked it. Because he wasn't doing a thing to stop it.

Especially when Margot pulled the napkin from her mouth. She made a face as she ran her tongue around inside her own mouth, tossing the bit of cloth to the side.

"Dry?" he asked, feeling as close to desperate as he'd ever been.

Because he wasn't used to this...*wanting*. He hadn't lied to her. Icelanders fucked. He certainly did and it had always been fun. Sometimes an intense kind of fun.

But it had never been like this, as if she was stripping away layers of his skin every time she met his gaze. Every time she frowned at him. Every time she came in that pink rush.

Even though she'd removed her gag, Margot didn't speak. She blinked once, then again, as if she was getting her bearings. And when she lifted her gaze to meet his, the gold in them was so brilliant he nearly looked away.

She was flushed and she was fierce and he wanted her in ways he didn't understand. He wanted to fuck her. He wanted to lose himself in her. He wanted *her*, all of her. Not just her nakedness, but every complicated thought in that fascinating head of hers.

She was breaking all his rules.

Margot reached over, put her hands on his chest and didn't say a word as she pushed him backward.

Thor could have fought her, of course, but he saw no reason to do such a thing. Not when he could fall back against the rug and let her climb over him and surrender himself to part of what he wanted.

He kept expecting her to say something. To challenge him in that way of hers. To analyze what had already happened and throw her buzzwords at him in that way she did.

Because he craved that, too.

But it seemed that she had taken his advice to heart, because she didn't say a word.

She simply…helped herself to his body as if he was the object.

Or, if he corrected himself, as if he was what she admired.

And she took her sweet time admiring him.

She used her mouth all over his chest. Her mouth and her hands and the seductive sweep of that lavender hair. She tasted him and she teased him, licking her way over his nipples and then tracing the outline of his pectoral muscles. She knelt beside him and explored each arm, and each leg, the way he'd done. She tugged off his loose trousers and threw them aside, and then she started all over again.

She kissed him everywhere except his cock and his mouth, and by the time she crawled back up the length of him and threw herself down beside him, Thor thought he might go out of his mind. He worried he already had. He thought his skin might crack wide-open with the force of his need—

And the only way he knew how to handle it was to get inside her.

Even though he already understood it wouldn't be enough.

She still hadn't said a word.

"Have you gone mute?" he gritted out, his control a pale shadow of what it ought to have been. He knew that, and even if he hadn't, he could hear it. He couldn't tell if it was anger or anguish or some passionate form of torment in between the two, but he couldn't keep it in. It spilled out of him as if of its own accord.

And the crazy part was, he couldn't seem to bring himself to care about that the way he should have. The way he knew he would, if he survived.

"Tell me what you want," she demanded, her voice husky from disuse.

And more, with something else that it took him long moments to realize was a kind of sheer, humming power that resonated inside him like the towering wall of the ferocious North Atlantic over a black sand beach.

Like home.

"You," he growled. "Now."

"You have to be more specific," she told him, and even though her lips curved, there was still that fierceness, a kind of wickedness that made every part of his body pull tight and hard.

She was a goddess. Gold and purple, flushed sweet cream.

Thor was lost.

"I need you beneath me, Margot," he managed to grit out.

He didn't know which one of them moved then, only that they were flipping around until he was on top of her at last, pressing himself into that sweet cradle between her legs.

They were both blessedly naked. And for a moment Thor held himself there, enjoying the simple perfection of her bare skin against his. The way his cock notched into her soft heat.

The anticipation.

"I'm beneath you," Margot said in that same demanding, daring way that lit him up everywhere they touched. And everywhere they didn't. "Now what?"

"I am not the one who hides behind words," he said, though everything in him shouted for him to simply tilt his hips, find her slick entrance and bury himself in her pussy at last. "Do you think I need to learn the same lessons?"

"I think that you're so certain you don't need to learn a thing that it probably means you do," Margot replied simply, that powerful current running through her and into him.

And the fact she was saying something he didn't want to hear didn't change that electricity.

If anything, it turned a simple charge into a lightning strike.

"I already told you. I'm fluent in all kinds of languages. My body isn't a mystery to me, Margot."

And as if he had to prove it, right there and then, he thrust himself deep inside her.

She groaned. He did, too. And for a moment the pleasure was so intense, almost excruciating, it was as if they had to freeze to survive the impact of it.

Thor held himself above her, his palms braced against the ground on either side of her head. And Margot was a flushed tangle of purple hair and bright eyes beneath him.

"But you have no issues, of course," Margot murmured, her voice soft but still infused with that note of power that made him think of the sea. "You have no needs. You're near perfect, just as you are."

There were a thousand things Thor could have said then, but he didn't. He pulled out, taking his time in making certain he dragged the head of his cock over all the parts of her he could, there in that tight channel where he'd already found each and every place that made her shiver. He found them all again. He reminded them both how well he fit. Then he thrust himself back in.

But Margot was still talking. "It's perfectly normal to run a hotel like this. To live in an antiseptic penthouse that echoes when you walk. You have no daddy issues at all. If we opened up a dictionary right this minute, we would find your picture next to the word *well-adjusted*. I'm certain of it."

He knew she was taunting him. And he thought he should stop it. Or counter it, anyway. He certainly couldn't allow it to go unchallenged—

But he didn't use words. He thought words were beside the point.

He used the deep thrust, then the slow drag out.

He used the angle of his hips and the way he moved them. He used the intensity of his pace and the way he could alter it at will to throw her toward the edge and then keep her there.

And keep her there.

She laughed, breathless and more than a little bit wild. And then she braced her hands on his chest as if that could stop this. As if anything could stop this.

"Here's what I know about you, Thor," Margot said, and her voice was thicker now. He could hear the little breaths that caught in her throat every time he surged deep within her, but she didn't stop. "You like to talk. You claim to be about the body, but the truth is that it's all mind games, isn't it? The only question I have is—who are you playing those games for, me or you?"

He shifted, going down on his elbows so he could press the wall of his chest against the glory of her breasts and make it all ache that much more.

"You're so cool. So aloof. You claim you listen to your body, but even while you fuck you're analyzing. Cataloging." Her gaze was a blaze of gold. "No wonder sex is your favorite form of recreation. You don't have to worry about true intimacy when everything is so clinical."

Thor didn't tell her what he thought about her sudden abiding interest in intimacy. He showed her. He picked up his pace, moving just fast enough so that she hitched up her knees on either side of him, putting her feet flat on the rug to give herself a little purchase to lift up and meet each thrust.

"You live in a sex hotel. You have this stark and empty penthouse all to yourself. You're so busy building walls around yourself that you don't even know you're doing it. Nothing can touch you. No one can know you. The more available you make yourself, the less you can be seen. But I see you."

Her voice broke then. And Thor wasn't thinking. He wasn't sure he was listening so much as he was withstanding the way each word she said burned into him, and scorched him deep inside.

And all the while he was lost in that sweet, delirious slide. He couldn't tell anymore if he was keeping to a pace or if he was simply losing himself inside her.

He couldn't tell if he was lost.

And he didn't care.

"I see you, Thor," she whispered again, and then everything was fire. There was a blistering light that ate them both alive, an electric madness that he didn't know whether to crave or fear.

He did neither. Both. He pounded into her and she met him, and he couldn't tell who was fucking who.

It was as if they were moving parts of the same whole, making a blistering storm all their own.

He felt her shake again, and he knew her now. He knew the way she came apart. He knew that tight, hot clench of her pussy around his cock. The way her thighs clamped down on the outside of his. The way she lifted herself to take more of him, all of him, arching her back to press herself even more firmly against him.

And Thor kept going. He fucked her through one orgasm, then straight on into another.

It was too hot. It was too *right*. He believed that she could see him and more, worse, he could see himself at last.

And when he released himself inside her, he knew beyond a shadow of a doubt that he was lost.

The trouble was, he understood as he heard himself shout out her name and tumble off into the madness of that storm they'd built, he didn't think he wanted to be found.

CHAPTER EIGHT

Margot woke slowly, a delicious sort of warmth all over her.

It took her a long moment, then another, to understand where she was.

Iceland. Thor Ragnarsson's famous sex hotel. Trapped at the notorious Hotel Viking by a blizzard, no less.

Which meant she'd actually survived the most intense night of her life.

She opened her eyes and found herself out on one of the low, wide couches in the main room in Thor's stark penthouse. She could hear his voice, though she couldn't see him from where she lay, sprawled out on the sofa that could have fit them both—and had, if she wasn't mistaken. She shifted, realizing as she did that he had tucked her under a thick duvet and that was what was keeping her toasty warm despite the fact she was still naked.

Margot sat up slowly, blinking as she looked around. There was still snow on the other side of the large windows, but the difference was that she

could see light out there as well. Far more light, anyway, than she had seen since yesterday morning in
Reykjavík.

It took her a moment to find Thor. He was far
away, down at the other end of the great space in
what she quickly realized must have been his office. He was speaking on the phone in rapid Icelandic, standing with his back to her and his gaze out
at the storm.

He had dressed. More than simply dressed. He
was wearing the kind of suit that made it perfectly
clear that he was a man of international clout. It was
dark and cut to flatter, making him look taller, somehow. More beautiful, if such a thing was possible.
He held one hand on the top of his head, as if he'd
started to rake it through his blond hair but had forgotten to complete the action.

And Margot was fiercely, fervently glad that he
couldn't see her. That she had a moment without
that piercing blue stare of his boring into her. That
she could take a breath or two to compose herself.
Hell, to *remember* herself. To try to put the jumble
of thoughts and sensation into some kind of order
without knowing he was watching her do it.

She had only the vaguest memories of what had
happened there before the fire after that last, intense
round of this game that didn't feel anything like a
game at all. She had no idea how long they'd lain
there together. She'd been slightly aware when he'd
moved them to the couch, and she knew that he had
slept there with her for some time. She had no mem-

ory of him leaving her, and even less of him covering her up.

She was almost certain it was morning, though she supposed it could be later on into the day, with all that snow.

Margot felt like a different person.

She found her fingers on her mouth, as if she expected to feel bruised there. But she thought that really, if there were any marks, they would be inside her. She felt torn apart. Rearranged.

Changed beyond recognition.

She pulled the duvet more tightly around her and took stock of her body, realizing with an uneasy sort of sensation that even her own limbs didn't feel like hers any longer.

Margot had dedicated her life to the pursuit of knowledge, but Thor had taught her—over and over and over again—how very little she knew about something as basic and fundamental as sex.

She'd spent her adult life studying something she had never experienced—not really, not like this or anything near *this*—and she suspected that, given time, she would find that horrifying. And maybe also sad.

She felt too many things, all at once, and her experience with that damned napkin had already taught her too well.

She didn't try to interpret them. She didn't try to analyze them.

It was as if they rolled through her, one wave and then the next. A deep kind of regret that she had never known what she was missing. That she had been so certain she was in the position to lecture on the topic of sex in the first place when all the sex she had ever had before had been so…deficient. There was an exultant kind of exhilaration that her body could do those things. That she could feel those things. That she was capable of so much she hadn't even known was possible.

Looking at Thor made her sad. Furious. Giddy. And so silly that she could feel a smile on her mouth for absolutely no reason at all.

One wave and then the next.

She felt ashamed that it had taken a gag in her mouth to teach her how to find her voice. She had a picture of herself in her head, that napkin in her mouth and her hand between her legs, and she felt it, too. The memory turned her on even as it made something in her stomach turn over, as if she thought she ought to find it sickening. But mostly it just made her hot all over again.

She *felt*.

And Margot had no earthly idea how she was ever going to manage to put these things she felt into any kind of order. How she was ever to make sense of them.

Thor finished his conversation and tossed his phone on the desk that spread there across the whole of one wall in a kind of nook that prevented her from seeing his numerous screens straight on. He didn't turn around. He stayed where he was, staring out the

window, and Margot thought she would give anything at all to see the expression on his face.

But when he turned, she had the sense that he'd
known that she was awake and watching him all
along, because his expression was wiped clean.

For a moment they only stared at each other, all
the rambling, empty space of the penthouse between
them.

Margot thought there was a whole lot more distance than that. And more, she could feel it gape
wider and more impassable inside her the longer they
did nothing but…look at each other.

When his phone rang again, it was a relief.

Thor held her gaze for a long moment. The ringing continued, but he didn't move to answer anything and she wasn't sure what she saw in his face.
It wasn't as simple as resignation. His eyes were too
blue for that. And she was sure that all that aloofness
she'd noticed before was different now.

Everything is different now, something intoned,
deep inside her.

His phone kept ringing.

"I have to take this," he told her, almost stiffly, in
a voice that didn't sound loud at all and yet managed
to echo down the length of the great room.

Margot inclined her head as if she was giving
him her permission. And she could see Thor didn't
like it. If she were a better person, she would have
offered to remove herself to the next room while he
handled his business.

But this was the man who'd encouraged her to put a fucking napkin in her mouth.

"Intimacy takes many forms, doesn't it?" she replied, also pitching her voice to carry. "It's really the gift that keeps on giving."

She saw temper flash across Thor's face, but he didn't argue with her any further. He turned back to his office and rummaged for something on his desktop. Not that anyone would have known it was the desktop. Margot hadn't seen the desk before, and it took her perhaps too long to realize that was because it was the sort of desk that could be hidden away in a cabinet. Imagine that. A whole life that could be easily tucked away from prying eyes whenever the mood took him.

It seemed she knew more about Thor than she'd realized. That she had been right on target, in fact.

Margot waited to feel a surge of triumph, but it was something else that moved in her, making her feel a little too close to a man who was standing as far away as it was possible to get from her while still being in the same sprawling penthouse.

"It's angled," Thor said, which made no sense. "You're not in the frame."

She didn't understand that, or why he hadn't answered that ringing, but then the huge, flat screen on the wall behind his desk area bloomed into life and color.

"Why do you always look like you're standing in a fucking morgue?" came a low, raspy voice with an American accent. Not just a random, unplaceable

American accent that could have been from anywhere, but one laced with hints of the South and a faint, dirty drawl.

Margot sank down on the couch, suddenly entirely too aware that Thor was *on a video call* and she was naked. Covered up in a comforter, sure. Out of frame, he'd said. But she was naked all the same, and that felt…wrong when there was another voice. And when it sounded like *that*.

"I assume you mean that my Nordic sensibilities offend you," Thor was saying in reply.

And he sounded…not quite like the man she thought she'd come to know over the course of a night that Margot felt had lasted several lifetimes already. Something scraped at her, thick and insistent, and she realized that he sounded like the Thor she had met downstairs last night. There in the bar, when he'd come up behind her and she'd thought he was nothing but another hotel guest. Who'd been attempting to hit on her.

It made her feel a little dizzy to think about how different things were now. How much a single night had changed them both.

"Sensibilities don't offend me, brother," the same voice replied.

"Aloha, motherfuckers," a third voice chimed in then. Richer, darker. And with a lilting sort of hint of an accent that Margot found unfamiliar but assumed went along with the Hawaiian greeting.

She peeked her head up over the back of the couch to sneak a look at the screen, hoping she really was out of frame. She assumed she must have been when no one said anything, and that allowed her to study the screen. It was split in two. On one side sat a very large, gorgeously muscled man bathed in sunlight with palm trees and blue water behind him. His eyebrows were arched and jet black, a fascinating contrast to his brown skin and the smirk on his surprisingly lush mouth. His black hair fell around his face, a little too long to Margot's way of thinking. A little too messy.

He wasn't beautiful, but he was purely carnal. Margot was surprised he didn't sizzle.

She was surprised she didn't, simply from looking at him.

The man on the other side of the screen was blond, though a darker, dirtier blond than Thor. He was also built out of lean, hard muscles and razor-sharp lines, like those fascinating cheekbones of his. And maybe it was his similarities to Thor that clued her in: his blue eyes, though a darker, moodier blue than Thor's; a tilt to his head that suggested he was up to no particular good; the kind of mouth that made Margot's mind seem to go blank for a whole beat or two.

She understood that these must be Thor's half brothers. Thor's famous half brothers, made objects of international interest the moment their existence had been confirmed at the reading of Daniel St. George's will six months ago.

Her heart thudded a little too hard for her peace of mind, but it wasn't because Thor's half brothers were so ridiculously attractive. It was because

Thor himself looked so…stern and disapproving as he glared at his screen.

"I thought *aloha* was a Hawaiian thing," the blond with the drawl said.

He was Charlie Teller, if Margot remembered her research into Thor correctly. The article she'd read about Daniel St. George's long-lost sons had made vague references to Charlie's brushes with the law and potentially dangerous associates. He didn't look dangerous on screen—or he didn't *only* look dangerous. He was grinning broadly, tipped back in a chair in a room somewhere. With terra-cotta walls that struck Margot as…insistent, somehow.

"It is a Hawaiian thing. *I'm* a Hawaiian thing."

That third voice was Jason Kaoki. She'd read about him, too. A local Pacific Island boy turned good, the fawning article had called him. He had gone off to college on the mainland on a full football scholarship and had even played a few years pro before sustaining the kind of injuries that had forced him into early retirement. He was rumored to be a major, if anonymous, philanthropist in Hawaii and other Pacific Islands. And then had come the will.

"You're not actually in Hawaii, though, are you?" Charlie asked. "I thought you were on some random ass island out there in the middle somewhere."

"Are you trying to throw down with me about some Pacific Island shit, you haole fuck?" Jason demanded, then belted out a big, broad laugh that seemed to warm up even this cavernous room where

Margot lay, far across the planet from his light and sea and palm trees, surrounded by snow and ice.

And a chilly Thor besides.

"As delightful as this questionable camaraderie is," Thor interjected coolly then, as if he could hear Margot's thoughts, "I believe this is meant to be a business call, is it not?"

"I'd tell you to chill out, brother," Charlie said, and Margot wondered if she was the only one who heard the sardonic kick in the way he used that word. *Brother.* "But I'm not sure that Viking ass could get any colder."

Jason laughed again and it had the same effect as before. Bright and loud, as if he didn't have a care in the world and didn't care what the idiots on his screen were talking about.

Though Margot imagined it would be a very foolish person indeed who failed to note the clever gleam in his dark gaze.

"I find Viking commentary entertaining," Thor said. "I do. But these conversations are supposed to be about money."

"I like money," Jason said, and he still sounded as merry. As lazy. "But how much can any one man have?"

"Meaning you're still holding out," Charlie replied, as if that was a code. "You might as well surrender, brother. The long arm of Daniel St. George reaches from beyond the grave whether you want it to or not. You can tell yourself whatever lies you

want, but believe me, you're going to end up building that hotel."

Jason smiled, big and broad, but Margot was
caught on the shrewd look in his gaze.

"You had a lot of good reasons to leave the mainland. I'm assuming Italy was one of those reasons.
Maybe your life choices on the mainland were another reason." Jason shrugged as if it was no matter
to him. As if he couldn't see the way Charlie's smile
became indefinably more dangerous. "But I like my
island the way it is."

"Jason is still holding off on development plans.
How is the Amalfi Coast treating you?" Thor asked
Charlie with no particular inflection in his cool
voice.

"Italian, Thor. It seems really fucking Italian."

There was more laughter, though somehow, it
didn't surprise Margot that Thor didn't join in.

"Everything continues apace here in Iceland,"
Thor told them. "Business is booming."

"Sex always sells," Charlie said with a shrug.
"And water is wet, the sun comes up in the east and
a douchebag is what a douchebag does."

"Is that life advice?" Jason asked.

"I'm a life coach in my spare time," Charlie drawled.

"We could all say a great many things about the
man, certainly," Thor said, an edge in his voice that
made goose bumps prickle along Margot's arms—
and also cut through his half brothers' laughter. "But
our father always had excellent taste in hotels."

"Don't call that asshole our father," Charlie muttered. "Jesus."

"He's nothing to me but one more haole," Jason said, which Margot interpreted as his agreement.

"I'm thrilled we agree on something," Thor said. "I'll send the usual email outlining our continued progress in our respective areas. Duty calls, gentlemen. Next week?"

"Next week," Charlie said with that same smile that the longer Margot looked at it, the less she thought was all that nice. "Every fucking week."

"Aloha, bitches," Jason said merrily.

And then there was silence when the screen went dark.

Margot stayed where she was. She was frowning toward the windows closest to her, shifting pieces around in her head, and it took her a moment to notice when Thor came to stand behind the couch. Next to her, but separated by the back of the couch.

And yet even though he had moved closer, it was as if he was on the other end of one of those video cameras. He looked as remote as if he'd carved himself from ice.

He made her feel shivery inside in a way that had nothing to do with sex, but felt a lot more as if she might tip over into tears at any moment. That closed-down look on his face made her hurt.

"Are you okay?" she asked quietly.

He looked startled, but only for a moment. Then it was straight back to ice and stone, shuttered and forbidding.

"It is a stipulation of the contracts we signed to take over the hotels our father left us that we hold these pointless conversations." He didn't sound like the man who had spent a long night weaving spells around Margot with his words alone. He sounded almost stilted. The way he had while he'd talked on his call. "Weekly."

"Does it stipulate that you have to be best friends on all those calls?" Margot pushed herself up, until she could cross her legs beneath her and sit up straight. "Either way, they didn't sound particularly awful."

"They are not awful. They are perfectly fine, I suppose, for full-grown men I am apparently related to and must now interact with as if we have some kind of history." Thor shook his head, but it was more as if he was shaking something off. "I do not understand brothers."

Margot thought that what he couldn't understand was connection, however new and strange, but she didn't say that. She didn't think it was the sort of thing he could hear at the moment. And probably not from her as she sat there, still sure she could taste that napkin in her mouth. "Have you met them in person?"

"The will was read in Germany." And once Thor said it, Margot remembered that she'd read that, too. The article had shown pictures of a law firm in Hamburg and paparazzi shots of men in dark coats and sunglasses. It was odd to think that she now knew what one of those dark-coated men tasted like. "The only thing more awkward than finding out that your father, who you never met and never wanted to meet, left you property you didn't want after his death is discovering that he did the same to others."

Margot wanted to touch him. She settled for her hands in fists in the duvet and a smile. "Do you think maybe he wanted all of you to band together and become some kind of family after he was gone?"

Thor laughed, though it was a far hollower sound than the laughter they'd heard from his half brothers. And it seemed to lodge between Margot's ribs. "He would have to have been delusional to imagine such a thing. But then, I think it is fairly clear that he was exactly that or he wouldn't have used his will to perform paternal acts in absentia. So who knows? Maybe this is what he thinks a family is."

"Thor…"

He was still dressed in that glorious dark suit of his and she considered it for a moment. He hadn't been wearing a suit yesterday. In her time in Iceland, come to that, she hadn't seen very many suits at all. They didn't go very well with the weather, for one thing. Which made her wonder why, exactly, Thor had chosen to throw one on this morning when he'd known he had to have this phone call with the half brothers he hardly knew.

She thought she could guess.

The idea that Thor, the strongest and most fascinating man she'd ever met, should feel the need to put on his armor before dealing with his family made a hot, prickling sensation threaten the backs of her eyes. Margot didn't dare let a single drop of moisture fall, but she had to blink a little too quickly to make sure.

And she gripped her duvet tighter.

"They say that a man is not truly a man until he teaches his son the sagas," Thor told her, after a long, taut silence. "I suppose it is another way of talking about fatherhood. But the man who taught me the sagas was my stepfather. Ragnar raised me. He taught me to read. He took care of my mother and me. He was a good man, always. In all my memories of childhood, I cannot recall a single time he drank too much or raised his voice. He was a big, kind, gentle man."

Margot was afraid to ask the next question. She had to force it out. "Is he…?"

"He died years ago, when I was twenty-five. He got a cough that wouldn't go away, and within three months, he was dead."

Margot searched his face and saw nothing. Only stone and ice and something harder still in the blue depths of his gaze.

"I'm so sorry," she said anyway.

"I am not telling you this story for your sympathy," Thor said with a kind of quiet menace that felt a lot like a kick to the gut, but Margot refused to show him that he'd landed a hit. "I always knew who my father was and it was not Daniel St. George. It was never Daniel St. George. I knew that name. I would have given anything not to know that name, but it was unavoidable. I hated him. But I never, not once, considered him my father."

Margot couldn't read him. There was a voice inside her that tasted a lot like panic, and it kept urging her to stop this. To go. To retreat from the tension, take a shower, pretend she couldn't tell that Thor was going through something.

But she couldn't bring herself to do it. "It makes sense to hate the man for leaving you."

Thor's mouth curved, cold and harsh. "You have to acknowledge a child in order to leave it, I think. Daniel St. George never condescended to do any such thing. I think I told you that my mother married Ragnar before I was born. But she never got over Daniel St. George. Never."

He shoved his hands into the pockets of his suit trousers, as if he didn't know what he meant to do with them. A kind of bitterness hung over him, like a cloud. She could see it in his eyes and in the twist of his lips. Worse, she could *feel* it, chilling her skin even though she still sat with the duvet wrapped around her.

"My mother is the one who drinks too much, Professor. And when she does, she cries. She becomes maudlin and bemoans all she has lost. Some might suggest that she lost nothing, but she never got over the man who left her without a second thought all those years ago. She spent the whole of her marriage to my stepfather nursing her broken heart. It was not something she bothered to hide. Her epic, eternal sadness, her inability to love Ragnar back, her grief—this was the third presence in our house. There was no point in making a child of their own because they not only had me, they had their very own ghost."

Margot thought of her own chilly upbringing. The pressure of her father's expectations. The way her mother had bent and contorted and still always proved that she was no match for the man she'd married. Margot's father had long since given up pretending he had anything but contempt for his spouse. And Margot understood now, in a different way than she had when she was younger, that she should be deeply ashamed that she, too, often had followed his lead because she and her mother had been engaged in a sick little competition to win the man's affection and regard.

It wasn't as if she wanted to hold her own family up as any kind of ideal. But there had never been any third parties in her parents' marriage or in the house where Margot had grown up. There had been no ghosts, only regrets.

"Did she ever see Daniel St. George again?" Margot asked gently, carefully. Because she didn't dare call the man Thor's father. She suspected that was a weapon he tolerated only when he wielded it himself.

Thor's gaze was so cold it made Margot's bones ache. "He had no desire to see her again, something that only became clear to her when he died. In many ways, he left her twice. He left her pregnant and alone, and then, all these years later, he left that will so he could slap her down once again by virtue of

ignoring her once more. And between you and me,
I am not certain she will ever fully recover."

"What do you mean?"

"It seems it took the callousness of the man's
will to finally make it clear to my mother what kind
of man he was," Thor said, all that bitterness and
icy chill making his voice sound different. Almost
scratchy. "The newspapers would have you believe
that it was an act of kindness. An old man reaching
out to the sons he'd abandoned and offering a kind of
olive branch from the grave. Perhaps my half brothers think so, I do not know."

"But you don't."

"I think it was one more demonstration of his
cruelty." Thor swallowed hard, and Margot had the
sense he could hear that scratchiness in his voice.
And hated it. "Because his will made it clear he knew
exactly who we were and where we had been, all this
time. He knew who had raised us and how. He knew
the details of our lives, which means he'd been paying attention, all these years. He could have made
contact at any point, but didn't. Daniel St. George
was interested in one thing only, and that was the
perpetuation of his name. Through his sons. He
didn't care who he'd made those sons with."

"Thor…"

"And do not deceive yourself. He has no interest
in the daughter he made, either. The only difference
between my overlooked half sister and the women
my father impregnated and abandoned is that my
sister was summoned to the will reading and left an

insult. Neither my mother nor anyone else was even mentioned. As far as Daniel St. George was concerned, they never existed."

"He sounds like a very sad, pathetic old man with dynastic pretensions."

Thor raked a hand through his hair, and it seemed he'd lost the battle with the emotion in his voice. It cracked. And it bled through into his blue gaze, too. "Now when my mother drinks, she does not regret the love she lost before I was born. She regrets the love she had all those years afterward that she could never quite accept. She regrets all those maudlin nights she cried for a man who cared nothing for her, while hurting one who did."

Margot hardly knew she meant to move, but then there she was, kneeling up on the couch so she could move herself closer to him. So she could reach out before she thought better of it and put her hands on his body.

She told herself not to pay any attention to that strange disconnection she felt because of it. Because he'd gone so cold overnight when she'd woken up warm all over.

Because she felt as if she knew him so well, and yet didn't know him at all, and she didn't have to have a hundred morning afters like this under her belt to understand that he likely didn't want to hear that.

"Thor," she said softly, amazed to find she could feel his heat through his clothes when she'd expected nothing but cold. "I'm sorry."

"You have nothing to apologize for. You weren't one of the players in this game." He looked down at her hands as if he couldn't make sense of them, there pressed into his sides. "I didn't build this antiseptic penthouse, you call it. I don't live here. This is a shrine my father built to celebrate himself. Hence the reflective surfaces. You heard my half brothers call it a morgue. He was a ghost throughout my childhood. Why not haunt my adulthood as well?"

"You're nothing like your father," Margot told him fiercely, and she didn't need the scientific method to achieve that conclusion. She knew.

"I never thought so. But then, Professor, the strangest things happen in sex hotels at the top of the world. A man who thinks he knows himself well might come to find that, unbeknownst to him, he has never been anything but a copy of the one man he hates above all others."

That shocked her, but she rallied. "I don't know what you're talking about. Nothing that happened last night makes you a man like that."

"It's all about intimacy, is it not?" Thor asked, a strange tension in his voice. She could feel it in the way he held himself. "Isn't that what we've been trying to fuck in and out of each other? And yet you can't live through a night like last night and not use it to take stock of all the other nights in your life, can you?"

"No," Margot said, and she didn't know if she was agreeing with him or denying what seemed to be coming next; what that knot of foreboding in her chest told her was surely coming next, no matter how she tried to hold on to him and the night they'd shared. With her fists.

"My father is famous for being a kind of sex god of his time. He has left the evidence littered about the planet in his wake. I have always been so certain that it was different when I did it. Because I am a different man. But perhaps that's the biggest lie of all and I am no different."

"Do you have a great many children out there that you refuse to acknowledge?"

"I have no children at all." Thor's mouth flattened. "As far as I know."

Margot told herself there was no reason she should feel so relieved to hear that. The man's sexual history was his business, not hers, and some people weren't parental…

But she had to fight to keep herself from grinning, because relieved was exactly what she felt.

"That's one difference," she said instead. "Another is that you're not cruel."

"You have no idea if that's true or not, Margot." And it was as if he tried to prove it then, with that expression on his face that made her wonder if he wanted her to hurt. To wonder. To fight to keep her breath from going shallow. "You have no idea how I plan to extricate myself from this situation. Will I let you down easy? Will I tell you lies? Will I simply make myself unavailable again?"

Her heart was slamming at her, but Margot kept her gaze trained on him. And for the first time since she'd woken up this morning, she wished she wasn't naked.

"You could do something truly revolutionary and choose none of the above," she suggested as evenly as she could.

"I promised myself two things," Thor gritted out. "One, that I would never be my father. And yet I realize that I have made myself his twin. I sleep around, without thought for the feelings of others. I have fun, so I assume they must be having fun as well. But how would I know?"

"You would know. Of course you would know."

It was almost funny to imagine he might not, after the attention he'd paid to…everything last night.

But he ignored her. "And second, I vowed that I would never become like my mother. A slave to emotions that ruined lives. My stepfather's. Her own."

"Yours?" Margot dared to suggest.

He didn't like that. That was clear, though all he did was stare down at her, his icy gaze glittering.

"And in one night, one single night, I have betrayed myself completely."

Margot moved again then, without thinking it through. Because she was in a panic, bright and searing, and she didn't know what to do except climb over the back of the couch and slide to the ground. And then she stood there before him, her hands gripping the jacket of his suit as if it was some kind of harness. As if she could lead him somewhere. As if she could muscle him into doing what she wanted—

Even if she didn't know what it was she wanted.

"This is what family is," she told him fiercely. "No one feels that they fit. Everyone thinks that they're missing something, somehow. If you're lucky, there's enough love in the mix that it all balances out, or so I hear, because it wasn't as if my father was any easier."

Margot felt disloyal saying such a thing out loud. Worse, she felt weak. As if in acknowledging that her father had been something less than ideal, she was showing her true colors after all. She was showing how little she had always been worth, just as her father had always suspected.

And if she'd been alone, that might have wounded her. That might have given her pause, at the very least. But she was too focused on Thor to care.

"Even if you followed in your father's footsteps, who cares?" she asked, because he'd handed her that napkin and freed her, somehow. And she wanted to do the same for him. "You're still not him. You'll never be him. You need to ask yourself why you think you have no choice in the matter."

She didn't miss the way her own words slammed into her, too. She didn't miss the fact that she'd never asked herself that question, either. What had she been trying to prove all this time? Why had she always allowed her father to make her feel, no matter what she did, that she didn't measure up?

And how could she tell Thor that he was the reason she was even capable of recognizing her own complicity in these things that had twisted her life around into something she wasn't sure she even wanted?

Margot didn't want to be a brain in a jar. She didn't want to hide in her words and her theories and her research.

She wanted to live her life, not study it.

With a quick breath for courage, she lifted herself up on her tiptoes and tilted her head back, because she knew exactly what she needed to do. She let go of his suit jacket and moved her hands up the hard-packed wall of his chest, every inch of which she'd tasted. Touched. And could likely re-create from memory, if necessary.

She looped her hands around his neck, letting her thumbs move over the splendor of his fine jaw.

"Margot."

Her name was a warning, but she didn't heed it. Instead, she lifted herself up even farther and went to press her lips to his.

But he stopped her. He reached up and took her upper arms in his hands, holding her away from him so she couldn't make contact.

"I want to kiss you," she said, and she knew, somehow, that it was more than a kiss.

That it was everything.

And more, she could see that he knew it, too. It was that gleaming light in his gaze, though his expression remained tortured.

It was everything, but he was keeping her from doing it.

"No," he said, as if the word was torn from him. "It's against the rules."

"I made the rules. I can break them, if I want."

"But I agreed to those rules. No kissing, Professor."

Margot didn't simply recognize the anguish she saw in his face then. She felt it, deep inside her. As if he was a part of her. As if he always would be, no matter what came next.

And she knew what was coming. She could see it. It was written all over him, and even though it was no more than they had agreed upon, it felt like the end of the world.

"Look out the window," he ordered her, though his voice told her things she knew he wouldn't. "The snow has stopped."

She didn't have to look. She didn't want to look. If she'd been paying attention to something other than Thor, she would already have noticed the sunlight beaming into the room, as crisp and cold as he was.

"You were trapped in my hotel while the storm ran its course," Thor said, as if he was handing down a sentence. As if he was throwing them both into prison, forever. "And now it has."

"Thor…" The next word stuck in her throat, but she forced herself to keep going, because she didn't care about power differentials when her heart was breaking into pieces. "Please…"

"We had an agreement, Margot," Thor said, and just like that, the torment on his face disappeared. She watched it go, leaving nothing but ice behind.

Until it was as if he had carved himself from the same volcanic rock that littered this island. It was as if he was nothing but sharp edges and the distant memory of ancient fires. As if the Thor she knew was gone. Or had never been at all. "And it's time for you to go."

CHAPTER NINE

EVERYTHING WAS FINE.

More than fine, as a matter of fact. Thor was not in the habit of having emotional responses to his sexual exploits, because there was no place for such absurdities in the face of a mere physical release, and he was determined that this should be no different.

Because it was no different, he told himself sternly.

The only thing that made his night with Margot unlike other nights he'd had was that she'd gotten a rare glimpse into the personal life Thor preferred to keep as private as possible—despite what everyone thought they knew about him, thanks to his successes and that damned will. It was an error he would have prevented if he'd thought it through that morning. And one he'd compounded by talking to her about things he never, ever discussed.

Never.

Thor had no idea why he'd done any of that—and he had no intention of ever repeating his mistakes.

There were some rules even he never broke.

The professor had left in a taxi Thor had ordered himself. And once she had gone, Thor took great pleasure in telling himself that he could breathe again. That the world made sense again. That the strange urges and feelings that he'd experienced during that storm were more about the storm than anything else. They weren't about Margot, because they couldn't have been.

Because that didn't make any sense.

That wasn't who Thor was.

Thor had spent the whole of his childhood watching the people in his life claim that love was the reason for all of their bad behavior. All of their weaknesses and vices. All of the cruelties they'd visited upon one another, whether by design or indifference.

Thor had no intention of falling into that trap himself. And he'd spent decades more or less immune to emotion, which was a terrific way to make certain he steered clear of it all.

This was no different, he assured himself. He was no different now than he'd ever been. It had been a long night, that was all.

He spent the next week congratulating himself on his wisdom in sending his purple-haired American on her way before he could confuse the issue further with more private thoughts he should never have shared with her.

And not only because he could see that sympathetic look on her face every time he closed his eyes.

Thor couldn't say he particularly cared for the revelations he'd had about how his behavior matched

Daniel St. George's famously debauched approach to life in general and women in particular, but he could handle that. After all, there was an easy solution if a man no longer wished to be the kind of man-whore Daniel St. George had always been.

And Thor quickly discovered that abstaining from the pleasures of the flesh was far easier than he ever would have imagined.

He removed himself from the hotel a few days after Margot left, telling his staff that a change of scene was in order.

It was good to get back to his house in Reykjavík. To remind himself that his real life wasn't that brooding hotel, but one stuffed full of his art, his books and all the things he'd collected over the years to show he was not and never would be his father. He had no interest in spending his life in an antiseptic warehouse the way Daniel St. George had.

Thor spent his nights in his clubs in the city, doing his usual rounds to make sure they were all running as smoothly as he liked. He made note of every detail about each place, then sent his thoughts and suggestions to his managers ahead of the monthly managers' meetings he insisted upon.

It wasn't until he found himself standing out on Laugavegur an hour or so before dawn one night, the bitter wind licking at him straight off the harbor, that he understood what he was doing.

He'd been so busy congratulating himself on taking a break from the hotel and his reputation that he'd somehow failed to notice that what he was really doing out here every night was looking for Margot.

And it was one thing to tell himself lies while he was tucked up in warmth and luxury. It was something else again when he was out in the thick, heavy dark of the approaching winter, just Thor and the night sky.

He found he didn't really try.

And the not trying felt a good deal like surrender.

Worse still, it appeared that his stubborn professor was full up on her research, because she was nowhere to be found. She wasn't in the bars or the clubs or any other of Reykjavík's hot spots—and this was Reykjavík. There were only so many places.

If she'd been out at night, conducting her interviews, he'd have run into her already.

Thor was standing out in the cold, pretending he was clearing his head after the loud live music he'd been listening to at the last bar.

He'd been pretending a lot of things lately, it seemed.

The truth was, Thor had been alone all his life, in one way or another. He had been alone in his parents' painful loop of unrequited love. He had been alone when he'd made his way in the world. He'd been alone when he'd built himself a tidy little empire and he'd certainly been alone throughout his adult life.

It had never occurred to him that there was another way.

And yet despite all of that, Thor had never been lonely.

Until now.

And he didn't know what the hell to do about it.

Margot locked herself in her bright and cozy little sublet, flatly refusing to entertain the dark emotions that traipsed around inside her. Instead, she threw herself into her work.

Because everything was different now. She could feel her shift in perspective like a kind of bone-deep tremor all throughout her body. It was a physical manifestation of what she'd done and said and felt that night at Thor's hotel and it made her hands ache. It made her legs feel weak even when she was lying down, scowling at her sloped ceiling, wishing herself asleep.

And she told herself she didn't mind if she carried the remnants of that night—and that napkin, and everything that had come after—with her forever. She knew she would. It was as if that night was a tattoo she wore on her skin, much brighter and more vibrant than the text she'd already put there.

Margot could choose to ignore the tattooed sensation and that trembling thing that lived in her now, every time she thought about Thor. Or she could try. But she was determined that her research reflect the change she'd lived through that night.

She flipped through all the notes she'd made on all those nights out in the city's bars and clubs. She listened to the voice recordings she'd made, imagining the faces of the people she'd met, and if she pretended that there wasn't one particular face that she saw above all, well…that was no one's business but hers.

She begged off from coffee dates and dinners her friendly colleagues invited her to and threw herself into her work with the kind of passion she remembered from way back in the last of her doctoral dissertation days.

That was the last time she had given herself permission to immerse herself in her research completely. She'd thrown herself into her dissertation and hunkered down with it until it was done at last. Until she couldn't quite tell the difference between the writing, the thinking and her. Until she wasn't sure where the words ended and she began, as a separate being.

Margot told herself it was a kind of freedom. Even a sort of bliss.

And she ignored the part of her that whispered that really what she was doing was hiding.

She restructured her arguments. She developed new theories.

"I still don't understand why you picked such a dramatically remote place to spend your sabbatical," her father told her with his usual condescension when she took a break from it all on Sunday evening to call her parents like the dutiful daughter she'd always been. "But I suppose Iceland is all the rage these days. As are treatises on sexuality, one supposes."

Margot burned with her usual shame and fury at that.

And normally she would have fallen all over herself to explain what she was doing. To try to make herself palatable to the one person alive who had never approved of a single thing she'd ever done—

But there was that tremor inside her. There was that ache in her fingers. There was the memory of the bluest eyes she'd ever seen and the approval in them that had made them seem lit on fire.

She wasn't the same person she'd been before she'd gone to Thor's hotel.

Maybe that was why she laughed instead of launching into the usual host of hurried explanations her father never paid much attention to anyway.

"I'm a tenured professor, not a teenager trying to be dramatic, Dad," she said, the same way she'd have laughed at a pompous student in one of her classes. "If the research I wanted to do could have been done in Des Moines, I would have gone there. I'm not in Iceland because it's trendy. I'm here because it's critical to my work."

Her father sputtered, and Margot braced herself for the flare of his temper—but instead, he handed the phone over to her mother quicker than he usually did.

Margot stood across the dark autumn arch of the planet, staring out her little window into the quickly coming night, and wondered why it had taken her so long to stand on her own two feet.

"What on earth did you say to your father?" her mother asked, muffling the receiver as if she was whispering. She likely was. Margot could see her as easily as if she was in the same house. Her mother was walking through the house from her father's study, back to the kitchen table, where she liked to spend her time. She read the paper there, listened to the radio and watched the kind of television that made Margot's father curl his lip in disgust.

Margot had always curled her lip in the exact same way at those shows, just to prove once again that she was nothing like her mother; that she was smart and intellectually curious and was worried about *weighty matters*, not the latest royal wedding or Hollywood scandal or silly movie-of-the-week.

"I think Dad forgets that he's not the only academic in the family," she told her mother, squeezing her eyes shut as if that could keep her from having to look at herself too closely.

Her mother let out a sound that could have been a sigh. Or a laugh.

"Your father forgets he's not the only academic alive," she replied after a moment. "It's part of his charm, really. But, Margot, you should know that no matter how he gets—and you know how he can get sometimes—he's so proud of all you've accomplished. We both are."

There was no reason Margot should have found herself blinking back tears at that. At another example of kindness from a person who she hadn't always treated well, so busy had she been trying to earn Ronald Cavendish's next distracted smile.

"I couldn't have done anything without you, Mom," she heard herself say, and it actually hurt as it came out.

Because it was true, and she hadn't understood that before. It was true, but Margot had been careening around all these years feeling superior to her own mother and the simple, steadfast love she'd always offered no matter the lip-curling or superiority complexes around her. Margot had always been so sure that kind of solidity and certainty was beneath her.

Maybe you've been emulating the wrong parent all this time, something inside her suggested. Harshly.

"I love you, too, honey," her mother was replying, sounding surprised—which also hurt. "Are you all right?"

If that wasn't an indictment, Margot didn't know what was.

"I'm perfectly fine," she told her mother.

And God, how she wanted that to be true, even if she wasn't sure she knew herself any longer. Maybe the truth was that she was finally figuring out the truth of who she should have been all this time.

No matter how much it hurt.

All in all, it was a full ten days later when she emerged, feeling shaky and strange, blinking her way into the bright, white light of a shockingly clear Reykjavík morning.

It was cold, the way it was always cold. She could feel the wind slice into her despite the fact she was wearing her heavy parka and good, warm boots. The air slapped at her face, making her eyes tear up and her skin feel chapped on contact.

Margot arranged her scarf to cover her mouth,

then shoved her gloved hands into her pockets as she headed down her little street toward the busier, more central part of Reykjavík. She took deep breaths of the thin, frigid air and told herself it was time to accept the fact that there was no more avoiding the one subject she hadn't wanted to address at all.

Not directly.

If she pressed her lips together, she could still feel that napkin there, teaching her a thousand things about herself she hadn't wanted to know.

And what a funny thing it was that she could be brought so low by a simple bit of fabric and the man who'd offered it to her. She felt humbled, altered, and she couldn't tell if that was a positive or negative—not even all these days and a new interaction with her parents later. Margot thought that really she should have objected. Surely every feminist bone in her body should have risen up in protest—

But that was the curious thing. She couldn't think of anything more feminist than locating her own voice, by any means possible. Did it matter how she'd gotten to that point? Or was she trying to complicate her own responses because she thought she should have reached it on her own?

Was what had happened to her problematic—or did she want it to be, so she could dismiss it? Or shame herself into denying the experience had changed her?

If another woman had told her that she'd had this same experience, Margot would have found it hugely concerning that a man had been the impetus for such growth. She knew she would have.

But that was minimizing the experience. And Margot didn't want to do that any longer. No more airs of intellectual superiority to conceal all her worst insecurities. And all the Bechdel tests and feminist manifestos in the world couldn't change the fact that it was the sex that had changed her.

And she was unaware of any way that a heterosexual woman could have life-altering sex without a man.

Which meant, of course, that there was no way not to put a man in the center of her own narrative. It was a notion that should have appalled her and yet…didn't.

Does it matter if we were both there at the center? she found herself asking as she walked down the cold streets. *Is sex only problematic when it's not intimate, or is it intimacy that's the real problem— because it knocks down all these barriers and leaves everyone both more and less than they were before?*

She could almost hear Thor's voice in her head as she turned that over and over inside her.

But then, the truth of the matter was that she could hear Thor's voice in her head all the time, and she wasn't sure she cared how problematic that was.

She hadn't believed in the kind of casual sex Icelanders engaged in before she'd experienced it herself. She still didn't. It was just that now Margot knew that it wasn't just hookup cultures or her generation's approach to dating that she found curious and flat. She had to look back at her entire sexual history and ask herself why she'd never understood that all the sex she'd ever had before Thor had...not been good.

Of course, she knew the answer.

She'd thought that the idea that sex could be fireworks and earthquakes, natural disasters and the northern lights all in one, were lies told in romance novels for the benefit of the feebleminded.

Margot had never imagined for a second that sex like that was—or could be, or maybe even *should* be—real.

"You got exactly what you asked for," she told herself resolutely. "A bit more than that, maybe, but no less."

Her lack of imagination was her own damned fault.

She made herself walk past the coffee shop nearest to her flat where she knew a number of her university colleagues spent their time, because she didn't want to talk about any of this.

That concerned her, too, if she was honest. She felt as if Thor had freed her. He'd allowed her to find her voice in ways she never would have imagined possible, but it had left her loath to engage in the kind of conversations she'd used to find so entertaining. She didn't want to take a tiny point and dig at it, poke at it, tear it apart.

Her life before that night in Thor's hotel felt so small now, as if it had shrunk in the wash while she hadn't been paying attention.

Was it academics that had gotten narrow over the course of these tenured years? Or was it Margot's approach to scholarship?

When had she turned away from big questions and lost herself in the minutia instead?

It was that old saying that everyone liked to trot out in weary tones, usually after contentious meetings, that academic politics were so vicious because the stakes were so small.

And Margot couldn't seem to remember why she'd decided that what she needed from her life was a steady diet of small stakes and meaningless arguments. Especially not now she felt turned inside out and made anew.

She found herself a seat near the window in a quaint coffeehouse, packed with cozy couches and overstuffed bookcases, and shrugged out of her parka. It was still bright outside and the light streamed in, piercing and blue and maybe a little too intense, but Margot liked the feel of it on her face.

She'd spent so long in the dark—all those nights out on the Reykjavík streets, or holed up in her flat. Or that long, stormy night in Thor's hotel, for that matter.

Or her entire life and field of study.

Margot had almost forgotten the simple pleasure of sunlight. The warmth of it and the way it washed over her like a caress. The way the light poured in through windows and made it hard to see anything but all that bright, hot sun.

And maybe that was why it took her longer than

it should have to notice the person who came to her side and stood there, backlit by the precious northern sunlight.

Margot shifted. Frowning by rote, she tried to make her eyes focus on the figure before her. She opened her mouth to comment on the numerous empty seats sprinkled throughout the coffeehouse at this hour on an indifferent Tuesday morning, but stopped herself.

Because her eyes might have been watering as she gazed into all that miraculous light, but her body knew exactly who she was looking at.

She felt herself shiver into instant awareness. She felt her pussy clench, then melt.

She knew.

Even before she lifted her hand to shade her eyes and really look at him, she knew.

"Hello, Professor," Thor said.

He sounded…not quite angry. Nothing quite so sharp. But he didn't sound his lazy, disengaged self, either.

Margot told herself there was no reason for her heart to flip around inside her chest at that notion.

"Thor," she said evenly, by way of greeting. "What are you doing here?"

He moved to the side so she could turn in her seat and look at him without having to stare directly into the sun. Not that it was any better. Thor was brighter by day. His eyes were too blue and the light picked up those impossible cheekbones and the mouthwatering line of his jaw. He wasn't dressed in that armored suit of his today, preferring boots and more casual trousers under the typical parka. He unzipped it against the heat in the coffeehouse, but he didn't sit down.

It took Margot a shockingly long moment to realize he was…whatever awkward looked like on a man like him.

Her stomach twisted into a knot, then flipped around deep inside her.

"Are you all right?" she asked.

"As a matter of fact, no." Thor stood there over her and she saw to her amazement that his big hands were in fists at his sides. She could hardly make sense of that, but there was no denying the way his eyes blazed when she lifted her gaze to his again. "I'm not all right, Margot. Where have you been?"

He did nothing to modify his volume or his tone, and Margot felt herself redden at the knowledge that the locals behind the counter might recognize him. Or even Margot, since she hadn't exactly been hiding her identity during all those late-night interviews.

She made herself smile. Politely. "I assume you mean that in a philosophical sense. Because I wasn't aware that I had to report my whereabouts to you. Or anyone else."

"You haven't been on Laugavegur, Margot. You haven't been accosting my customers. What am I supposed to make of that?"

"I don't know why you would care where I am." It cost her to keep her feelings off her face, but she thought she managed it. "You do remember that you told me to get out of your hotel, right?"

"We agreed that you would be there only as long as the storm continued. The storm had ended, so it was time for you to get back to your life. It didn't mean you needed to drop off the face of the planet."

"I didn't drop off the face of the planet."

"It's been ten days."

He said that as if he was outraged that she might not know how long it had been, and that made the knot inside her catch fire.

"Thor." Margot indicated the seat across from her, nodding toward it, afraid that if she let herself she would…explode. Or something equally terrifying. "Would you like to sit down?"

"I would not like to sit down, Margot. What I would like is an explanation. Any explanation will do. Where have you been? Have you been hiding? Licking your wounds?"

That knotted thing pulsed, electric and so intense it bordered on pain.

"What wounds do you imagine I should be licking?" she asked, and she wasn't managing to keep herself calm and expressionless any longer. She could hear it in her voice and had no idea what was on her face. What felt revolutionary was that she didn't care. "You're the one who threw me out. Because I had the temerity to worry about your emotions, if I recall correctly. Not a mistake I plan to make again."

"That's the trouble," Thor threw at her. "I don't make mistakes and I don't have feelings."

"People don't generally track other people down

in coffeehouses to shout at them about things they *don't* feel."

He looked as if she'd hit him. And she watched as he took one of those big fists and tapped it against the center of his chest.

"I don't want to feel this, Margot," he thundered at her. "I don't want to *feel* any of this. I don't want you inside me, so deep I don't remember my own damned name."

CHAPTER TEN

THOR FELT UNHINGED. BROKEN.

This was not how he operated. He did not skulk around the neighborhood he was pretty sure a past lover lived in, on the off chance that he might catch sight of her the way he had today. He did not make scenes. He certainly didn't lose his cool at past sexual partners—not least because he had never felt that deeply about any one of them.

But this was Margot. Everything was different with Margot.

He was different with Margot.

Thor had learned entirely too many things about himself over the past ten days. Chief among them that he'd been lying to himself for the bulk of his life without ever realizing it.

"I don't know what you're talking about," she was saying now, though the way she had her chin tilted into the air told him what a liar she was. "You must have told me a hundred times how Icelanders operate. All handshake, no feelings, because you're so *evolved*."

"While you, of course, hide away in this or that ivory tower to protect yourself with your research. Is that right?"

"As a matter of fact, that's exactly what I've been doing for the past ten days," she replied loftily. "Research."

Thor felt the edges of his vision go a little wobbly. "I beg your pardon. Exactly what kind of research?"

Margot smiled, sharp and edgy. "Why? Would it bother you if I spent every single one of the past ten nights conducting your favorite form of research with every Icelandic sex god I could find? Handshake after handshake?"

Thor wanted to deny it, of course. Because he was not a jealous man. He'd never understood those who were, when there were always other women, other lovers.

But there was only one Margot and he was already a mess, so why not admit it? It wasn't as if he was doing a great job of hiding it.

"Yes," he bit out. "It would bother the hell out of me."

And that sat there between them then, ugly and real.

Thor didn't know which one of them was more shocked. He, who had never been the slightest bit jealous of anyone or anything, thought he ought to have been appalled that such a sentiment existed inside him—much less had exited his mouth.

And he was quite certain that his progressive professor would have a similar take.

Margot cleared her throat, though her eyes looked darker than usual.

"I don't believe in possessiveness," she told him, though he thought her voice was awfully weak.

"Neither do I." He shrugged. "And yet here I am. Feeling more than a little fucking possessive, Margot. The question is—what are we going to do about it?"

She blinked, and he watched the way she sat up straighter, as if she was as affected as he was—but was hiding it better. And it was amazing how much he wanted that to be true.

"You mean, other than having a serious conversation about the deleterious effects of toxic masculinity?" She frowned at him. "Speaking of which, did you follow me here?"

"It's more accurate to say that I saw you on the street and decided to come say hello. Perfectly acceptable and social, no? Or is that not something you Americans understand?"

Her frown deepened. "Why were you on *this* street?"

"Here's the problem," Thor said then, because he didn't much like where this was going. "I should feel toxic, but I don't. I feel alive."

He expected her to descend into a full-on scowl, but instead, she pulled in a breath as if he'd landed a blow. It was another thing Thor should have hated but found he didn't.

"You flipped a switch in me and I can't turn it off," he told her. "I haven't seen you in ten days, and yet you're the only thing I see. You know how I feel about ghosts, and yet you haunt me. Is this what you mean by toxic, Margot? Because I have the terrible feeling that it is something far more insidious."

She sat straighter in her chair and tilted that chin of hers higher, as if that would keep him from noticing that she'd gone a little pale. "Like what?"

Thor knew it was a taunt. A dare.

He should have hated it. He should have hated all of this.

But he couldn't quite get there, because this was Margot. This was who she was and who he was, too, when he was with her. He could go ten years without seeing her and he knew it would be exactly like this. She was bracing and she was beautiful and he was never going to get past this. Never.

The longer he looked at her, the less he wanted to.

"At first I told myself I didn't care because I have never cared before." He gazed down at her, as if he could change what happened that easily. "I came into the city and took my usual tours of my bars. My clubs. There's nothing new or special about it. I go back and forth between Reykjavík and the hotel all the time and I take my pleasure as it is presented to me. I like sex, as you might have comprehended."

"I don't believe in sexual jealousy," she told him loftily, but he could see the color high on her cheeks and the way her lips formed a flat line.

"I don't believe in it, either. But you don't have to believe in something to feel it, do you?" Margot scowled at him, and that eased the hard knot in his chest that had been getting harder, sharper, thicker by the day. "But this is what I'm trying to tell you. No one would do. No one interested me. It isn't that I haven't touched another woman since you, Margot. It is that I haven't had the slightest urge."

"I don't know how you want me to respond to that. You can't possibly expect me to take responsibility for your feelings. Nor, I hope, are you anticipating that I will congratulate you on a little spell of abstinence."

"You are all I see," he told her again, more intensely this time. "At first I told myself I was looking for a woman who interested me, whoever she might have been. One night passed. Two nights. Three. And soon I was forced to admit the truth. I don't want another woman. I want you. Only you. Tell me what I'm supposed to do with that."

She made a noise that could have been anger. All of this was new to Thor. He couldn't recall having this kind of overwrought conversation with anyone. Ever. It veered too close to the sort of maudlin carrying-on that he associated with his mother, when she'd had far too much to drink.

But it was early in the morning. It was bright and clear. He was perfectly sober.

And Margot might have been looking at him as if she didn't comprehend a single word he was saying—but he could see her hands there in her lap, balled up into fists so tight that he was certain her fingernails would leave marks on her palms when she unfurled them.

And he knew, somehow.

Just as he'd known during that long, epic night they'd spent together. He might not know what she wanted. But he seemed to have no trouble at all in-tuiting what she needed.

And maybe it didn't matter that it took him a little longer to figure it out for himself.

"Let me tell you how I've spent the last ten days," he told her. He didn't care that he was a recogniz-able figure in the city, or that at least two patrons in this coffeehouse were likely filming him as he stood here, making a fool of himself. She had put that napkin in her mouth. The least he could do was use his voice, too. "First I looked for someone to help me forget you. But that didn't work, because I do not think it will be possible to forget you. When I finally admitted that to myself, I began to look for you. Yet you were nowhere."

"Not that it's any of your business," she said, her voice tight and her body stiff and unfriendly, "but I locked myself in my flat with my research. My re-search notes, that is. Today is the first day I've come up for air."

He recognized that sheen of moisture in her eyes. It told him she knew exactly the gifts she'd given him. And how could he help but try to be worthy of them?

"You think I don't understand this," he said qui-etly. "But I do. It's too complicated. It's too over-whelming. It's not at all what you wanted. Don't you think it took me by surprise, too?"

"I'm sure you have nights like that all the time."

"You know I don't. And neither do you."

"It was a really great handshake," she said, and there was something stark on her face. It made Thor feel raw inside. Scraped out. Hollow. "And I appreciate you coming to tell me that you had the same experience. But it was only a handshake, Thor. That was the agreement."

"I want a new agreement."

The winter sun was streaming in through the coffeehouse's front window, making Margot look ethereal. Otherworldly. As if she was one of Iceland's magical creatures, brought to life there before him. Her lavender hair seemed to glow like some kind of halo around her and that mouth of hers was enough to send him over the edge.

She looked wild. Hurt.

His.

And that was the part he concentrated on when she shook her head, shoved back from her table and surged to her feet.

"No," she said fiercely, her voice low and shaking at the edges. "I can't. One taste was more than enough. I don't want any more. I can't take any more."

Thor was close enough to see the very moment her frown trembled into something else, her face falling as the emotion in her eyes tipped over at the edges.

And he could tell that it horrified her. He saw it on her face in that split second before she pushed past him and threw herself out into the cold.

But Thor had suffered through ten long days and even longer nights. He'd had no choice but to accept who he was.

It was easy to beat himself up for his excesses and call himself Daniel St. George the Second.

But the truth was, Thor was like his father. His real father, Ragnar. The man who had fallen in love once and had never been dissuaded from that path, no matter what. The man who had loved Thor's mother and Thor himself with a quiet steadfastness that Thor could still feel inside him, as if that love was in his bones. As if it *was* his bones.

A man only truly falls in love once, Ragnar had told him once. *But if he is lucky, once is all he needs.*

Thor had always thought that was just another example of the kind of pure foolishness he wanted nothing to do with.

Then he'd met Margot and everything had changed.

He hadn't fallen apart that night in his hotel, though in many ways that was what it felt like.

He was terribly afraid he'd fallen a whole lot further.

And it was entirely possible that he was more like his lost, lamented father than he wanted to admit. To Margot, their one night might have been exactly that—one night.

But there was only one way to find out, and he didn't much care if it offended her sensibilities.

Thor threw open the coffeehouse door and went after her.

* * *

Margot told herself she was blinded by the winter sunshine, but that was a lie.

She was crying and she hated it, so she ran.

She ran away from the coffeehouse. From Thor.

From all the intense emotions that swirled around between them until she thought she might choke on them—and then what would become of her?

She ran until her lungs hurt, until she ran out of pavement, and found herself there at the edge of the harbor. There were big, broken-up chunks of ice floating out in the water and snow-covered mountains in the distance and every inhalation made her nose hurt. When she turned back around, she knew she would be charmed all over again by the brightly painted buildings clustered together that made up Europe's most northern city. It was easy to fall in love with Reykjavík.

But when she turned around, the only thing she saw behind her was Thor.

"Why are you following me?" she demanded, but she hardly recognized her own voice. Or the dark things that flooded her, as if she was a different person. The kind of person whose heart leaped at the sight of him. The kind of woman who wanted things she'd been taught to think were bad and wrong and beneath her.

Such as a beautiful man she couldn't stop thinking of chasing her through a city because he'd learned her. He knew her. And he'd taught her something, too—that her mouth would always argue when her body wanted nothing more than to surrender.

That mouth of his curved as he gazed down at her, as if the cold didn't bother him. "Tell me to leave you alone, Professor. Tell me that is what you want, and you will never see me again. I promise."

And of course that was what she wanted. It was what she needed, because she couldn't concentrate when he was near her and she shouldn't want the things he made her yearn for. She turned into someone she hardly knew when he was near. And anyway, she had work to do and papers to write and a life to get back to that didn't involve tall, dangerous Vikings who looked at her as if she was the only light left in this cold place.

Or the only light in him.

And as she stood there on the edge of the world, trapped between the frigid harbor and the thousand summers she saw in his blue eyes that seemed to gleam even brighter out here in all the remarkable daylight, she couldn't seem to say a word.

"You've ruined me," she whispered after much too long had passed and she thought the things she really, truly wanted were written all over her anyway.

Thor laughed at that. As if it—she—delighted him. "I believe I will take that as praise."

"Philosophically, I'm deeply opposed to these old, tired heterosexual norms," she seethed at him, because her heart kept pounding at her, but she couldn't seem to stop her mouth. She had managed it only once in as long as she could remember—but she

didn't want to think about that now. Not here. "I'm
outraged that any of this is happening. I don't want to
feel these things, either, Thor. I spent my life deeply
certain that I could never, ever feel these things."

"Funny. You tasted straight to me."

Margot knew she was lost because that sang in
her, then settled like wine and heat in her pussy,
which had never been confused about this man. And
still wasn't.

But she wasn't ready to surrender. Not again.

"I never reacted to any man like all the songs said
I should—or the movies, the books, the fairy tales.
I always assumed that really, deep down, I wasn't
like all the girls who felt those things. I thought I
was different."

Because she'd wanted, desperately, to be different,
she could admit to herself here. Now. She'd wanted
to distinguish herself from the other girls she knew,
and one way to do that was to create a lot of theoreti-
cal sexualities. She'd tried any number of them on
for size, at least in her head. Because she'd wanted
to be smarter, yes, and she'd wanted to impress her
father. But more than anything, she hadn't wanted
to feel ordinary.

And the fact that she'd only ever been attracted to
men had seemed like a minor detail, nothing more.

Thor reached over and took a strand of her hair
between his fingers, then seemed to concentrate on
wrapping it around and around into a kind of thick
purple ring.

Even the hair, Margot could admit to herself

here, had been another way to prove she wasn't like the herd.

She didn't understand how this man could make her feel profoundly ordinary in a way that made something in her glow like molten heat, simply because he was a man and she was a woman—and unlike anyone else in the world, ever, just because he was looking at her as if she was made of pure magic.

"What does *different* mean?" he asked almost idly. "It sounds like an unnecessary label. Why don't you permit yourself to feel whatever it is that you feel without worrying what word to use to describe it."

"You kicked me out," she flared at him.

"You can tell me that I hurt your feelings, Margot," he said quietly, his blue gaze touching hers as if he knew. As if she was still naked when she was with him, no matter what she was wearing. "You don't have to pretend you don't care."

Margot swallowed. Hard.

"I care," she whispered.

She felt as if she'd screamed out her feelings to the whole of Iceland. As if she'd revealed so much of herself that she might as well really have been standing there in the cold, as stripped down as she'd been in his hotel. And she thought that if he smirked at her, if he made some kind of joke, if he did anything at all, she might not survive it.

But Thor only smiled.

"I know. And I'm glad."

"Because it gives you the upper hand?" she asked

sharply, because she was afraid of that, too. She was afraid of everything.

"Pay attention, please, Professor." He tugged on her hair, a sharp little bite that echoed everywhere. "I don't want the upper hand, necessarily. What I want is you."

Something wild and sharp shot through her. Her first thought was that it was some kind of virus, taking out her knees right here in public.

It took one long breath, then another, to realize that it was joy.

She wasn't sure she'd ever felt anything like it before.

But she also wasn't sure she dared let herself believe it. "You had me."

"It turns out that one night was too brief a time. I am thinking of something longer. To allow for far more…research opportunities. Perhaps a year?"

"You can't possibly mean that. You hardly know me."

"I know you," Thor corrected her. And there was something about the way he said it. About that pure confidence in his gaze and stamped all over his face, as if he was telling her one of the Icelandic sagas. "I may not know every detail. There are a thousand stories we have yet to tell each other, but we will, in time. Still, I know you. And what's more, Margot, you know that I do. You were there. You know exactly how intimate we were over the course of one long night. You know what it meant."

She heard a ragged sound and only dimly understood it was her. Her breath. Her heart. She couldn't tell the difference.

"I don't know what you mean."

"I mean that I want you. In my bed. In my life. All of the above."

"I don't believe in things like this," she told him fiercely, while her heart clattered in her chest. "I don't believe it's possible. One night is just one night, and it doesn't magically turn into..." But she couldn't say that word, no matter how blue Thor's gaze was. "A relationship is a deep friendship over the course of time. It's an egalitarian partnership. It's supporting each other, learning how to be disappointed in each other. It's choosing to stay with another person despite all the weight and baggage of reality and experience."

"That sounds like a prison sentence." Thor's voice was dry, though his blue eyes danced with laughter. "Here in Iceland there was a survey. Most of us said, when asked, that we refused to deny the existence of trolls, elves and other magical creatures."

"I've heard that statistic. I think it was on the flight I took over here, in fact. But I don't think—"

"I was raised on the sagas, Margot," Thor said. He shrugged, though his gaze never left hers. "Trolls and elves make as much sense to me as the aurora in winter, the white nights of summer and, yes, a single night that feels like forever. Why not? Who are you to determine how much time is enough to know you need another person in your life?"

"Because it's supposed to be hard!" she threw at him.

But this was Thor. He only smiled back at her as if these were love songs she was singing, not arguments she was trying to make. "Why?"

Margot felt as desperate as she had when she'd decided to strip off her clothes in his bedchamber because he'd dared her to enact her consent. As desperate as she had when he'd presented her with that napkin.

"Because I know who I am," she told him, the words spilling out of her mouth before she could think better of them and hold them back. "I'm a disappointment. Don't you understand? I'm glad you threw me out of your hotel. I'm glad it was only one night, and that you didn't let me kiss you. It's for the best. I think what we should do is agree to let this just be a memory. It's better that way. You don't want any part of who I really am, I promise you that."

He looked singularly unmoved by her confession. "Why not?"

"Every boyfriend I've ever had left me because I'm too independent."

"I'm an Icelander. We are the most feminist country in the world. Ask anyone. I was raised to prize independence in a woman, and I do."

"That's what they all said, but that's not what they meant." She shook her head, scowling at him. "I'm selfish. I lose myself in my work and I don't come out, sometimes for ten days at a time. I disappear, sometimes when I'm standing right in front of another person. I live in my head."

"Not always," Thor drawled, and she hated the fire that licked over her because it wasn't his mouth. His clever hands.

"I'm serious. I can't possibly give you what you want. I can't give—"

"Professor. All of this carrying-on because you don't want to admit that you are besotted with me is unseemly." He shook his head sadly, though his eyes danced. "I don't require you to make any declarations. Not now. Someday soon, I'll tie you up, shall I? And see what sort of truths I can coax out of you with my mouth. My hands. My cock, which we both know full well you love unreservedly."

Margot felt too hot. Too weak. And she wanted too much.

For the first time in her life, she wanted everything. The kind of relationship she'd described, steeped in reality. And the fantastical relationship she'd decided a long time ago wasn't possible. Sex like dying and being reborn, over and over and over again. Orgasms and laughter and a man who took her breath away without even trying.

She wanted it all.

"I'm not at all comfortable with those sorts of power dynamics," she lied.

Thor laughed. "I don't believe that any good comes out of deciding what you are and are not interested in. Or standing here, at a clinical distance, coming up with rules to live by. What's the point?

You could make a list of things you're opposed to in bed, and maybe you mean it, but it's all abstract. When there is only me and you, alone, who can say what might happen? Why must we decide now?"

"I hope that's a roundabout way of saying that if you get to tie me up, I can tie you up, too."

"I don't know how you have failed to recognize that I do not have the—what do you call them—*hang-ups* that you seem to have." Thor's grin was pure wickedness, and Margot couldn't pretend she didn't want to bathe in it. In him. "You can do whatever you like to me. In fact, I encourage it. But I need more time. More than one night, one storm."

And the world seemed to spin all around her, too bright and too cold, so fast and so wild that she should have felt dizzy.

But Thor's gaze was steady. And so blue. And somehow, he helped her feel solid. Sturdy.

And there were so many things she wanted to say. Arguments she wanted to make and justifications she wanted to throw out between them, to get a little breathing room. To gain a little perspective.

Because you'd rather be in control than be happy, a voice inside told her.

And sounded entirely too much like her mother.

Thor's fingers were still in her hair. And he wanted her.

Not just for another night. A year, he'd said.

And that was the only word that made any sense at all.

She didn't believe that anyone could fall for someone that fast, except she had. *They* had. She couldn't believe that intimacy was possible without time and trust, but she knew that night had proved otherwise.

She knew too many things that couldn't be true, but somehow were.

Maybe she was only trying to argue because she didn't know what else to do.

Margot remembered the stark, empty penthouse in the hotel. How panicked she'd been when she put that napkin in her own mouth. And how quiet she'd gotten inside once she'd surrendered to it.

She did the same thing now.

She breathed out, long and slow. She surrendered. She moved closer to Thor, tipped her head up and let her gaze meet his.

And this time, when she pushed herself up onto her toes, then pressed her lips to his, he didn't stop her.

And that was how she kissed Thor for the very first time.

First it was a press of lips, as sweet as it was soft.

"Professor, I am not a fairy-tale princess in a drugged slumber," Thor said against her mouth. "I want more."

"Then take it," she invited him, because she understood now, with his taste in her mouth.

Surrender wasn't weak at all. Surrender was strong. It required the strength and the suppleness to bend without breaking. It required grace.

It required a heart full of trust. It required faith.

Thor angled his head and everything changed all over again.

Fire. Heat. And that greedy yearning that had been eating away at Margot since the moment she'd looked up to find him at her table in the middle of that storm.

He took and he took, as if he'd waited whole lifetimes to taste her like this. She found her hands in his hair and felt his around her face.

Still she kissed him, as if her life depended on it, too.

As if all this time, and no matter her brain or her job or her thoughts to the contrary, she had been something less than whole.

Wandering around, acting as if she knew things, when all the while her life had been leading her here. Right here.

To a perfect kiss from the perfect man, draped in all this bright, impossible sunlight in the middle of a cold fall, here at the top of the world.

"I am no professor," Thor said against her mouth, so she could feel the way his curved into a smile. "But this feels a whole lot like forever."

She couldn't help herself from smiling back, wide and filled with that joy so sharp it almost hurt.

"Come," she said, a thousand forevers in her voice, pumping like heat in her veins, and settling hot and needy between her legs. She took his hands in hers and tugged him along with her as she started for her flat. "I'll show you."

And that was exactly what she did.

CHAPTER ELEVEN

A YEAR LATER, Margot sat once again in the dimly lit bar of Hotel Viking, tucked away in a booth that offered her a view of nothing save the sea.

That surly, northern sea that crashed against the volcanic rocks far below, over and over again, with a kind of focused ruthlessness that made her shiver.

Much like the man she'd come here to see.

It had been the best year of her life.

Margot had spent the rest of her sabbatical in Reykjavík, but everything had changed. Thor took her to the house he kept in the city itself, where she learned more about him from the things he'd collected—and the distinction he drew between his true home and that hotel penthouse—than she'd known about some of the men she'd had entire relationships with.

He had encouraged her to give up her flat. She had refused, obviously, then had spent the whole of the next semester regretting that choice. Because she had been back in Iowa then, teaching and resuming her real life, and it had felt as if she'd left everything that mattered to her across the planet.

It didn't matter how many times Thor came to visit her. It didn't matter how many cold Iowa winter mornings she woke to find her favorite Viking there in her bed in the little house she kept within walking distance of the university.

Because there were always the mornings that followed. The mornings when she woke up and missed him so much it felt as if she might never be whole again.

Margot spent a lot of time interrogating her feelings, which she could only call operatic in the extreme, but that was the craziest part.

All the interrogation in the world didn't change them.

"I have a confession to make," she'd told Thor on one of their video calls, which she found torturous. She could see him. She could lose herself in the blue of his gaze, the sharp blades of his cheekbones. She could let his voice wrap around her. But she couldn't touch him, and it stunned her how much that hurt.

"That sounds ominous," he'd murmured in reply, lounging before her in all his indolence. "Not least because neither one of us is Catholic."

"There's a visiting professorship at the University of Iceland." She threw it out there, as if she'd been shooting a gun. "I applied. And, unless you have an objection, I start in the fall."

"What objection do you imagine I would have?" Thor had shaken his head, those eyes of his gleaming bright. "I will, of course, miss these mad flights into the American heartland at least once a month. I will miss the distance between us, which both of us have enjoyed so much. Do these count as objections?"

"You might feel differently when—"

"Professor." His smile had lodged inside her, where it always turned over and became heat. "Come."

Margot hadn't waited for the fall. As soon as classes had wrapped up in the spring, she'd packed up her house, put most of her belongings into storage and gone back to Reykjavík.

She had moved into the same flat and had pretended to not quite hear Thor's disgust on that subject.

But it hadn't mattered.

Because they had spent the whole of the previous spring semester building exactly the kind of friendship she'd always imagined a relationship should contain. They'd spent hours and hours talking through screens. They'd cooked meals together, separated only by the screens of laptop computers. They'd told stories, had drifted off to sleep with their electronic connections still open between them and had learned all the day-to-day truths about each other's lives. The routines. The drudgeries and small triumphs. The irritations and sweetnesses in turn.

Had that been all they did, Margot still would have counted it as the most successful and exciting relationship she'd ever had.

But, of course, there had also been the visits.

She had flown back to Iceland for her spring

break, where Thor had been as good as his word. He had asked her to trust him, and she had.

And he had stripped her down, blindfolded her and introduced her to his dungeon.

Where he had tied her up, made her cry and cry out, until she hardly knew who she was.

Then he had taken the blindfold off to reveal that there was no one else in the Hotel Viking dungeon but the two of them.

"I thought the point of a place like this was committing to a performance," Margot had said when Thor had finally untied her. "I expected a crowd."

"I would never toss you before a crowd without asking you first," he had murmured. "If public sex intrigues, only say the word."

But the truth was, Margot didn't particularly want to share him.

Something she thought she'd proved when she had taken her time returning the favor, tying Thor up so she could have her way with him.

Until they were both shaking.

It had been hard to sit still on her flight home, reliving all those delicious, deliriously intense moments with him.

Just as it had been hard to go back to that real life of hers that didn't seem to fit her anymore.

Because she wanted him.

If anything, time made it worse.

They spent the long, bright summer together again in Reykjavík. In her flat. At his house. And then back at the hotel, when Thor felt they needed that little touch of opera.

Summer days rolled into those Iceland summer nights, bright as day, with a sun that never quite dipped below the horizon.

"Why doesn't this drive you crazy?" she had asked one night.

They had enjoyed a remarkably European evening. They had gone to a classical concert at Harpa, the iconic concert hall on the water in Reykjavík. Then they'd indulged in a late dinner. They had walked back to Thor's house at midnight that looked like noon.

Then they had enjoyed each other for dessert.

And had gone back for seconds.

"Do you mean the white nights?" Thor had asked, from where he stood beside her at the windows she'd opened because she still couldn't get used to all the light at two in the morning. "Or the fact you still refuse to consider living with me?"

"We've gone over this. Virginia Woolf—"

"I own a hotel, Professor. If you must have a room of your own, you have a variety to choose from."

"I want to enjoy the summer," she had whispered, fiercely.

Because, she realized now as she stared out at the surging sea, holding a glass of wine to her lips without tasting it, she hadn't expected it to last.

She had told herself, over and over again during the spring semester and again this long summer, not to get too comfortable. Not to put too many expectations on him. Or herself.

Summer had ended. The night had returned and then started to take over.

Margot had started her new job, and that had taken a lot of her concentration at first. She had thrown herself into the work, and a part of her had known full well that this was usually the breaking point. Her previous relationships had always shattered over the amount of time she dedicated to academics.

So it had been something of a surprise that Thor had no problem at all with how much she worked.

"I can't see you again until next week," she had said once, scowling at him in the street outside her flat. "I can't ask you up, as I'm getting up too early in the morning—"

"Professor. You wound me. Perhaps you have forgotten that I'm a vastly wealthy and terribly busy man."

"I haven't forgotten that. Why are you mentioning it?"

"It is not an act of surrender to share your schedule," he said drily. "On the contrary. It is how two busy people make sure they see each other when they can."

Margot had never known anyone like him.

When he told her that he would never resent her career, the truth was, she hadn't believed him. In her experience, that was the thing that men said—until the moment they wanted something and couldn't have it because she was tied up with work.

But Thor had a busy schedule of his own. Sometimes he needed to stay at the hotel rather than in town, even if that meant he couldn't see Margot. Sometimes he traveled out of Reykjavík. He always invited her along, but it never seemed to irritate him if she had to decline the invitation.

As the days passed, Margot began to believe.

That everything Thor had told her—that first, glorious night, and all the days thereafter—was true.

"You look entirely too pleased with yourself," came his voice then, washing over Margot the way the tide caressed the rocks below.

She took her time looking up at him. Up, then up some more.

He was beautiful. He was her Viking, summer blue eyes and the heat in them that she knew, now, was all for her.

"I was thinking about independence," she said.

This was a man who wanted her, always. She knew it when his gaze lit with that laughter she craved. She knew it when he lowered that big body of his to sit next to her on the banquette.

He wanted her body. He made that clear, nightly.

But he also adored her mind.

And somehow, she realized a little bit breathlessly, over the course of this past year he had fused the two together.

Somehow, he had made her whole.

Though it was more than that. It was the two of them, together.

Together, they could do anything. Long distance. Operatic sex. Quiet laughter. The inevitable fights. The intense makeup sessions.

Anything.

"Are you planning to assert your independence?" Thor asked. "While naked, a man can only hope."

"I always thought that I had to choose," she said. She had meant to keep her voice even. Steady. But then the words came out of her mouth and there was nothing steady about them.

The steady thing was the way Thor looked at her. It was the way he waited to see what she might say next. It was his body pressed against hers, ready to keep her safe no matter what came next.

"I never believed that I could have everything," she told him. "You're supposed to be impossible."

And he gazed at her for what felt like another forever or two. Then, slowly, he smiled.

"I love you, too, Margot."

That took her breath away.

But then she scowled at him, all the more ferociously when his smile widened.

"You don't even have to think about it. You're just going to throw that out there."

"Professor." Thor shifted in his seat, and Margot thought he was going to face her, that was all. But instead he lifted her up off the seat, holding her with that ease that never failed to make her wet and hot and needy, before settling her down astride his lap.

"Catch up. I was in love with you before morning. But you needed a year to think about it."

"Nobody falls in love overnight."

But her voice was too thready. Too insubstantial.

"I did." His blue eyes blazed. "We did."

She could feel his cock between them, proud and ready, she couldn't seem to keep herself from moving her hips so she dragged her aching pussy over that hard ridge. She knew no one could see them, not with the high back of the banquette seat to block them from prying eyes—but tonight, she wasn't sure she cared.

"Thor…" she whispered.

As if his name really was a prayer.

Thor settled his big hands on either side of her face, smoothing back the hair she still kept lavender, not because she thought it made her different but because he loved it.

"I love you," he told her, and his voice was as hard and sure as the volcanic rock the hotel sat upon. "I want you in every way a man can want a woman. I want to marry you. I want a family with you. I want to take care of you and let you take care of me in turn. I want to possess you and protect you, but only if you promise you will do the same for me."

"I promise," Margot whispered. And she leaned forward, tipping her face to his. "I love you, Thor."

"I know you do, Professor," he said, there against her mouth. "You had to think your way into it, that is all. Have I passed all your tests now?"

Margot wanted to argue. She opened her mouth to tell him that there were no tests, there was only time—

But that would have been a lie.

"I might have loved you that first night," she told him, solemnly, as if they were exchanging vows. Perhaps they were. "But I love you even more for waiting all this time."

"Professor. Margot." Thor's voice was soft, but that look in his eyes made a loud, chaotic kind of joy tumble through her. "I will always wait for you."

She kissed him then, because she was his.

And more wonderful still, he was hers. Truly hers.

"I love you," she told him again. Because now that she had said it, now that she had finally said it, she wanted to say nothing else. "I love you."

And for a long while, there was nothing but that love. His mouth on hers. His hands holding her jaw where he wanted it, while she tortured them both with the slick, soft roll of her hips.

Until Margot was tempted to imagine that they'd made their own storm.

That they would always be the storm, this storm, perfect and wild and beautiful, and entirely theirs.

Thor stood in a rush, taking Margot with him and setting her on her feet.

"I have plans for you," he told her, and she could feel the dark promise in his smile wind through her. "All you have to do is make a single, simple choice."

Margot smiled, because none of the choices Thor offered her were simple.

They were always far more complicated than they seemed.

But they always made her scream.

She held his gaze, realizing that she'd trusted him like this from the start. Some part of her had recognized him the moment she'd seen him. Some part of her had known.

Margot didn't believe in love at first sight.

But she'd spent enough time in Iceland now to know that only a fool bet against magic in a place like this.

"Up or down?" Thor asked her, lazily.

Heat licked over her skin. Her nipples stood, aching. And her pussy was already wet with greed.

Up meant the penthouse, in all its stark beauty, where every touch felt sacred and usually ended in prayers to some or other god.

Down meant the Hotel Viking dungeon, where there was nothing to do but turn the sacred inside out.

"You choose," she told him, because she didn't need rules and boundaries to love him. Not anymore.

This was love. And love was trust.

This was who they were.

It was who they'd been that first night, little as Margot had wanted to admit it. It was who they would always be, together.

Thor's smile sent flames racing all over her, and he was still smiling when he bent his head.

And when she surged to her toes to kiss him this time, Margot knew why he had always tasted like this.

At last, she knew.

Because Thor tasted like forever.

And forever started now.

* * * * *

PLAY THING

NICOLA MARSH

MILLS & BOON

For the strong, empowered women who embody the
heroines I like to create.

Know what you want and strive to get it. Be bold.
Be courageous. Be true to yourself.

CHAPTER ONE

CHARLOTTE WAITED UNTIL the boss from hell hung up before slamming down the phone and sticking out her tongue. Childish, but it made her feel good.

She glared at the phone, wishing it would disintegrate so she wouldn't have to talk to him again. Yeah, like that would help. She also had an inbox full of emails from Mr Alexander Bronson, asshole extraordinaire.

The guy was demanding, arrogant and clearly had been put on this earth to make her life a misery.

As if to emphasise the point, an email pinged into her inbox with a gut-churning subject line: One last thing.

Sighing, she opened the email. And stopped breathing.

Forgot to mention, Charlie, I'll be arriving at the Sydney office tomorrow to follow up on my ideas to reconfigure staff. I look forward to meeting you then.

He didn't sign off. He didn't need to. Superior beings from other planets were above mere mortals.

Alexander Bronson, here, in the flesh, tomorrow. Torturing her. Tormenting her. Teasing her.

Charlie. No one ever called her that. She hated it. She'd told him so. Which ensured he never called her anything else. No Miss Baxter for him. Uh-uh. The CEO of countless accountancy firms around Australia, the wunderkind who took ailing companies and turned them around, had an informality about him that won friends and influenced lowly accountants like her.

The kicker was, her boss might be demanding and expect perfection, yet she couldn't help but admire his work ethos. She respected him for it, she identified with hard work. It was all she knew in her lacklustre life. Which made it all the more annoying that a small part of her looked forward to their daily phone calls and his infernal teasing.

Could she be any more pathetic? The highlight of her day was talking to her cocky boss who seemed to make it his life's work to tease some kind of response out of her.

Her cell rang and she glanced at the screen, dithering about whether to take the call. She adored her Aunt Dee but she couldn't cope with any outlandish requests today. She had to prepare for her imminent meeting with the charming Mr Bronson tomorrow.

Mentally chastising her goody-two-shoes conscience, she picked up the cell and stabbed at the answer button.

'Hey, Aunt Dee, I'm at work so can't talk long—'

'Dear girl, I know you're at work.' Her aunt sounded

breathless, like she'd jogged up a flight of stairs. Unlikely, considering Dee equated exercise with the devil's work. 'But I need your help and it's urgent.'

Charlotte instantly felt guilty that she'd contemplated ignoring her aunt. Dee had raised her when her flaky parents couldn't be bothered, preferring to travel the world in search of the next village in dire need of education. Dee rarely asked for favours so the fact she needed help meant this could be serious.

'Sure, whatever you need. Is everything okay?'

Dee inhaled a loud breath. 'Not really. My friend Queenie has had a nasty fall and broken her hip. She's alone, with no one to care for her animals, so I need to drive up to Byron Bay now. But the owner of the building where I keep stock for my business is coming to inspect it later today and I need to vacate the lease space.'

Her heart sank. As if this day couldn't get any worse. Sorting through her aunt's questionable 'stock' for her kinky online business wasn't one of her favourite activities on the planet. Aunt Dee had enlisted her help on more than one occasion to stuff envelopes for orders and Charlotte blushed just thinking about some of the apparatus people used in their sex lives.

'You need me to pack everything up and store it at home?'

Dee sighed in relief. 'Could you, sweetie? It would mean I could be at Queenie's today rather than tomorrow and she really needs me.'

Charlotte's inner child wanted to say 'I need you' but that was selfish and untrue. She'd learned from an early age to depend on no one but herself. She valued her independence, wore it like a badge of honour. Except that lately, her closest friends Abby and Mak had found great guys, leaving her to ponder whether being alone was something she cherished because she could or because she had to.

Shaking off her melancholy, she said, 'Leave everything to me.'

'You're a lifesaver, Charlotte.' Dee made smooching sounds. 'Not sure how long I'll be gone, maybe a few weeks. I'll let you know.'

'Okay—' but Dee had already hung up, leaving Charlotte to face the inevitable.

An afternoon of packing up vibrators, nipple clamps and edible underwear.

Oh, goody.

CHAPTER TWO

ALEXANDER BRONSON HADN'T been back in Sydney for a year and as he traversed the Harbour Bridge he couldn't help but glance at the Opera House on his left and remember the first time he'd been there. The first time he'd felt like he'd finally broken free of the shackles of his past.

Sydney had a unique vibe, far removed from his claustrophobic upbringing in outback New South Wales. It was the city where he'd studied, where he'd launched his career, where he'd ensured he'd never have to end up like his father.

His unofficial home, a boutique hotel in the Central Business District, beckoned. But first he had to check out his last property for the day, a warehouse on the outskirts of the glitzy eastern suburbs. He'd already been to Manly, Mosman and Balmoral Beach today, ensuring his investments were running smoothly. This last warehouse had to be cleared asap for a new tenant to move in tomorrow and his manager had informed him there'd been some kind of hold-up.

He didn't suffer incompetence lightly. He liked order in all aspects of life. Which was why he'd sort out this complication today and face the shake-up at The Number Makers tomorrow.

Crazy name for an accountancy firm. Then again, considering the mess the initial owner had made of the business, it didn't surprise him. Thank goodness for workers like Charlotte Baxter. Working offsite could be tough, but she'd made everything much easier than expected. He admired her work ethic, the way she questioned him and proposed solutions to problems he might not have anticipated.

He also liked the way she brought out the worst in him.

She sounded so prim and proper, so damned disapproving, he couldn't help but tease her.

He shouldn't make assumptions but he knew her type. Conservative wardrobe. Conservative views. Conservative life. She probably had an equally reserved husband, well-behaved kids and knitted on her lunch break. Though this was at odds with the fact that he'd registered her marital status as single when he'd dug deeper into his rising-star employee.

He'd deliberately called her Charlie during their first call and she hadn't hesitated in reprimanding him—ensuring he never called her anything but. Because there was an underlying hint of playfulness in her sharp reprimands and retorts, as if she wanted to cut loose but didn't know how.

Not that he was the guy to help her do it, but if he could make his work environment more pleasant, he was all for it. He'd had enough of morose, stifled environments back home to ensure he went out of his way to foster the opposite in all aspects of his life ever since.

Oh, yeah, he was looking forward to meeting the woman who'd smoothed his entry into the company. He had grand plans for her. Management plans. Because The Number Makers needed to be turned into a profitable business again and that meant appointing qualified staff. Staff like his introverted Charlie.

He couldn't wait to meet her.

CHAPTER THREE

CHARLOTTE STEPPED INTO her aunt's rented space in a cavernous warehouse and immediately wished she'd said no to helping out.

She wasn't a prude, but seeing evidence of how much fun other people had in their sex lives always made her feel lacking somehow.

Her aunt's online business, Dee's Delights, did a roaring trade in all things sexy. From dildos to condoms, beads to fetish wear, her aunt dealt in it all. And if the lavish lifestyle her aunt enjoyed was any indication, many people were return customers.

Dee had told her about the business when Charlotte turned eighteen. Initially mortified that her aunt even knew what a cock ring was, Charlotte had studiously ignored anything to do with her aunt's line of work. Now, at the ripe old age of twenty-five, and never having had a long-term boyfriend, Charlotte wondered if having to handle all this stuff today was the universe's way of telling her to lighten the hell up.

Thankfully, most of the raunchier stuff still resided in boxes, leaving her to pack only the vibrators, handcuffs and lingerie. She'd booked a courier for six tonight, meaning she had three hours to get every box filled and taped.

As she held up a pair of fluffy fuchsia handcuffs and smirked, she glimpsed a full-length mirror on the inside of a partially open wardrobe door. Probably a remnant of the last tenant—she couldn't imagine her aunt wanting to try on any of her merchandise and didn't want to—but the moment the idea of trying stuff on popped into her head she couldn't dislodge it.

Her gaze fell on the lingerie. A turquoise chemise with lace overlay. A purple halter baby-doll. A wet-look corset. A pink body stocking. An ebony faux-leather bustier and thong.

Heat flushed her cheeks as she picked up the latter and held it up. Would her sedate life change if she wore stuff like this? Not that anybody would see it, but it might give her more confidence to shake things up a little. And she wanted that, craved that, with every cell in her lonely body.

Her flatmate Mak had jetted off to New York with her delectable guy Hudson last week, leaving her more alone than ever. Charlotte rarely dated, didn't go out clubbing and preferred reading to sexting. On the odd occasion she dipped her toes into the dating pool, she went for boring guys like...her. Because ultimately, that was the kind of guy she could see herself marrying, having kids with and with whom she could build the kind of life she'd never had. Secure and happy, with a house she could grow old in, surrounded by a family of her own making.

She'd found the house but wasn't having much luck with the guy.

Before she could second-guess her crazy decision she pulled the elastic off her ponytail and ran her fingers through her hair. She took off her glasses, toed off her flat pumps, unbuttoned her white shirt and unzipped her grey pencil skirt. The warehouse air had a chill, making her skin pebble as she stripped off her sensible cotton underwear. Or maybe her goosebumps had more to do with the naughty thrill of slipping on the thong and bungling her way into the bustier with detachable lace collar.

When she'd done up the last hook, she took a deep breath and padded over to the wardrobe. Opened the door wider. Took a peek in the mirror. And gasped.

Her reflection didn't shock her as much as the sight of a tall gorgeous guy in a suit staring at her with obvious appreciation.

'Who the hell are you and what are you doing here?' She spun around, covering her bits even though they weren't really exposed.

Her handbag and cell were on the table laden with boxes, too far away to make an emergency call if she had to.

Damn, why had she been so stupid? She could've dressed up—or undressed in this case—in her flat where she'd be storing the boxes, not here where any pervert could wander in.

'I could ask you the same question,' the handsome stranger said, stepping inside the room and closing the door.

Uh-oh.

Being alone in an empty warehouse in raunchy underwear with a man, no matter how attractive, wasn't good. She had more sense than this. She blamed her stupid impulsiveness on the realisation that her life was so empty she actually looked forward to verbally sparring with her irritating boss daily.

She'd wanted to cut loose for just one moment. To feel what other women felt wearing underwear like this. She hadn't banked on having an audience for a foolish moment of bravado.

'Get out,' she yelled, sidling towards her clothes, fear making her heart pound in her ears.

'I own this place so that's not going to happen.' His curious gaze fell on the table, where the vibrators and lingerie lay scattered. 'You, on the other hand, need to tell me what you're doing here and why my warehouse has turned into a sex shop.'

There was something vaguely familiar about his condescending tone and she hoped to God he wasn't a client whose taxes she'd done.

'Don't be ridiculous, this isn't a sex shop. My aunt rents this space, from you apparently, for her online business and she asked me to pack everything up so the new tenant can move in tomorrow.' She gestured at the merchandise, belatedly realising she'd left herself exposed when a glimmer of interest lit his gaze. 'So if you leave me to it, I'll be out of here in a few hours.'

'Well, aren't you the little helper,' he drawled, his

gaze starting at her toes and working its way upward, a slow, leisurely perusal that made her nipples harden.

Her body's reaction startled her. She'd never reacted to any man like this before, let alone a stranger. She read about this kind of thing in the romance novels she devoured by the boxful: the shy woman instantly attracted to the commanding man. It was a seduction game she fantasised about but knew could never happen to her. They called those novels fiction for a reason.

Yet here she was, standing in front of a guy she didn't know, letting him look his fill. And enjoying it.

When he reached her eyes, what she saw made her knees wobble a tad. Desire. Passion. Lust. The kind of lust she'd never, ever seen in a man's eyes when they looked at her.

'Is trying on every outfit part of you *helping* out?'

His obvious desire discombobulated her and when he grinned the smug smile of a guy who knew exactly the effect he had on her, she made an impulsive decision to make him pay. She might be inexperienced and naive when it came to sparring with a man but that didn't mean he could toy with her.

'My old corsets and bustiers are worn out so I thought I'd replenish my stocks.' A blush heated her cheeks at the blatant lie but once she started she couldn't stop. 'It's a tough job looking this good for the men of Sydney but somebody's gotta do it.'

He laughed, a rich, deep rumble that reached down into her chest and filled the lonely ache that resided there.

'Does that include me, considering I'm a man and I'm in Sydney?'

Charlotte had never played games with any guy. She didn't flirt and she didn't elicit grand passion in them. But something about this stranger made her feel like she could do both.

'Why, do you think I look good?' She rested her hands on her hips in a blatant invitation for him to look his fill again, wondering what magic powers the lingerie held to make her this bold.

'Honey, you have no idea.' He stalked towards her and her newfound bravado fled. She edged towards the table, needing her cell within reach. But like an eternal klutz she stumbled and would have fallen if he hadn't been by her side in a second. Strong hands steadied her, held her upright, made her yearn for things she had no right to crave.

Up close, he was even more startlingly good-looking: dark wavy hair, blue eyes the colour of Bondi on a clear day, chiselled jaw dusted with the faintest hint of stubble, the perfection marred by a small scar on the underside of his chin. And when he smiled again…oh, boy, she felt it all the way down to her toes and a few choice places in between.

She cleared her throat, trying to summon outrage at being held by a stranger while dressed like a stripper. 'Let me go.'

But her command sounded soft and uncertain, falling flat if his amused smirk was any indication.

'Do you want me to?'

He quirked an eyebrow, daring her to deny the invisible energy zapping between them.

She couldn't explain it. She didn't do casual sex; could count the number of times she'd actually had sex on one hand because it had been unremarkable. She didn't believe in instant attraction or one-night stands. Or having vertical sex with a hot stranger in a warehouse.

This wasn't her.

But what if it could be?

For a moment, she wondered where that voice had come from. Her conscience didn't encourage her to go wild. Quite the opposite, in fact.

And where had it got her? Alone and craving a relationship.

What if she did something so out of character that she could never go back to the person she was? Would that give her the kick-start she needed to *make* the life she wanted happen instead of *waiting* for it to happen to her?

'I don't know you… I mean, I'm not good at this… and I don't usually do this kind of thing with strangers—'

He kissed her. His lips were commanding, his skill obvious in the way he exacted the right amount of pressure—not too hard, not too soft…

A kiss to her meant a meshing of lips, the occasional tongue, a bit messy and nothing to rave about.

What this guy could do with his tongue…the moment it invaded her mouth and touched hers she couldn't think. Couldn't breathe. Couldn't do anything but hold onto his lapels and press against him, desperate for contact.

His relentless assault on her lips made her tremble with longing. He changed the pressure, he nipped her bottom lip so hard it bordered on painful, and then he soothed it with a seductive sweep of his tongue.

A fleeting thought pierced her passion haze: could a woman orgasm from a kiss? Because she throbbed so startlingly from his mouth on hers that it had to be scientifically possible.

His fingers threaded through her hair, grazing her scalp, and she moaned at the tingling sensation it elicited. He took it as a sign of encouragement, spinning her around and hoisting her onto the table. She gasped at the cold plastic against her bare butt and he broke their kiss to stare at her in wide-eyed wonder.

'I don't do this. Sex with a stranger.'

'Me either,' she said, breathless and slightly husky. Wishing he hadn't stopped. Wishing she had the guts to articulate how badly she wanted him to continue.

His hungry gaze locked on her, daring her to follow through on what they'd started. 'So what do you want to do?'

He'd given her an out.

She should take it.

Her entire life revolved around rational, well-considered decisions. Weighing up facts. Making safe choices.

Where had it got her?

Single and not loving it. Her sex life was lived vicariously through erotic romance novels, craving an elusive something that would jolt her staid life; something like this crazy, exciting interlude to give her confidence a boost and ensure she could follow through on finding her perfect guy.

Staring into this guy's amazing blue eyes, she wondered if maybe karma had delivered exactly what she needed.

Her throat tightened but she had to get the words out, had to take a chance for once. 'I want to do this.'

Before her common sense kicked in, she placed her hand on his abs. Low enough to be suggestive. High enough he could end this now and walk away if he wanted to.

His low groan raised the fine hairs on her arms as he nudged her knees apart, stepped between them and slid his hands under her butt, sliding her towards him.

She gasped as he ground against her, hard and insistent, while his hands palmed her breasts. The softest whimper filled the air and through a hazy fog of want, she realised it had come from her.

She wrapped her legs around him and he responded by rolling her nipples between his thumbs and forefingers, making her go a little crazy. She writhed against him, wanting more. He plucked at her nipples, sending a sizzle to her core.

If his touch felt so good with the stupid faux leather as a barrier, what would it feel like to be naked? She wanted to find out but he had other ideas.

'Lie back,' he said, placing a palm between her breasts and gently pushing. 'Prop on your elbows so I can see you.'

The guys Charlotte had been with didn't issue orders. They got the basics done without a word.

She liked being told what to do. Liked the gleam in his eyes when she did exactly as he wanted. She eased back until she rested on her elbows, uncertainty making her shiver as he hooked his thumbs under the elastic of the thong. He tugged gently, lowering it, leaving her naked and vulnerable.

She'd never felt so exposed. But her protest died on her lips as he locked gazes with her at the same time he slid a finger inside her.

Reverence widened his eyes, as if she'd bestowed a great gift on him, and her flutters of worry faded beneath his ministrations.

Another finger slipped inside her, rhythmically sliding in and out as his thumb circled her clitoris. Slow. Steady. He was driving her insane with the feel of him and the way he met her gaze. Uncompromising. Confident in his ability to satisfy her. Seeing her, really *seeing* her.

'You are so frigging beautiful,' he muttered, his tone barely above a growl, and she gritted her teeth to stop from groaning out loud as the pleasure built. She tensed her muscles and began spiralling out of control. She blanked her mind until all she could focus on was him. His touch. His fingers. His stare.

Her orgasm crashed over her, so strong, so unexpected, wiping her out. She couldn't hold back, her yell loud and triumphant.

She expected to be swamped with mortification the second her body stopped pulsating. But nothing happened, other than a relentless yearning to do it all again.

'Thank you,' she murmured, sounding oddly formal.

'You're welcome.' His smile widened as he reached down and unzipped. 'If you want, there's more where that came from.'

Charlotte's jaw dropped open. She'd heard of the fabled internal orgasm but equated it to other fanciful, elusive things, like unicorns and fairies.

Apparently her mystery man believed in all things mystical and she watched in unabashed fascination as he unsnapped his trousers and pushed them down along with his jocks.

Showing her proof of exactly why he could be so confident.

Wowza. She might not have seen many erect penises but the ones she had made this one look like a giant. With a wicked-looking head.

She smiled at her joke and he quirked an eyebrow.

'It doesn't bode well that you take one look at me and want to laugh.'

A killer sense of humour and a big dick. She'd hit the jackpot. Ding, ding, ding.

'I'm out of my comfort zone here. Can't you give a girl a break?'

'Thought I already had.' He winked and she laughed, surprised at how easy this felt.

The few other times she'd had sex had been awkward, without a hint of banter. She liked this, liked feeling like a wanton goddess splayed before a sex god.

'This is crazy. You know that, right?'

He nodded, fishing a condom from his wallet and rolling it on with an expertise that indicated he'd done it many times before. 'Crazy is good.'

He set about proving it, sliding into her with a force that made her gasp. He grabbed her butt, lifting it slightly so he could drive into her on an angle that ensured he hit that fabled sweet spot. He thrust into her over and over with a relentless force that had her surging up, reaching for him.

She held onto his shoulders as he half lifted her off the table, his penetration deeper, his rhythm faster. The pleasure bordered on pain and she bit his shoulder as she came again, stunned by the ferocity of it.

He tensed and groaned a second later, his fingers digging into her butt so hard she might not be able to sit for a week. She didn't care. She didn't care about anything other than this euphoria making her feel as if she could do anything.

He held her for what seemed like an eternity before gently lowering her to the table and withdrawing. She felt the loss immediately. Craved more. Mentally chastised herself for being stupid.

He turned away, giving her time to put her clothes on while he took care of business. She didn't like seeing his back. Not when their fronts had connected so well.

Remorse, swift and stabbing, flooded her.

What the hell had she been thinking, having sex with a stranger?

However, when he turned back to her, his expression open, his smile satisfied, she couldn't be sorry.

'You were incredible.' He cupped her face between his hands and brushed a soft kiss across her lips.

To Charlotte's horror, the burn of impending tears stung her eyes and she blinked, forcing a smile as she pushed him away.

'So were you,' she said, sounding flippant, while inside a little part of her crumbled at his unexpected tenderness. 'But I really need to get this tidied up now.'

It was a curt dismissal he didn't deserve but she had to get him out of here before she cried.

'Sure, I hear the landlord is a slavedriver.' He seemed completely unfazed by her rudeness but he stared at her with a newfound intensity that bordered on uncomfortable. 'Maybe I'll see you around?'

'Maybe,' she ground out, refraining from adding, 'like never.'

Scorching sex with a stranger hadn't been on her to-do list today but now that it had happened…did she feel different? More confident? More womanly? Just *more*?

She had no freaking idea because in seizing the moment, she'd moved so far out of her comfort zone she'd ended up on another planet, one where good girls did bad things and didn't regret it. Especially when that bad thing had been oh, so good.

But no matter how incredible her momentary lapse had been, it couldn't happen again. She needed to move on and refocus on the priorities in her life.

Like finding a genuine guy who'd want more than a quickie on a table in the back room of a warehouse.

He paused at the door, as if he wanted to say something. Ask for her phone number? Ask her out to dinner? Her inner romantic yearned for some gesture to indicate that this hadn't been just sex to him.

She should have been relieved when he half shrugged and held up a hand in farewell before closing the door behind him.

She wasn't. All she could think was that she'd found the bad boy she'd been craving but had let him go far too easily.

CHAPTER FOUR

ALEX HAD DONE something bad.

The kind of bad that could get him a lifetime membership to hell alongside the naughty guy with horns and a pitchfork, ensuring he danced on hot coals for all eternity.

On his first day back in Sydney, he'd envisaged having a quiet afternoon inspecting his property investments.

He hadn't expected to have sex with the woman he'd earmarked to take The Number Makers into the future.

Even now, hunkered behind a solid wooden door in a rather ugly office, he couldn't believe he'd been stupid enough to have sex with Charlotte Baxter.

Not that he'd recognised her until it was too late, with her hair down, no glasses and wearing the kind of lingerie to fuel wet dreams.

Because the woman he'd researched online once he'd taken this job looked nothing like the woman he'd had scorching sex with in that warehouse.

The headshot on The Number Makers website depicted a prim woman wearing a bland white blouse, minimal make-up, steel-rimmed glasses and a dorky headband, with her hair pulled tight in a high ponytail.

Never in his wildest dreams had he expected Charlotte to be wearing leather underwear and looking nothing like her picture when they first met.

There'd been a vague familiarity about her at the time, but he'd put it down to wishful thinking. His little head overriding his big one because he'd wanted to get laid and the intriguing woman in the leather underwear had seemed up for it.

It wasn't until they'd done the deed that the truth had detonated. The moment he'd heard her say, 'I really need to get this tidied up now,' he'd known.

Charlotte had used that same phrase many times over the last few weeks when he'd assigned her tasks. Usually in reference to cleaning up work, where she had to deal with the mess left by the old manager.

When it came to work, she'd always been agreeable. It was only when he tried to be friendly, to get to know her better, that she became abrupt and shut him down.

I really need to get this tidied up now.

Fuck. He'd been struck dumb when he'd realised he'd slept with an employee. That was when he'd taken a closer look and realised that without the uptight hairdo and the glasses, she had the same eyes. A captivating slate grey that held secrets.

Like the fact she could masquerade as a vixen after hours once she shed her librarian persona.

He should have trusted his gut that she looked vaguely familiar, should have taken a closer look at her face. Unfortunately, he'd taken one look at her lithe body and lost it. Not because she was a bombshell—she had small, pert breasts thrust heavenward by that saucy bustier, a trim waist, slim legs and an ass that fitted in his hands nicely.

No, he'd lost it because he'd seen something in her eyes…a wistful yearning, a war waged between boldness and fear, like she wanted to jump him but didn't know how.

It had captured his interest like nothing else.

After he'd realised her true identity, he hadn't been able to get over the startling contrast between the woman he'd imagined and the woman who'd made him hard by fixing those cool grey eyes on him.

He could read most people. But after he'd twigged that he'd screwed Charlotte, he couldn't fathom how the hell she'd been so into it. How did a no-nonsense woman switch from being contained at work to confident enough to strip down, try on raunchy underwear and fuck a stranger in a warehouse? It left him completely baffled.

She'd intrigued him during their many phone conversations and he'd wanted to see how far he could push her. He'd deliberately teased her over the last few weeks, chuckling at the curt shutdowns she reserved for him—and probably every male on the planet.

To think how she'd responded to his touch…at the time, he hadn't been able to explain rationally his over-the-top urge to possess her. Sure, he'd been too busy to date lately and hadn't had sex in three months, but he'd never been driven by urges before. Celibacy didn't bother him, especially when he had a new job in the pipeline. Yet he'd taken one look at Charlotte—not that he'd known it was her at the time—and wanted her.

His cock hardened and he shifted in the uncomfortable ergonomic chair. First item of business on the agenda at The Number Makers: change the furniture and make it more comfortable for staff so they wanted to stick around and work.

Though when he met Charlotte in a few minutes' time and she realised who she'd had scorching sex with on a table in a back room of his warehouse, he had a feeling nothing would make her stick around.

He had to convince her otherwise.

Her work spoke for itself. She went above and beyond for her clients. She put in extra hours without expecting remuneration. She carried the load for her team. And she'd completed every task he'd set for her over the last few weeks. He'd been testing her, seeing how willing she was to take on extra work and she'd passed.

He hoped to God she wouldn't quit because he hadn't kept his dick in his pants.

Worse, he couldn't get the image of her splayed on that table out of his head. He'd never seen anything so damned erotic as a woman he'd just met being so willing and eager. She'd been absolutely wanton and it had turned him on big time. Later, when he'd discovered her identity, it had made him wonder how he could have gotten her so wrong. Had that bold, fiery woman always been hidden beneath her brusque exterior? And if so, what would it be like to coax her to come out and play again?

He couldn't afford to think that way. He'd made a mistake by sleeping with an employee, a mistake he had no intention of replicating.

But the fact he couldn't stop thinking about her, had lain awake most of last night because of it, didn't bode well for when she entered this office shortly.

He needed to focus on work. On making The Number Makers a strong, viable company. The more money he made, the further he left his old life behind. He couldn't afford a slip-up.

But what if he'd already slipped up in slaking his unexpected lust for her?

CHAPTER FIVE

CHARLOTTE LIKED TICKING off tasks in her head.

Pack up Aunt Dee's merchandise? Check.

Have the boxes couriered to her flat? Check.

Enjoy sizzling sex with random stranger? Check.

Even now, the next morning, heat surged to her cheeks every time she thought about what she'd done in that warehouse.

She, the queen of introverts, having two mind-blowing orgasms with a guy whose name she didn't even know.

It had been preposterous. Ludicrous. And so freaking incredible that she'd found herself smiling at random times last night, and several times first thing this morning.

After he'd left and she'd got over her funk at doing something so completely illogically bizarre, she'd expected embarrassment and shame to follow her initial remorse. It hadn't happened. Instead, she'd felt oddly empowered, like she'd taken control of her sexuality and wielded it in a way she'd never anticipated.

Of course it hadn't lasted and by the time she'd got

home, her newfound boldness had faded and humili-
ation had set in.

How could she have done that?

Obsessing about sex with a stranger was the last
thing she needed, especially when she had to meet
her pain-in-the-ass boss in person for the first time
in ten minutes.

Her confidence had taken more hits than a boxer
over the years and while her sexy encounter yesterday
had given her a momentary boost, she'd reverted to
type today, envisaging their first meeting to be more
of the usual: him demanding, her deferent.

To give herself confidence she'd dressed to impress today, wearing her version of a power suit. A
deep burgundy knee-length skirt, an ivory silk blouse
that tied in a bow at the neck, a fitted black jacket and
low kitten heels. She'd even gone all out and straightened her hair. Not in any effort to impress Alexander
bloody Bronson but to ensure she exuded self-assur-
ance when she faced her nemesis.

Okay, so she was being a tad overdramatic, but
he'd really riled her these last few weeks, barking
orders, demanding perfection and teasing her with
that ridiculous nickname. Charlie. Made her sound
like a boy. And hit a little too close to home because
of how asexual she felt at times, languishing in her
single life and wishing things could be different. That
she could be different.

Courtesy of that sexy stranger yesterday, maybe
she could be.

That was what her brain-fade in that warehouse

had ultimately been about: embracing her dormant sexy side, indulging in a little excitement, seeing exactly what she was capable of if she let go a little. Because, although she craved a stable, loving guy, deep down she wanted him to rock her world in more ways than one.

Trying not to cringe with embarrassment at the indignity of having sex with a man whose name she didn't know, she gathered her files, checked them for the third time to ensure she'd stacked them in alphabetical order then rested her electronic tablet on the top, ready to show Mr Bronson exactly how competent she could be.

She hadn't seen him arrive but the receptionist assured her he'd been holed up in the old manager's office since early this morning and hadn't opened his door since.

She'd be the first staff member he would interview.

'Woo-hoo, lucky me,' she muttered, glancing at the old-fashioned round clock opposite her desk. She valued punctuality so surely her new boss would be impressed if she arrived five minutes early for their meeting?

Not giving herself time to ponder the upcoming face-to-face she'd been dreading ever since he'd told her of his arrival in Sydney, she swept up her work in her arms and headed for his office.

The receptionist mouthed 'good luck' and Charlotte grimaced in response, before knocking twice on Mr Bronson's door.

When she heard a clipped, 'Come in,' she opened

the door and stepped inside. He had his back to her, his butt resting on the desk while he spoke into a cell pressed to his ear.

Her first impressions: dark wavy hair a tad too long to be conventional, broad shoulders, designer suit, nice ass.

Wow, that guy yesterday must have really done a number on her if one of the first things she noticed about Mr Tall, Dark and Demanding was his ass.

She closed the door and crossed the room, mentally reciting all the ways she'd like to torture him in response to how he'd tortured her over the last few weeks.

However, all thought fled when he ended his call and turned to face her.

Shock rendered her muscles useless and the files in her hands tumbled to the floor, along with her tablet, the numbness flooding her body soon replaced by something far more sinister.

Soul-deep, soul-destroying mortification.

Because the boss she had to impress to keep this job, the boss who'd made her life hell with his demands, the boss who could make or break this company, was the sexy guy who'd turned her world upside down yesterday in the warehouse.

CHAPTER SIX

WHEN ALEX TOOK on a new client he threw himself into the business of rejuvenating that company one hundred per cent. He'd gained a reputation as astute, driven and results-focused because of it. Clients came to *him* these days. He rarely advertised. And he'd treated The Number Makers job with the same industrious approach. Meaning he'd researched the key players before he started. Meaning he knew Charlotte Baxter was dedicated, conscientious and goal-orientated before she walked through his door.

He also knew she'd probably want to eviscerate him once she got past the shock.

'Need some help?' He didn't wait for a response, moving around the desk to squat and gather up her files. It would give her time to compose herself, as a small part of him felt like a complete bastard for springing a surprise of this magnitude on her when he could have called her last night and warned her.

If he'd been blown away when he'd realised the truth yesterday he could only imagine how she'd be feeling now.

When he stood and placed her files and tablet on the desk, she still hadn't moved but some of her colour had returned.

'Why don't you have a seat and we'll talk?' He laid a hand in the small of her back and she jumped as if he'd electrocuted her.

He didn't know whether to be flattered or appalled.

'I know this is awkward, but it doesn't have to be—'

'You *knew*?' She sank onto the chair opposite, her eyes wide and accusing, her mouth open slightly, shell-shocked. 'I mean, yesterday, when we...you know...you knew who I was?'

Hell.

Alex had intended on coming clean but not this soon. He'd wanted to smooth the way, reassure her that what had happened wouldn't interfere with their working relationship at all. But one look at her mouth twisting in disgust told him he'd be fighting a monstrous battle to convince her to stay, let alone listen.

'Charlie, look—'

'Don't call me that,' she growled. 'Don't you dare call me that.'

She shook her head, sending a sleek fall of hair over one shoulder. He preferred the way she'd looked yesterday, tousled and make-up–free, and the fact she'd gone to so much trouble today to impress her new boss made him feel bad anew.

'Let me explain.' He laid out his hands, palms up, like he had nothing to hide. Yeah, like that would placate her. 'I know I should have said something yesterday. I'm a businessman and I'm good at what I do, so I researched this company before taking on the job.'

Her eyes narrowed, fiery slate slits pinning him with a disdain he deserved. 'What do you want, a medal?'

He bit back his first instinct to laugh. Good to know she had a sense of humour beneath that austere front. Along with lingerie designed to make a man lose his mind.

'What I'm trying to say is, I didn't recognise you when I set foot in that warehouse. You had your hair down and glasses off and were wearing that lingerie…'

Crap, how could he explain the next bit without sounding like a total sleaze?

'And?' Disgust had given way to audible animosity. He hoped it was an improvement.

'You blew me away and I couldn't control my baser instincts. We had phenomenal sex, but it wasn't until you said something afterward that I realised who you were.'

He could have sworn her upper lip curled in derision. 'And what was that?'

'You said "I really need to get this tidied up now", referring to your aunt's merchandise in the warehouse, but it's a phrase you've used often in reference to tasks I've set you over the last few weeks.'

Her frosty expression didn't change, as if she was unsure whether to believe him or not, but she gave a begrudging nod and he pinched the bridge of his nose, searching for the right words to make her understand. 'I was honest about one thing yesterday. I don't do things like that, meet women and have sex with them in under ten minutes. But seeing you like that…it blew my mind.'

At last, a breakthrough, when her rigid shoulders relaxed a tad. Not a complete thaw but he'd work on it, whatever it took. He needed Charlotte on board for his revamp of this company. And if having to work alongside this intriguing woman while he did it was a side benefit, he was all for it.

'You seriously couldn't control yourself around me?'

Out of all the responses he'd imagined, that wasn't it. She sounded hesitant, slightly awed, as if she couldn't believe he'd want her.

Some asshole must have really done a number on her for her confidence to be that low. It made him want to vault the desk, sweep her into his arms and show her exactly how sexy she was.

'You're incredible, and when I saw you I wanted you.' He shrugged, hoping the simple truth would appease more than an apology. 'And at the risk of having you fling that tablet at my head, seeing you strut in here only reinforces that snap judgement I made yesterday. But I know we have to work together and we're professionals. So let's chalk up yesterday to what it was—phenomenal, impulsive, amazing sex between consulting adults—and move on to business.'

She stared at him, dazed, but the faint pink in her cheeks indicated he'd hit the mark by articulating just how incredible it had been between them.

'You expect us to work together and pretend like nothing happened?'

She'd lost the biting, sarcastic edge and it gave him hope.

'I don't know about you, but I'm not that good a pretender.' He steepled his fingers together and rested them on the desk, trying to project a professional picture, when forgetting what they'd done in that warehouse was the furthest thing from his mind.

Seeing her again, sitting opposite him in her conservative work attire, only made him want to see what was under it all the more. Would she be wearing lace? Satin? Or that risqué leather again?

Damn, not helping the hard-on situation.

'But doing the best job I can for this company is important to me and I want you to work alongside me to achieve that goal. Can you do it?'

He half expected her to tell him to stick his offer. To tender her resignation and sue the pants off him.

Instead, after a long pause where she studied him with disconcerting intensity, she nodded.

'I can do this if you can.'

Hot damn, that almost sounded like a challenge.

As if she thought he couldn't work with her without reverting to the horny caveman he'd been yesterday. He'd show her.

But in agreeing to keep this all business, he'd be deprived of some serious pleasure.

Their first encounter had been colossal.

What would prim Charlotte be like if she really let go?

CHAPTER SEVEN

CHARLOTTE LEFT THE office in a daze. She couldn't return to her desk to focus on work and pretend her carefully ordered world hadn't just been tipped on its head.

She'd had sex with her new boss.

Not just sex. Amazing, stupendous, multi-orgasmic sex. The kind of sex she'd only ever read about but never dreamed could happen for real.

As she walked aimlessly in the bright Sydney sunshine, she remembered one of the last things she'd said to her flatmate Mak before she'd left to take Broadway by storm.

'I need a bad boy. Some big, bold, annoying, arrogant guy to rattle my cage.'

Well, she'd got her wish and then some.

In what weird alternate universe, in what giant cosmic twist of fate, did she have the best sex of her life only to discover she'd have to work alongside the hot guy who'd rocked her world? The guy who held her dream of owning her perfect house in the palm of his hand and had the power to make or break it with a snap of his talented fingers?

It didn't seem possible. But it was and now Alexander Bronson expected her to work with him and act like he hadn't been inside her in the most intimate way?

Impossible. Improbable. Improper.

Because Charlotte couldn't forget, despite what she'd told him.

She blamed him, for saying all that stuff about how badly he'd wanted her and how he couldn't control himself around her. As if she were some glamorous femme fatale who inspired that kind of passion in a man. She wished.

There'd been a moment when she'd first seen him behind his desk, an infinitesimal moment, where she'd seen hunger in his eyes. As if he still wanted her. It should have sent her running. It didn't.

For the simple fact she liked feeling wanted.

Men didn't turn their heads to stare as she walked down the street. She didn't inspire sexist wolf whistles or lewd comments. And the one and only time she'd succumbed to searching for a date online, she'd taken down her profile from the app after a day when she'd received a mortifying two less-than-stellar requests.

Besides, she valued her job. She needed her job. And she couldn't walk away now, not when she was so close to realising one of her long-held dreams.

Having nomadic parents, being raised by a kooky

aunt, meant Charlotte craved security like nothing else. And the quirky cottage on the outskirts of Sydney that she'd fallen in love with represented that to her.

A home.

A house all of her own, where she could establish the life she wanted before following the rest of her dreams: a husband, kids, the works. Charlotte wanted it all and knew the only way she could make it happen was to go after it.

It wouldn't be easy, finding her perfect guy. She knew this, considering she'd have to date regularly to discover what she really wanted in a man and her track record in the dating stakes had been abysmal until now. But the house was a first step in the right direction and somehow, with her twisted logic, she thought that once she had the house she could set about finding a guy happy to live in it.

She almost had enough for a deposit, enough for the bank to take her seriously for a hefty loan application. Just another fortnight and she could start living her dream.

But to do so, she had to tolerate working with Alexander Bronson.

'You can do this,' she muttered, kicking at a stone on the footpath, as her cell buzzed in her pocket.

She fished it out, her palms growing clammy as his name popped up on the screen. She'd entered it the moment she'd left his office, ensuring she could ignore his calls if needed.

But this wasn't a call; he'd sent a text.

Have ordered morning tea for staff. Please pick up
the order from Le Miel on your way back.
Will be good to have staff bonding session.
Alex

Charlotte muttered an unsavoury curse under her
breath and shoved her cell back in her pocket. She
didn't need a staff bonding session. She'd already
bonded with her boss and it had been so damn monumental she couldn't forget it.

Le Miel was a café they often used for work func-
tions, and she figured he'd probably got the recom-
mendation from the receptionist. Heading there would
be good—she needed a friendly ear and Abby was
a great listener. Though what her friend would say
when she heard about the events of the last few days...
Charlotte picked up the pace. The faster Abby talked
sense into her, the better.

Ten minutes later, she had two bags filled with
Abby's delectable pastries ready to take back to the
office. But she couldn't leave without talking to her
friend so she perched at her favourite table, ordered
a cappuccino and waited.

Abby always popped out from the kitchen when
she visited, which was several times a week. Charlotte couldn't resist her friend's melt-in-the-mouth
beignets, croissants and *pain au chocolat*, eternally
grateful for her fast metabolism that ensured a thirty-
minute walk a day burned off the calories.

That leather bustier yesterday had been tighter
than her usual size—a moderate B cup—so maybe

she should lay off… She stopped eyeing up a giant almond croissant and sipped at her coffee instead, wishing she hadn't thought about that damn lingerie. She blamed it for her entire lapse in judgement. That, and Alex's inherent hotness.

Alex.

That was what he'd said to call him. Informal, casual, implying intimacy.

Hell, it was going to be a tough four weeks, waiting until the wunderkind yanked the accountancy firm out of the mire. It could only be a good thing, ensuring she had a job to support her impending loan. But four weeks of working alongside the guy who'd haunted her dreams last night would be torture.

'Hey, Char, what brings you by this time of day?' Abby collapsed into the chair opposite after placing a plate of freshly baked strawberry tartlets on the table between them. 'Your firm only ever orders afternoon tea and only then infrequently.'

'The new boss is trying to suck up to the employees.'

Abby smiled. 'So how is the boss from hell? Is he as intimidating in person as he was on the phone to you all these weeks?'

She'd whined about Alex for weeks—his condescending teasing, his constant demands, his infernal tasks—and Abby had been a sympathetic ear. Which would make what she had to divulge all the more shocking. Her friend would think she'd lost her mind.

'Uh… Alex is good.'

Abby's eyebrows shot up. 'That's interesting.'

'What?'

'You've never called him anything other than nasty names before. What's with the breathy tone? Is he hot?'

'You don't know the half of it,' Charlotte muttered, wishing she'd grabbed the morning tea order and made a run for it.

Abby grinned and rubbed her hands together. 'I sense a story.'

'Yeah, a horror story.' Charlotte sighed and internally debated how much to tell her friend.

'That bad, huh?' Abby patted her hand. 'Why don't you tell dear Abby all about it?'

Charlotte usually laughed at her friend's corny joke whenever she used that line. She barely mustered a wan smile today.

'I had sex with him.'

The tartlet Abby had halfway to her mouth fell to the floor and landed upside down with a small splat. 'What did you just say?'

'You heard me.' Charlotte grimaced, hating the way her stomach churned. She could have blamed it on hunger, considering she hadn't eaten a thing since last night, but she knew better. 'I did something crazy yesterday and now the karma gods are paying me back big time.'

Abby gaped at her and she didn't blame her. Charlotte hadn't had a date in all the time she'd known her so the fact she'd just announced she'd had sex with her boss would be as unbelievable as flying to the moon.

'I think you better start at the beginning.' Abby

grabbed a serviette, scooped up the smashed tartlet, and placed it on the table. 'Though you'll have to make it the quick version because I've got another batch of croissants in the oven.'

Charlotte inhaled a breath and blew it out. Yeah, like that would calm her nerves. Thinking about what she'd done was bad enough. Articulating it would make it all too real.

'Short version. My aunt got called away to Byron Bay to help a sick friend. She had to urgently vacate the warehouse she rents to store her merchandise and asked me to do it. So I was there, packing stuff, when the hottest guy on the planet walked in and we ended up having sex.'

Jeez, it did sound crazier spoken out loud.

Abby, astute as ever, eyed her with speculation. 'You're not telling me everything. Why would you have sex with some random stranger, hot or otherwise?'

Heat flushed Charlotte's cheeks as she remembered exactly how hot sex with Alex had been. The way he'd looked at her, the way he'd touched her, the way he'd pounded into her…her insides clenched at the incredible, erotic memory. 'Well, I was in a weird mood, lamenting my rather pitiful social life, so decided to try on some of the lingerie.'

Abby let out a whoop of laughter. 'No way. He walked in on you?'

'In faux leather, no less. Bustier and thong. A real eye-opener.' Her sardonic response elicited more laughter.

'So you're blaming the lingerie?'

'If only.' Charlotte shook her head, wishing she could blame her lapse in judgement on something so trivial. 'The lingerie made me feel bold but it was more than that…he really *looked* at me and I liked it.'

'Oh, sweetie.' Abby leaned over and hugged her. 'You're beautiful. The guy has good taste.'

She snorted. 'I'm average at best and he must have thought I was easy in that get-up.'

Abby frowned and tut-tutted. 'Why do you put yourself down like that?'

'Habit,' Charlotte wanted to say, but she wisely kept silent. Abby had always chastised her for being self-pitying and Charlotte agreed it wasn't an attractive trait. Didn't mean it stopped her from lamenting her lack of a love life in her quieter moments.

'Anyway, I lost my head, had the best sex of my life, then walk into my new boss's office this morning and realise he's the hot-sex guy.'

'I can't believe this.' Abby's eyes widened, her expression awestruck. 'It's like something out of those romance novels you devour.'

'I know, right?' Charlotte couldn't help but smirk. 'Who knew I had an inner vixen?'

Abby squared her shoulders, her nod emphatic. 'Well, I think it's great. About time you had some fun.'

'It's not going to happen again.'

Despite that tiny, insistent voice deep inside that whispered how great it would be to feel that good again.

'How did he react when he saw you this morning?'

'Not surprised.'

Abby startled. 'You mean he knew? About you working for him?'

Charlotte nodded, anger quashing her momentarily lapse into wistful. 'Yeah. He's good at his job. Has a mega reputation in the accountancy world for taking ailing firms and turning them around. So he researched me. In his defence, he said he didn't recognise me—'

'I bet he didn't,' Abby chortled.

'I'd taken my hair down and my glasses off before trying on the lingerie, trying to get into some vampy character to see if I'd feel any different, so I guess I didn't look anything like my work picture.' She dabbed at pastry crumbs with her fingertip, pushing them around the plate, embarrassed to admit how she'd been role playing for a brief moment in time at that warehouse. 'He said he only recognised me later, when I used a phrase I've been using a lot in our business dealings.'

'Well, I'm assuming it wasn't *take me now*?'

Charlotte shot Abby a death glare and she laughed.

'He sounds like a bad, bad boy, not telling you the truth immediately when he recognised you.' Abby snapped her fingers. 'Hey, isn't that what you said you wanted before Mak left, a bad boy?'

'Yeah, be careful what you wish for.' Charlotte rolled her eyes. 'Now I have to work with that bad boy for a month and pretend he didn't rock my world. Several times.'

Abby beamed. 'You go, girl.'

Charlotte managed a wry smile. 'The only place I'm going right now is back to work with some of your amazing pastries, so the ratfink can try and buy us off with treats.'

Abby's smile faded. 'You'll be okay, yeah? Working with him?'

'I'll be fine,' Charlotte said, hoping her conviction lasted when faced with the prospect of working one-on-one with her dishy boss for the foreseeable future.

CHAPTER EIGHT

ALEX FOUND HIS gaze drifting to the elevator all too often as he mingled with staff in their cubicles. Charlotte should have been back by now and the longer she stayed away, the more he wondered whether she had done a runner.

Not that she struck him as the flighty type. Not if her work record was any indication. But if she'd been half as rattled as him after their earlier meeting...

Damn, he hadn't expected to be so affected by her. He'd been prepared to make his confession, ensure she understood and move on to work. He hadn't expected to be so confused.

His visceral reaction to seeing her again startled him. His gut had griped like he'd drunk too much fine cab sav when he'd seen her in that professional get-up. There'd been nothing remotely sexy about her skirt, blouse and jacket, but when she'd looked at him—albeit in stunned horror—he'd felt it like a kick in the head.

It had something to do with her eyes. Those cool, grey orbs held a world of secrets and he'd love to discover each and every one.

Yeah, like that was going to happen.

Alex had a job to do. Turn this company around. And Charlotte was a big part of making that happen.

As if thoughts of her had conjured her up, the elevator doors slid open and she stepped out, laden bags in each hand. The staff clearly looked forward to Le Miel's delights because they flocked to her, quickly taking the bags and heading for the mini conference room where they'd set up cutlery and crockery.

Her gaze homed in on him like a radar and he felt that kick again. It unsettled him and he reacted with a goofy grin. It didn't go over well if her raised eyebrow and supercilious expression were any indication.

He crossed the office, determined to set her at ease. They had a lot of work to do. 'Thanks for picking up the morning tea.' He gestured towards the conference room. 'Shall we?'

She didn't respond, other than a curt nod. He much preferred the warm, willing woman he'd held in his arms yesterday but knew her frosty counterpart would be much more conducive to work.

He followed her into the conference room, not surprised when she kept her distance. He chatted with staff, made small talk, discovering that Edgar had worked here the longest, an impressive twenty-four years, that Suzie had five kids, that Viola would happily take a redundancy to go farm alpacas and that Charlotte was the glue that held everyone together.

Staff raved about her, vindicating his choice to make her the new manager. She had smarts, kindness and respect, three traits that would ensure she excelled in the job.

But appointing her in that role meant they'd be working a lot closer together for his time here. The old manager had been responsible for running the place into the ground almost single-handedly and a lot of work had to be done to ensure it prospered again. He was up for the challenge. Would Charlotte be?

If she could barely stand to be in the same room as him, he doubted it.

As some of the workers drifted back to their cubicles, she finally approached him. 'You did a good thing with this morning tea, thanks.'

'Good working relations are important to me.'

Her eyes widened imperceptibly, pinning him with what he'd quickly come to recognise as her signature scepticism.

He hadn't meant it as anything other than what it was: a declaration to foster a solid work ethic. But she glared at him as if he'd made some gross sexual innuendo.

'We need to talk,' he said, making a grand show of glancing at his watch. 'You're a team leader here and I need to pick your brains about some of the ideas I've been kicking around.'

'Sure.' Her brisk nod was as terse as her response. 'I've got clients all afternoon so does first thing in the morning suit?'

Usually, he'd insist they work through dinner but in this case he'd be better off keeping his distance for now.

'Fine, see you at nine.'

She stared at him a second too long, as if she couldn't quite figure him out. That made two of them. Because as Charlotte stalked out of the conference room, he couldn't tear his gaze off her ass, the memory of how it had felt in his hands making his palms tingle.

After all his self-talk, he still wanted her.

Not good.

The smart thing to do would be to lock himself away in his office for the rest of the day, but that plan was shot to shit when he reviewed the latest performance reviews.

Staff cuts would have to be made if certain sectors of the company didn't start shouldering their load.

Which meant he had to play hardball.

He called the staff back into the conference at one and made his usual speech when he arrived at companies like this one.

'Thanks for taking a few minutes out of your busy day.' He pointed at the empty conference table. 'Sorry I didn't have time to organise a banquet lunch too.'

A few titters echoed through the group and he continued. 'As you know, I'm here to ensure The Number Makers becomes a viable company moving forward and the go-to accountancy firm in Sydney's eastern suburbs. To do that, the profit margins need to improve alongside work productivity.'

He paused, letting the implication sink in. He heard the sharp intake of breaths, the furtive glances, the stricken expressions. This part of his job sucked.

'I'm still in the process of reviewing all person-nel's billable hours but I won't sugar-coat this. Cuts may need to be made.'

A paper clip bouncing off the carpet could have been heard at that point, the silence was that pro-found.

'Rest assured, that will be my last resort, but I wanted to be upfront with you on the first day so we all know where we stand.'

Feeling like an ogre trampling Lilliputians, he tried his best reassuring smile. By the number of round eyes fixed on him, it didn't work.

'I'll be moving forward with a plan of action over the next week. In the meantime, keep up the good work.'

Damn, that sounded trite and condescending, con-sidering he'd virtually threatened some of their jobs. He'd avoided making eye contact with Charlotte dur-ing his little speech but as the staff trickled out of the room, he couldn't resist.

Her reaction surprised him. That gleam in her eyes almost looked like admiration, before she turned her back and followed her co-workers out.

It gave him hope. Maybe this could work out after all.

If only he could stop staring at her cute ass.

CHAPTER NINE

WHEN ALEX HAD called the staff into the conference room at lunchtime, Charlotte had expected a pep talk.

She'd been impressed by his team-bonding exercise at morning tea and hadn't been afraid to tell him. It boded well that they'd resorted to polite indifference. She could do this. Work alongside him. Without constantly thinking about how damn incredible he'd felt inside her.

Yikes. That was the fifth time this afternoon she'd let her mind slip back to yesterday. She blamed him. If he didn't keep strutting around the office looking delectable in a navy suit, pale blue shirt and trendy stripy tie, she wouldn't be reminded of how hard his muscles had felt beneath that suit when she'd hung on for the ride of her life.

'Not helping,' she muttered as she prepared for the last client of the day. A call-up that she usually would have postponed until tomorrow considering she'd officially clocked off thirty minutes ago.

But with Alex's less than encouraging speech ringing in her ears, she needed to prove her indispensability and what better way than working late?

Her co-workers had skedaddled at five, either too intimidated by Alex's threatening speech or too stupid to care. Whatever their reasoning, it didn't affect her. She had a job to do: to prove to the boss she'd inadvertently shagged that she'd become essential to taking the company forward.

Hopefully, taking on an unexpected client and working late would go some way to convincing him she'd do whatever it took to consolidate her position.

She also had an ulterior motive. If she impressed him with her work and appeared keen to toe his new company line, it would show him she'd forgotten their encounter. That it meant little in the grand scheme of their working relationship.

Utter bollocks, but it was her excuse and she was sticking to it.

Her new client turned out to be an ex-rugby league player who needed a new accountant to manage his business interests, a string of lucrative pubs. He dwarfed her office with his height and broad shoulders, which she couldn't help but notice in the vest top he wore, with shorts that accentuated well-toned legs.

In the past she'd surreptitiously ogle a guy like this, lamenting the fact he'd never notice a girl like her beyond her mathematical skills. But today, something had changed. The client openly flirted with her—and she enjoyed it.

Maybe the wild sex she'd had with Alex had given her a much-needed confidence boost, maybe wearing sensuous satin underwear for the first time made her meet the guy's eye when she'd usually look away. Whatever it was, she liked feeling this empowered. It boded well for chasing her dream.

'You've done a great job with keeping accurate records.' She turned the computer screen towards him. 'This is the program we use so whatever you need, don't hesitate to get in touch.'

His wolfish smile revealed a row of startlingly white teeth. 'Does that include calling you after hours?'

Her inner vixen did a little shimmy that he'd be remotely interested in her 'after hours'.

Her inner accountant shut down that vapid vixen quick smart.

'I'm available to answer your accountancy questions from nine 'til five.'

'Pity,' he said, his grin widening. 'If you ever fancy a drink, drop by one of my pubs and the staff will let me know you're around.'

'Thanks.' She stood to escort him to the door. 'But I don't mix business with pleasure. It's unprofessional and you wouldn't want someone like that handling your finances.'

He managed a rueful shrug while she hoped her nose wouldn't grow from telling that whopping great lie.

Because she had mixed business with pleasure, even if she hadn't known it at the time, and she couldn't stop thinking about it. Worse, how it might feel to do it again.

'I'll be in touch,' she said, waiting until the elevator doors had slid shut to toe off her shoes, pick them up and head to her office to pack up her things.

She'd almost reached her office when Alex's door flung open and she jumped. 'I thought you'd left with everyone else?'

'And leave you alone with that Neanderthal? Not bloody likely.' He almost growled, a deep frown marring his brow. 'You shouldn't smile at men like that. It gives them the wrong idea.'

'Excuse me?' The shoes fell from her fingers as outrage made her stand tall. 'My job is to make clients trust me enough to feel safe having me handle their money. That includes being polite. Which includes smiling.'

She flashed him her broadest, fakest smile. 'See? Nothing wrong with it. And while I understand you're the head honcho around here for the next month, I'd appreciate it if you would credit me with some business nous and butt the hell out.'

Probably not the smartest way to end her first day with the boss but he'd got her so damned riled she could barely see straight. God, the guy was insufferable. He'd reverted to the condescending know-it-all he'd been over the phone for the weeks they'd corresponded before actually meeting.

'In my office. Now,' he barked, turning his back on her and stalking into it.

Charlotte had two options. Flip him the bird, pick up her shoes and leave. Or do as he said so she could keep the job that was so important to her.

She chose the latter. But still flipped him the bird.

When she entered his office, he stepped around her and slammed the door shut.

'Just so you know, windows become reflective at night with the lights on in here,' he said, so close she could smell his distinctive aftershave, some expensive heady blend of citrus and spice. 'In case you ever needed to make rude signs at me in the future.'

Horrified, Charlotte felt heat scorch her cheeks. He'd seen her.

'Listen, we rub each other the wrong way—'

'Do we?' He spun around to face her, still so close she could touch him if she were so inclined. 'I think the way we spark off each other has more to do with battling residual sexual tension.'

Damn, why did he say the S word? She could handle thinking about their encounter in her head, barely. Having him articulate it made it all too real. She needed to forget their sizzling connection, not remember.

'We agreed to forget about that,' she said, resorting to the same proper tone she'd used to put that rugby dude back in his place.

'We did and we will.' He glared at her, as if this buzz between them were all her fault. 'We're both professionals and I'm sure we can act like it.'

'Good,' she said, with a terse nod, but why didn't she believe him?

He sounded strained, as if articulating their need to keep things between them strictly business-focused was an effort.

'Maybe we should have dinner together? Clear the air, establish a better working rapport?'

'Dinner?' She made it sound like he'd invited her to eat rat poison with a side of nails.

The corners of his mouth twitched. 'You do eat, don't you?'

Yeah, but not with him. If keeping her mind on work in the office with him around was hard enough, trying to pretend she didn't want him over dinner would be impossible.

Sharing a meal implied camaraderie and intimacy, two things she couldn't associate with him. She had willpower; she wasn't a saint.

'I might have other plans.'

A blatant lie but it should let her off the hook.

To her surprise, anger darkened his eyes as he dragged a hand through his hair, appearing perplexed for the first time today. 'Don't tell me it's that rugby Neanderthal.'

Oh, my. Was that why he'd acted so crazy about her smiling at that client? Was he jealous?

No freaking way.

So she pushed him a little. 'Could be.'

His brows knitted together in a formidable frown. 'It's unprofessional to date clients.'

'And it's unprofessional to shag the boss but hey, we've already been there, done that, haven't we?'

She flashed a sickly sweet smile, silently berating herself for taunting him. A stupid, naive move when his gaze dropped to her mouth as if he envisaged the perfect way to shut her up.

Uh-oh.

'Alex, whatever you're thinking, you know this can't happen for a number of reasons. We just agreed to keep things professional because we're grown-ups. So get that look out of your eyes—'

'Damn it, I don't want to do this. I don't want to muddy our working relationship. But there's something about you…' He reached out, as if to touch her, before thinking better of it. 'I need to focus one hundred per cent on getting this company back on track and you're messing with that.'

He shook his head, his expression tortured. 'I can't get you out of my head and that lack of concentration is going to affect how I operate.'

His honesty impressed her and a small part of her couldn't help but be thrilled that a guy like him found a girl like her remotely memorable enough to distract.

'We can't,' she said, sounding less than convincing and they both knew it.

'You feel it too, don't you?' He took a step forward, invading her personal space, making her lean towards him inadvertently. 'Tell me you don't.'

Charlotte hated lies, but in that moment it was her only option. She opened her mouth but nothing came out. Instead, his gaze dropped to her lips again. Intense. Focused.

A second before he kissed her.

She should protest. She didn't. He had access to her mouth and he used it to wield his seductive power, the kind of power she'd never experienced before with any other man.

His tongue teased and taunted. Hot, long sweeps that demanded she match him. And she did, with more eagerness than she could have imagined.

His arms clamped around her waist and hauled her to him so she could feel every hard plane. And one very hard appendage.

She had to stop this before she lost her mind as well as her job. Her hands slid between them, her palms flat to his chest. She should shove him away. She didn't, enjoying the feel of his hard chest beneath her hands too much. Her fingers flexed slightly and he groaned into her mouth, his arms tightening in a vice-like grip.

He backed her towards the door, where he flicked the lock and hit a button that brought the blinds down over the windows.

Only when she nipped his bottom lip did he break the kiss, raising his head to stare at her in a daze.

She knew the feeling.

'I've wanted to do that all damn day,' he muttered, his gaze dropping to her mouth again before returning to her eyes. 'The way you kiss? Just as hot as yesterday.'

'Alex—'

'Fuck, even the way you say my name makes me crazy.' He rested his forehead against hers, as if trying to transfer his thoughts. If they were anything like hers, three letters could sum them up: XXX.

'Do you want me as badly as I want you?' He lifted his head and eyeballed her, daring her to disagree.

'I'll be honest and say my work has suffered today because I can't stop thinking about you.'

'Maybe you're just a crap boss?' she deadpanned, biting her bottom lip to stop from laughing out loud at his outraged expression.

'You'll pay for that,' he said, grinding his hips against hers in a way that left little doubt as to the punishment he had in mind. If that were the case, she'd be bad every day. 'So what are we going to do?'

She knew what she wanted to do. Tear his clothes off. Push him into the nearest chair. Straddle him. Ride him until she could hardly walk.

But despite the sexy satin beneath her sedate clothes, Charlotte was still the same shy, sensible woman she'd always been. A woman who never broke rules. A woman destined for a quiet, utilitarian life, the opposite of her parents.

She'd chosen to wear the frivolous underwear today to see if the confidence garnered from yesterday would continue. It looked like it had, but not in the way she'd expected.

She'd wanted to impress her boss. Little did she know she'd already done that by spreading her legs for him yesterday.

She inwardly cringed. No matter what she wore beneath her clothes, no matter how much she got off on the power trip of feeling sexy yesterday, she couldn't change who she was. Not for this guy, not for any man.

So she said, 'I'm going back to my office, packing up my things and leaving.'

But she didn't move. She willed her legs to do something; they didn't respond. Her palms still splayed against his chest and his pelvis nestled against hers like they fitted. It felt good. Better than good. Having his body plastered to hers, her lips still tingling from his kiss, felt freaking fantastic.

For a girl who didn't feel this way very often—try never—it was difficult getting her head to work in sync with her heart.

She craved romance. Yearned for the buzz of electricity, the spark, that special something that ensured every day seemed brighter.

Once she'd got over the shock of her sexy stranger being her boss this morning, she had to admit she'd felt more alive. Secretly checking him out at morning tea. A pep in her step at lunch. Her stomach falling away when she'd seen his name pop up in her inbox.

Ludicrous. Ridiculous. Preposterous. The kind of dangerous reactions that could derail a woman's prudent plans.

Having him admit he felt this buzz between them too should make her happy. It didn't. Because as she stood in the circle of his arms, her heart still pounding, she'd never felt so confused.

She never threw caution to the wind. Never took a risk. Her parents did enough of that for all of them.

She weighed options, made calculated decisions. But all she could think now, with him staring at her with open speculation, was that she had to take a gamble eventually and maybe she should bet on him.

'Do you really want to leave?' His hand drifted up

to her face, cupped her cheek. 'Because if that's what you really want, I'll let you go and we'll never speak of this again. But after what just happened, despite all our protestations to keep things strictly professional, I think we might need to reassess.'

He was right, damn him. He might have bamboozled her but they had to get this sorted.

'I think we have good intentions to focus on work and we said all the right things, but that kiss...' Her hand drifted towards her mouth, her fingertips tracing where his lips had branded her. 'It's going to be tough. But I can't risk any fallout if we do something crazy like indulging in a...fling.'

Damn, even saying the word made her blush. She would never be the type of woman to indulge in a no-strings, brief affair, but having to work alongside Alex for the next month or so would sorely challenge her previous belief systems.

'What do you mean?'

'I need this job. A reliable, stable income is all important to me at this stage of my life and I can't let anything derail my plans.'

Crap, could she sound any more pompous? But she had to make him understand that while her body craved his, her mind couldn't be swayed.

'Does that mean you'd be up for a fling if we separated business from pleasure?'

She should have known he'd focus on that one word.

Fling.

For her, it conjured visions of a confident woman

making demands on a hot guy. Having him at her beck and call. Indulging secret fantasies. Being naughty and wanton.

And couldn't be further from her if she tried.

'I don't think I'm fling material,' she said, her voice embarrassingly wavering.

'You're an incredible, sensual woman who's making me go a little crazy.' He made loopy circles at his temple. 'We can call it a thing rather than a fling if that helps?'

She laughed, wishing he weren't so damn appealing.

He grinned back at her. 'If you're worried about us working together while we indulge this *thing* between us, don't be. I'm discreet. I can separate business from pleasure. And I plan on there being a lot of the latter if you come on this wild ride with me for the time I'm here.'

Four weeks. Twenty-eight days of hedonistic pleasure, the kind of which she only ever read and dreamed about. That was what Alex was promising her.

She'd never been so tempted.

But she couldn't shake her rational side. Indulging in a fling thing wasn't her style. Then again, no guy had been her style lately. Man drought would be an understatement.

'So this is a casual thing?' How she could sound so cool she had no idea, considering how loudly her blood pounded in her ears.

His eyes lit up, considering she'd acknowledged

she might be interested. 'I'd never lead you on. I'm here for a month then I'll move to the next job. It's what I do. I hate being in one city, one town, for a long time. So yeah, it's casual.' He paused for emphasis. 'A monogamous casual fling thing, because I don't sleep around.'

His honesty blew her away. No man had spoken to her like this before. The guys she'd dated in university had been quiet, recalcitrant types as backward as her. They'd date a few times, end up in bed, with barely a spark. A bit of fun, a light-hearted distraction from the onerous study load.

None of those guys had lasted a month because she'd been a realist. Why waste time on someone that didn't do it for her?

Here was a guy, offering her a whirlwind, exciting four weeks and she was dithering.

Deep down she knew why.

She had her dream house in sight, which meant she had to go after the rest of her dream. The right guy. The kids. The dog. The herb garden. The veggie patch. The comfortable, steady life she'd always wanted.

And having a short-term fling, no matter how incredible the guy, and the sex, wasn't conducive to achieving it.

But she'd whined and moaned to her friends about this very thing, a lack of excitement in her life. Now she had six-three of hot male offering it to her on a platter and she couldn't say yes?

The pressure of his palm against her cheek increased slightly as his thumb brushed her bottom lip in an erotic sweep. 'No pressure, Charlie, this is entirely your decision, whatever you want to do.'

Damn, she must be in a bad way if him calling her Charlie sounded like an endearment rather than a taunt.

'I want…' *you*, she wanted to say. But the admission stuck in her throat.

So she quashed her rampant nerves, told her common sense to shut the hell up, broached the short distance between them, to show him what she wanted by slamming her mouth against his.

As her nerve endings fired to life again and he groaned into her mouth, she knew there was no turning back now.

CHAPTER TEN

ALEX HAD NEVER put himself out there like that with a woman before. Laying it all on the line before they started up.

Usually, he'd woo them a little, enjoy the sex, get to know them, see if a casual thing was worth pursuing. With Charlotte, he'd had the scintillating sex and bypassed the rest. And despite his initial misgivings that getting involved beyond work could pose a problem, he knew in his gut that this thing between them was worth pursuing.

He'd been impressed when she'd taken on a new client after hours and had decided to wait to speak to her. He hadn't expected to witness her morph into some kind of starstruck groupie around that rugby player. He'd seen guys like that before, had handled accounts for some of them. Big, beefy meatheads used to wielding their fame to get any woman they wanted then dumping them to move on to the next.

Alex had thought Charlie would cut the boof-head down to size. Instead, he'd watched her escort him into her office, then smile and chat as if they were old buddies, feeling the uncharacteristic stab of jealousy all the while.

It didn't make sense. He never got so involved with any woman that he cared who they spoke to or how they did it, yet with Charlotte he'd found himself willing those damn elevator doors to close on the rugby player's ass so he could talk to her.

Her work ethic impressed him. The sex yesterday had blown his mind. But what did he really know about her beyond that?

He'd invited her into his office to talk. To show her that he was more than a guy who took advantage of a woman by fucking her. To get to know more about her in the hope of figuring out why she had such a hold on him when he barely knew her.

She wasn't his type. He preferred tall, leggy blondes. Charlie was a petite, slim brunette. Maybe that was the attraction? Opposites in every way? But he wasn't that shallow and knew it was more than that.

For the first time in a long time he found himself intrigued by a woman to the point that he couldn't get her out of his head.

So when she'd flipped him the bird, her defiance adding to her aura of mystery, he hadn't been able to resist her.

Worse, he'd found himself blurting out how much he wanted her and how long he wanted her for. Real smooth. Not.

He'd expected her to protest when he couldn't resist kissing her. He hadn't expected her whole-hearted response, let alone her agreeing to his terms.

What was it about this reserved woman that pushed his buttons in a major way?

She kissed him with unabashed enthusiasm, as if she couldn't get enough.

The feeling was entirely mutual.

Her hands slid down his chest, tentative at first. Skimming the waistband of his trousers. Sliding around his hips. Coming to rest on his ass, squeezing lightly.

He chuckled and eased away from her lips. 'Are you feeling me up?'

'Absolutely,' she said, her cheeks flushed, her eyes bright. 'Seeing as you so kindly explained how this thing between us will work, let me clue you in on how I see it working.'

God, he loved this feisty side of her, hidden beneath the pulled-back hair and the sedate clothes.

'Go ahead, fill me in.'

'You're absolutely right about keeping this a secret because if word got out I'd lose my credibility. And I want you to promise me that whatever happens in your revamp of this place, you'll only judge me on my work performance.'

He raised his hand in the way he'd seen countless witnesses do on courtroom TV dramas. 'Promise.'

'And before you go getting the wrong idea about me, yesterday was an aberration.'

Confused, he lowered his hand to rest it on her hip again. 'What do you mean?'

A deep crimson blush stained her cheeks. 'I don't wear raunchy lingerie. I don't have spontaneous sex. I don't do anything particularly adventurous, so if you think I'm some wanton sex goddess because of my crazy behaviour yesterday then you're wrong, and I don't want you getting the wrong idea because that lingerie was false advertising—'

'Whoa. Slow down. Take a breath.'

Could she be any more adorable? He knew she wasn't the kind of woman to have a quickie with a stranger because of how delightfully flustered she'd been since. Even now, with her heightened colour and her bumbling rambles, she gave off an awkward vibe, as if she couldn't quite believe she couldn't resist him.

'I like you.' He hoped she accepted his intimate smile at face value, that he wasn't giving her some generic spiel to get into her panties again. 'I want to have fun with you while I'm in Sydney. No expectations.'

She took a long time to respond. 'But what if I disappoint you?'

She spoke so softly he wondered if he'd heard right. The woman who'd worn leather underwear yesterday and kissed him as if her life depended on it today must have some serious self-esteem issues to blurt something like that.

It saddened him, to think she didn't know exactly how amazing she was.

'Nothing about you could ever disappoint me,' he murmured, sliding his hands up her sides to rest on her shoulders. 'You're spectacular.'

'I'm average on a good day,' she responded drily, her lips quirked in a wry grin. 'But I can work it when I put my mind to it.'

He chuckled, loving her sense of humour. 'You know, I had every intention of ravaging you on my desk, right here, right now. But considering we already did the hot and steamy part yesterday, how about we backtrack a little and get to know each other?'

Her eyes widened until he could see the tiniest of green flecks amid all that grey. Like freshly mowed blades of grass against a slate path. Striking.

'Like a date, you mean?'

She sounded puzzled, as if she couldn't figure out why he'd want to spend time with her. Yeah, some prick must have dented her confidence real good. He could kill him for it.

'Yeah, if you want to call it that.'

A tiny furrow appeared between her brows. 'What do you want to call it?'

'Extended foreplay.' He winked, relieved to see her frown clearing. 'Trust me, sitting opposite you at some restaurant or café, sparring with you, wondering what you're wearing beneath your clothes, will make it all the sweeter when I get you naked later.'

Her breath whooshed out in a little exhalation as her colour deepened. 'Just so you know, I'm out of my depth here.'

'You don't date?'

'Rarely,' she muttered, her honesty surprising him again. 'But I like you.' The beguiling pink in her cheeks turned crimson. 'And I really like what we did yesterday. So yes, I'll go on a date with you.'

Alex had never met a woman so straightforward.

The kind of women he dated were glamorous, confident and a tad whiny. They'd never articulate how much they'd enjoyed sex let alone admit they were insecure.

Charlotte was refreshing. His life might be ticking along just the way he wanted it, no roots in one place, constant travel, a healthy bank account, a stellar career, but he knew there'd been a certain repetitiveness to it lately.

Then he'd walked into that warehouse yesterday and boom! This woman had rocked his well-ordered life and hadn't stopped since.

'I haven't been to Sydney in a while. Do you want me to get some recommendations for a restaurant or would you like to choose?' He wiggled his ass. 'I'm happy to be in your capable hands.'

As if she only just realised she still had his ass cheeks in her hands, she jumped and released him, making him chuckle. 'I prefer simple food over fancy.'

'Me too.'

She gnawed on her bottom lip for a moment, making him yearn to do the same. 'I love the freshness of Vietnamese food. Do you like it?'

'Love it.'

Frankly, he'd eat a plate of roasted cockroaches if it meant spending the evening getting to know her better.

'There's a little hole-in-the-wall café near my place. I practically live there.'

She tried to wriggle out of his grasp and he released her. But not before swooping in for another kiss. He liked her gasp of surprise, that he could catch her off guard. By the reserved front she presented he guessed that didn't happen very often.

She responded to him immediately, as she had earlier, open-mouthed, clutching at him, eager. Major turn on. Huge.

He wrenched his mouth away from hers before he reneged on his plan to take things slower after the fiery start they'd had.

'I'm hungry,' he said, tucking a strand of hair behind her ear. 'Vietnamese first.' He leaned in to whisper in her ear. 'You later.'

He heard the faintest of stifled moans and it shot straight to his straining cock. They had to get out of here. Now.

'Come on.' He grabbed her hand and opened the door, studiously avoiding glancing at the desk and thinking how badly he wanted her spreadeagled on it.

That particular fantasy would have to wait for another day.

CHAPTER ELEVEN

CHARLOTTE HAD LOST her mind.

Giving into an impulse for sizzling sex with a stranger was one thing. Agreeing to have a short-term fling with him was another.

She'd been powerless under his onslaught of charm.

You're spectacular.

She was so far from spectacular it wasn't funny, but when Alex looked at her, he made her feel wanted in a way she'd never experienced.

He had this hold over her she couldn't explain. As if she could do anything and be anyone around him.

Maybe it was the transient nature of their liaison. Maybe it was the fact he was totally wrong for her. Whatever it was, she'd agreed to spend time with him for the next four weeks and she'd never felt so alive.

Even now, sitting across from him at her favourite Vietnamese restaurant, the place seemed less dingy and the prawn spring rolls more delicious.

'Do I have mint in my teeth?' He paused with a

lettuce-wrapped spring roll halfway to his mouth. 'You're staring.'

'Just admiring the view.'

She shrugged, like it meant little being so open, when in fact she wasn't used to giving men compliments.

He smiled and she felt that same little hitch in her chest since she'd first laid eyes on him strolling into that back room at the warehouse. 'If you're trying to soften me up, you don't have to.' He crooked his finger and leaned forward, cupping his mouth to say in an exaggerated whisper, 'I'm definitely easy so you can have your wicked way with me later.'

She laughed, a loud burst that had her slapping her hand over her mouth.

'You've got a great laugh, don't stifle it.' He tilted his head, as if studying her. 'I may be pushing my luck here, considering you've already agreed to hang out with me for my time in Sydney. But I want you to make a concerted effort not to hold back with me, okay?'

He relaxed into his chair again. 'I like spontaneous.' His eyes fixed on her mouth, making her tingle all over. 'Like how you were yesterday, giving in to your first impulse. Go with that.'

She knew he wasn't just talking about the sex. But as long as she couched their fling in purely physical terms, she could protect her heart.

Because that was her greatest fear in agreeing to be reckless. That he'd walk away without looking back, just as he'd stipulated, while she'd be left nursing a slightly broken heart because she'd been dumb enough to fall for him despite trying otherwise.

'I'm not that person,' she said, mortification making her voice wobble a tad. 'I carefully consider options and make calculated decisions. It's what makes me a good accountant. But socially...' She grimaced. 'I'm awkward. Guys know it. Which is why I've never had a long-term boyfriend and haven't dated since uni.'

His mouth dropped open and the spring roll in his fingers plopped onto his plate. 'Never?'

She bit her bottom lip and shook her head, embarrassment making her want to slink under the table. 'I finished uni three years ago. Since then I've been establishing myself professionally and working towards buying my own home.'

She held up her thumb and forefinger an inch apart. 'I'm this close to achieving my goal. I've found my dream house. So I guess working hard doesn't leave much time for dating.'

He looked at her with a blatant scepticism she found disarming. 'You finish work at five. That leaves plenty of time to date.'

Charlotte wished she'd never started this. There was honesty and there was revealing too much. She'd done the latter. Now she'd have to tell him the rest, every mortifying moment.

'I prefer fictional men to the real thing. They don't disappoint.'

The corners of his mouth quirked. 'Care to tell me why I'm the exception?'

Her infernal blush returned, probably making her cheeks glow an alarming fire-engine red. 'You'll laugh.'

He held up his hand. 'Promise I won't.'

She'd come this far, she had nothing to lose in telling him all of it. Besides, she couldn't embarrass herself more than she already had. 'I'm close to putting a deposit down on my dream house. Which means I can follow through with the rest of my plans.'

'Go on.'

'I don't want to live in the house alone. I want a husband. Kids. The works.' She sighed at how embarrassingly corny it sounded articulated out loud to a man of the world like Alex. 'The kind of family life I never had.'

His eyebrows rose. 'Your parents are dead?'

They might as well be for all the time she'd spent with them growing up. They'd missed her first day at school, countless award presentations, the day she made the softball team, her graduation. She'd never forgiven them for it.

'They're teachers for an international welfare organisation. I got dumped on my aunt Dee from the time I could walk and talk. Well, not that early, but they left when I turned six. They've flown in to Sydney on a whim a few times over the years, never announcing their arrival and they fly out again just as fast. Other people's kids are more important to them than their own.'

He quickly masked his initial appalled reaction. 'You're their only kid?'

She nodded, bitterness making her nudge her plate away. 'Aunt Dee is amazing. She's quirky and fun and loving. She raised me, and I consider her more my mum than my biological mother.'

Pity darkened his eyes. 'She's the one who runs the online business that rented space in my warehouse?'

'That's the one.'

His lips eased into a full-blown smile. 'I have to meet her, if only to thank her for giving her niece excellent taste in lingerie.'

She gave him a look. 'You know I don't wear that stuff all the time.'

'Actually, I don't.' He lowered his voice and it rippled across her as if he'd caressed her skin with his fingertips. 'But I intend to find out, every single day for the next month.'

The bitterness clogging her throat evaporated under the onslaught of his charm. 'You're definitely the bad boy I pegged you for.'

Realisation lit his eyes and he snapped his fingers. 'So that's why you agreed to this fling. The good girl wants a bad boy before she settles down.'

'Something like that.'

'In that case, honey…' He held out his wrists to her, as if ready for handcuffing. 'I'm all yours, do your worst.'

She loved his overt flirting, the easy way he made her smile. 'Keep eating, otherwise the main course will never arrive.'

While he did as he was told and she savoured the

succulent prawns in their crispy pastry shells, she couldn't help but feel glad she'd told him everything.

Well, almost everything.

He'd find out the rest soon enough, when they made it back to her apartment for dessert.

And she wasn't thinking about Abby's delectable pastries in her fridge.

This fling could be just what she needed before settling down to the serious business of finding her dream man to go with the dream house.

As long as she didn't cast Alex in that role, she'd be fine.

She'd never be so foolish as to do anything like that.

CHAPTER TWELVE

MAYBE ALEX'S IDEA to have dinner before getting his hands on her had been a bad idea. He'd envisaged extended foreplay; he hadn't expected to want to simply…touch her.

Not in a sexual way, but when she'd started telling him all that stuff about her folks and her lack of experience with men, he'd wanted to bundle her into his arms and never let go.

And that wasn't him.

He could deal with fun and flirty. Dangerous and dirty.

Emotions, he steered clear of. They bred dependency and complications and contempt. He'd seen what they'd done to his dad and he lived with the fallout of that tragedy every frigging day. It drove him, that unrelenting desire not to end up like his father—depressed, suppressed, a shadow of his former self before he ultimately ended his life.

Growing dependent on one person for happiness was a fool's errand. He sure as hell was no fool.

Hearing Charlotte talk about her folks had reminded him of how long it had been since he'd visited his mum. He rarely returned home to the outback town in northern New South Wales that held nothing but bitter memories. But he flew her to whatever city he was working in once a year, out of obligation.

On those tension-fraught visits they made polite small talk like two strangers. Something he guessed they were, considering the yawning emotional gap between them since his dad's death.

They never spoke about him. Ever.

He'd tried. Once. After the funeral. She'd shut him down. And Alex had maintained the awkward status quo for the last eight years.

'Can I get you anything?' Charlotte propped in the doorway between her small kitchen and lounge room, where he'd taken a seat as instructed when they'd entered her flat.

The place was neat yet cosy. Minimalist furniture. Bright rugs. Overflowing bookshelves. The contrast encapsulating this intriguing woman perfectly.

'Yeah. You. Naked. Here.' He patted his lap, his grin lascivious.

He liked seeing her smile. She should do it more often, to alleviate those shadows that lurked behind the grey depths of her eyes.

Her honesty over dinner had surprised him. Telling him about her inexperience with men, her frugal dating history, her parents… He'd wanted to know more about her since their initial encounter. He guessed he'd got his wish.

But at what cost? Growing closer to Charlotte, a

deepening of intimacy beyond sex, could only end in disaster. She'd virtually told him as such, in her revelation about her dream.

She almost had the house, then she wanted the man.

He could see it so clearly. Some clean-cut man in a respectable profession. Probably a teacher. A banker. Maybe another accountant. Moving into Charlotte's dream house, making perfect babies, to go with her perfect life.

She deserved her dream.

Then why did the thought of her settling for sedate when she hadn't really lived yet bug the hell out of him?

He could have settled. Had the life his parents had. Marriage, mortgage, a kid. But he'd seen what that life could turn into and he wanted no part of it.

Ever.

'I was asking if you wanted a drink. Or dessert?'

'Only if I can eat it off you.' He stood and stalked towards her, one thing on his mind to obliterate the mood that thinking about the past never failed to elicit.

'On that note, I have a surprise for you.' She pointed at the sofa. 'But you have to sit and promise not to move.'

'Not promising anything,' he said, but he did as she instructed, intrigued by this playful side of her.

'See those boxes?' She pointed to an open door leading to a bedroom, filled to overflowing with boxes. 'That's all the stuff I packed up yesterday and there might just be more things I can try on and model for you, if you're game?'

He made a strangled sound and flopped back on the sofa. 'Stop. You're killing me.'

She laughed, a soft provocative tinkle that had him eyeing her with newfound respect. 'I figure that I became this hot, confident woman wearing that lingerie, it can't hurt to try again, right?'

'You don't need any of that stuff,' he said, suddenly serious amid their light-hearted banter. 'The way we sparked? That's all you, babe.'

She flushed, her smile coy. 'Thanks, but I need to do this for me, okay?'

He nodded. 'Okay. Should I give scores out of ten for these outfits?'

'Only if you want me to use those painful-looking clamps I spied yesterday around a certain part of your anatomy.'

He winced and she laughed again. 'Be back in a minute.'

While he spent his life on the road and adventure was his middle name, sexually he'd never been into the kinky stuff. Or half the apparatus he'd glimpsed at the warehouse yesterday. Give him an armful of warm, sexy woman and he was a happy man. About to get happier as Charlotte peeked around the door, her cheeks a fetching pink.

'I'm not so sure about this…' She trailed off, sucking in her bottom lip. 'Nice in theory but now that I'm wearing it, I'm still a chicken at heart.'

'You're not a coward.' He eyeballed her, hoping

to convey with one look how attractive he found her, with or without the sexy lingerie. 'You're a strong, confident woman who's taking control of her sexuality and indulging in a little fun. Nothing scary about that.'

His words hit the mark as her head tilted up and she opened the door wider.

Leaving him gobsmacked.

If that faux-leather black number she'd worn yesterday had turned him on, this sheer red chiffon thing shot him into the stratosphere.

It looked like an extremely short nightie that ended at the tops of her thighs, held up by the thinnest spaghetti straps. It fell loosely from top to bottom, making it shapeless. But the fact he could see straight through it, revealing dips and curves, and some equally sexy underwear, made him want to sit up and howl.

'Too much?'

She sounded uncertain and doubts clouded her eyes again.

He had to show her exactly how incredible she was.

'You're exquisite,' he said, surging to his feet. He had to get his hands on her. Now.

'Uh-uh.' She waggled her finger at him. 'You're just looking for now.'

'Spoilsport,' he muttered, sinking back into his seat, adjusting himself as he did so. 'If I'm only allowed to look, how about you take off that bra?'

He expected her to refuse. When she didn't, flicking the clasp in front, tugging her arms out of the loops, and letting it fall to the floor, his hopes soared. This shy woman had untapped depths of sensuality he had every intention of exploring in minute detail.

'Wow.' He stared in reverence at her dark nipples clearly visible through the see-through chiffon. Her breasts were perky, the areola perfectly defined. He wanted his mouth on them so desperately his cock throbbed.

'If you like that…' She hooked her thumbs into the elastic of her panties and pushed them down to her ankles, kicking them off in a cute move that would have looked practised coming from any other woman.

She straightened, her arms hanging loosely by her sides, her expression uncertain, as she let him look his fill.

And he did. He stared at the neat thatch of hair at the apex of her thighs. At those tempting nipples. Finally he reached her face.

When she slowly raised an eyebrow, as if taunting him with a 'what are you waiting for?' he practically leapt off the couch and vaulted the coffee table to get to her.

'What about the rest of the fashion show?' She grinned, as if she knew exactly how much she turned him on.

'Sweetheart, we've got a month for you to show me every goddamn scrap of underwear in those boxes but, right now, I need you real bad.'

To prove it, he grabbed her wrists and held them overhead as he had her up against the doorjamb, her eyes wide pools of shimmering desire.

'You are so frigging sexy,' he murmured, a second before he claimed her mouth.

She tasted sweet and decadent, like the after-dinner mints they'd enjoyed at the restaurant, her soft moan of pleasure firing his libido into overdrive. As if it needed the help.

He slid his hands under the nightie, seeking her breasts. A soft handful. Perfect. He rolled her nipples between his thumbs and forefingers as he plundered her mouth, loving how she strained against him, eager, wanton.

Her pelvis ground against his cock and he slid one of his hands lower to find her wet and wanting.

He delved between her slick folds, found the hard nub and rubbed, toyed a little, teasing her with his fingers, savouring the incoherent sounds she made. She was so responsive, so damn ready for him that it made his cock ache to be inside her.

She made soft mewling sounds as her excitement built and he circled her clit faster, stunned by how fast she climbed towards climax. His fingers continued to toy with her, to delve, and when she came apart he swallowed her cry of release, needing to be inside her so badly his balls ached.

When her body softened, his lips eased off the pressure, their kiss growing softer, gentler.

'You make me feel so good,' she murmured, burying her face against his shoulder, making something inexplicable tighten in his chest.

He got that urge again, to wrap his arms around

her and hold on. To protect her. To cherish her. Like a goddamn knight.

To distract from the bizarre feeling in his chest, he got down to business. Unzipped. Condom on. Palmed her ass and lifted her a tad higher for easier access. Then he slid into the hilt. It was tight, wet heaven, her glorious pussy clenching around him like it would never let go.

She nipped at his shoulder as he withdrew and thrust again. Over and over. Swirls of pleasure pooling in his lower back. Making his balls lift. His cock so damn hard he felt invincible.

Her soft pants spurred him on. She scored his back as he drove into her with the mindless intensity of a man hell-bent on reliving the mind-numbing release he craved.

'So, so good,' she whispered. 'Amazing.'

Then she bit his shoulder, hard, and he came with the force of a hurricane slamming into him, spinning him around, leaving him disorientated.

At some point his forehead had connected with the doorjamb and when he could muster the strength he lifted it to find himself staring into Charlotte's grey eyes glowing like molten pyrite.

He wanted to speak. To tell her how damn unusual it was for him to have this kind of physical connection with a woman so soon.

He liked sex. He'd had a lot of it since his late teens, when he'd lost his virginity to a farmer's daughter three years his senior on a hay bale at the back of a shearing shed.

Casual sex had never steered him wrong. So what
was it about Charlotte that made him feel as if what
they'd shared, twice now, went beyond fucking?

'You're something else, you know that, right?'

Lame, as far as compliments went, but it had the
desired result when she beamed at him.

'So does that mean you're up for another fashion
parade tomorrow night?'

He laughed and tightened his hold around her
waist. 'Babe, give me thirty minutes and you can
model the rest tonight.'

Her hand skimmed his chest to settle over his
heart. 'Make it fifteen and you've got a deal.'

'Hot damn,' he muttered, brushing a kiss across
her lips, wondering how she'd managed to shatter his
focus in just over twenty-four hours.

Usually, when he started at a new company, he'd
remain one hundred per cent focused on getting the
job done. Since yesterday, when he'd strolled into
that warehouse and seen this shy accountant in her
raunchy get-up, his intentions to concentrate on work
only had been blown to smithereens.

He needed to get back in the game, ensure The
Number Makers became a viable proposition again.

But when Charlotte's hand drifted from his chest
and slid lower in that quiet, determined way she had,
he thought, *tomorrow. I'll regain focus tomorrow.*

CHAPTER THIRTEEN

CHARLOTTE OPENED HER eyes at six a.m. every morning without the aid of an alarm. She'd do five yoga stretches in bed, a few ab crunches to get the blood pumping then head for the shower.

But something felt different this morning as her eyes fluttered open. More light streamed through the blinds, streaking the ceiling with slashes of gold and sienna. She blinked several times, stretched. Only to encounter sore muscles. All over her body.

What had she been doing…in an instant it came flooding back. Dinner. The crimson lingerie. Alex.

Bracing for the uncharacteristic sight of having a man in her bed, she gathered her meagre courage and rolled her head to one side.

Nothing.

Alex had gone.

Disappointment swamped her, making her choke up. Stupid, considering she understood the terms of their arrangement but when he'd agreed to spend the night she'd envisaged all sorts of crazy scenarios, like waking up next to him, cuddling, kissing, more…followed by breakfast.

Annoyed by her sentimentality, she pressed her fingertips to her eyes, took a few deep breaths then opened them.

To find Alex propped in the doorway, wearing nothing but a towel and a smile, holding a cup of coffee.

'Morning,' he said, sounding way too chipper as he crossed her small bedroom to place the coffee on the side table. 'You were sleeping so soundly I didn't want to wake you.'

She wouldn't have minded him waking her if he'd done it with his hands and tongue but she kept that gem to herself. Just over a day in this guy's company and she'd turned into a sex maniac. Then again, considering what Alex could do in the bedroom…or the doorway…or the warehouse…a girl could be forgiven for focusing on getting down and dirty.

'What time is it?' The aroma of rich coffee beans tempted her and she reached for the cup.

'Six-forty.'

'Crap, I'm going to be late.' She sipped too deeply and scalded her tongue. 'Ouch.'

'Slow down, I hear the boss is lenient.'

His lopsided grin made her want to say 'screw work and come back to bed' but he'd returned to the doorway and she didn't know what this meant.

Was he regretting staying the night?

Was he in a hurry to leave?

Was he second-guessing his decision to have a fling with her?

'Thanks for the coffee,' she said, blowing on the steaming liquid before taking a slower sip this time. 'I can't function without a caffeine hit in the morning.'

'Same here.' He gestured at the towel. 'Hope you don't mind, I had a shower.'

'No problem.' She cradled the mug, letting the warmth infuse her to stave off a sudden chill.

Not that there was anything inherently wrong with their casual conversation but their exchange held nothing of the ease they'd experienced last night. Even during dinner, when she'd revealed all that stuff about her folks and her penchant for stability, there hadn't been this stiltedness.

She didn't like feeling like this. She was awkward enough around people, especially men, without adding to it.

He cleared his throat. 'I'll see you at the office.'

A statement, not a question, as he swivelled and strode back to the bathroom, where he would no doubt put his clothes on before beating a hasty retreat.

The unexpected sting of tears annoyed her anew. What the hell had she expected? For them to go into the office together?

She'd been the one to stipulate a strict privacy policy if they decided to indulge in this mutual attraction. The last thing she needed was anyone at work getting a hint of anything improper going on between her and the boss, not when there was a possible promotion in the foreseeable future.

But she'd be lying to herself if she didn't admit

to expecting...*more* from their first morning-after encounter.

If they were this wooden now, how much worse would things be in the office? Had she been a fool to even contemplate separating business from pleasure?

She could do it. Could he?

Drinking the rest of her coffee, she waited for him to leave. The bathroom door opened in two minutes, indicating his desire for a speedy escape.

He stopped in the bedroom doorway, wearing the same clothes as last night yet managing to look impossibly fresh and gorgeous.

She waited for him to speak, to say something to banish the unease hanging like a pall in the air.

After what seemed like an eternity, he gave her a brusque nod. 'See you later.'

She waited until she heard the front door close before slumping back onto the pillow and muttering some very unsavoury names under her breath.

Whether directed at him or her, she had no idea.

CHAPTER FOURTEEN

ALEX COULDN'T STAND people who brought their problems to work. He had a firm belief that what happened outside office doors should stay there, which was why he had more than a few qualms about indulging in a steamy affair with Charlotte and not letting it interfere with their working relationship.

What a crock.

On all counts.

Because he'd certainly brought his mood into work with him today. An unsettled, God-awful mood he hadn't been able to shake since he'd first opened his eyes this morning to find a sexy, slumbering Charlotte next to him, looking like an innocent angel he'd willingly corrupted.

He hadn't wanted to spend the night. He never did. Sex he could do. Intimacy, not so much. But he'd been so knackered after his first day at The Number Makers, not to mention two sensational bouts of postdinner sex, that he'd dozed after their second time in her bed and slept right through.

Another first, not waking several times. He never

had a good night's sleep. Probably because the phone call regarding his dad's death had come through at one thirty-seven a.m. all those years ago and he'd slept fitfully ever since.

He hated the phone ringing at night, but had learned to cope considering overseas business calls rarely happened during the day because of time zones. But the harsh jangle grated on his nerves, never failing to catapult him back to that night when he'd heard his mum's tremulous voice imparting the devastating news.

He'd known things had been rough for his dad, had witnessed his depression first-hand. The stifling atmosphere in the house he'd grown up in was one of the reasons he had escaped as soon as humanly possible.

But the moment his mum had articulated the doubts surrounding the death, that it might have been suicide, the guilt had set in.

Had he done enough when he'd been home? There had always been a wedge between him and his dad, an invisible barrier that had prevented them from getting close. He'd blamed his dad for being deliberately distant and he'd used that as an excuse not to visit home as often as he should after he'd left.

Which of course led to the inevitable questions: would his dad be alive if he'd visited more often?

Alex had refused to let the guilt eat away at him, but in the wee small hours, when he couldn't control his subconscious, the guilt festered and manifested in the form of soul-destroying nightmares that ensured he rarely slept well.

But last night with Charlotte curled into him like an affectionate kitten, he'd slumbered soundly. When he'd woken, feeling more rested than he had in years, the sight that had greeted him had taken his breath away.

Dark, natural lashes fanning her cheeks. Her lips parted, emitting tiny puffs of air. And the sheet draped across her waist, leaving her breasts bare.

He'd looked his fill, even though it seemed voyeuristic with her fast asleep, but he couldn't help it. Something about her inherent innocence captivated him in a way he hadn't expected after their first sizzling encounter.

How could a reserved, introverted woman be so fiery and uninhibited in bed?

Even though he hadn't known her identity when he'd first entered that warehouse and seen her in that racy lingerie, something about her had captured his attention. He'd glimpsed a hint of vulnerability despite her bold outfit and that contrast had snagged his interest like nothing else.

Interestingly, his desire for her hadn't abated since. If anything, after last night, he wanted her even more and that was what had sent him running from her bed before she woke.

Because while he'd been staring at her like a perv he'd started feeling…stuff. The kind of scary, terrifying stuff that confused the hell out of him, considering he'd known this woman for a grand total of two days.

It didn't make sense. He didn't do touchy-feely. He

never invested emotionally in any of his liaisons. Yet waking up next to Charlotte had him wondering what it would be like to do this more often.

He'd hoped a cold shower would clear his head. It hadn't. If anything, his heart had still pounded madly when he'd peeped in on her before making coffee. Perhaps what he'd needed was a caffeine shot to really wake up. If anything, that had been the beginning of his downward spiralling mood because all he'd been able to think about as he'd propped against her kitchen bench waiting for her machine to fire up was how for the first time in for ever this sense of domesticity didn't frighten him.

It had been enough to have him bolting out of her apartment asap. She'd seen it too, his fear. Had stared at him in blatant confusion when he'd handed her a cup of coffee and that confusion had given way to hurt when he'd retreated.

He didn't do morning-afters for a reason and having Charlotte look at him like he'd stabbed her in the heart reinforced why.

He never should have stayed the night.

Waking up next to her, battling the urge to linger, had discombobulated him ever since.

He'd avoided her for the last four hours, not wanting to inflict his mood on her further. Thankfully, he had a shitload of work to get through so the employees thought nothing of him being holed away. But the fact he'd deliberately ignored Charlotte all morning after the evening they'd shared didn't sit well with him.

He wanted to make it up to her without giving her the wrong idea.

What idea's that, dickhead? That you might actually like her?

'Shut the fuck up,' he muttered, his inner voice not doing him any favours.

Two days. He'd known her a grand total of forty-eight hours—he didn't count the numerous phone calls to discuss business over the last few weeks. Because the Charlotte who'd sounded so uptight and prim on the phone that he hadn't been able to resist teasing her was nothing like the real woman in front of him.

In the flesh, Charlotte Baxter was something else.

With a frustrated growl, he opened the folder containing the first lot of staff performance reviews. While he liked the freedom of moving from one company to another and the challenge of making it viable again, he hated this part of his job.

Sitting across from long-time employees who weren't performing to the best of their abilities; seeing the fear in their eyes; dealing with their overt hostility.

He'd seen it all in his time, from new hires who'd told him to stick his job up his ass and walked out, to the desperate breadwinners who'd do anything to keep their job, to the old-timers who knew if they were sacked they wouldn't find new employment.

Doing performance reviews at The Number Makers wouldn't be any different and, in the mood he was in, this had the potential to go pear-shaped. He'd be better off leaving the reviews until later and focusing on something less fraught, like client referrals.

He stared at the phone, dithering over whether to call Charlotte. She could help. She could give him an insight into the current system beyond the obvious.

Another thing he'd learned in his travels: figures didn't always tell the whole story and he wanted to ensure he did this right.

With a resigned sigh, he picked up the phone and stabbed at her office number. If the old manager had her on speed dial he must have conferred with her regularly. Then again, considering the hatchet job he'd done, maybe not. If the old fool had relied on Charlotte more often the company wouldn't be ailing.

When she picked up and responded with a cool, 'Yes? Can I help you?' Alex wished he hadn't rung her. Hearing her voice served like a kick to the head, his instantaneous reaction making his chest twang and his fingers dug into the wood of the desk while he clutched the phone to his ear with the other hand.

'Are you busy?'

'Always.' Her clipped response catapulted him back to the many times over the weeks she'd sounded just as dismissive, as if he was an unwelcome intrusion.

'Could you spare fifteen minutes to help me with something?'

She hesitated, as if remembering the last time she'd entered his office, and not wanting a repeat performance.

'Sure,' she finally said, her tone demure yet aloof. 'I'll be there in five.'

'Thanks.'

He hung up and let out a long breath. His plan to keep business and pleasure separate was fast becoming blurred if his visceral reaction to hearing her voice was any indication.

Even her terse, sharp responses reminded him of last night and the breathy way she'd murmured his name as he'd plunged into her, the whispers of want as he'd teased her with his tongue, the soft pants as her excitement had escalated.

'Hell,' he muttered, focusing on the documents in front of him and seeing nothing. The figures swam before his eyes as all he could see was Charlotte sitting up in bed, sleep tousled and adorable, staring at him with expectation.

He didn't like expectations where women were concerned. For the simple fact he could never live up to them.

He'd outlined their arrangement so clearly, had been adamant he'd stick to it. But he hadn't banked on Charlotte getting under his skin, and knowing he had to see her shortly to discuss work meant he had to get his act together. Pronto.

A knock sounded at his door and he called out, 'Come in,' putting his game face on. The one he hoped conveyed professionalism, not the one that showed his inner turmoil.

She opened the door and strode into his office, defiantly meeting his eyes as if she expected him to bring up last night.

As if he would.

However, as his gaze flicked over her, taking in the calf-length grey fitted skirt, pale blue blouse and plain black pumps, all he could wonder was what lingerie she wore under the sedate outfit.

Which took him straight back to last night, exactly what he didn't want.

'We've got a lot of ground to cover,' he said, sounding way too abrupt as he gestured at the seat opposite. 'I need your input on the client referral system.'

She quirked a brow, impressively imperious, as if his attitude didn't impress her one bit. 'Why should my opinion matter?'

'Cut the crap,' he barked, instantly regretting it when her eyes widened in shock. 'Sorry, that came out wrong. I'm grouchy because of these.'

He pointed to the paper stack in front of him. 'I hate doing appraisals. It's the worst part of my job, coming into a new company and making the hard decisions based on performance. So I'm leaving these until later and dealing with the easier stuff first.'

He picked up a folder he'd set to one side and waved it at her. 'By the way, this is yours and in case you're wondering it's beyond reproach. I'm not surprised the old manager suggested I liaise with you over the last few weeks.'

His apology and subsequent explanation for his terseness meant little considering her rigid posture didn't soften one iota. The frostiness turning her eyes a glacial grey was a dead giveaway too.

'I know how proficient my work is. I do a damn good job for my clients.' Her nose tilted in the air slightly and for the first time this morning he felt like smiling. Her snootiness was beyond cute. 'But if you think you'll get my help on the appraisals too, I'm not a tattle-tale.'

'I'm not that unprofessional. I'd never put you in that position.' He placed her folder off to one side. 'Like I did with you, I won't take the manager's word for it. I'll observe staff, check their billable hours versus productivity. I set you tasks over the last few weeks, made you jump through proverbial hoops and you proved your worth. That's what I'll do with the other staff.'

He drummed his fingers against the stack of files in front of him. 'I've done my homework on each and every employee. I know their strengths and weak-nesses. But not everything is obvious on paper and I want to see first-hand what they're capable of. But for now, can you offer insight into this referral system?'

The disapproval pursing her mouth vanished. 'Fine, what would you like to know?'

For the next thirty minutes, Alex worked through the files, gaining more insight into the client referral system than he'd hoped for. As he already knew from her previous work, Charlotte articulated her opinions clearly and used facts to back them up.

She didn't mince words or show a hint of senti-mentality for the old system, which surprised him. She might be an astute businesswoman but he'd fig-ured she had a soft core and would try to sway him towards keeping the old system.

Her objectivity would make her perfect managerial material, just as he'd suspected.

When he'd closed the last file, she stood. 'Is there
anything else?'

'No, that'll be all, thanks.'

She turned on her heel and stalked towards the
door as if she couldn't wait to escape. He didn't blame
her. Keeping business and pleasure separate was one
thing, treating her with palpable coldness another.

It wasn't her fault he was in a funk.

Well, it partially was, but he was the one with
the intimacy issues. She could obviously handle their
scorching after-hour activities while maintaining a
cool politeness at work, no problems at all.

'Charlie,' he called out, wanting to say something,
anything, to make this awkwardness better.

However, as she turned and stared at him, a master of the poker face, he couldn't come up with one,
single thing to say to make any of this better.

So he settled for a lame, 'Thanks for your help,'
which she acknowledged with a brief nod before barging out of his office and slamming the door.

Reinforcing a clearly delineated line between the
pleasure they'd shared last night and the business of
today.

He should be happy. He wanted it this way.

Then why did he feel like flinging a stapler through
the window?

CHAPTER FIFTEEN

CHARLOTTE COULDN'T STAND being in the office for another moment so at the conclusion of her meeting with Alex she grabbed her bag and laptop, told Reception she'd be working offsite for the afternoon, and hightailed it out of there.

She ran the gamut of emotions as she headed for Le Miel. Annoyance. Anger. Hurt. Self-doubt. And back to anger again.

How could he treat her like that?

She could have handled indifference but his obvious coldness had her doubting the wisdom of letting this man into her life, albeit only on a physical level.

She'd felt it before he'd bolted from her apartment, had put it down to the usual morning-after awkwardness. Not that she'd had much personal experience of it but she'd been floundering before he'd appeared in her bedroom bearing coffee.

When he'd fled, she'd made a decision to keep her distance at work and had managed to avoid him all morning. She'd been almost relieved when he'd called her into his office to work, thinking it would give them both the opportunity to laugh off last night and get down to business.

She'd been wrong.

He'd been brusque to the point of rudeness and even though he'd apologised, it hadn't eased the hurt deep inside.

She hated feeling so fragile, her latent insecurities ready to flare with the slightest provocation. She knew where her lack of self-worth stemmed from and it didn't make it any easier to deal with. Being abandoned by her parents at a young age ensured she'd always felt not quite good enough.

What was it about her that made them choose poorer children worldwide over their own child?

She'd always been a model child, a quiet kid who did exactly as she was told, with an innate sense of righteousness that ensured she wanted her parents to be proud of her.

She remembered bringing home a certificate her fourth week at primary school, a pink cardboard star for neat handwriting, being friendly to other kids and staying back to clean up at lunchtime. She'd loved that star, had clutched it to her chest with pride, not caring that gold glitter had become embedded in her jumper. When she'd presented it to her folks after school, they'd smiled, ruffled her hair and returned to scanning websites for their next lost cause. They'd never noticed that the pin on the corkboard hadn't stuck and the star had tumbled behind their desk. They hadn't cared.

She should have known then that nothing she did

would ever be good enough, that they'd leave her regardless and it had been almost a year to the day afterward that they'd left her with Dee.

She'd felt lacking ever since.

Unfortunately, her inbuilt insecurities affected all aspects of her life. She didn't feel confident with men so she'd never had a boyfriend. She didn't feel like she belonged in the trendy world of fashion, cafés and clubs, so she'd never had girlfriends. Sure, she'd hung out with fellow nerds at school and uni, quiet, diligent types who preferred studying to partying, who caught up for the occasional coffee, who were happy to share books but not much else. Acquaintances more than friends, the type of girls happy to hang out but only if it involved study load.

She hadn't minded at the time, or so she'd told herself to banish the desolation that swept over her at the oddest of moments, making her solitary existence seem so hollow. It gave her time to focus on achieving her goals. It didn't fill the forlorn ache in her heart.

Mak and Abby had been her first real friends and that had only come about because Mak had been her flatmate and nobody said no to the exuberant, bubbly dancer. Mak had brought her out of her shell a tad and had introduced her to Abby, but while she valued their friendship, she still felt different from those girls. They were determined and bold and confident, three things she could never be no matter how hard she tried.

She always felt inherently lonely.

Being dumped by her folks ensured she retreated

from everyone, knowing that if her own parents could leave her others could too. She couldn't depend on anyone. Even her exuberant aunt Dee, who'd smothered her with love and attention, couldn't shake her unswerving sense of self-preservation.

Depending on others could result in her being alone and devalued. Again.

Which was why Alex's callous treatment now rankled so damn much. During their sizzling encounters he'd made her feel assured and she already liked it too much to be good for her.

She should never have agreed to a fling.

For someone who weighed decisions carefully, she'd sure lost her mind a little the day she'd had sex with a stranger, then followed that up with a steamy night with the promise of more.

So she'd responded in kind in the face of his hostility. Answered his questions regarding the referral system. Showed no emotion. And envisaged strangling him with one of the whips she'd glimpsed in her aunt's paraphernalia a few days ago.

Stomping into Le Miel, she had a craving for the biggest croissant Abby could create and one of the patisserie's signature hot chocolates. The more sugar, the better. She needed sweetening up today.

She also needed her friend to talk some sense into her, though she knew deep down she was well past that. For the simple fact that even after the way he'd proved how he intended on keeping business separate from pleasure, she still wanted him.

Last night reinforced that.

She'd never, ever felt that way.

Strong, confident, empowered.

The kind of woman who could actually inspire passion in a man. A woman confident in her own skin. A woman capable of taking pleasure as well as giving it.

She'd never been so brazen. Touching him everywhere. Kissing his ticklish spots. Exploring the hard planes of his amazing body with her hands. Sex with Alex was an eye-opening experience and then some.

She could attribute her feistiness to the lingerie.

She knew better.

Alex made her feel that way. As if she could demand gratification and seek it, could fulfil her deepest desires and his.

She likened it to shedding some of her reservations and being reborn. Wobbly and uncertain at first, but gaining confidence with each mind-blowing encounter.

It felt fan-freaking-tastic.

Maybe she should be thanking him for being so cold today. It reinforced that they were one way in the bedroom, another out of it. Smart people who could keep their sensual life separate from real life.

And if she was completely honest with herself, it was the most exciting thing she'd ever done.

Considering her residual insecurities, having this fling would be good for her. She could get it out of her system and, when Alex left, focus on finding her for ever guy.

A sound plan. If she could only ignore the deep-seated niggle that sex with Alex might have ruined her for any other man.

'Idiot,' she muttered, plonking her bag onto a chair and her laptop on the table.

'Talking to yourself isn't a good sign, you know.' Sean, the young guy who waited tables in the afternoons, grinned. 'How've you been, Charlotte?'

'Good,' she said, the trite response sounding like the hollow lie it was. 'Is Abby around?'

He shook his head. 'She had to fill in for a pastry class at the local cooking school.'

She didn't know whether to be peeved or relieved. Talking to her logical friend always served to calm her when things threatened her equilibrium, but she'd already told Abby about her first encounter with Alex and didn't want to rehash the events of last night.

Because last night had been special.

Dinner at her favourite Vietnamese restaurant had been the extended foreplay he'd predicted and she'd barely tasted the sublime food when all she'd been able to think about was sampling him later.

And sample she had. It had been stupendous.

She wanted more.

But at what cost to her pride?

Could she really put up with his insufferable arrogance at work then melt in his arms at night?

Doubtful.

She wasn't that good an actress, despite her new-found vamp powers.

'What'll you have?'

Snapping back to the present, she said, 'The biggest almond croissant you've got and a mega-large hot chocolate chaser.'

'Done.' Sean beamed, his fresh-faced enthusiasm making her feel a hundred years old. 'Not many women eat as much as you do. It's cool.'

'I think I should be insulted.' She smiled at his horror-struck expression. 'I'm kidding. I like food.'

And was blessed with a fast metabolism. One of the few good things her parents had bestowed on her.

'Coming right up,' he said, beating a hasty retreat, and Charlotte settled in for a few hours of work.

Only to discover she'd left her client files at the office.

'This just gets better and better,' she mumbled, reaching for her cell.

She'd get the office junior to bring the files to her, and send back an afternoon tea treat to the office in return. After leaving a message with Reception, she fired up her laptop and made a start, only stopping to demolish the melt-in-the-mouth croissant and slurp down her hot chocolate.

The sugar rush instantly comforted and as she waited for her files she wondered if Alex would call her tonight and if so what her response would be.

Fight or flee?

She had no idea.

CHAPTER SIXTEEN

ALEX'S MOOD DIDN'T improve after Charlotte left his office. If anything, it worsened because all he could think about was her wounded expression and it killed him that he'd put it there.

He'd treated her with a coldness bordering on contempt and all because he couldn't get a grip on his out-of-control reaction around her.

The entire time she'd been sitting opposite him, so prim and reserved, he'd wanted to rip open her blouse and check out the bra beneath it.

He'd wanted her spreadeagled on his desk, her panties around her ankles, so he could feast on her.

He'd needed to be inside her so damn badly it hurt.

So he'd done the only thing possible to hide his rampant lust: be cool to the point of abruptness.

She'd noticed. He'd seen it in the disapproving purse of her lips. Lips that had explored almost every inch of his body last night.

'Fuck.' He thumped his desk. Like that would help.

He had to see her away from the office, make amends for his boorish behaviour. He'd be honest, tell her how rattled he'd been this morning to wake up next to her, that it wasn't in him to deal emotionally so he never spent the night and he'd reacted badly because of it.

They'd worked through lunch so maybe he could ask her out for a coffee. But his plan hit a snag when he discovered she'd left the office to work offsite for the afternoon; to escape him, no doubt. Not that he blamed her. He'd been a stupid bastard, the way he'd handled this entire situation.

However, his luck took a turn for the better when he happened to be at Reception when a call came through from Charlotte, asking for files to be brought to her.

She expected a junior to do the job.

He had other ideas.

'I've got a meeting in the city so I'll drop those files off,' he said, pleased that the receptionist didn't find it odd that the boss wanted to do such a menial task.

'She's at Le Miel.' The receptionist handed him a stack of files with an elastic band around them. 'Tell her that if she doesn't send back afternoon tea for the crew she won't get her files next time.'

Alex smiled. 'Shall do.'

He liked the camaraderie among the team here. After working at many companies he'd witnessed his fair share of backstabbing and undercutting but workers at The Number Makers seemed to have a surprising bond despite the uncertainty in this economic climate.

Not that he'd be around beyond a month but he valued loyalty and it went a long way to helping him make the tough decisions when the time came.

Battling Sydney's mid-afternoon stream of traffic, he made it to Le Miel in thirty minutes. He had no idea what Charlotte's ties were to the patisserie but from what he'd heard she frequented the place a lot.

As he strode towards the shop and saw a young hipster guy grinning at her with obvious fondness, he hoped that wasn't why.

An uncharacteristic stab of jealousy made him falter. Had his foolish behaviour driven her into the arms of another guy? An old boyfriend perhaps?

However, the closer he got he realised the hipster couldn't be older than late teens. Considering Charlotte had to be mid-twenties tops it wasn't completely out of the question that she'd hook up with a young guy.

But she'd told him she hadn't dated since university and he knew he was being an idiot, jumping to stupid conclusions when he should be barging in there and making up for his behaviour.

Knowing he couldn't afford to botch this up, he pushed the glass door and entered gastronomic heaven. The aromas hit him first. Cinnamon, sugar, vanilla, and for a startling moment he catapulted back to the past. He remembered running into the kitchen back home after school, the same smells making him salivate as his mum took a batch of freshly baked cookies out of the oven.

He'd perch on a stool at the island bench, where

she'd have a glass of icy chocolate milk waiting for him, and get his wrist playfully slapped while trying to sneak the cookies before they'd cooled.

Those had been good times, when his dad had still been employed and his mum would ask him about his day and he'd regale her with funny stories, like the time a goat got into the classroom and ate his teacher's curriculum, or the time the principal chased the school bully all the way down to the dam and fell in.

She'd laugh so hard. One of the few times he'd see his mum laugh, which was why he'd tried so hard, often inventing stories just so he could see her happy.

Because young Alex knew that once his dad entered a room all the happiness drained out of his mum. They'd seemed to sap each other of any form of lightness and it had spiralled downward until his dad hadn't been able to take it any more.

When he'd got the call about his dad's death, the first thing he'd wondered was if he could have done more. If he'd stayed around, would his dad have had more reason to live? They'd had so little in common and when his father had rebuffed his constant overtures to be mates, Alex had stopped trying. Alex loved sports, his dad had hated them. Alex liked hiking beyond the farm, his dad had stayed within its boundaries, rarely venturing outside.

Losing his job had changed his father and for someone already on a slippery slope into moroseness it had pushed him over the edge. Alex had eventually decided to leave his dad alone, counting down the days until he could flee the oppressive house. He'd escaped Rocky Plains as soon as he finished high school and his dad had died four years later.

He didn't want to think about how his parents had co-existed after he left. He didn't want to surmise that his absence had thrust his parents together more, that their obvious friction would have quadrupled and that had ultimately led to his dad's demise.

'Alex?'

He blinked at the sound of his name, disconcerted by his memories, to find Charlotte staring at him.

Her eyes narrowed. She wasn't pleased to see him. 'What are you doing here?'

'I brought your files,' he said, fishing them out of his briefcase and laying them on the table beside her laptop.

'Uh, thanks.' She stared at him as if he'd personally delivered a ticking time bomb. 'Don't you have more important things to do?'

'Considering how I screwed up this morning, nothing's as important as making things right with you.'

His honesty surprised her, her sharp intake of breath followed by a subtle wariness as she eased back into her chair. As if she was trying to put as much distance between them as humanly possible.

She pinned him with a direct stare. 'Are you talking about the way you ran out of my apartment or the way you treated me in your office?'

She didn't flinch away from the truth. He admired that.

'Both,' he said, grimacing. 'Though they're linked.'

'Let me guess. You're trying so hard to keep business and pleasure separate that you had to prove you could leave my bed in the morning and treat me like a lowly employee at the office.' Disgust underpinned her accusation and he didn't blame her.

He shook his head, her insight not surprising him. She had a way of homing in on the truth without sugar-coating it. It was refreshing, when most of the women he'd been involved with in the past were master game players who couldn't admit the truth if it bit them on the ass.

'It's more complicated than that.'

She waited, not saying a word, her scepticism palpable.

'I don't do sleepovers,' he blurted, folding his arms. Yeah, as if that would stop the insistent urge to reach for her every time he was around her. 'So when I woke next to you this morning, it unnerved me and I didn't handle it very well.'

To his relief, the corners of her mouth twitched. 'Sleepovers involve popcorn and ice cream and horror-movie marathons and pyjamas.' She schooled her expression into a faux innocence he found delightful. 'And we had none of those things, so technically it wasn't a sleepover.'

'God, do you know how badly I want you right now?' he murmured, curling his fingers into fists under his arms to stop from reaching for her. 'You're this beguiling contrast of aloof one second, teasing the next. It's driving me nuts. I can't think. I can't concentrate, for wanting you.'

'Stop doing that.' She jabbed a finger at him. 'You

can't go from making me want to slug you for your arrogance to making me want to straddle your lap.'

He stifled a groan. 'And that's another thing that drives me crazy about you. How blunt you are. I like it. A lot.'

'So what are we going to do about it?' Her eyes darkened to pewter, her dilated pupils making him want to yank her onto his lap, other customers be damned. 'Because here's another dose of that bluntness you seem to like so much about me. I won't tolerate being your play thing in bed then being given the frosty treatment in the office. It's not doable.'

She waggled her finger at him and he wanted to capture it and suck it into his mouth. 'I understand we need to keep business and pleasure separate. Heck, I stipulated it. But there's a difference between being polite co-workers and the way you treated me this morning.'

'Agreed.' He glanced around, saw that no one seemed to be the slightest bit interested in what they were doing, and snagged her hand. 'I hated how cold I was to you in the office this morning, especially as my mood had more to do with me not being man enough to face my fears. Forgive me?'

Her lips parted on a surprised O and he'd never wanted to kiss any woman as badly as he wanted to kiss her at that moment.

'What fears?'

'Babe, you have no idea.' He raised her hand to his mouth and brushed a soft kiss across the back of it. 'I don't do commitment. I don't do emotional connection. I don't stay in one place long enough to make those things happen—'

'Which is why you don't sleep over.' She snapped the fingers of her free hand, shooting him a shy glance. 'So you've never stayed over at a girl's place, ever?'

'Plenty of women, never girls,' he deadpanned, earning a whack on his arm.

She laughed and the rich sound of genuine amusement lightened his heart. He'd been worried coming here that he might have screwed things up between them beyond repair but he should have known she'd be as magnanimous in this as she was in the way she'd handled every onerous task he'd thrown her way over the last few weeks.

'So we're okay?' He squeezed her hand before releasing it. 'You'll still work your way through that lingerie box for me?'

'Only if you're lucky.' She winked, her playful side so at odds with the woman he'd assumed she'd be from their business dealings that he couldn't help but stare. 'For now, I need to get back to work and you need to take afternoon tea back to the office.'

'You can come back with me, now that you know I won't bite your head off?' He waggled his eyebrows suggestively. 'Or we can skive off work for the rest of the afternoon and do naughty things to each other in private?'

Colour stained her cheeks but he glimpsed the gleam of excitement in her eyes. 'I have a lot of work to do and there'll be less distractions around here.'

'Okay, suit yourself.' He shrugged. 'But just so you know, I'm always up for that naughty stuff, any time.'

She took a long time to answer and when she did, it was worth the wait.

'Later.'

That one word pepped up his mood considerably and he made it his goal to show her exactly how crazy she drove him *later*.

CHAPTER SEVENTEEN

TRUE TO HER WORD, Charlotte had ploughed through a stack of work that afternoon. She'd completed tax assessments on three client files, a monumental task considering the level of complication. It had served its purpose.

Keeping her mind off Alex.

And she'd done the same thing for the next few days, working offsite, immersed in client files, determined to impress with her work ethic—and keep her hands off him.

She'd been blown away that he'd shown up at Le Miel to apologise, even more so by his honesty. And secretly thrilled that he'd spent a night with her earlier in the week, a first for him.

She shouldn't read too much into it. He'd probably been tired and fallen into a deep sleep. But the fact he'd acknowledged it meant something to her; that despite all his protestations about being unable to connect emotionally, maybe a small part of him already had.

They'd made their agreement, so the fact he'd spent

the night shouldn't be such a big deal, yet why did it feel as if it was?

It made her wonder. Had she sensed something that day at the warehouse? That this guy could pleasure her in a way no man ever had? That for once she'd rather live a fantasy, no matter how brief, rather than read about it?

An outlandish, ludicrous supposition, especially as she only dealt with facts and figures on a daily basis. But even when she'd learned her sexy stranger's true identity, she hadn't shied away from him. She'd tried; he had too, with their initial conversation to keep things professional.

She guessed she should be grateful that they were both adult enough to confront their unrelenting attraction and do something about it without letting it interfere with work. Well, not much anyway. Because every time she completed a task, every moment she had between clients, her thoughts drifted to Alex and how badly she wanted him.

It defied logic, this constant yearning to have him. She'd gone from celibate to sex maniac in no time.

Thanks to Alex.

She wanted to show him how much she appreciated his honesty and his apology earlier that week.

And she knew just the way to do it.

However, she dithered for a full hour and a half after her naughty idea first struck. She headed home and cleaned counters in the kitchen, scrubbed the bath, even disinfected the toilet, her least favourite job on the planet. Doing the most menial of tasks couldn't dislodge her idea and she pondered it.

Doing something so outrageous as turning up at his workplace on a Friday night with seduction in mind...baffled her. How could she, the queen of low self-confidence, do something like that, let alone think it?

Seduction was for self-assured women who knew what they wanted and weren't afraid to grab it.

Isn't that you lately?

'Dumbass voice of reason,' she muttered, sifting through the lingerie box for the hundredth time.

Silk and satin slid between her fingers, soft and sensuous, as she imagined Alex experiencing the same tactile sensations if she wore this stuff and he touched her...

With a frustrated growl, mind made up, she snagged what she needed, had a quick shower and headed back to the office before she could change her mind.

With a new boss intent on making changes, a few people would have stayed back to work late but most would have left by seven-thirty.

Even if a few foolhardy souls remained, Alex's door had a lock.

She'd texted him before she left home on the pretext of a work discussion to ensure he'd be at the office. He'd responded with a flirty 'work or *work*?' She'd left him guessing, responding that she'd be there in fifteen minutes.

She'd made it in ten.

After swiping her card through security, she entered the office, to find all the lights dimmed and not a workaholic in sight.

Good.

She'd worn flip-flops, easier to slip off, and a white cotton dress she'd picked up for ten dollars many moons ago.

A dress with a zipper down the front.

She'd bought it on impulse, when Mak and Abby had been hassling her to go clubbing with them. But she'd got the flu and hadn't been too sorry to miss out on yet another social occasion where she would have felt gauche. So she'd never worn it, as it made her feel slightly vulnerable having that zipper on it. As if it could slide down at any time and reveal more than she intended.

Tonight, that was exactly what she hoped for.

For someone who'd ignored her sexuality for so long, she'd turned a little slutty. And was enjoying every minute of it, despite her usual self-doubts rearing their ugly heads at inopportune moments.

She could see it so clearly: being in her fifties, still living in her dream cottage that she hoped to put a down payment on in a fortnight, her kids dropping around for a visit, cooking up a storm, but still remembering during the odd illicit moment how she'd turned into a vixen for that brief period at twenty-five before she settled down.

In her daydream she could envisage a husband too, the perfect guy who'd come home at the end of the day and slip his arms around her waist from behind while he nuzzled her neck.

She'd turn, secure in the circle of his arms...to find Alex staring at her with blatant lust.

Charlotte stumbled and slammed her palm against the nearest desk for support.

Alex couldn't be her dream husband.

He wasn't husband material.

He'd made that perfectly clear.

Mentally chastising herself for mixing up her daydreams, she traversed the office on steadier legs. With every step she shed shy Charlotte and morphed into her new sexier self, the kind of woman not averse to wearing scandalous lingerie with the aim to seduce.

Alex had articulated a particular fantasy to her.

She had every intention of making it come true.

He hadn't closed the door completely and muted light spilled out through a crack. She paused on the threshold and took a few steadying breaths to quell her rampant nerves. Wearing racy lingerie and a zippered dress might be a confidence boost, but going through a full-on, office-based seduction was another thing entirely.

Her arms tingled, nerve endings firing, and she shook them out. Rolled her shoulders. Yeah, like that would loosen her up. She did a few calf raises and managed a rueful smile. She wasn't warming up for a Zumba class; she was intent on getting Alex warmed up.

Before her meagre bravado fled entirely, she pushed open the door. And her lungs seized.

Alex was sprawled across the sofa to the right of his desk, intently studying a financial report. His hair was ruffled, like he'd run his hand through it several times. He'd lost the tie and undone the top two buttons on his shirt, leaving a tantalising glimpse of bronzed chest. He'd rolled up his shirtsleeves too, revealing strong forearms.

She had a thing for good arms on guys. Arms capable of handling a woman. She didn't mind a broad chest and firm ass either.

She flushed from head to toe as she recalled exploring much of his body that night he stayed over. Trailing her fingertips over all that gorgeous tanned skin, skirting over ridges and dips, mesmerised by the sheer beauty of the man.

And he was. Absolutely beautiful. Not an adjective used to describe men usually, but in Alex's case it fitted.

He glanced up at that moment, caught sight of her and smiled, sending her pulse into overdrive. 'Hey.'

She cleared her throat and managed a sedate 'hey' right back at him, as she entered the office and closed the door.

His eyes widened imperceptibly as she flicked the lock.

'Are you here to take advantage of a hard-working man?'

'Something like that,' she said, crossing the room

to his desk, where she proceeded to remove items and stack them on the floor in neat piles.

'What are you doing?'

'Spring cleaning.'

He laughed and when she risked a sideways glance at him, she knew he knew. Her hands shook as she carefully lifted the PC screen and placed it next to the other items.

Only when the desk was completely clear did she turn towards him and crook her finger. 'Come here.'

He stood so fast the file on the sofa tumbled to the floor and documents scattered. He didn't care. He advanced towards her, the intent in his gaze making her skin pebble.

'Nice dress,' he said, stopping two feet in front of her.

'You think?' She shrugged, as if his proximity didn't affect her in the slightest, when in fact her heart thudded and the crispness of his aftershave flooded her senses, making her heady.

'Yeah.' He reached out and toyed with the zipper tab. 'I like this.' He inched it down slowly, the rasp of metal sharp in the air heightening her anticipation. 'Easy access.'

'That was the whole idea.'

She met his gaze boldly, feeling as if she were having an out-of-body experience as he lowered it all the way and pushed the dress off her shoulders, leaving her standing in a sheer white lace teddy that revealed more than it hid.

'Fuck me,' he murmured, his gaze heated as it ze-roed in on her rigid nipples.

She wanted to say 'I intend to' but some of her brazenness fled when he reached out and touched between her legs.

And discovered the teddy was crotchless.

'You are something else,' he said, a second before his mouth crushed hers.

There was nothing soft or seductive about his kiss. He plundered her mouth. Ravaged her. His tongue mimicking what she yearned for him to do lower. Long, hot, open-mouthed kisses that had her clawing at him, desperate to gain purchase before she slid in a boneless puddle to the floor.

His hands spanned her waist and hoisted her onto the desk. She gasped as her butt hit the cool wood and he nudged her knees apart, stepping between them.

'Do you have any idea how much time I've spent fantasising about this very thing since you entered this office early in the week?'

Buoyed by his blatant lust, she nodded. 'You told me that first night you wanted to ravage me on your desk, so here I am.'

He shook his head, as if in a daze. 'How did I get so lucky?'

She raised an eyebrow. 'You could get luckier?'

He didn't need the encouragement, as he eased her down with one hand until she was propped on her el-bows, watching him watch her.

He didn't break eye contact as he peeled the teddy

from her crotch to her stomach, leaving her bare to him. He knelt, reverent, and placed his mouth to her.

Feasted on her. Licking and sucking. Nibbling and nipping. He lapped at her, his tongue an exquisite torture as desire made her tremble. When his teeth scraped across her clit, she whimpered. And when he sucked, her hips jolted off the desk.

He drove her wild with his mouth as she climbed fast and furiously towards an orgasm that ripped through her so hard she almost passed out.

Her eyes had drifted shut at some point and when her eyelids fluttered open Alex towered over her, poised between her legs, unzipped and sheathed, his gaze hungry and focused.

'Look at me,' he demanded, as he slid into her inch by glorious inch, slowly, languorously, as if he had all the time in the world to pleasure her.

She bit her lip at the exquisite pressure of him filling her so completely. Then he started moving. Slowly at first. Withdrawing with infinite patience. Thrusting in hard. Maintaining this steady pace with a determination that defied logic.

How could he be so controlled when all she wanted was for him to pound into her like their previous encounters?

'You're determined to drive me nuts, aren't you?' She writhed and arched her hips upward but he held them down.

'It'll be worth it, sweetheart.'

And damn him, he was right. Because this time her orgasm built slowly. Tension made her muscles tighten and her spine buzz. Her skin rippled with sensation, as if a thousand butterflies were dancing across it.

She watched him, his jaw clenched, a vein pulsating at his temple, his gaze focused on her. Only her.

She eyeballed him, wondering if he knew how damn good he made her feel, and whatever he saw in her eyes drove him over the edge as he pounded into her so hard she half lifted off the desk. His fingers dug into her butt as he stiffened and groaned, her orgasm crashing over her a second later.

They hadn't broken eye contact and for several long moments they stared at each other in stunned silence. At least, that was how she felt. Stupefied. Caught up in some weird alternate universe where she shed her shyness and thought nothing of seducing a hot guy on his desk.

'Have you had dinner?'

Of all the things she expected him to say after their mind-blowing encounter, that wasn't it.

'No.'

'Me either.' His lopsided grin made her heart twinge in a way it shouldn't. 'I think I've worked up an appetite. Want to grab a bite?'

Charlotte should say no. She shouldn't get into a pattern of indulging in date-like behaviour whenever they had sex, because it could only lead to expectations. Expectations far removed from their clear-cut fling. Expectations that would result in her wanting things she shouldn't.

'Stop over-thinking this.' He reached forward and

traced the faint frown line between her brows. 'I like hanging out with you. We have to eat. Let's do it to-gether.'

'Okay.' She found herself agreeing all too quickly. So much for not fostering expectations. 'I might need to go home and change first.'

'Why?' His fingertips traced a line from her brow, down her cheek, along her jaw, to her neck. From there, his hand drifted lower, between her breasts, across her ribs, coming to rest on her stomach where the teddy lay ruched up. 'This way, I'll know exactly what you're wearing beneath that dress and I'll look forward to taking it all off you later.'

Her insides clenched at the thought of more as a slow, lascivious grin spread across his face. 'I think your body agrees with me.'

She blushed. Of course he'd felt that, considering they were still engaged below the waist. How could she do this, lie sprawled across a desk, having a post-coital chat, not in the least bit self-conscious? It defied belief how this man could befuddle her to the point she shed her inhibitions.

'If you want to eat, we'll have to get dressed,' she said, adding a pelvic wiggle for good measure.

'If you keep doing that, we're not going anywhere,' he said, but slid out of her and took care of business while she redressed.

As she slid the dress zipper up, she caught sight of her reflection in a glass cabinet behind the desk. That was when reality set in.

Did she really think she could pull this off, playing a vamp only interested in one thing?

Because every time they had sex, Charlotte knew a small part of her craved more. The way he made her feel when he pleasured her…she had a sneaking suspicion that no other man would come close. And if that were the case, was she setting herself up for a major fall?

What if her dream guy didn't do it for her like Alex?

Spending more time with him would only reinforce this, which meant she had to get away.

Now.

'Sorry, can't do dinner, have to go,' she blurted, making a run for the door.

'What the—?'

'See you tomorrow.' Her fingers fumbled the lock for a second but then she twisted it, opened the door and fled.

CHAPTER EIGHTEEN

ALEX HAD NO idea what the hell had just happened.

One second he was on a high after having amazing sex on his desk, the next he was watching Charlotte flee his office after reneging on their dinner plans.

'Hey, wait up,' he yelled, giving chase. Thankfully, he caught her just before the elevator doors slid shut by sticking his hand between them.

They slid open to reveal her staring at him wide-eyed, her lips compressed in a mutinous line.

'What happened back there?'

'Nothing. I just remembered I have stuff to do.' She shook her head, soft brown waves tumbling over her shoulders, making him want to bury his nose in it and inhale the fruity fragrance of her shampoo.

'Let me guess. Feed your cat.' He snapped his fingers, trying to turn down the sarcasm but more than a tad annoyed at her sudden urge to flee after what had just happened in his office. 'But you forget that I've been to your flat and you don't have a cat. So what's up?'

'Can't you just let this go?' Colour suffused her

cheeks and she folded her arms across her chest. Like that could ever distract him from her perfect, pert breasts.

'No. It's not in my nature to give up.'

When the elevator doors started pinging because he had his arms braced against them, he said, 'I'm coming with you.'

She glared at him, frown lines crinkling her forehead. 'I want to be alone.'

'No, you don't. You want to mull over what just happened. Maybe you're freaked out by how powerful the connection is when we have sex?' He stepped into the elevator and patted his pocket to ensure he had his cell and car keys. 'Don't be. Sex is rarely that good and when it is, you have to embrace it.'

He shot her a cheery wink. 'I have.'

'That's because you didn't have a choice,' she snapped. 'I strutted into your office like some ho and practically stripped in front of you.'

Her confession seriously rattled him. Was mortification behind her abrupt turnaround? He knew her inexperience with men could be an issue but the way she'd responded to him so far had convinced him that she'd shed her inhibitions.

He had to slow this down. Had to show her that he liked her for more than her body. Which he obviously hadn't done a very good job of so far.

'You're overwhelmed, I get it, but don't ever think I see you as anything other than a strong woman willing to embrace her sexuality.'

Her mouth softened at his declaration and he continued. 'I like being with you. That's it. No hidden agenda. No ulterior motives. So how about we take this down a notch? Grab takeout and go somewhere that makes you comfortable?'

A refusal hovered on her lips. He could see it in every rigid line of her body. So rather than waiting for a response, he stepped completely into the elevator and stabbed at the button for the ground floor.

'You don't need to answer, just give me directions,' he said, watching the lit numbers on the console count down. 'Anywhere you want.'

When she still didn't speak, he risked a glance at her. She slowly turned towards him, her expression solemn.

'I feel like a big, greasy hamburger with a side of fries.'

Trying not to let his elation show that she'd capitulated, he nodded. 'Sounds good.'

When they reached the ground floor and exited the building, her continuing silence didn't disarm him so much. Whatever thoughts were going through her head were enough to scare her into this funk so he'd bide his time, feed her, then try a different tack.

That was when it hit him.

He never put this much effort into wooing a woman.

Especially not when they'd already done the deed.

Enough of a thought to send him into a funk too. Maybe he should cut his losses and run while he still could? The thought of working alongside her for the next three weeks, being forced to pretend platonic was fine; keeping his hands off her was a big ask.

He couldn't do it. Not when every time he sat at his desk he'd be bombarded with memories of her splayed across it.

Damn, he'd never get that image out of his mind.

She'd surprised him by taking the initiative, by boldly entering his domain with the sole purpose of seducing. It had turned him on big time. As for that dress and teddy, he hoped he could convince her to try on every single one of those decadent items from her aunt's kinky online store.

Not tonight. Tonight, he had to convince her that a fling didn't necessarily equate with making her feel cheap, that he valued their connection.

He'd assumed he'd already demonstrated that by taking her out to dinner earlier in the week but he should have known that with her inexperience she'd revert to type and withdraw.

When they reached the basement car park he placed a hand in the small of her back and guided her towards the right. 'We'll take my car.'

That way, she couldn't drive off and ditch him.

Surprisingly, she didn't protest and waited until they'd reached his car, opened the door and slid onto the passenger seat before speaking. 'Thanks.'

'For what?'

'Putting up with my freak-out.'

He grinned. 'Gorgeous, that wasn't a freak-out. That was you floundering after having the best sex of your life with a master.'

Her eyebrows shot up and the corners of her mouth eased into a semi-smile as he'd intended. 'A master, huh?'

'You can call me sir.'

With that, he closed the passenger door on her grin, walked around the car and slid into the driver's seat. They lapsed into a comfortable silence as he headed for the nearest fast-food outlet and ordered big. When they had a paper bag of burgers and fries, along with chocolate milkshakes, between them, he finally asked, 'Where to now?'

'I'll direct you,' she said, pressing her hand to her stomach. 'And I'm not averse to you speeding a little, because those smells are making me hungry.'

He had a constant appetite around her but it sure as hell wasn't for food.

'How far?'

'Ten minutes.'

Thankfully, it was less in the evening traffic and they soon pulled up in a deserted parking lot on a beachside cliff top, completely isolated by a ring of trees.

'What is this place?' He hadn't been to this part of Sydney before, a trendy suburb on the outskirts of the affluent east.

'Eat first, talk later,' she said, tearing open the first bag, snaffling a fry and stuffing it into her mouth. 'Mmm…good,' she murmured, throwing in an appreciative moan that shot straight to his dick.

He'd heard her moan like that before, usually when he was thrusting inside her, her head thrashing from

side to side, as if teetering on the brink between pleasure and pain.

Damn, he needed to eat pronto before he hauled
her into the back seat and had his wicked way with
her again.

'I didn't pick you for the junk-food type.' He un-
wrapped a burger, took the top off and removed the
pickles.

'About the only good thing my parents ever gave
me was a fast metabolism.' She raised her hamburger
in the air. 'So I can eat as many of these as I want and
not get fat. My friends hate me.'

He wanted to delve further into that offhand comment about her folks but he didn't want her to clam
up again, not when she'd only just started talking.

'You've got a rocking bod. I'm very appreciative,'
he said before taking a bite out of the burger and wishing he were nibbling on her.

She mumbled something unintelligible but he
glimpsed happiness in her eyes.

They demolished the burgers and fries in record
time—he couldn't remember the last time he had fast
food, and thought it must taste better because of her.

'Shall we partake of our beverages outside?' He
did a funny little half-bow that had her smiling at his
faux formality.

'Sure, I've got something to show you anyway.'

They fell into step beside each other, slurping at
their milkshakes, as they ducked between an opening in the trees and crossed a grassy knoll with a
gradual incline.

'So this is one of your favourite places, huh?'

'It will be when I make an offer very soon.'

Offer? They crested the knoll and came to a road, lined by modest houses on the opposite side.

'There. That one,' she said, pointing to a weatherboard Californian bungalow two houses to the left. 'That's my dream house and I'm going to buy it.'

He heard the wistfulness in her voice, and the pride behind her declaration.

'Good for you.'

His response fell flat as she half turned towards him. 'You don't like it?'

'I didn't say that.'

He didn't have to, considering his less than enthusiastic response was far from complimentary.

He hated feeling this way, oddly uncomfortable, staring at the small house with its newly painted white boards and ecru-trimmed windows. A towering eucalyptus smack bang in the middle of the neat lawn, edged by flowerbeds. Complete with a goddamn picket fence, a ludicrous duck-egg blue rather than white.

But something about the thought of Charlotte living out her dream here, without him, didn't sit well.

Not that he wanted to be part of anyone's long-term dreams, but just a week into their hot fling he didn't want to think about it ending.

'You asked to see my go-to place and this is it,' she said, the hurt in her voice making him want to slap himself upside the head. 'I've been coming here almost daily for the last four weeks because it makes me feel good.'

He understood that. Airports made him feel that way. Tangible proof of his transient life, just the way he liked it.

He didn't like becoming connected to anything or anyone for too long, because he'd seen first-hand how that bred contempt and eventually led to the disintegration of anything good.

He wasn't fool enough to believe that all marriages were like his folks', but being cut off emotionally had become so ingrained for him that he wasn't interested in trying to rectify it. Getting too attached, letting himself feel, meant that when life got hard, as it inevitably did, the fall would be all the harder. He was many things; a masochist wasn't one of them.

'Isn't the Sydney housing market booming right now?'

His unspoken question hung between them: if this dream house was so damn good, why hadn't it sold during that time?

'It is, but the owner's asking price is too high.' She ditched her milkshake in the nearby trash and wrapped her arms around her middle, as if seeking comfort. 'I've spoken to the realtor and told him my bottom line. He thinks he can get the owner to budge a little. So in the meantime I pray every night that the place won't get sold out from under me.'

She sounded so forlorn he couldn't resist touching her, resting his hand lightly on her shoulder. She didn't shrug it off, a good sign considering the way he'd doused her enthusiasm.

'Your dream is my nightmare,' he said quietly, knowing he had to come clean if he was to have any chance of spending more time with her.

'You don't own a house?' She studied him with an intensity that unnerved.

He shook his head. 'Plenty of investment properties but not a house I call home.'

'That's sad.'

He bristled at her audible pity. 'I had a home, the one I grew up in, and it sucked. So I promised myself the day I finally escaped that claustrophobic house in a dead-end town, and all the crap it held, that I wouldn't put myself in that kind of situation again.'

She paused, as if searching for the right words, before finally responding. 'A house can be a base. A place to put down roots. Nothing more.'

'That's bullshit and we both know it.'

Wishing he'd never revealed so much, he ditched his milkshake too and thrust his hands into his pockets. 'You made some offhand comment about your folks before. And you told me they travel the world. So no prizes for guessing that's why you want a stable base so badly.'

He didn't feel bad homing in on her weak spot, if the way she frowned was any indication. 'We all want the opposite of what we had growing up. For me, that's freedom. For you, it's stability.'

He gestured at the bungalow. 'I'm happy for you chasing your dream, truly, I am. But I see a woman who's led a quiet life, probably deliberately to be the opposite of her parents, who's willing to settle too soon before she's really experienced half of what's out there.'

He threw his arms wide, knowing he'd said too much when she turned away, but not before he'd glimpsed a sheen in her eyes.

Crap. He'd made her cry.

To her credit, he saw her shoulders draw back and her spine straighten before she turned back to him. 'And what's out there, Alex? What's the big attraction with living out of a suitcase, moving from place to place, never having time to build strong friendships and a steady relationship?'

Feeling like an absolute prick for trampling all over her dream when she'd had the guts to open up to him about it, he said, 'I just don't want you missing out on fun before you settle down.'

When anger flared in her eyes, he rushed on, 'Don't get me wrong, investing in Sydney property is like taking out shares in a gold mine. But taking on a hefty mortgage at your age before you've travelled and done all that exciting stuff is huge and I don't want you missing out on all that.'

She tilted her head to one side, studying him, and he had an uncanny feeling she could see right through his bullshit.

Because the moment he'd articulated how he didn't want her missing out on adventure, he'd envisaged her having those adventures with him.

An outlandish thought, so far from left-field it

wasn't funny, but the moment it popped into his head he could see it so clearly. If she'd awakened sexually with him, what would it be like to show her more? To show her the world?

He didn't want stability but he wouldn't be averse to having a wondrous woman by his side on his travels.

Ridiculous. He'd known her a grand total of five weeks, four of those via telephone and email.

So why the hell was he contemplating something so bizarre?

Not to mention one salient point.

He'd earmarked her as the new manager for The Number Makers, a secure job that would ensure she could afford the dream house in front of him.

Managerial accountants didn't throw away their sensible dreams to follow a whim.

Shaking his head to clear it, he reached for her, relieved when she let him hold her hands. 'You know what? Forget everything I said. Maybe I'm a little jealous, seeing evidence of how much more evolved you are when I'm a thirty-two-year-old wanderer who will never settle down for anything.'

He must have finally said the right thing because the tension from her face drained away. 'You're jealous?'

She sounded incredulous, an improvement on the hurt, so he continued.

'I think so.' He squeezed her hands. 'At your age I was still partying hard while building my empire.'

The corners of her mouth quirked. 'You don't have an empire.'

He released one of her hands to tap his temple. 'Up here I do. And it's a magical place, filled with nubile women and endless dollars hanging from money trees and a dashing, handsome king who does what he wants when he wants.'

'That's some imagination.' Her wry smile lightened his heart. 'I guess we agree to disagree on what constitutes a future.'

'Yeah.' He tugged on her hand, drawing her close. 'And thank you for showing me your dream. I'm happy for you. And I'm sorry for raining all over it with my bluntness.'

'I like bluntness, just like you do,' she said, resting her head against his chest. 'We don't have much time together so why waste it pussyfooting around and playing games?'

As Alex slid his arms around her waist and hugged her tight, he got that feeling again. The one he'd had earlier when he'd thought of her living her dream life in this place. Like indigestion burning his gullet, only stronger.

'We don't have much time together.'

Usually, he'd be relieved she knew the score.

So what the hell was his problem?

CHAPTER NINETEEN

CHARLOTTE HAD TO get this relationship back onto familiar footing before she made a complete ass of herself.

She never should have brought him here.

What had she expected? That he'd take one look at her dream house after knowing her for five minutes and fall headlong into her happily-ever-after fantasy?

She was an idiot.

An idiot who now had to distract herself fast before she blubbered all over him.

So she did the one thing guaranteed to get this fling back on track.

Focus on sex.

'Come with me.' She grabbed his hand and tugged, half jogging back to the car.

He was only too happy to keep up with her, one of his long strides matching two of hers. This eagerness to pleasure each other was good. It kept her mind focused on the physical, not leaving her much room to dwell on the unanswered questions buzzing around her head like pesky flies.

What had happened in Alex's past to ensure he never wanted to put down roots? Why did he consider his childhood home and town claustrophobic? Who had caused such emotional damage that at thirty-two he refused to settle down?

And the doozy, why did he have to go and plant that seed of doubt, that maybe taking on a big mortgage before she'd done exciting stuff like travel was a mistake?

She had a goal. A dream. And nobody, especially some charming wanderer, would distract her from it.

She needed this house.

She needed a clear-cut plan for the future.

She didn't need to be swayed, no matter how tempting the momentary vision of freedom he'd planted in her head.

What would it be like to chuck in her job to go travelling for a year? To not worry about getting up to the annoying buzz of an alarm, to spend her days exploring new cities rather than stuck behind a desk using her mathematical skills, to meet new people and expand her social group?

For those few moments Alex had lectured her about his concern for her settling too soon, she'd envisioned a different life.

It could be wonderful.

It could also result in her ending up like her folks, with nothing to show for their years of work, and there was no way in hell she'd be inflicting that kind of life on her children.

They reached the car and she perched on the bonnet, the metal still warm beneath her butt. She took charge, grabbing his lapels and tugging him close, her kiss clumsy but effective as he groaned and nestled between her thighs, the material of his trousers rasping against her skin in a delicious chafe.

She decided then and there to frame this dress.

'Let's get inside the car,' he murmured, nipping her earlobe before sucking it into his mouth and toying with it using his tongue.

She shivered at the sensation flooding her body and wrapped her legs around him in response. 'No. I like feeling this…exposed.'

He grinned, his teeth almost luminous in the moonlight. 'A risk-taker, huh?'

'Only with you,' she said, meaning it.

For a guy she hardly knew, Alex made her feel safe in a way she never would have thought possible.

It took her ages to warm up to people usually, which explained why she hardly had any friends.

Mak had been her flatmate, and so overtly exuberant and friendly that Charlotte had eventually had no choice but to let her into her heart. Abby had been Mak's friend, a co-worker initially, and it seemed inevitable that the three of them had started hanging out.

She missed Mak terribly, but didn't begrudge her friend chasing her dream to dance on Broadway. She missed Abby too, considering her job at Le Miel and her sexy man Tanner kept her too busy to hang out as often as they used to.

Maybe that was why she'd let Alex into her life so

quickly? Loneliness. Then again, she'd been lonely for most of her life courtesy of her inherent insecurities, so maybe she was grasping at any excuse for her wanton brazenness when it came to this man?

'You're killing me, sweetheart.' He rested his forehead against hers. 'I don't have another condom on me.'

For a second she contemplated saying *screw it*, but her rational side wouldn't be denied. While she hadn't slept with anyone in years, a guy who looked like Alex who embraced a wandering lifestyle certainly wouldn't have been celibate.

'I'm clean, in case you were wondering,' he said, as if reading her mind, 'but I don't do unprotected sex.'

He hesitated, as if unsure whether to say more, before adding, 'I don't see kids in my future so I won't risk it.'

As if she needed another reminder of why they could never be anything other than a short-term fling. But knowing they could never be more than this and having it shoved down her throat were worlds apart.

She could have pointed out that condoms weren't foolproof and considering she wasn't on a contraceptive—she'd need to have regular sex to consider it—they were playing Russian roulette every time they did the deed.

But this wasn't the moment to lecture. She needed to stop the questions pinging in her brain and sex with Alex was guaranteed to do that.

'We can do other stuff,' she said, with a coy toss of her head, a move she'd never tried in her life but which seemed to work as his gaze brightened.

'We could get arrested for public indecency by doing *other stuff* out here.'

She didn't want to explain that she came here every night to stare wistfully at her dream house and no one else ever did, so she unwound her legs and slid off the bonnet.

'There's always the back seat?' She raised an eyebrow in invitation and thankfully he didn't need to be asked twice.

'You're incredibly naughty,' he said, opening the door and waiting for her to scoot across the seat before joining her. 'I like it.'

He closed the door and activated the locks, his gaze inscrutable in the darkness as clouds scudded across the moon. 'Lie back.' His command held a hint of desperation, like he couldn't wait to go down on her.

'No.'

She needed to be in control this time. She needed to prove to herself that she had a handle on this thing developing between them because, deep down, their connection was more than sex and they both knew it.

Scooting closer, she placed a hand over his zipper and the sizeable bulge beneath it.

His sharp intake of breath hissed out slowly as she eased the zipper down, the rasp of metal teeth unlocking the only sound in the car.

'Charlie…'

She had no idea if his warning growl meant stop or hurry up so she reached inside his jocks and wrapped her fingers around velvet steel.

'Fuck,' he muttered as she took him out and slid her hand up and down experimentally, getting a feel for what he liked by listening to the changes in his breathing.

When she brushed her thumb over the head he jerked slightly.

'You like that?' She did it again, savouring the power that came with making a man like Alex needy.

'I like everything you do to me,' he said through gritted teeth as she squeezed harder.

'Good,' she said, leaning forward to lick him.

His hips lifted off the seat slightly. She took it as a good sign.

She'd never done this before and while she had reservations about putting something so big in her mouth, she wanted to experience everything she could with this incredible man.

Tentatively she wrapped her lips around him. He tasted musky, almost sweet, and she lapped a little. He moaned again and rested his hand on her head, his fingers twining in her hair a little.

Emboldened, she took him deeper into her mouth, as far as she could without gagging, leaving her enough room to fit an entire hand around what was left over.

No surprise why he felt so damn good inside her.

She started to move, slowly at first. Sliding him

out of her mouth and back in, her fist moving in synchronicity.

He liked it, if his low groans were any indication. She liked it too, liked lapping him, licking him. Her very own Popsicle. She almost giggled at the thought but didn't want to kill the mood. Or choke.

Besides, giving her first blowjob was having an unexpected effect on her. She'd never expected to be this turned on.

She shifted restlessly and, as if sensing her need, he leaned sideways and slipped a hand between her legs. It wasn't the most comfortable positioning, being squished into the back of a car, her knees on the floor with her head in his lap, him half draped along the backseat, one hand on the back of her head, the other doing wicked things between her legs, but they made it work.

As he zeroed in on her clit and rubbed it, she automatically picked up the pace, sucking harder as her head bobbed and her hand pumped.

His hand tightened on the back of her head, tugging painfully at her hair. She didn't care, as the pleasure built from his other hand's ministrations. Pushing her higher, faster, than ever before until she fell over the edge into blissful oblivion.

With a garbled cry he followed, the heat of him in her mouth like nothing she could have anticipated. It was so damn sexy.

After unkinking their bodies like a couple of contortionists, she sat next to him, content to rest her head in the crook of his shoulder.

'You're incredible,' he said, turning his head to brush a kiss across her forehead. 'And just full of surprises.'

'You ain't seen nothing yet.'

Her flippant response lost some of its impact when she ended on an embarrassing hiccup and he eased away, searching her face for some clue as to her emotional state.

Good luck with that, she thought, as she had no idea how the hell she'd ended up here, in the back seat of some hot guy's car, giving him head when she wanted to give him her heart.

But she couldn't and that ensured there'd be more focus on sex, less dwelling on things she couldn't have.

'What's wrong?'

He placed a finger under her chin and tilted her head up. Not that he'd be able to read much in the dim interior. She'd never been more grateful for clouds covering the moon in all her life.

'Nothing.'

'You know I'm going to keep pestering you until you tell me, right?'

Already feeling too fragile, she couldn't withstand an interrogation, so she settled for a half-truth.

'That's the first time I did *that* and I'm wondering if I was okay.'

She only just heard his muttered, 'What the fuck?' as he swivelled to face her completely.

'You mean…' He cleared his throat, more stunned than she'd expected. 'That was your first blowjob?'

'Uh-huh.' She shrugged, as if it meant little, when in fact she was more than a little curious to hear his evaluation.

Not that she wanted a score, per se, but a little feedback wouldn't hurt for future reference.

'Babe, what you did with your mouth and your hand…' He shook his head, as if trying to clear it. 'Phenomenal.'

She grinned like he'd presented her with a gold medal for fellatio. 'Really?'

'Really.' He grinned back at her and at that moment the clouds cleared the moon and she spied a glint in his eyes in the resulting light flooding the car. 'Though maybe I should lie and say you were average, which means you'd need to do a hell of a lot of practice?'

'I'm sure I could find willing subjects for that,' she deadpanned, unprepared for his hand to shoot out and tweak her nose.

She squealed and swatted him away, but they ended up mock wrestling and laughing and falling on top of each other.

'This is nice,' she said, when they finally drew apart to catch their breath.

'Us being in the back seat?'

'Us playing and swapping banter after sharing something intimate.' She laid a hand on his chest. 'I never expected to feel this comfortable about sex, especially after not knowing you that long, but I feel good being with you like this.'

'Feeling's mutual, sweetheart.'

He enveloped her in a squishy hug and while she knew his endearment didn't mean much, in that moment, in the circle of his arms, her heart squirming with neediness, she wished it did.

CHAPTER TWENTY

ALEX DROPPED CHARLOTTE back at her car at work, followed her home to ensure she got there safely, then slunk off into the night like a goddamn coward.

She'd asked him to stay.

He'd cited work.

Yep, a coward. A lily-livered, low-bellied coward who couldn't face seeing her any longer tonight in case he blurted the truth.

How seeing her dream house scared the shit out of him.

He'd acted like a real prick too, spouting all that crap about her settling down too soon before experiencing life. Then had to backtrack when he'd seen how badly he'd hurt her.

He should have taken her home then. Instead, he'd been the recipient of the best head of his life. She'd blown his mind, literally, yet while he'd been coming down from his high all he'd been able to think about was her in that damn house without him.

Or with him.

And that was what had him in such a funk he'd

hightailed it away from her flat so fast his tyres had spun.

Because the moment she'd shown him that damn Californian bungalow with its garish blue picket fence, he'd pictured her on the front step and him coming home to her. Or maybe the other way round.

She'd be a kickass manager when he promoted her so maybe he could stay home for a while and stop flitting. Whip up gourmet meals for his hard-working woman. Have an open bottle of red on the dining table waiting for her at the end of a long day. Be a supportive sounding-board. Draw her a bath…

He couldn't have any part of that.

When he reached his hotel in record time, he showered and dressed, slapped some aftershave on his cheeks and ran a comb through his hair.

He knew what he needed to get him out of this funk.

He needed to remind himself of why he chose this kind of life and how good it made him feel.

So he headed for the one place that could guarantee him a shot of reality anywhere in the world.

The hotel bar.

It didn't matter where he stayed in Australia or the UK or Asia, he always frequented the hotel bar. Not because he had a drinking problem but for the special brand of camaraderie that could only be found among fellow nomads.

People who loved to travel. People who had wanderlust in their veins. People who valued adventure over stability.

Right now, he needed to be with his people.

Entering the bar, he headed for a vacant stool smack bang in the middle of the trendy stainless-steel bar running the length of the room. His vantage point offered him an uninterrupted view of the bar and a glittering Sydney Harbour Bridge casting sparkles on the water.

Pretty, but he wasn't here for the view. He needed to talk to fellow travellers, swapping tales of their wanderings, desperate to be distracted from the crazy thoughts that seeing Charlotte's dream house had conjured up.

A young barman sporting enough facial piercings to make him wince stopped in front of him. 'What can I get you?'

'A glass of your best Shiraz, please.'

The barman's eyebrow rose, elevating three rings higher than the rest. 'It's four hundred a glass?'

'That's fine.'

A good red would soothe his soul and loosen his tongue. Because now that he was here he didn't feel like talking all that much.

A fellow businessman in a designer suit sat on his right while an older woman in a severe black dress sat on his left. They both stared at their cells, their thumbs flying as they tapped out messages. The guy had an untouched Scotch in front of him, the woman a G&T. He recognised their harried expressions well. He usually wore one himself, striving to get deadlines done before moving on to the next challenge.

The barman didn't take long to deposit his wine in

front of him and after the first sip Alex relaxed. The rich flavour of aged grapes slid over his tongue, the perfect end to a startling day.

Why had Charlotte shown him her dream house?

It was the one question that continued to bug him and raised a whole heap of other questions he'd rather not contemplate.

Did she have a hidden agenda?

Was she mistaking sex for something more?

Or was she trying to prove that, no matter how sizzling their encounters, ultimately he wouldn't be good enough to be the man she settled down with?

The latter shouldn't bother him, but it did. He'd known that feeling of worthlessness before, with his parents, where nothing he did or said seemed enough to vanquish the pall of sadness that hung over their household.

And he'd tried, boy, had he tried.

He'd got the best marks, trained hard to be chosen captain of the football team in winter, the cricket team in summer. He'd started working at the local ice-cream parlour at age fourteen to take financial pressure off them. Hell, he'd even helped shear sheep to help his dad during a busy season, when he hated those smelly woolly things.

He'd busted his ass in an effort to make his parents happy. Nothing had worked, and in the end his dad had killed himself anyway.

'Man, what a day.' The businessman on his right flung down his cell and picked up his Scotch. 'Ever feel like you're a hamster running on one of those goddamn wheels?'

Alex nodded and raised his glass. 'All the time.'

The businessman clinked his glass. 'To hamsters.'

Alex grinned and took another sip as the businessman tossed back his entire glass. He stuck out his hand. 'Alex.'

'Richard.' They shook hands before his new bestie gestured at the barman for a refill. 'You travel much?'

Alex nodded. 'All the time. I'm an accountant by trade but these days I take ailing companies and get them back on track.'

'Impressive.' Richard raised a fresh Scotch in his direction. 'This is my fifth hotel on the eastern seaboard in ten days and, as much as I like a change, I'm exhausted.'

'What do you do?'

'CEO of my own security company. We protect anyone and anything.'

'Is that your motto?'

'It should be.' Richard took a healthy slug of his Scotch. 'Let me ask you something, Alex. Do you ever take a vacation?'

'Rarely,' Alex said, surprised the admission saddened him when he usually couldn't care less. He spent enough time on the road not to care but it struck him that sitting in hotel bars swapping stories with strangers wasn't the same as lazing by a pool reading for pleasure not business.

'You should.' Richard frowned and pinched the

bridge of his nose. 'Or you'll end up like me. Wealthy but wiped out. Single and hating it.'

Alex reckoned Richard couldn't be more than fifty-five. Would that be him in another twenty-odd years, cynical but burned out, rueing his bachelor-hood?

So much for bonding with fellow travellers. Richard was a real downer.

Richard wiggled his ringless third finger. 'I take it you don't have a ball and chain waiting for you at home?'

Alex shook his head. 'Footloose and fancy-free.'

Usually, he revelled in his singledom. So why did his proud declaration sound so hollow?

'I was you once, a good-looking young buck taking on the world.' Richard shrugged and downed his second Scotch in as many minutes. 'Never would've thought it'd ever lose its appeal.'

Shit. Dear old Dick was a real killjoy. 'I like being a nomad, travelling when the whim takes me, making a cool million or two.'

He threw it out there defiantly, daring Richard to disagree.

Alex liked his life. He liked living on his terms, not someone else's. As for the future, it would be solid because he'd have financial security to see him well into old age, without having to dwell on the unhappiness of his partner dragging him down.

Richard rolled his eyes and half leaned across him. 'What about you, honey? Are you a nomad too?'

Alex tried not to cringe at Richard's casual use of

'honey' for the austere businesswoman now looking down her snooty nose at the two of them.

But to his surprise, she didn't fling her drink in Richard's face as Alex half expected. Instead, she smiled and it softened the severity of the lines bracketing her mouth and eyes. 'I travel a fair bit for work but I have a doting husband waiting for me with my slippers and cigar when I get home.'

Alex laughed and Richard managed a rueful chuckle.

'Don't mind him.' Alex jerked a thumb in Richard's direction. 'I think he's had a long day.'

Richard grimaced. 'Make that a long two weeks. Hotels suck.'

The woman raised an eyebrow. 'You don't like travelling?'

'It lost its appeal a long time ago,' Richard said, studying her with open curiosity. 'What about you?'

'I love it.' Her eyes brightened with enthusiasm. 'There's nothing like a pristine hotel room at the end of a long work day or a hotel bar like this one for meeting interesting people.'

Richard grunted his disapproval and Alex nodded. 'I agree.'

'To fellow wanderers.' She tapped her wine glass against his and they both took a sip as Alex wondered if he'd stumbled into some kind of alternative reality, where the woman was the angel perched on his left shoulder and Richard the devil on his right.

The woman had a similar mind-set to him, Richard the opposite. And rather than mixing with these people bringing him the clarity he sought, he couldn't help but feel even more confused.

He could have been holed up in Charlotte's flat right now, with an armful of warm, willing woman.

Instead, he'd blown her off to reassert his independence.

What kind of an idiot did that make him?

CHAPTER TWENTY-ONE

CHARLOTTE DIDN'T WANT to be alone tonight.

With her emotions pinging all over the place after the odd evening with Alex she knew she'd be up all night, brooding and mulling.

She needed a friend. But when she'd reached out to Abby she hadn't anticipated having to meet her at the nightclub owned by Abby's boyfriend Tanner.

As she entered Embue, the *doof-doof* beat pierced her eardrums and she wished she'd stayed home after all.

This so wasn't her scene.

Beautiful people mingling, beautiful bodies dancing, making her feel decidedly ugly in her plain black dress, the only fancy outfit she owned. Like she needed a reinforcement of how average she looked on a good day.

She'd begged off going out with Mak and Abby so many times until they'd finally left her alone. They gently teased her for being a nerd, for ending up a spinster unless she got out there and met guys. She'd laughed along with them but little did they know the real reason she remained a social hermit.

She felt lacking in all areas of her life.

Sure, she could hold her own at work, but socially she didn't know how to act or make small talk or flirt.

She'd never learned how.

Being an introvert at school ensured she'd never had friends. She'd spent the bulk of her downtime around her aunt's motley crowd: artists, musicians, flamboyant transvestites. She'd loved mingling with these interesting people but they too had made her feel insignificant. Not deliberately, but because she couldn't help but compare herself to their ostentatious lifestyles while she toiled away at her homework ensuring she achieved the dream: becoming an accountant. Woo-hoo.

But it had been more than that. She'd seen these people drift in and out of her aunt's life and figured that if her vivacious, charming aunt couldn't hold onto friends, what hope did she have?

In her experience—with her parents, with her aunt's friends, even Mak—people ultimately walked away. So it became easier to shut herself off, expecting little, giving the same.

Somewhere along the line, her self-worth had become wrapped up in this lack of serious bonding and it had spiralled out of control ever since.

She hated being a loner and feeling this unworthy but until Alex she'd felt powerless to do anything about it.

As she watched lithe, sinuous bodies wind around

each other on the dance floor, a yearning so strong it took her breath away made her light-headed.

Those couples exuded sex. They wore their sexuality like a badge of honour, while she'd just given her first blowjob in the back seat of a car and skedaddled, overjoyed when Alex hadn't pushed to spend the night.

Tears stung her eyes and she blinked rapidly. Coming here had been a mistake. But falling for her fling was a much bigger one.

That was what had her so melancholy.

Pining for Alex.

Ridiculous, as she barely knew the guy and he'd made it more than clear he wasn't interested in anything more than a fling. Heck, the way he'd reacted when she'd shown him her dream house should have served as a stark warning that he could never be the guy for her.

He'd bolted because of it, had cited work as an excuse not to come home with her. Ouch. But even his obvious reticence in getting too close hadn't served to give her the wake-up call she needed.

She wanted him.

For more than a few weeks.

For the simple fact he made her feel like a different woman. A woman who could take charge in and out of the bedroom, a woman willing to step outside her comfort zone, a woman not afraid to take risks.

But it would be beyond foolish to pin her hopes of evolving into a new woman on a guy destined to leave without a backward glance. Which explained her current funk.

'Screw this,' she muttered, spinning on her low heels to head out, when she glimpsed Abby waving at her from an alcove tucked behind the main bar.

She glanced at the exit longingly, but she'd reached out to her friend and it would be poor form to ditch her now.

Squaring her shoulders, she marched through the crowd of beautiful people as if she belonged. She wished.

'I'm so glad you're here,' Abby squealed and enveloped her in a hug. 'I can't believe it's taken you this long.'

Charlotte remained silent as they disengaged and Abby waved her over to a plush gold velvet chaise longue. 'What would you like to drink?'

She bit back her first response of 'soda' and decided to live a little. 'A vodka and lime, please.'

'Coming right up.' Abby spoke into a Bluetooth-thingy clipped onto her collar.

'What is that?'

Rueful, Abby shrugged. 'Tanner sets me up in here so I don't have to fight my way to the bar.'

'And fend off the inevitable guys who'd flock to you,' she said drily, garnering a laugh from her friend.

'You might think he's possessive, I prefer to think of him as protective.'

'He's a good guy,' Charlotte said, though she wouldn't admit in a million years that she found Tanner intimidating.

With all those tattoos and that perpetual glower she found him formidable. Sexy, but scary. She could never handle a guy like that but her friend did it with ease.

'Yeah, he is.' Abby's eyes gleamed whenever she mentioned her boyfriend. She got this glow, the kind that could never be emulated by any skincare. 'So what's happening with you and that dishy boss?'

'We're hanging out,' Charlotte said, and promptly burst into tears.

'Oh, no, honey.' Abby pulled her into her arms, squeezing tight, while Charlotte cried out some of the tension making her feel so confused.

She rarely cried. She'd learned from a young age that tears were futile and did nothing but make her look puffy-eyed. She'd cried a lot when her parents had first left her with Dee but her aunt had never mentioned her red, swollen eyes.

Instead, Dee would ply her with sodas and cupcakes, and cuddle her incessantly to make up for her parents' callous disregard of a child's tender feelings. In the ensuing years, when her parents hadn't come back no matter how hard she'd sobbed into her pillow at night, her tears had eventually dried.

So finding herself in the midst of a crying jag was as disorientating as discovering she might be falling for her fling.

Abby didn't say anything, just held her, until her sobs petered out.

'Sorry about that,' Charlotte said, when her friend released her. She scavenged for tissues in her handbag and tidied up her face as best she could, knowing she must look a fright but was too drained to care. 'Must be that time of the month.'

Abby's raised eyebrows implied she didn't buy her pathetic excuse for a second. Their drinks appearing saved Charlotte from having to say anything for a moment but the second the waiter disappeared Abby swooped.

'Okay, start talking and don't stop 'til you've told me everything.'

'Not much to tell.' Ha. Understatement of the year.

'Last time we spoke, you'd had sex with him at that warehouse before you knew he was your boss.' Abby pinned her with a probing stare. 'I'm assuming you've done the dirty again?'

Charlotte sighed, hating the inevitable twang in her chest whenever she thought about the connection she shared with Alex. 'Several times.'

'And?'

'And I said I was okay with a fling but I don't think I'm built that way.' She ended on an embarrassing hiccup and squeezed her eyes shut to stave off more tears.

'Oh, Char.' Abby draped an arm over her shoulders and squeezed before releasing her.

When Charlotte opened her eyes, Abby stared at her with determination.

'Hope you don't mind, but I'm your friend and I'm going to be blunt, okay?'

Even the mention of blunt had her remembering Alex saying that was one of the traits he liked about her. She wondered how much he'd like it when she channelled that signature bluntness into dumping his ass before she got in any deeper.

'Do your worst.'

'For as long as I've known you, you've never been out with a guy. You don't date. You don't socialise. Don't you think letting go a little with this guy, who obviously pushed your buttons enough you had sex with him on first meeting, is a good thing?' Abby hesitated, plucking at her bottom lip, before continuing. 'I know you envisage the grand happily-ever-after. We all do. It's in our DNA or something. But having a fling before you settle down can be the best thing for you.'

'You're right, I know you're right.'

Hadn't Charlotte given herself the very same pep talk? But using cool logic to explain away her raunchy behaviour and keeping Alex at an emotional distance seemed much easier in theory.

'Maybe I'm confusing lust with a stronger emotion?' Charlotte shrugged, as if her concerns meant little when in fact she needed all the help she could get. 'I've never felt this way about a guy before so perhaps I'm in over my head?'

And terrified that, no matter how hard she tried to dress up this thing with Alex as a fling, she'd find it difficult to walk away at the end.

A frown slashed Abby's brow. 'Have you discussed your fears with him?'

'Hell no. He'd end things instantly.' She screwed

up her nose. 'Alex is a "no muss no fuss" kind of guy. He travels a lot. Doesn't stay in one place too long.'

Abby nodded, ponderous. 'And he's been upfront with you from the start about an expiration date on this fling?'

'Uh-huh.'

'Hmm…' Abby sipped at her cocktail, some bright pink thing with bubbles that would give Charlotte an instant headache. 'Honestly, Char, I don't know what to say. I want you to keep having fun with this guy because it's good for you. But your tears indicate you're already emotionally invested, which can only end badly for you when he leaves.'

Charlotte managed a watery smile. 'You've just articulated exactly how I feel. But without giving me a solution.'

Abby took another healthy slurp of her cocktail, like the alcohol would give her clarity. 'Is there any chance… I mean, do you think he feels more for you beyond the obvious?'

In her more deluded moments, when he cradled her in his arms as if he never wanted to let go, Charlotte liked to think so.

But she'd given up believing in fairy tales a long time ago, around the time her folks dumped her with her weird aunt so they could travel the world, and the only fantasies she believed in these days occurred between the pages of her favourite novels.

'He's made it more than clear we're short-term, nothing more,' she said, wincing. The facts hurt.

'Then you've got a decision to make,' Abby said,

clasping her hand and squeezing. 'Keep having fun and take what you can get. Or end it now before you get hurt.'

Charlotte smiled in gratitude at her friend, not stating the obvious.

What if it was already too late?

CHAPTER TWENTY-TWO

HANGING OUT IN the hotel bar last Friday night hadn't given Alex the emotional distance he'd needed from Charlotte. In fact, it had only served to reinforce how much that part of his life had lost its appeal. Not good.

So he reserved his cowardice for the office and ensured he avoided her all week.

Sure, they discussed work projects when needed but he told her he needed time to organise the new staffing hierarchy going forward and thankfully she believed him.

He'd referred three new clients to her too, all involving a lot of work to ensure she stayed busy.

And stayed away from him.

But all that was about to change because somehow he'd been so swamped for the last few hours that he hadn't noticed the time and now they were the last two people in the office on a Friday night again.

Damn.

He remembered the last time this had happened, every erotic moment replaying in his mind like a dirty movie.

His cock thickened just thinking about it and he snuck a surreptitious glance at her as she crossed the outer office to the photocopier.

There was nothing remotely remarkable about her outfit today. Calf-length navy skirt. Pale blue shirt. Negligible heels on navy pumps. She fitted the stereotype of a dedicated accountant but he knew what lay beneath that sedate exterior and he clenched his hands into fists to stop from barging out there and tearing off her outer layers.

She stabbed at a few buttons on the photocopier then leaned forward, drawing the skirt tight across her ass. Alex bit back a groan, his cock at full attention now and making sitting uncomfortable.

He couldn't see a panty line at this distance and imagined her wearing a thong. Black satin. Smooth. Slippery. Easy to hook aside as he spread her legs wide, bent her over that copier and entered her...

Fuck.

He stood and stalked around his desk, chastising himself for being a fool but unable to stop this relentless desire for her.

She chose that moment to glance over her shoulder, her gaze knowing, as if she knew he'd been watching her.

He made it as far as the door to his office when her bold stare zeroed in on his cock, an obvious bulge in his trousers.

Her tongue darted out to sweep her bottom lip in a gesture so provocative he felt it all the way to his balls.

This woman was fire and ice.

Hot and cold.

Temptation and reservation.

She was something else.

His cell rang at that moment. A smart guy would have ignored it and followed through on the lust pounding through every inch of him. But he'd turned into a dumb schmuck lately and the cause was staring at him with a beguiling mix of daring and defiance.

Taunting him. Challenging him.

So much for avoiding her. He wanted her so damn badly his vision clouded with it.

But giving in now wouldn't end well for either of them, not when he knew in his gut that Charlie wanted more from him than he could give, so he managed a terse nod, swung around and closed the office door.

'This is bullshit,' Charlotte muttered, furious for allowing herself to be dragged into Alex's stupid game again.

He'd been doing this all freaking week, business one minute, casting lustful glances her way the next.

She. Was. Over. It.

They couldn't go on this way. Something would snap. She had a sneaking suspicion it would be her. Or his neck if he ever let her close enough again to wrap her hands around it.

Not that she didn't appreciate his faith in her work ethic. She'd never been so challenged professionally, with the three clients he'd referred her way taking up most of her time. With a little luck she'd be in line for a big promotion to the coveted managerial role that would ensure she could afford her upcoming mortgage and then some.

She had a feeling he was grooming her for it and while she understood his reticence for discussing it, she couldn't help but hope. But all the work in the world couldn't distract from how much she missed their physical contact, how much she craved his touch.

It wouldn't be so bad if she didn't have to see him every day, strutting around the office in those designer suits that moulded his body to perfection, smiling at everyone, being charming and affable because that was who he was.

What would it be like to be that confident? To draw people to you without trying? To be a natural extrovert who never knew the agony of uncertainty and awkwardness?

She'd accepted who she was a long time ago but she'd be lying if she didn't admit to being a tad jealous of people like Alex who breezed through life without a care in the world.

So after a long week she'd decided to stay behind tonight in the hope they could have a word. Maybe get supper together. Maybe indulge in something more.

Because she'd come to a decision after her chat with Abby last Friday.

She would take what she could get while she could and ensure she waved Alex away with a light heart when he walked out of her life.

She'd wanted this.

She'd called the shots at the start.

No use getting the proverbial cold feet because her long-term dreams and her current fantasies had got mixed up.

Clarity wouldn't come from mulling and second-guessing.

Clarity would come from screwing her brains out and walking away from this fling a well-satisfied woman.

She'd sensed him watching her earlier, had been delighted to discover he still wanted her as badly as she wanted him, the evidence of his desire making her salivate.

But he'd closed the door on her, deliberately shutting her out.

'Good luck with that, buddy,' she said, kicking at a leg on her desk as she channelled her indignation into tidying up.

She wanted to be ready to execute her plan the moment he tried to make his escape.

He made her wait a full twenty minutes before exiting his office. He paused on the threshold, uncertain, as he glanced at her picking up her satchel and turning off her office light. She kept her back to him, not wanting him to see the first part of her plan until it was time.

He didn't move as she headed for the elevator.

If he didn't follow her in, her plan would be scuttled. But it would also be a good indication that maybe she'd read this situation all wrong and he'd cooled things off between them ahead of schedule.

She pressed the elevator button to go down and by the time it arrived and the doors slid open, he still hadn't moved.

She stepped inside, thankful this old building didn't have cameras in the elevators, and held the button to keep the doors open.

Then she turned around.

His eyes bugged as he caught sight of her blouse, unbuttoned to the waist, revealing a sheer creamy lace bra.

She'd been wearing provocative lingerie all week in the hope he might get to see it and if this didn't do the trick, nothing would.

Her finger cramped from pressing the elevator button and just when she'd given up hope he bounded towards her and almost skidded into the elevator in his haste to join her.

'Going down?' She arched an eyebrow, biting back a triumphant smile as he launched at her. One hand splayed behind her head, the other on her ass, his lips crushing hers.

Her finger slipped off the button as he backed them into the corner of the elevator, his hard cock hitting her sweet spot and making her whimper.

He ravaged her mouth as she clung to him, devouring her as if he'd never get enough. Nipping at her bottom lip. His tongue sweeping into her mouth. Challenging. Commanding.

Charlotte was so damned turned on she momentarily wondered if she could come from kissing alone. But then he wrenched his mouth from hers, pausing long enough to hit the stop button. The elevator juddered to a halt but they were just getting started.

'You are so fucking hot,' he murmured, rucking up her skirt and smoothing his palms up her thighs. 'Do you have any idea what you do to me?'

She palmed his cock through his trousers. 'I think I do.'

He plucked at her panties, almost tearing them off in his haste, his urgency delighting her. Emboldened by his obvious desire, she unzipped him and slipped her hand in. 'I want you inside me. Now.'

He slipped a finger between her slick folds, another, and groaned. 'You're certainly ready for me.'

She bit back her retort, 'always', because that sounded too permanent and she didn't want to scare him off, not when she wanted him this badly.

'So wet, so sweet.' His fingers slid in and out, sweeping over her clit every third stroke, before gliding in again. Sure, masterful strokes designed to ratchet her excitement to unbearable levels.

'Inside. Now,' she gasped, as he slipped a third finger inside her, stretching her, alighting her nerve endings.

He claimed her mouth again as he sheathed himself in record time before plunging into her to the hilt. The back of her head thunked against the elevator wall. She didn't care, the fleeting pain diluted in a wave of pleasure spreading from her core upward.

He plundered her mouth as his fingers clamped onto her ass, hoisting her higher so she could wrap her legs around him. He thrust into her repeatedly, thick and long and oh, so good. Filling her in a way she'd never imagined in her wildest dreams.

With every slide out, with every thrust in, he hit her sweet spot. Over and over until she hovered on the edge of an orgasm so powerful her back spasmed.

Then he changed the angle of his hips and she plummeted over and into a free fall of carnal bliss so intense she screamed.

He kissed her, swallowing her cries of release and groaning his own into her mouth, his fingers digging into her ass so tight she'd have bruises for sure.

She didn't care. She didn't care about anything right now but the way Alex made her feel, wishing she could feel this good all the time.

'How long are you staying around for now?'

The moment the question slipped from her lips she regretted it. In her post-sex stupor she'd over-stepped a line they'd agreed on at the start. And in adding in that one significant word 'now' she'd im-plied that because of their involvement he'd extend his time in Sydney.

Crap, she'd screwed up, big time.

'I'll be gone once the project here is done, another few weeks max,' he said, his cool tone chilling her as he withdrew from her, physically and emotionally.

He turned away, giving her time to fix herself up. How kind of him. A gentleman now that he'd had his way with her.

Okay, so that was grossly unfair. She'd seduced him and when he shut down as she'd expected she blamed him.

'Can you press the button, please? I need to get home.' She sounded so prim, so proper, she inwardly cringed.

'Sure.'

The elevator lurched as it started its descent again as they stood side by side, watching those infernal numbers count down.

How could they have such a strong physical connection but anything further resulted in this frigid standoff?

When the doors opened into the car park and they stepped out, Charlotte mustered her best nonchalant expression. 'See you tomorrow—'

He kissed her, a mere brush of his lips against hers, his tenderness almost undoing her completely.

When he pulled back, she couldn't read the turmoil of emotion darkening his eyes. 'I'm taking you out on a date tomorrow night. Pick you up at your place around seven.'

With that, he spun on his heel, leaving her confused and gaping and wondering what the hell had just happened.

CHAPTER TWENTY-THREE

ALEX HAD NEVER been so torn in all his life.

He wanted to give Charlotte a night she'd never forget.

He wanted to let her down gently.

He wanted to express how incredible she made him feel but that it had to end.

He knew that, after last night. The moment she'd asked how long he'd be staying around for, he'd known. She'd invested far too much into this fling and the damnedest thing was, maybe he had too.

Easier to break it off now, before he ended up breaking her heart.

He didn't want to hurt her. She was too special for that. And he knew that was exactly what would happen if they continued spending time together.

The sex was sensational but somehow, whenever they hooked up, he was left wanting more and if her post-coital question in that elevator was any indication, she did too.

She'd left him no choice.

He had to end it.

Tonight.

He could have done it last night but it would have been too callous after they'd just had sex. Besides, he knew Charlotte was a hearts and flowers kind of girl. That damn house she coveted so badly told him that.

So that was what he'd give her tonight. A night of romance, a night a special woman like her deserved. Then he'd take her home, give her a chaste kiss, and end it.

She'd understand. They'd both known the fleeting nature of this going in and he hoped that once she got the promotion she'd be too busy to give him the evil eye at work.

Another two weeks and he'd be out of here, leaving Sydney behind and heading to Auckland for a conference before weighing up his options. He had companies in Perth, Adelaide and Melbourne begging for his attention and he hadn't decided which one to tackle first. Maybe Perth would be the best option, the other side of the country so he wouldn't be tempted to hop on a plane and return to Sydney if he lost his mind and ended up pining for Charlie.

'Idiot,' he muttered, jabbing at her doorbell.

He had a clear-cut plan.

He had to stick to it.

The door opened and he sucked in a breath. Charlotte stood before him wearing a purple strapless mini dress that hugged every curve of her body. She'd curled her hair and it fell in soft waves over her shoulders. She'd used smoky make-up on her eyes and a plum gloss that made her lips shimmer.

Fuck. She was a knockout, determined to shatter his limited self-control.

He couldn't screw her tonight, it wouldn't be right, but damn it was going to be hard to keep his hands off her when every cell in his body clamoured to be all over her.

'You look incredible,' he finally said, when he unglued his tongue from the roof of his mouth and stepped forward to place a kiss on her cheek. 'Stunning.'

'Thanks.' She blushed and tugged on the hem of the dress self-consciously. 'My flatmate left a stack of dresses behind when she moved to New York so I raided her wardrobe.'

He bit back his first response, 'You should do it more often,' for the simple fact he wouldn't be the beneficiary of seeing her metamorphose into a sex goddess after tonight.

The thought left him feeling winded.

Thankfully, she didn't notice anything amiss as she turned to grab a black clutch and her keys off the hall table. When she turned back he'd managed to get himself under control and forced a lazy grin that belied the churning in his gut.

'Where are we going?'

'It's a surprise,' he said, placing a hand in the small of her back and guiding her down the path towards his car. He could feel the heat of her skin through the thin material. It didn't help his rampant libido straining to let loose.

'I'm not usually one for surprises but in your case

I'll make an exception.' She cast him a flirtatious glance from beneath mascaraed lashes and damned if he didn't want to drag her into the back seat again.

'Are you flirting with me, Miss Baxter?'

'I may be, Mr Bronson.'

He opened the passenger door and waited for her to slide in before leaning down. 'You're something else. You know that, right?'

An odd melancholy clouded her eyes, as if she sensed this would be their last hurrah. 'I'm hoping you mean that in the nicest way possible.'

'I do,' he said, startled to inadvertently recite those two little words that personally terrified him.

He slammed the door and stalked around the car, determined to keep this evening light-hearted. It was the least he could do before letting down the first woman he'd actually cared about in a long time, if ever.

They made desultory small talk on the short drive to the exclusive harbourside restaurant where he'd made reservations. When they pulled up out front and he handed over his keys to have his car valet parked, her eyebrows rose.

'I heard it takes a year to get into this place. How did you manage it?'

He tapped the side of his nose and winked. 'It's not what you know, it's who you know.'

When she continued to eye him with suspicion, he said, 'I called in a favour from an old buddy.' He quickly added, 'And before you think I bring all my dates here, you're the first.'

'I'm flattered,' she said, but didn't sound like it. In fact, ever since they'd arrived here, she'd seemed uneasy.

He waited until she'd stepped from the car before asking, 'What's wrong?'

She hesitated, as if unsure how to answer. 'Don't get me wrong, I think it's fantastic you brought me here, but I guess it just reinforces that once I buy the house I'll never have a chance to do fancy stuff like this.'

Of all the things she could have said, he hadn't expected that. He didn't want to have any deep and meaningful conversations tonight. He wanted her to have fun so she'd remember him fondly and not as the asshole who dumped her.

Her response virtually echoed the concerns he'd expressed when she'd shown him her future home.

Had she actually heard what he'd said and was reconsidering making such a huge commitment before she'd experienced all that life had to offer?

A flare of hope had him wondering what it would be like to be around for her awakening, before he mentally kicked himself in the ass for going there.

Even if Charlotte had reconsidered taking on a huge mortgage, that didn't mean he'd be up for anything beyond short-term. Whatever the time limit on their relationship, he'd eventually end up leaving; and eventually breaking her heart. No way in hell would he be responsible for that.

Determined to make tonight special for her, he smiled. 'You'll be whipping up fancy meals in your very own kitchen. How cool will that be?'

She managed a wobbly smile. 'You're right. Maybe I'm being a chicken because I'm going to put down a deposit next week.'

'That soon?'

Why did the thought leave him so hollow?

She nodded. 'It's exciting yet terrifying at the same time.'

Her bottom lip wobbled a tad and he captured her chin in his hand, tilting it up slightly. 'Hey. This is your dream. Don't ever doubt yourself, because you're incredible and you can do anything you damn well set your mind to.'

A fact he was all too aware of as she stared at him in open adoration.

Fuck. He'd been so intent on not breaking her heart some time down the track, what if it was too late?

'Let's eat,' he said, sounding gruff as he released her, but as they entered the restaurant he couldn't shake the feeling that no matter how special he tried to make tonight, it wouldn't make an ounce of difference.

She'd end up hating him by the end of it regardless.

They reverted to small talk after they ordered: the rosemary-skewered Tasmanian salmon with a cauliflower cumin salad for him, the oven-roasted pork belly with a semi-dried tomato mousse for her. The meals arrived surprisingly fast and he watched Charlotte devour hers. He loved her healthy appetite: in all areas of her life.

Sadly, he couldn't taste a thing. Because the longer he sat across from her pretending this was just a regular date between two people who were crazy about each other, the harder it was to fathom that they wouldn't be indulging in this banter any longer. That he wouldn't be able to kiss her, to touch her, to bury himself deep inside her.

This was bullshit.

Of his own making.

'What's wrong?' She placed her fork and knife neatly together in the centre of her empty plate and nudged it away. 'You're distracted.'

'Sorry.' He grimaced, not wanting to tell her the truth now, like this, but finding it increasingly difficult to hold back.

'Is it work? Is there a problem?' She gestured around the restaurant, featuring floor-to-ceiling windows with stunning views of Sydney by night, the glow from nearby buildings reflecting off the water like glittering fairy lights. 'Is that why you brought me here, to soften me up before you deliver bad news?'

He shook his head. 'Nothing like that.'

'Then what?'

She searched his face for answers he was reluctant to give. Hell, they hadn't even made it to dessert yet.

'I wanted tonight to be special.' And that was all she'd be getting out of him until he took her home. This wasn't the place to break unpleasant news.

Her eyes narrowed slightly. 'There's more.'

He should have known she'd be intuitive, picking up on his mood no matter how hard he tried to hide it.

Thankfully, her cell rang at that moment, a momentary reprieve as he gathered his thoughts.

She quickly glanced at it, one eyebrow rising. 'Sorry, I have to take this, it's my aunt.'

'Go ahead,' he said, pushing away his half-eaten meal.

He watched her expression change from happiness at hearing from her aunt to concern, though he couldn't hear much of her murmured conversation as a pianist started up.

When she hung up, her cute nose crinkled. 'I'm sorry to do this after you went to all the trouble of getting us a booking here, but I have to go home.'

'Is everything all right?'

'My aunt's biggest client, a regular who keeps her in business, has an urgent order to be filled and I have to do it tonight to ship first thing in the morning.'

He tried not to laugh.

Her aunt's kinky sex-toy business had saved him from blurting the truth here. But his relief was short-lived, that phone call only delaying the inevitable.

'Do you mind if we leave now? As it is it's going to take me all night to sort everything.'

'Sure,' he said, gesturing at a waiter for the bill. He wanted to offer to help but he knew that spending the next few hours beside her as she sorted through that quirky lingerie and more wouldn't be conducive to ending things. 'Let's go.'

She worked on her cell for the entire drive back to her flat, doing an online search for the courier companies her aunt usually used, making bookings.

It gave him a chance to mentally rehearse what he'd say when they arrived at her flat but he never got the chance because her cell rang again when they reached her doorstep, her aunt issuing more orders.

When she hung up, she pecked him on the lips. 'Sorry, I really have to get started. I'll see you tomorrow.'

With that, she left him staring at a closed door.

So much for manning up and ending it tonight. He'd have to psych himself up another time.

Sooner rather than later.

CHAPTER TWENTY-FOUR

As if Charlotte needed a reminder of how thoughtful Alex was, he sent her a text the next morning saying she could take the day off if she needed it after her all-nighter.

Considering she'd got a grand total of two hours' sleep once she'd filled the massive order for her aunt's business, she took it. She fired back a quick Thx, am exhausted, will c u soon. Meaning tomorrow. Or tonight, if she plucked up the courage to text him later this afternoon and ask him to come over.

She didn't like how they'd ended things last night.

He'd obviously gone to a lot of trouble to organise a special dinner date for her but she'd sensed his reticence at the restaurant, as if something was bothering him.

She'd caught him staring at her a few times when he'd thought she wasn't looking and she hadn't been able to fathom the odd look in his eyes.

He'd been about to open up to her, she just knew it, when her aunt had called, and while she loved Dee she could have strangled her at that moment.

He hadn't offered to help her either, which was another red flag.

What was going on inside that handsome head of his?

Increasingly sleepy, Charlotte curled up in bed, read three-quarters of the latest bonkbuster that had her riveted and dozed for an hour or so. When she woke, morning had given way to afternoon and she felt as lacklustre as she had before sleep.

Something kept niggling at her, something about last night, a feeling she hadn't been able to shake since she entered that fancy restaurant.

It bordered on…disappointment. That she'd never be able to do anything like that again. That she was giving up a lot for her dream house—like expensive dinners and spa days and vacations—and ultimately, she wondered whether the sacrifices would be worth it.

She wanted that house. Craved it. Damn Alex for planting those thoughts in her head, that she'd be missing out on something if a house financially tethered her for life.

Only one way to shake off her funk.

Visit her baby.

So for the umpteenth time over the last few weeks she found herself parked opposite the Californian bungalow that had captivated her from the first moment she saw it online.

She could see her life behind that picket fence so clearly.

Coming home at the end of a long day, letting herself in the front door, toeing off her shoes and padding barefoot along the polished, honey-coloured boards to the cosy kitchen where she'd pour a glass of wine before sinking into her sofa in the lounge room.

The lounge had an open fireplace and, while Sydney winters weren't terribly cold, she couldn't wait to curl up with a book in front of it.

Throw in the stand-alone clawfoot bath that was big enough for two people and a modern double shower, a small sunroom that backed onto a tiny cottage garden and a reading nook on the veranda she'd immediately coveted, and she could hardly wait.

As she continued to stare at her dream house, she waited for the inevitable buzz of excitement, that slightly breathless feeling that made her tingle every time she visited.

Today, it didn't come.

Probably overtired, she knuckled her eyes, yawned, took a deep breath and stretched.

It didn't help.

Odd. Her house—she'd come to think of it as hers the last few days as she finalised her mortgage at the bank—appeared as charming as ever. She loved the ecru-trimmed windows, the fresh painted exterior, the duck-egg-blue fence. It looked like a home, not just a house, the kind of home she'd craved since she was a child, her nose buried in a book while Dee chattered incessantly, choosing to live in fictional worlds rather than her own where her parents didn't give a damn about her and preferred living in a tent than in a proper house with their own daughter.

But as she stared at her house, the doubts crept in.

Was she doing the right thing? Tying herself to a life of debt with no money left over for travel or indulgences? Ensuring that bricks and mortar consumed her life? Making sure she did it tough until she found the dream man to fulfil the rest of her fantasy and help shoulder the load?

What if that didn't happen? Or what if the guy she met didn't want to live in this house? What if he didn't want to take on the responsibility of a big mortgage alongside her? What if he preferred going out to frugal dinners at home?

A wave of nausea swept over her and she swallowed.

She'd had it clearly planned out. Get the house first; the rest would follow. A carefully calculated decision she'd been more than happy about.

Until Alex.

He'd done this to her. He had her wishing for things she'd never wanted before. Fun. Frivolity. Fantasies…

'Damn you,' she muttered under her breath, thumping the steering wheel for good measure.

It didn't help. Sadly, she had a feeling nothing would because, no matter how many times she envisaged her life in this house, she couldn't help but see Alex, in the garden, in the kitchen, in the bedroom, front and centre in her happily-ever-after scenario.

And he'd made it more than clear that would never, ever happen.

Which left her totally screwed.

CHAPTER TWENTY-FIVE

ALEX KNEW HE was in big trouble when he mooned around the office for the entire day, unable to concentrate on work because Charlotte wasn't around.

Pathetic.

Since when had he turned into some lovesick schmuck who couldn't think about anything but a woman?

*Love*sick?

Fuck. The moment the word popped into his head, he knew he had to get out of here. Had to do something drastic to shake himself up.

He didn't love Charlotte.

He didn't have it in him to love anyone.

Not any more.

So he did the one thing guaranteed to give him the wake-up call he needed.

Booked a trip home.

It would take too long to drive to the tiny outback town not far from Broken Hill, the isolated mining town over seven hundred miles west of Sydney, so he booked a flight leaving that night and made arrangements to be away from work for two days.

It was a crazy, impulsive thing to do, considering he hadn't been back to Rocky Plains since his father's funeral many years ago and had vowed then never to return.

But he needed to do this. Needed a reminder of why he could never have what Charlie wanted.

Charlie… He should tell her he was leaving. Then again, they had a casual thing. He didn't owe her any explanations and it sure as hell wouldn't make their imminent break-up any easier if he started treating her like a girlfriend he had to check in with.

Scowling, he gathered his things, gave curt instructions to the receptionist regarding the work to be delegated, and headed for the airport. He didn't even stop at his hotel to pack. He wouldn't be staying in Rocky Plains long enough to warrant a bag.

At the airport he flipped his cell over and over in his hand, wondering if he should give his mum a heads-up of his impending arrival, before ultimately deciding against it.

She wouldn't care one way or the other if he showed up. She never had, not since he'd left home for university without looking back.

They had a polite relationship. One maintained out of obligation rather than any real emotion. He knew why.

He couldn't help but blame himself for his father's death and couldn't bear to see the judgement in his mother's all-knowing stare, like she blamed him too.

Even if the coroner and local police force had been unable to establish whether his father had drowned in the family dam by accident or had committed suicide, Alex knew the truth.

His dad had lost the will to live a long time ago.

He'd seen evidence of it every single miserable day, growing up in a household where his dad couldn't give a flying fuck about him no matter how hard he tried and his parents hated each other yet did their utmost to hide it.

The flight took two and a half hours and landed in Broken Hill around eight p.m. As he stepped off the small plane, the heat hit him first. Descending like a heavy, oppressive cloak, stifling every living thing beneath it.

He'd travelled the world and had welcomed the warmth of the tropics. But the outback heat was something else entirely and it made him want to claw off his tie and guzzle a litre of water.

He hired a car, made the thirty-minute drive to Rocky Plains and checked in to the first motel he could find, then spent an hour lying on the rickety bed, staring at a ceiling mottled by water stains. Rain in these parts was rare but when it came it bucketed down in a relentless torrent.

He hadn't thought this through.

Back in Sydney, he'd been so desperate for a reality check that he'd bolted. Now that he was here, listening to the raucous laughter of beer drinkers from the bar next door and the occasional hoon doing burnouts up the main street, he wished he'd never come.

He must have fallen asleep from sheer exhaustion

and over-thinking at some point, because when he woke sunlight streamed through the dirty window set high in the wall.

Time to head home and face his mother.

After grabbing an OJ from the motel's vending machine, he drove the ten minutes to his family's farm. Not a working farm, per se, just a small homestead, a barn and a dam on a few acres of land stuck in the middle of nowhere.

He hated it.

The isolation had always got to him and being an only child hadn't helped. When he wasn't being forced to endure his parents' less than scintillating company he'd been left to wander alone. Riding his dirt bike along tracks. Taking pot-shots at cans with an air rifle. Swimming in the dam.

His heart sank as he turned into the pocked drive. He'd never understand why his mother had chosen to stay here after his dad's death, stuck in the middle of nowhere, left to wallow in bad memories.

She'd be home. She always was. His dad had worked on the railway in Broken Hill; she'd tutored kids online. It had worked, until his dad had lost his job and ended up moping around the house.

That was when things had turned really ugly and he'd been glad to finish high school the year after and escape.

She must have heard the car because by the time he'd parked and got out she stood on the back step, waving at him.

He didn't deserve the huge smile that lit her face.

He didn't deserve anything bar a scathing lecture for being such a shitty son.

His feet dragged, just as they used to, as he approached the back veranda. 'Hey, Mum.'

Her smile widened. 'This is a nice surprise.'

In the few seconds before she enveloped him in a hug, he noticed several things. Her greying hair had been coloured a natural-looking blonde that softened her face. She wore make-up. And the perpetual frown lines that resided between her brows had eased.

His mum looked younger than the last time he'd seen her two years ago. The last time he'd flown her to Brisbane for three days, part of his obligatory son duties. She'd sensed his heart wasn't in it, like the other times he'd made the hollow gesture and she'd returned home after one night. He didn't blame her. He'd felt nothing but relief.

She'd mentioned a new man in her life back then, a new pub owner in town. He hadn't wanted to know the details but had wished her well. If anyone deserved happiness after the shit she'd put up with over the years because of his dad, she did.

When she wrapped her arms around him and the faintest waft of cinnamon reached his nose, he had a sudden urge to bawl. He clung to her, his intention to keep their reunion brief lost amid a wave of emotion he could almost label regret.

Why had he stayed away so long?

When she released him, her eyes were damp. 'Come in and I'll make you a cuppa.'

He had a hankering for something a lot stronger

but tea would do for now. As he stepped inside, he was catapulted back in time. He remembered entering this kitchen every day after school, ravenous for his mum's delicious baking but eager to escape to avoid the inevitable awkwardness between his folks after his father lost his job. He'd cram choc-chip cookies in his mouth, snaffle a few for later, drink half a carton of milk, then bolt for his room on the pretext of homework. He'd keep his ears plugged to drown out potential arguments. Would listen to music half the night. Had done whatever it took to cope.

'Are you going to stand there all day?'

He blinked, to find himself still hovering in the doorway, and shook his head slightly to clear it. 'Memories,' he said, entering the kitchen and inhaling deeply. 'Still smells amazing in here.'

'That's because I bake every day.' She bustled around the kitchen, the familiarity of her movements making his throat clog so badly no amount of clearing would ease it. 'Not for me, of course, but I donate baked goods to the church every week and they sell them.'

Alex hated his first thought: why was she so altruistic now when she had barely been able to utter a civil word to his father all those years ago?

'So what brings you by?' She placed a cup of tea in front of him, along with a plate piled high with cookies, a slice of apple cake and a lamington. 'Is something wrong?'

Of course she'd jump to that conclusion. He never came home.

'Everything's fine, Mum.' Her baking smelled divine but he lost his appetite as he realised he'd have to give her some semblance of the truth to explain his unexpected arrival. 'But I realised I've been avoiding this place for a long time now…and I wanted to see you,' he belatedly added, feeling like a bastard when her face fell.

'Well, whatever your reasons, I'm glad you're here.' She sat opposite and sipped her tea, wariness in her gaze as she studied him. 'It's been too long.'

Her subtle chastisement hung between them and he searched for the right words to make her understand why he'd stayed away. Bitterness, resentment and a long-festering indignation burned in his gut, making him feel slightly sick.

'Why did you stay, Mum?'

He blurted the question, unable to remain silent a moment longer. He wanted to ask her so much about the past but knew it would be futile. What was the point of dredging up rotten memories that would only serve to drag them both down?

But he had to know the answer to this one question. Had to know why she'd chosen to stay when he couldn't wait to get away.

'Because this is my home,' she said, with a shrug. She stared into her tea, unable to meet his gaze, her mouth downturned. 'I loved it. I always loved it, even when your father was around and trying his best to make me hate it.'

She lifted her head to eyeball him, her stare surprisingly defiant. 'I stay here because it reminds me of how much I tolerated and how far I've come.' She tapped her chest. 'I'm proud of being a fighter, not a quitter.'

Like you.

Though she didn't say it, he saw the accusation in her eyes and it served like a kick in the guts.

'I didn't quit, Mum. I chose to walk away from a place that held nothing but bad memories.' He gestured around the kitchen. 'You chose to stay for your reasons, I chose to leave for mine, so don't make me feel bad because of it.'

She deflated a little. 'I'm not trying to make you feel bad.' She shook her head, tendrils that had escaped her ponytail clinging to her face. 'I just can't understand why you stayed away so long, why you didn't come back to see me.'

Her voice rose and ended on a squeak she quickly covered with a cough. 'I'm not laying a guilt trip on you. I appreciated those plane tickets you bought me over the years so we could catch up in the city. But I guess I just really want to know why you've returned now.' She held up her hand before he could respond. 'And don't give me some cock and bull story about wanting to see me, because if you'd wanted to do that you would've visited any time over the last two years since I last saw you.'

Suitably chastised, and fast running out of excuses, he folded his arms and compressed his lips into a mutinous line.

She guffawed, a loud bark of laughter he'd rarely heard from his mother growing up. 'Your father used to get the same stubborn expression when I asked him a question he didn't want to answer.'

Alex didn't want to revisit the past but his mum had given him the perfect opening and he took it. 'Did Dad kill himself?'

Shadows descended over his mum's eyes, blanketing the earlier defiance. But he had to know. His original intention to come here, to remind himself why he could never lead a staid life stuck in one place too long, had been briefly superseded by his thirst for the truth. Growing up in this household, stifled by moroseness, hadn't been healthy. Getting answers could be nothing but cathartic.

'I can't say for certain but from his mind-set in the days leading up to his death, yes, I think he committed suicide.'

How could his mum sound so stoic? As if she were chatting about their pet dog that had accidentally drowned in the dam years before his dad.

'What was different about those days before he died?'

Alex couldn't let it go, no matter how much he feared the answers.

'Your father suffered from depression, as you know—'

'Actually, Mum, I didn't know, because both of you pussyfooted around the issue in front of me. You stomped around here with a stern face and Dad slunk around like he was scared of his own shadow. I frigging hated it!'

His mum blanched, staring at him with hollow

eyes, devastation etched into every line on her face, as if he were a stranger. Which technically, he was. In staying away all these years for his own peace of mind, he hadn't stopped once to think how it had affected hers. She'd always sounded so calm during their chats on the phone, cool to the point of detachment when she came to the city, like she didn't care whether she had a son or not.

But maybe she'd done the same as him, withdrawn, removing herself from the situation emotionally rather than physically.

'I didn't want you to bear the brunt of it like I did,' she said, so softly her voice quavered. 'I tried to hide so much of his behaviour from you.'

A sliver of foreboding pierced his resolve to know the truth. 'What behaviour?'

She sighed, her shoulders slumping as she hugged her middle. 'Your father always had depression. I knew it when I married him and in a way that quiet staidness about him drew me in. He always medicated to stay on top of it, but after he lost his job on the railway and was home all the time he cut back. Said the meds were affecting his taste and sight and other aspects of his life.' She blushed and Alex really didn't want to go there. 'The fewer meds he took, the more unstable he became. Moody. Argumentative. Angry for no reason…'

She gritted her teeth and half turned away, but not before he glimpsed hardships he never knew had existed. Regret that he hadn't known mingled with anger at his obtuseness, clawing at his gut until he felt as if he were being ripped apart from the inside out.

He didn't want to know how bad it had been but he'd started this, he couldn't back down from the truth now.

'Did he ever hit you?'

His fingers unconsciously curled into fists beneath the table at the thought of his mum possibly enduring physical abuse when he'd had no bloody clue.

She bit her bottom lip, as if she'd already said too much. 'No. But the senseless arguments were hard to take at times.' Her tremulous voice broke his heart but before he could offer useless comfort, her head came up, her defiance admirable. 'I hated your father at times for the way he treated me, but I loved him too. It's why I stayed and told him in no uncertain terms that if he didn't get back on his meds and see a counsellor, I'd kill him myself.'

Shell-shocked, Alex dragged in several deep breaths. It did little to quell the sickening churning of his gut. 'I had no idea.'

'Exactly how I wanted it.' Some of the tension holding her shoulders rigid eased. 'Our marriage wasn't pretty and I'm sorry you were privy to most of it. I tried to hide my bitterness but it spilled out sometimes and your father saw it. Those were the days I wondered if my loyalty and love were misplaced...' She shook her head. 'But I'm a fighter. I stuck around to help him and because I stick by my vows.' She smiled at him. 'You were another very valid reason to stick around. I wanted to give you the home life I never had.'

Fuck, this was crazy. He knew his mum had been a foster kid but to stay in a dead-end marriage with a depressed man because of him? Like he needed any more guilt.

'You shouldn't have put up with him for me.'

Damn, he sounded ungrateful, but she didn't bristle as he expected.

'You don't understand because you don't have a child. When you do, you'll get it.' She placed a hand over her heart. 'What you feel in here? You'll do anything for your child.'

'And I repay you by escaping and never looking back.' He scowled, hating the guilt seeping into every cell of his body. He'd been a selfish bastard, so hell-bent on running from his past he hadn't stopped to think what it would be like for those left behind, particularly his mother. 'I'm sorry, Mum. For everything.'

He huffed out a long breath. He'd come this far, he had to tell her the rest. 'I blamed myself for Dad's death for a long time, figuring if I'd made more of an effort to be the son he wanted while I was here that he would've been happier. And later, after I left, that I should've visited more often.'

Her hand trembled as she briefly touched his cheek. 'Your father had a mental illness. We both did as much as we could, so never blame yourself for a decision that was ultimately his to make.'

She smiled and it chased away the darkness of

memories shrouding her. He remembered those rare smiles, when she'd look at him with pride and love, like she couldn't quite believe he was hers. He'd loved those smiles. Those brief fragments in time when he could pretend his mum was happy and, in turn, he was too.

She'd done it all out of loyalty. To her marriage, to his father and to him.

He couldn't fathom that depth of caring for another person, maybe he never would.

If having a partner and child meant sacrificing a part of his soul, he wanted no part of it.

Her hand steadied as it cupped his cheek. 'You're a good boy. Always were, even if you have a funny way of showing it.'

He wanted to promise he'd visit more often. That he wouldn't be an absentee son any more. But he didn't intend to make promises he couldn't keep, despite the best intentions, so he settled for divulging the truth considering she'd done him the same courtesy.

'I came home because I met someone and she wants this kind of life.' He screwed up his nose and gestured at the kitchen. 'She wants the house and the garden and the mind-numbing stability. And I needed a reminder of why I'd run away from all that and why I can't share any of that with her.'

His mum tilted her head to one side, studying him with an intensity that unnerved. 'She wants all that other stuff, but does she want you?'

That was the kicker.

He didn't know.

He'd presumed to think she wanted him as part of her happily-ever-after scenario but what if he'd misread the situation? What if she really was happy with a short-term fling, getting all the raunchy stuff out of her system before settling down with some sedate bloke who'd give her the long-term security she craved?

God, he'd been a fool.

And the worst part was, now that he'd come home and talked to his mum, sitting in this kitchen that calmed rather than antagonised, remembering good times more than bad, he realised that having a place to put down roots mightn't be such a bad thing after all.

The thought of being stuck in one place, with one woman, terrified him. The fear of their relationship growing stale, the fear of growing complacent, the fear of drifting apart. His worst frigging nightmare come to life.

It had happened to his folks but now he knew the truth. His father's problems had been organic, stemming from a mental illness, and his mother had stayed by choice. Sure, she'd done it out of love—for him and his father—but to tolerate that kind of a marriage seemed like a massive sacrifice.

Alex didn't have it in him to be so giving. To fall in with another's life plan when he had his own.

But what happened if he kept drifting, until he woke up one day and realised he'd given up a wonderful woman for a life of…nothing?

His mum hadn't run when the going got tough.

Maybe spending his whole life running away from possible heartache wasn't the answer for him either?

'I think the expression on your face says it all.' His mum laid her hand on the table, palm up and he didn't hesitate to place his hand in hers. 'Sounds like you've faced a few of your fears in coming back here. Why not go all the way and take a chance on love?'

Alex squeezed her hand, unable to find the words to respond.

He didn't love.

He couldn't.

But what if he already did?

CHAPTER TWENTY-SIX

YESTERDAY, CHARLOTTE HAD thought it kind of sweet that Alex had been so considerate and given her the day off.

Last night, she'd waited for his call. Or a text. Or something. When she hadn't heard from him, she'd assumed his sweetness extended to being solicitous about her fatigue and leaving her alone to have an early night. Then she'd turned up at work this morning to discover he'd taken two days off, without leaving a word of his whereabouts.

Not so sweet after all.

It shouldn't bother her because technically they weren't in a committed relationship and he didn't need to check in with her regarding his whereabouts. But it did. Which proved how involved she really was despite all her assertions to the contrary.

Only one way to get him out of her head: focus on work.

She'd hardly been in the office for thirty minutes and all the talk centred around promotions. Her co-workers insisted she was a shoo-in for the new man-

agerial role and while she feigned bashfulness she
knew deep down they were right.

She'd completed every task Alex had set her before
he'd arrived in Sydney. She'd gone the extra yard for
clients. She'd gone above and beyond in all aspects
of new case files.

She deserved this promotion.

If he announced it when he got back she wouldn't
hesitate to make a deposit on her house. She could
hardly wait.

'Where's the Proudman file?' she called out to the
receptionist when she couldn't find it on her desk.

'Alex was working on it before he left.' The receptionist jerked her thumb towards his office. 'It's
probably still on his desk.'

'Thanks.' Charlotte breezed into Alex's office like
it was the most natural thing in the world when every
time she set foot in here her heart started pounding
and bucking like a wild thing.

That desk...

Even after he left she'd never be able to look at it
without blushing. Never in her wildest dreams had
she thought she could be the type of woman who had
sex on a desk, let alone at her workplace. But she'd
gone kind of crazy the moment she'd met Alex and
the insanity hadn't let up since.

She hated contemplating the end of their fling but
it had served its purpose. Being awakened sexually,
feeling confident in her own skin when it came to
men, would ensure she could socialise and date with-

out gaucheness. After all, she'd have the house soon enough, a solid, dependable man had to follow.

When she found herself inadvertently running her hands over the desk she shook her head to clear her musings and started searching for the Proudman file. Alex must have left in a hurry because files were stacked on top of documents in disarray, with seemingly no order to any of it.

She started tidying up, putting the files on one side, documents on the other in a neat pile. A heading on one of the documents snagged her attention. *Promotions.*

She shouldn't look at it. She wouldn't. But curiosity got the better of her and she risked a quick glance. And froze.

He'd listed promotions in order from managerial positions down.

Her name wasn't at the top.

He'd given her job, the one she'd busted her ass to get, to Dennis, the guy she'd mentored when he first arrived three years ago.

In what warped, twisted world did some guy with less experience than her get to be her boss for the foreseeable future?

Anger surged through her, making her fingers flex and the paper crinkle. Damn. She quickly smoothed it out and slid it to the bottom of the pile, sorting faster through the files until she found the one she wanted.

Alex had given her job to someone else when he'd hinted several times it would be hers.

Was he punishing her somehow?

If so, for what?

Anger soon gave way to a familiar emotion, one that consistently rattled her confidence and made her feel unworthy.

Undeserving.

Yet again she'd done her best but had been found lacking. And this time, because she'd been stupid enough to drag her bruised heart into the equation, the fallout would be so much worse.

Like her parents, Alex had deemed her not good enough.

It cut deep, all the way down to her soul.

Shaken to her core, she returned to her office. Sat at her desk. Pretended to work when in fact she spent the next hour staring out of the window envisaging all the ways she could punish her boss.

Starting with ending this thing between them.

What had she been thinking, to indulge in a brief, irrational and futile affair that could only end badly?

Now, not only would she have to deal with a pining heart—because yeah, she'd been stupid enough to fall for him a little—she'd have to tolerate working beneath a guy who had the promotion she deserved.

'Crap,' she muttered, thumping her desk with both fists. It did little but make her hands sting. Better than her eyes, as she dragged in several breaths to stave off tears.

This was what came of harbouring hopes.

This was what came of fooling herself into believ-

ing things could be different this time, that she'd be
enough, that she wouldn't be found lacking.

She'd been a fool.

But no more.

The moment Alex got back, they were O.V.E.R.

CHAPTER TWENTY-SEVEN

ALEX WISHED HE'D had the balls to confront his past earlier. He'd never felt so light, as if a weight had been lifted from his shoulders. Seeing his mother, getting answers to questions that had plagued him for years, had ensured he had a clearer vision for the future.

He didn't have to shy away from commitment for fear of ending up like his folks.

He just had to change the boundaries of what would make a relationship work for him.

As he stood outside Charlotte's flat and waited for her to answer his knock, he rocked on the balls of his feet, excitement making him edgy.

He hadn't bothered texting her when his plane had landed. He'd wanted to surprise her.

The proposal he had for her was that damn monumental. Huge. Life-changing. If she agreed.

She would. He'd do everything in his power to convince her.

He knew she felt more for him than she let on. He'd seen it in her eyes so many times. And in the way she'd opened up to him about her hopes and dreams.

They could make this work. He had no doubt. They both just needed to have a little faith.

She took an eternity to answer and he knocked again, louder this time. When she finally opened the door, all the air whooshed out of his lungs.

She wore a towel. A large bath sheet that hid more than it revealed, but he knew what was beneath it and that was enough to drive all rational thought from his head.

'Hey,' she said, but he didn't give her time to say much else as he entered, kicked the door shut and reached for her.

He glimpsed wariness in her eyes—she was probably mad at him for taking off without letting her know where—and something far scarier. Sadness. As if she knew their time together was coming to an end.

Not if he had his way, so he set about showing her just how special she was to him.

He hauled her into his arms and crushed his mouth to hers, savouring the way she instantly opened to him, their tongues tangling as if they hadn't kissed in years. It had only been a few days but it felt like for ever and he slid his hands under her towel, grabbed her ass and hoisted her up.

She made cute mewling sounds as he turned and backed her up against the door. Small whimpers of appreciation when he slipped a hand between them to touch her clit, the swollen nub slick already.

Their kiss deepened to the point he couldn't breathe. He didn't care, as his thumb circled that nub with precision, until she came apart on a loud moan.

Her hands clutched at his shoulders as he sheathed himself and slid into her, her welcoming tightness something he'd never tire of. As if she were made for him.

His fingers dug into her ass as he lifted her higher, changing the angle, making him a little insane as he drove into her. She wrapped her legs around his waist, squeezing him tight and a groan ripped from somewhere deep inside.

Every thrust, every plunge, took him closer to the edge. Too fast. Not fast enough. The exquisite friction of his cock inside her set off a reaction that blanked his mind until all he could focus on was her. This. Now.

At some point his mouth had drifted across her jaw, to her ear, where he murmured exactly what he was feeling at that moment. 'I could fuck you like this for ever.'

With a strangled cry, she angled her head and claimed his mouth, her back arching, her pelvis moulded to his. It was enough to drive him over the edge, the white-hot explosion of heat behind his eyeballs blinding him to everything as he came harder than ever before.

She sagged against him, limp in his arms. He held her close, knowing with a certainty he could never walk away from her, no matter how much the thought of anything long-term freaked him out.

When his arms started to ache from holding her up, he gently eased back so she had no option but to lower her legs to the floor. She'd lost the towel at some stage, leaving her gloriously naked. He took a moment to appreciate her creamy expanses of skin, her taut nipples, her perfect breasts.

'God, you're beautiful,' he said, brushing a kiss across her lips. 'Be back in a minute.'

He cleaned up in the bathroom, splashed some water on his face to wash off the plane journey and by the time he came back out she sat perched on the edge of an armchair, fully clothed in yoga pants and a hoodie.

'I much prefer you in that towel,' he said, sitting on the sofa and patting the empty spot next to him.

When she didn't move, he realised she hadn't spoken a single word since he'd arrived.

'Are you okay?'

'I'm fine.'

She didn't sound it, her voice tight and controlled. 'Busy day and I'm beat.'

'Same.' He ignored the faintest clang of alarm bells in his head. Usually after they'd had scintillating sex she'd be all over him, wanting to touch and cuddle. Today, her stiff posture and thinned lips were giving him a distinct hands-off signal.

She was mad at him for taking off without an explanation, so he'd give her one.

'I flew home for a few days. A last-minute trip. Sorry for not telling you.'

One eyebrow raised a fraction. 'You don't owe me any explanations.'

Ouch. She really was pissed.

So he continued. 'I needed to see Mum, clarify a few things.'

'Good.' A brief, one-syllable response that sounded far from it.

'I came straight here from the airport because I want to ask you something.'

He took a deep breath.

Here goes nothing.

'When I leave Sydney I want you to come with me. Live on the road for a while. Share a few adventures...' He trailed off when she stared at him in open-mouthed shock, and not the good kind.

She looked seriously annoyed, as if he'd inconvenienced her somehow, her stare bordering on loathing.

Fuck.

Had he misread their relationship? Had he got the situation all wrong?

He'd assumed she felt like him, that she'd want more beyond a short-term fling. His offer, to have her become a part of his life, was the closest he'd ever come to a long-term commitment with a woman.

Facing his fears rooted in the past had liberated him, had given him the courage to embrace a new future, with her.

But what if she didn't want him?

'Say something,' he said, hating the hint of desperation in his tone.

She clasped her hands in her lap so tightly her knuckles stood out, a frown slashing her brows. 'Is that why you did it?'

'Did what?'

'You're going to appoint Dennis Boage to the managerial position so I'll be more likely to chuck in my job and come travelling with you on a whim?'

She didn't shout. He could have handled irrational anger if she'd yelled. But her cold, frosty tone scared him as much as the bleakness in her eyes.

'What are you talking about?'

'I saw it!' She leaped to her feet, finally showing some sign of defiance. 'Your list of promotions, with my name beneath his.'

She stalked around the coffee table to stand over him, hands on hips, magnificent in her ire. 'You know how much that promotion means to me, how much owning that house means to me, then you go and pull something like this?'

He stood slowly, disbelief warring with indignation. Did she think so little of him that she'd believe him capable of messing with her career to suit himself?

'You think this is some kind of stunt?' It was his turn to rein in his anger as icy-cold disdain flooded his veins. 'I came here straight from the airport because I couldn't wait to be with you, to ask you to continue this amazing connection we share. And what do I get? Accusations.'

He muttered, 'Fuck me,' under his breath, unable to comprehend he'd read this situation so wrong.

This was why he didn't do emotional commitment. Ever.

'Maybe if you hadn't gone snooping on my desk, you would've been more amenable to my proposition?' She stiffened at his jibe and he continued. 'Or maybe not, considering you think so little of me.'

He shook his head. 'That document you saw? It was a list I'd made in the early days when I accepted the job. Decisions made purely on recommendations from the old manager. But I don't work like that. I told you so.' He thumped his chest. 'I make my own decisions. You saw me do it. I evaluated everyone fairly. Including you.'

He jabbed a finger in her direction. 'You said you were fine with us having a fling outside work. You said it wouldn't blur any lines.'

He backed away from her, her stony expression shattering what little hope he harboured. 'I call bullshit. Because I've definitely kept work and play separate. Can you say the same?'

He strode for the door, willing her to say something, anything, that would resolve this. Waiting for her to say he'd got it wrong. That she did care for him. That she'd love to travel and have adventures and be his partner for however long.

When he reached the door, she still hadn't spoken.

So he walked away from her without looking back.

CHAPTER TWENTY-EIGHT

THE INITIAL NUMBNESS that invaded Charlotte's body after Alex left soon gave way to tremors, the kind of shaking that made her flop onto the sofa and hug herself tight.

Light-headedness made the room spin a little and nausea made her stomach gripe.

She felt sick, like she'd ingested rotten sushi, something she'd inadvertently done once and had never forgotten. That bout of food poisoning hadn't made her chest ache, though. She could barely breathe through the pain constricting her lungs, like a band around her ribs progressively tightening.

Alex had come here to offer her the world.

She'd flung it back in his face.

She'd never forget his expression once he'd told her the truth.

Total and utter contempt.

The tears she'd been holding back trickled down her cheeks. The second time in a week she'd bawled. So much for her deeming it a wasted activity when it was much better to get on with the job. Set goals.

Work hard. Don't lament a lack of a family/boyfriend/ love life.

But she'd never felt like this before. Bereft. Aching. Grieving for the loss of something—someone— wonderful.

Her laptop beeped on the table, the screen lighting up to indicate she had an incoming video call. From her parents.

Crap.

They rarely called her. Except the obligatory birthday and Christmas. So this call out of the blue could only mean one thing.

Trouble.

She stared at the screen, tempted to ignore the call. But the unexpectedness of it made her anxious and she didn't need one more thing to worry about when she lay awake all night.

Dabbing at her eyes with the hem of her hoodie, she squared her shoulders. She could do this. She'd made an art form of feigning indifference towards her parents for many years, pretending their abandonment didn't hurt.

She stabbed at the answer button and waited for their faces to appear on the screen. Where were they at the moment? Spain? Morocco? Nepal? She lost track of their destinations after a while, only giving their postcards a cursory glance before stuffing them into a box.

Initially they'd given her such joy as a child, cards featuring interesting pictures from exotic locations. She'd run to the mailbox every day in the hope to receive one. But as time passed and her parents didn't return she'd grown to hate those postcards, tangible proof of her two closest biological links not giving a crap about her.

She could count the number of times they'd flown back to Sydney to visit her on one hand. They'd left her with Dee the day after her sixth birthday and had returned at two-yearly intervals, usually staying a week max, until she'd turned sixteen. By then she hadn't been able to hide her dislike and they'd stopped visiting.

But those frigging postcards still arrived like clockwork. No digital correspondence for them. Were they truly that clueless, that they couldn't comprehend how each and every one of those little cardboard rectangles acted like a knife to her heart, a reminder of how they'd turned their back on their only child?

Their faces finally appeared on the screen and she forced a smile. 'Hey, nomads.'

She rarely called them Mum and Dad these days. It didn't feel right as they were so far from being parental it wasn't funny.

'Hi, darling.'

Another falsity. They always called her darling and it grated as badly now as it had in her teens.

Quashing her residual bitterness, she said, 'Is everything okay?'

'Everything's fine,' her mum said, not looking a day older than the last time they'd video-called five months ago. Her blonde hair had a few streaks of grey but her hazel eyes fairly sparkled with joy.

Half her luck. 'We just thought we'd call and tell you our news.'

Charlotte's heart sank. She'd grown immune to her parents' 'news' over the years, which usually revolved around them trying to conquer some new far-flung destination.

'What news?'

Did they believe she genuinely sounded upbeat or could they tell she faked it? After what had happened with Alex, she didn't care. Her life was falling apart and they didn't have a clue because they hadn't been around long enough to get a read on their own daughter.

'We've been awarded a grant to open a small school in Papua New Guinea.' Her mother leaned into her father, who stared down at her like she hung the moon. 'It's an incredible opportunity to work with the kids there and the best part is, we're closer to you.'

Her mum rubbed her hands together as her dad leaned towards the screen. 'Isn't that great? We can pop in for a visit more often. See our best girl.'

A long-festering resentment burned her gut. Their best girl? She was their only girl and they'd never given a crap about her.

'We miss you, darling.' Her mum blew her a kiss, her dad doing the same a moment later. 'Maybe you could come and visit us? See what we do? Get a feel for the sacrifice we made in leaving you behind but how much we've helped those less fortunate?'

As they both stared at her with such unabashed

happiness, Charlotte felt the first stirrings of something akin to yearning.

What would it be like to live life to the fullest like her parents? To want to do good for others? To not care about owning possessions or saving for the future? To live out of a suitcase, unconcerned about mortgage repayments or bills or superannuation?

She'd always scoffed at their lifestyle, believing them to be frivolous and foolish in their inability to plan for the future. She'd labelled them selfish for following their own path and abandoning her to do it.

But hearing them say they'd actually made a sacrifice to leave her behind to help others less fortunate resonated.

She'd never considered that. She'd been too absorbed in her self-pity party for one, attributing their gadding about to selfishness, not selflessness.

How she'd yearned for normal parents growing up. Parents who attended information nights. Parents who pretended to be the Easter bunny, tooth fairy and Santa. Parents who gave a damn.

Dee adored her, always had, and the feeling was entirely mutual. She hadn't wanted for anything and her aunt had become the mother she'd never had. But no matter how nurturing Dee had been, Charlotte had never been able to get past the fact that her own parents preferred caring for strangers rather than their own child.

'Is everything okay?' Her dad leaned closer to the screen again, a habit she found endearing at times. 'You look upset.'

'I'm fine, Dad.'

But she saw the look her folks exchanged, as if they didn't buy her excuse for a second. Great timing for them to suddenly discover the parental gene.

'How's work?' her mum prompted, her usual inquiry whenever they spoke. They didn't have much else in common and her mum had discovered early on not to ask about her social life—or lack of one.

'Fine.'

'That's your second fine in thirty seconds.' Her dad waggled his finger at her. 'A sure sign you're not.'

Charlotte had no intention of divulging the mess she'd made of her love life so she changed the subject. 'Tell me more about this project in Papua New Guinea.'

It worked like magic, her parents taking it in turns to tell her about the school they envisaged, growing increasingly animated as they spoke.

Charlotte barely heard half of what they said, too busy watching their body language. They constantly touched, leaned into each other and finished each other's sentences. Her dad kissed her mum twice, once on the top of her head as she snuggled into him, once on her cheek when she gazed up at him in adoration.

That was when it hit her.

Maybe them travelling the world together hadn't been about abandoning her at all.

Maybe they didn't need anyone else in their lives, they were that connected.

How many couples still appeared so in love after twenty-nine years of marriage? She couldn't think of any. Her co-workers constantly bitched about their spouses and Dee had divorced at twenty-four after eighteen months of marriage.

Yet here were her folks, appearing truly happy in their life choices. She might never forgive them for abandoning her, for choosing their lifestyle over her, but it made her realise something.

Their enthusiasm for life shone through in their words and actions. They practically glowed with it.

She'd made it her goal to be the opposite of them, to do the opposite. Choose security and stability and a house over travel and adventure. Build a nest egg rather than squander what little money she had. Find a staid, dependable man and have a relationship based on trust and friendship rather than any grand passion.

She'd had it all planned out.

So why did she feel like she'd short-changed herself somehow?

Maybe she should be trying to emulate her parents' marriage and lifestyle, not shy from it?

Alex had offered her the opportunity and she'd rejected it. For a guy who'd been totally upfront about not doing long-term commitment, it must have taken a big turnaround for him to ask her to go with him.

She'd been so damn angry at the time, so sure he was dangling a relationship in front of her to make up for the fact he'd taken away her promotion and thus affected her future mortgage and dream house.

But what if she was wrong?

What if Alex had asked her to accompany him on

his travels because he felt their connection went far deeper than sex?

She felt it. Why couldn't he?

'I think your plans sound wonderful, Mum and Dad, but I have to go. Sorry. We'll chat soon.'

And she meant it, disconnecting before they could ramble on further.

She had things to do. Important things.

Starting with showing Alex that she *was* the kind of woman to take risks.

CHAPTER TWENTY-NINE

ALEX HAD DONE many impulsive things in his lifetime.

Buying a house wasn't one of them.

But he had to do this, because if he didn't he'd lose Charlie completely and that wasn't possible.

After he'd stormed out of her flat, he'd driven aimlessly, determined to clear his head. He'd taken a wrong turn down one of Sydney's infamous one-way streets and ended up having to go over the Harbour Bridge to Manly. He parked, slipped off his shoes and socks, rolled up his trousers and walked along the beach. Something guys in suits rarely did by the number of odd glances garnered from passers-by.

He had no idea if it was the fresh sea air, the feel of sand between his toes or the simple art of walking for pleasure rather than as a means to get somewhere, but by the time he got back to his car his anger had given way to determination.

He'd shied away from commitment his entire life. He'd made many excuses, mostly to himself, not to get emotionally involved with a woman. But he wanted to have more than a fling with Charlotte and if she hadn't accepted his first offer, this time he'd make her an offer too good to refuse.

She valued stability, he didn't.

What if he could meet her halfway?

It took him two hours to get the deal done. Sign the paperwork. Make it legit, so he could present her with tangible proof of how far he was willing to go for her.

He had no idea if he'd ever tread down the marriage road—he couldn't shed all his neuroses at once—but admitting he loved her would be a good start. It would be enough for now.

With the relevant documents tucked firmly in his breast pocket, he hightailed it back to her flat.

To find a decrepit set of three suitcases outside her door.

Fuck. The sight of those forlorn cases almost undid him. She was leaving? Maybe she really didn't love him after all?

A steely resolve he'd used many times in the business arena overran his momentary doubts.

Only one way to find out how she felt, once and for all.

He pounded on the door, surprised to find it swung open.

'Charlie?' he called out, entering the quiet flat.

'In here,' she answered, her voice drifting from behind the semi-closed bedroom door.

After shutting the front door, he went in search of her. He pushed the bedroom door open and stopped when he saw the bomb site that her bedroom had become.

Piles of clothes lay in disarray on the floor. Shoes covered any unused space. And three designer suitcases bearing a renowned emblem took pride of place on the bed, open and ready to be stuffed.

'Going somewhere?' He gestured at the cases, his heart sinking. Had she started packing for the move to her dream house?

'Yeah.' She flung a plain grey dress that had seen better days onto a pile behind her.

'Where?'

'Not sure yet,' she said, shooting him an uncertain glance. 'That depends on you.'

'Me?'

He couldn't acknowledge the tiny flare of hope. Not yet. He'd already made the mistake of assuming too much and look where that had got him. Absolutely nowhere.

'Well, I couldn't very well accompany you on an adventure with those tatty old cases so I invested a sizeable chunk of my house deposit on new luggage.' She gestured to the cases on the bed. 'So you'd better still take me on your travels, otherwise I'll be stuck with these very expensive pieces and nowhere to go.'

Alex could have whooped for joy.

She felt it too. This crazy, indescribable, heady feeling that defied belief or explanation. The kind of feeling that prompted them to do outlandish things, like squander her house deposit on designer luggage. Like him buying a house.

'I'm taking you wherever I go,' he said, aiming for nonchalance as he slid the sale documents out of his pocket and handed them to her. 'But first, you might like to take a look at this.'

'Airline tickets?' Her soft smile shot something straight to his heart, something that lodged and he'd never be able to shake off.

This incredible woman was willing to give up her dreams to be with him. He'd make damn sure he was worthy of her faith in him.

'No. Check it out.'

She unfolded the paper, her eyes scanning it quickly and he saw the exact moment reality hit.

'You didn't,' she whispered, her hands shaking a tad as she re-read the document, then let out an ear-piercing squeal. 'You bought my dream house and put it in my name?'

'Yeah. Seeing as you doubted my intentions, I had to do something outrageous to prove how much I love you.'

'You love me...' she murmured, shaking her head as if to clear it. 'I can't believe this.'

'Believe it, babe,' he said, kicking clothes out of the way to get to her. 'This way, you'll always have the house. And who knows, maybe one day you'll let me live in it with you. But in the meantime, let's go wild. Take some time off. Travel. Have fun.' He stopped two feet in front of her, yearning to take her in his arms. 'Knowing that you'll have a managerial role when you get back to The Number Makers.'

Her bottom lip wobbled and tears filled her eyes. 'You are the most incredible man I've ever known and I can't thank you enough for all you've done for me.'

'Pfft. Buying a house is nothing—'

'I'm not talking about the house and you know it.' She stepped forward and rested her palms against his chest, staring up at him in wonder. 'You've awakened me sexually. You've given me self-confidence. You've made me feel worthy for the first time in my life. And most of all you've made me take a risk and fall in love with a wanderer.'

He grinned like an idiot. 'So you love me too, huh?'

'Oh, yeah, and I intend to prove it every which way in every city in every country we visit.' She slid her palms up slowly, to cup his face. 'And don't worry, I'm not packing anything but kinky lingerie.'

He laughed, wrapped his arms around her waist, picked her up and swung her around until they were both dizzy.

When they came to a stop, he rested his forehead against hers. 'My very own play thing, complete with raunchy accessories. How did I get so lucky?'

'You're about to get a whole lot luckier,' she said, moving the suitcases off the bed before pushing him onto it and straddling him. 'For the rest of your life, if you'll have me.'

'So I'm your dream man?' He propped himself up on his elbows, watching with lascivious intent as she peeled off her T-shirt and flung it onto the floor.

'You're every dream and fantasy I've ever had rolled into one.' She unclipped her bra at the back and it followed the same route as her T-shirt, leaving her delectable breasts bare to him. 'And I can't wait to share every adventure together.'

He reached for her, wanting her to fill his hands the way she'd filled his heart. 'Starting now...'

* * * * *

COMING SOON!

We really hope you enjoyed reading this book. If you're looking for more romance, be sure to head to the shops when new books are available on

Thursday
1st November

To see which titles are coming soon, please visit
millsandboon.co.uk

LET'S TALK
Romance

For exclusive extracts, competitions
and special offers, find us online:

f facebook.com/millsandboon

◎ @millsandboonuk

𝕏 @millsandboon

Or get in touch on 0844 844 1351*

For all the latest titles coming soon, visit
millsandboon.co.uk/nextmonth